Praise for

Kathy Reichs

ALSO BY KATHY REICHS

ADULT FICTION
Déjà Dead
Death du Jour
Deadly Décisions
Fatal Voyage
Grave Secrets
Bare Bones
Monday Mourning
Cross Bones
Break No Bones
Bones to Ashes
Devil Bones
206 Bones
Spider Bones
Flash and Bones
Bones Are Forever
Bones of the Lost
Bones Never Lie
Speaking in Bones
The Bone Collection
Bones Buried Deep (coauthored with Max Allan Collins)
A Conspiracy of Bones

NOVELLAS
Bones in Her Pocket
Swamp Bones
Bones on Ice

YOUNG ADULT FICTION (WITH BRENDAN REICHS)
Virals
Seizure
Code
Exposure
Terminal

NOVELLAS
Shift
Swipe
Shock

Kathy Reichs

THE BONE CODE

A TEMPERANCE BRENNAN NOVEL

SIMON & SCHUSTER

London · New York · Sydney · Toronto · New Delhi

First published in USA by Scribner, an imprint of Simon & Schuster Inc., 2021
First published in Great Britain by Simon & Schuster UK Ltd, 2021

This paperback edition published 2021

1 3 5 7 9 10 8 6 4 2

Simon & Schuster UK Ltd
1st Floor
222 Gray's Inn Road
London WC1X 8HB

Simon & Schuster Australia, Sydney
Simon & Schuster India, New Delhi

www.simonandschuster.co.uk
www.simonandschuster.com.au
www.simonandschuster.co.in

A CIP catalogue record for this book is available from the British Library

Paperback ISBN: 978-1-4711-8892-3
Export Paperback ISBN: 978-1-3985-0733-3
eBook ISBN: 978-1-4711-8891-6
Audio ISBN: 978-1-3985-0032-7

Printed and bound in Great Britain by CPI Group (UK) Ltd, Croydon, CR0 4YY

For Paul Aivars Reichs
Thanks

DNA neither cares nor knows. DNA just is. And we dance to its music.

—Richard Dawkins

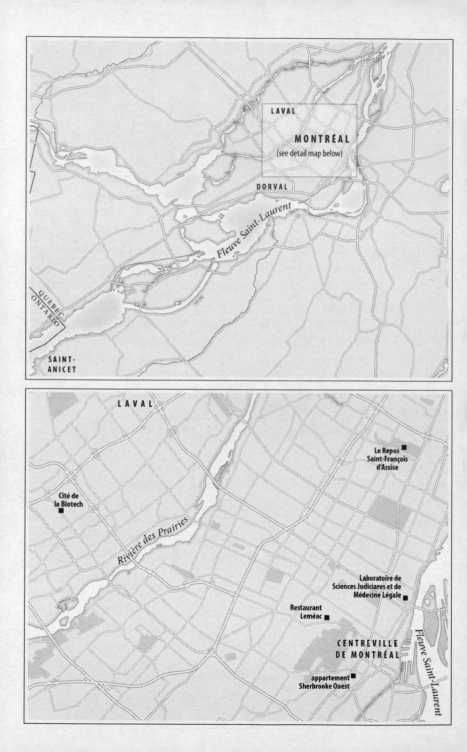

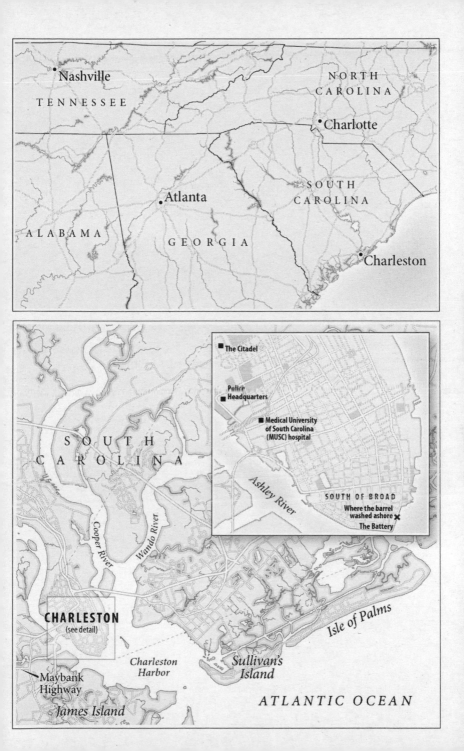

THE BONE
CODE

1

Tuesday, October 5

The kid was dead. No doubt about that. The 911 caller thought so. The ER reported her DOA. The toxicologist showed cause. The ME signed the certificate.

The kid was dead. That wasn't the question.

The phone rang. I ignored it.

Beyond my window, the sky was a chaos of gunmetal, smoke, and green. The wind was blowing angrier by the second.

I'd have to go soon.

The palette on my screen mirrored the turmoil outside. Within the gray backdrop of flesh, the bones burned white as Arctic snow.

I'd been analyzing the X-rays for almost two hours, my frustration escalating with the storm.

One last glance at the final plate in the series. The hands. Then it was adios.

I forced myself to concentrate. Carpals. Metacarpals. Phalanges.

Suddenly, I sat forward, the gusts and thickening darkness forgotten.

I zoomed in on the right fifth digit. The left.

The phone rang. Again, I paid no attention.

I shifted back to the cranial views.

A theory began to take shape.

I was poking at it, twisting the idea this way and that, when a voice at my back caused me to jump.

Framed in the doorway was a woman not much bigger than the subject of the films I was viewing. Standing maybe five feet tall, she had gray-streaked black hair drawn into a knot at the nape of her neck. Thick bangs brushed the top of tortoiseshell frames not chosen for fashion.

"Dr. Nguyen," I said. "I didn't realize you were still here."

"I was completing an autopsy." Slight accent, mostly Boston but with an undercurrent of something more exotic.

Nguyen had taken charge at the Mecklenburg County Medical Examiner's office only recently, so she and I were still testing the waters with each other. Though not exactly effervescent, she seemed organized, fair, and earnest. So far, so good.

"Is that the Deacon case?" Nguyen's gaze had shifted to my screen.

"It is."

"You're advising the family?"

"Yes." Seeing her raised eyebrows, I added, "The request came from an attorney named Lloyd Thorn. I hope you don't mind me viewing the films here."

"Of course not." Nguyen flicked a wrist, as though to brush away the thought. Maybe to help her change tack. "Inara is now a Cat Three storm and moving faster than predicted. A mandatory evacuation has been ordered for all coastal counties, and it's expected to sweep inland."

"Ain't climate change grand?"

Nguyen ignored my quip. "I'm closing the lab. Mrs. Flowers has already left. She plans to head into the mountains to stay with a cousin."

Eunice Flowers has been the MCME receptionist since Gutenberg began cranking out Bibles. The first to arrive each day, she is normally the last to depart.

"There's a woman in the lobby who wishes to see you. Mrs. Flowers told her you were unavailable, but she insists on waiting."

"Who is she?" A glance at the phone showed the message signal flashing red.

"I've no idea. Or why she ventured out in this weather."

"I'll talk to her." Feeling a flicker of guilt for disregarding Mrs. Flowers's calls.

"Don't linger too long," Nguyen warned.

"No worries." Moving the cursor to close the X-ray file. "My cat is probably dialing a rescue hotline as we speak."

"I'm certain Charlotte is safe." Lacking conviction. "We're much too far from the coast."

I said nothing, recalling similar thinking back in '89. And Hurricane Hugo.

Though it was only 3:20 p.m., little light filtered in through the lobby doors or windows. All was quiet inside the building. Save for the security guard, not in evidence but undoubtedly present, I seemed to be the only person left on the premises.

The woman sat in the chair opposite Mrs. Flowers's command post. Her feet, shod in sensible oxfords, rested primly side by side on the carpet. She appeared to be studying the laces.

My first thought: the woman was the dowdy aunt from Peoria. A ratty shawl wrapped her from shoulder to calf, and a floral print scarf, tied babushka style, covered her hair. A curved-handled umbrella hung from one wrist, and a frayed tweed tote sat centered on her lap.

My second thought: why the cold-weather gear when the thermometer that day had registered an unseasonable eighty degrees?

Upon hearing my footfalls, the woman lifted her chin, and her babushka'd head rotated slowly, tracking my approach. The rest of her body seemed clenched in a knot.

Drawing close, I noted that the woman's eyes were pale—not

the usual blue or green but a shade closer to that of honey in a jar. I estimated her age at sixty-five minimum. Mostly based on the attire. The scarf hid much of her face.

"I'm Temperance Brennan. I apologize for your wait."

One hand rose to clutch mine. Though blue-veined and knobby, the intensity of its grip took me by surprise.

"Thank you so much. Thank you. I understand. Yes, of course. I've waited a long time. I don't mind a bit more."

Using the umbrella for support, the woman started to push to her feet. I gestured her back down. "Please. Don't get up."

I placed my briefcase on the floor and perched on the adjacent chair, pointedly not settling back.

"So, then. You are . . .?"

"Oh, dear me. Excuse my rudeness. I should have introduced myself at the outset. My name is Polly Susanne Beecroft."

"It's nice to meet you, Ms. Beecroft. I—"

"It's Miss. Don't give a patoot about titles." The breathy "p" fluttered the silk framing her face. "If one never married, what's the harm in saying so? Don't you agree?"

"Mm."

"But please, call me Polly."

"How can I help you, Polly?" I asked, wanting to wrap this up quickly.

"I hope you will excuse my rather cheeky approach." The honey eyes locked onto mine. "I've come to implore your help."

"I am a forensic anthrop—"

"Yes, yes, of course. That's why I believe you're the person I need."

"I'm listening."

"It's a bit of a tale."

I gestured encouragement I didn't feel.

Beecroft drew a quick breath, as though to begin. Seconds passed. No words left her lips.

"Don't be nervous," I reassured.

Tight nod. Then, "My twin sister died last year, bless her soul. She was seventy-three years old."

I now knew where this was headed. Still, I didn't interrupt.

"Harriet married but was widowed young, so she never had children. She began studying art in her thirties, from then on was totally caught up in her painting. I'm afraid she and I were not fruitful like the Bible instructs." Quick grin. "Following Harriet's death—"

"Miss Beecroft—"

"Polly. Please."

"I'm very sorry for your loss, Polly. But if you have issues regarding your sister's passing, you must raise them with the coroner or medical examiner who signed the death certificate."

"Oh, no. Not at all. Harriet died in hospice of pancreatic cancer."

OK. I was wrong about the purpose of Beecroft's visit. Realizing that and, I'll admit, a tad curious, I said nothing.

"Since I was Harriet's only kin, it fell to me to clear out her home. She lived in Virginia, in a small town not far from Richmond. But that's unimportant. While going through her things, I discovered several items that have troubled me greatly."

The overhead lights wavered, then steadied.

"Oh, my." One liver-spotted hand fluttered up and hovered, like a moth suddenly free and confused.

"Perhaps this could wait a day or two, until the storm has passed?" I suggested gently.

But Beecroft wasn't to be dissuaded. "May I show you what I found? I'll be oh so brief. Then it's off I go."

An image fired in my brain. My near-octogenarian mother struggling to control an umbrella in a gale.

"Did you drive here, Polly?" I asked.

"Oh, heavens. No. I came by taxi."

Crap.

"Do you live in town?"

"I have a condo at Rosewood. Do you know it?"

I knew it well. Mama had recently moved to Rosewood. I now had an inkling how Beecroft had made her way to me.

I also had an inkling that the frumpy garb was misleading.

Rosewood is a nine-acre complex modeled on George Vanderbilt's nineteenth-century getaway in Asheville. Life in the three-towered extravaganza did not come cheap. Beecroft had means.

"Taxis may be scarce in this storm." *Crap. Crap.* "How about you outline your concerns as I drive you home?"

"I couldn't possibly impose."

"It's on my way." It wasn't.

"That's so terribly generous. I knew you would be a kind person. Very well. But first you must see something."

The kind person watched Beecroft dig an envelope from the tote and draw three photos from it. Withholding two, she offered one to me.

"This was made in 1966. I'm with my sister. We were feeling a bit naughty that afternoon."

The picture was in color though somewhat faded. A close-up and obviously posed, the shot had been snapped outside on a sunny day. Two teenage girls stood behind a wall with only their heads visible, chins and forearms resting on the top row of bricks. Each had chestnut hair, worn center-parted and ear-tucked. Each had the odd honey-colored eyes.

Both girls grinned mischievously while staring straight into the lens. They looked identical.

I studied the image, feeling a vague sense of unease. Of recognition? But that was impossible.

Beecroft's words cut into my thoughts. "—didn't take as many photos back then. Not like today, with young people capturing every second of their lives, posting images of themselves flossing their teeth or cleaning the pantry or torturing the cat, or whatever. Really. Does anyone care about such triviality? But do forgive me. I digress.

"The quality has deteriorated, but our faces are still quite clear. I'm on the left, Harriet is on the right. We were eighteen at the time. We'd just graduated from high school and been admitted to Vassar. But that is also irrelevant. How I do go on."

Beecroft offered another photo, this one encased in a protective sleeve. I laid the first on the table beside me, took the second, and observed it through the plastic.

The sepia tones and white cracks suggested that this image was considerably older. As did the formal pose and style of clothing.

But the subject matter was similar. Two teenage girls looked straight at the camera, one seated, one standing with her hand on the chair back. Both wore high-necked, long-sleeved dresses with complexly draped ankle-length skirts. Neither smiled.

The resemblance to Polly and Harriet Beecroft was uncanny.

I looked up, seeking explanation.

"That's my grandmother and her sister," Beecroft said. "They, too, were twins."

My eyes dropped back to the picture.

"That portrait was made in 1887. They were seventeen years old."

"They look exactly—"

"Yes," Beecroft said. "They do. Did."

Then Beecroft handed me the final photo.

Hollow silence echoed around us, punctuated by the rumbles of the mounting tempest.

I heard nothing. Saw nothing but the image in my hand.

I swallowed, too shaken to speak.

2

Both Carolinas have miles of coastline, so hurricanes aren't uncommon. Wilmington. New Bern. Myrtle Beach. Charleston. At one time or another, each has been slammed.

Charlotte is up in the piedmont, so largely safe, but if a hurricane or snow warning is issued, the Queen City goes berserk. Schools and courts close. Supermarkets empty. Generators and batteries disappear. Usually, it's then a big fizzle. We sweep up and resume bagging groceries, meeting clients, and driving carpool.

I'm not an alarmist. Far from it. But the weather that day appeared determined to live up to the hype. The rain was holding off, but the barometric pressure felt about a billion pounds per square inch, with gusts growing more belligerent by the second.

A shawl and a babushka aren't aerodynamically suited to wind, but the oxfords were a prudent choice. Though the walk to Beecroft's entrance was challenging, we managed.

Normally, I'd have checked on Mama, but she was away on one of her spiritual healing adventures. Arizona? The Catskills? I wasn't sure. Made a mental note to phone her.

From Rosewood, it wasn't far to Sharon Hall, the turn-of-the-century mansion-turned-condo-complex in which I own a unit called the annex. No one knows when the tiny two-story structure was built. Or why. The annex appears on none of the old deeds or property maps. I don't care that its tale is forever lost to history. In fact, the enigma is part of the appeal.

I moved into the annex following the collapse of my marriage and during my occupancy have changed little save bulbs and filters. Until recently. Now a spiffy new study occupies space that for eons had served as an attic.

For the briefest instant, an image flashed. Craggy face, heart-spinning blue eyes, sandy hair losing out to gray.

My chest tightened. Thoughts of my new roommate, Andrew Ryan? Or the fierce blast of air that rocked the car?

A brief note about Ryan, Équipe des Crimes contre la Personne, Sûreté du Québec. Since he worked homicide for the SQ, the police in La Belle Province, and I am the forensic anthropologist there for the LSJML—the Laboratoire de Sciences Judiciaires et de Médicine Légale—the *lieutenant-détective* and I have collaborated on murder investigations for decades, working out of the same headquarters in Montreal. Somewhere along the way, we began to date. Then we began to, well, more than date. Now we live together. Sort of.

More on that later.

After arriving at the annex, I muscled the car door open. It shut itself. Hunched forward, I hurried inside, hair whipping, briefcase twisting this way and that.

"Birdie?" Setting my purse and case on the counter.

No response from the cat. Not surprising. Climatic extremes upset his feline psyche.

"I'm home, Bird."

Still nothing.

Like the MCME lobby, the interior of the annex was unnaturally dark for midafternoon. I hit the wall switch and turned on a dining-room lamp, then climbed the stairs to my bedroom. As I was yanking

off my Nikes, a small white face peeked from beneath the bed, ears
flattened as low as possible.

"Chill, big guy. It's just a little wind."

Birdie studied me, wary. Perhaps irritated. Hard to tell with cats.

Or maybe he was picking up on my own anxiety. The weather
really did look bad. Should I stay and ride it out? Or head for a motel
in the foothills?

A gust fired a volley of gravel against the side of the house. The
cat face withdrew back into its refuge.

"Fine. I'll see what the experts are saying."

Returning to the kitchen, I located the remote and navigated to
the local twenty-four-hour news station. Hit mute as I waited out
a guy offering to clean my gutters. An ad for Bojangles chicken. A
promo for an upcoming Panthers game.

Eventually, the feed cut to an anchor seated behind a glass-topped
desk with tiny lights looping its front-facing surface. John Medford.
I'd met him a few times at charity fundraisers. Knew his pompadour
was higher than his IQ.

Over Medford's right shoulder, a graphic showed a regional map
framed by another array of twinkly lights. An alarming green blob
hovered to the southeast of Charlotte. A chyron at the bottom of the
screen stated: *Inara is coming!*

I activated the sound. Medford's voice was neutral, his brows
canted at just enough of an angle to show appropriate concern.

"—at least one model shows her slamming into Charleston, then
being squeezed between the clockwise circulation of a high-pressure
system out in the Atlantic and the counterclockwise push of low
pressure in the Mississippi Valley. Sound familiar to you longtimers
out there? It should. That's the combo that sent Hugo barreling at us
back in 'eighty-nine. Of course, just one model is saying that. Others
see the storm skimming the coast, then hightailing it offshore. But it's
always best to be prepared."

A bullet list appeared beside the map. Medford worked through
the points, putting his folksy touch on each.

"I'm sure y'all know the drill, but it never hurts repeating. Should Inara come our way, stay inside, preferably in an interior room—maybe a closet or a bathroom—and away from windows, skylights, and glass doors."

OK. Birdie had me there.

"If flooding threatens your home, cut the electricity at the main breaker. If you lose power, turn off your major appliances—you know, the air conditioner, the water heater—big-ticket items you don't want damaged. And you'd best not use small appliances, either, including your computer."

Shit. Did my laptop and mobile have juice? As I dug both devices from my briefcase and plugged them in to charge, Medford droned on.

"I'm figuring we'll be fine here in Charlotte, but it could be a real boomer over at the shore." Encouraging smile. "Stay tuned. I'll be back in thirty with an update."

The station went to another commercial break. I hit mute again and was reaching for my cell phone when it rang. Warbled, actually. After checking caller ID, I answered.

"Hey, Ryan."

"*Bonjour, ma chère.*"

"You still up in Yellowknife?"

After retiring from the SQ, Ryan went into business as a PI. At the moment, he was investigating something having to do with diamond mining and claims. And one unhappy party. I didn't ask.

"Yes, ma'am. Today's high will be minus fourteen."

"Celsius."

"*Ç'est frette en esti.*" Translation: bloody cold. "I'm hearing reports of a wee squall down your way."

"The models are all over the map. As usual. Some suggest Inara could hit the Carolinas. Others have her heading west to Keokuk."

"Where's that?"

"Iowa."

"That's not true."

"It is. It's the southeasternmost city in the state."

Ryan ignored that. "Any chance Charlotte could be in the cross-hairs?"

"Highly unlikely."

"It has happened."

"It has."

"How's the Birdcat coping?"

"Poorly. Listen, Ryan, I appreciate you checking in, but I have to finish up an analysis involving a potential child endangerment. Maybe homicide."

"Potential?"

"It's complicated."

"For years, I was a cop."

"It said so right on your badge." Referencing one of Ryan's favorite new lines.

"It did."

"OK." I organized the basics in my head. "The victim lived here in North Carolina. Last week, she was found dead in her home. An autopsy showed no evidence of trauma, but toxicology testing revealed lethal blood alcohol levels."

"Where were the parents?"

"Off sailing the Caribbean."

"How old was the vic?"

"The detective zings straight to the core."

"Former detective."

"Right. The victim—her name is Tereza—came to the U.S. via a Bulgarian adoption agency in 2012. At the time, the parents were told she was seven years old. But they claim to have subsequently uncovered records listing Tereza's date of birth as 2000, not 2005. That would make her twenty when she died, not fifteen."

"An adult, not a minor."

"Bingo."

"So perfectly legal to be home alone. What's the problem?"

"Tereza told everyone she was born in 2005. The agency insists that's the case."

"The kid had no friends?"

"She arrived in the States speaking no English, so the parents decided on homeschooling. Over the years, that arrangement continued because of behavioral issues. Not sure what those were."

"So your vic had little contact with anyone outside the home."

"Exactly. She was a very small person and, at the time of her death, was claiming to be a minor, dressing like a kid, acting like a kid. The parents say it was fraud from the outset and that Tereza was a sociopath who scammed them for years."

"Let me guess. Some DA disagrees and is determined to prosecute."

"Child abandonment, child endangerment, negligent homicide. Who knows what else? The parents' attorney, a guy named Lloyd Thorn, insists his clients are guilty of nothing but kindness. He says they provided Tereza with a home free of charge. That they just couldn't take her abusive behavior any longer."

"So they did what?"

"Took a prolonged vacation, hoping she'd move out as they'd suggested. They figured she'd be fine on her own."

"Where are they now?"

"Under arrest in Saint Croix. Thorn contacted me yesterday after he got access to X-rays taken when Tereza suffered some sort of fall last year."

"Are the films useful?"

"Very. I have a theory, but I want to do a little more research before I talk to Thorn. He's phoned me four times in the last two days. The guy's very high-pressure."

"And I know how you respond to bullies."

"Keep that in mind, detective."

"*Oui, madame.*"

"We could lose power anytime, so I want to wrap this up."

"Conditions are that bad?"

"Electrical outages are SOP here."

"Ring me in a couple of hours?"

"Sure."

"Maybe talk dirty?"

"Goodbye, Ryan."

After disconnecting, I verified several points online. Then I turned to my osteology and genetics textbooks.

Every now and then, I got up to peer out a window. Or to check back with our folksy weatherman. Each time, Medford's eyebrow angle was slightly more acute.

I was doing one last round with the X-rays when something bulky skittered across the lawn and slammed a wall with a muted thud. The annex went dark.

And I was as certain as I'd ever be regarding Tereza.

Time for some serious battening.

Inspired by Medford's second bullet point and Birdie's instinctual choice of refuge, I dragged bedding into the annex's most interior room, a windowless closet with a low, sloping ceiling wedged below the staircase. I added my mobile and laptop, a gallon of water, a box of granola bars, my current Karin Slaughter book, and Birdie's food and drink bowls.

A quick sandwich by flashlight, a trip to the head, then I went in search of the cat. He was not enthused about being hauled out from under the bed.

The rain started as I was descending the stairs. No timid first wave of tentative drops, the deluge came all at once, full force and sideways, like water blasting from a high-pressure nozzle.

Easing my grip, I allowed the cat to catapult from my chest into the improvised storm cellar. He shot behind a row of stacked boxes, eyes like Frisbees, fur and tail in full upright mode, an odd mewing noise rising from his throat. I crawled in with him and closed the door.

"It's OK, Bird. We've got plenty of food."

Stretching out on my makeshift bed, I tried to relax. Eventually, the cat joined me and curled at my knee. I reached down to pet him. His entire body was trembling.

For the next several hours, Birdie and I listened to the cacophony of pounding rain and howling wind, muted but unmistakably wild. I wondered how extensive the damage would be. The cat's thoughts were undoubtedly traveling a different path.

At some point, I drifted off. Awoke to the sound of an exploding transformer.

Feeling the cat tense and resume shaking, I started to stroke him, slowly and gently. As my hand worked its magic, my thoughts looped back to my afternoon visitor.

Polly Beecroft and her sister, Harriet, were monozygotic twins, meaning they'd developed from a single fertilized egg that split early in embryonic development. Since the women shared identical DNA, they looked alike. No biggie. The chance of having identical twins is around three or four in every one thousand births.

I felt the tiniest easing of tension in Birdie's body. My touch was having the desired effect. Or he was running out of steam.

Polly's grandmother and her great-aunt were also identical twins, born in London in 1870. Polly had showed me a portrait of them, one named Sybil, the other Susanne Bouvier. They, too, had looked like clones of each other, and both had looked exactly like Polly and Harriet, born eight decades later.

Something shattered in the yard. Birdie's shaking kicked back into high. I decided to think out loud, adding my voice to the stroking, partly to benefit the cat, partly to block the bedlam outside.

"Susanne and Sybil traveled to Paris in 1888, and after a month in the city, Sybil vanished without a trace. To this day, no one knows what happened to her.

"Polly's grandmother, Susanne, went on to emigrate to the U.S., marry, and have children. Polly's mother was born in 1909. Polly and Harriet came along in 1948.

"Here's the strange part, Bird. In addition to Sybil's disappearance, of course. Polly also showed me a picture of a death mask."

Birdie rolled to his back. I took this as an indication of interest.

"Death masks were popular in the nineteenth century, before

people had cameras. They were kind of like ceramic selfies, created to help friends and family remember the deceased."

I made that part up, but it sounded reasonable. Birdie didn't question my explanation.

"Polly didn't know where Harriet had gotten the photo. And she had no idea of the mask's current whereabouts. Are you ready for this? The death mask in Polly's picture looked exactly like her. Like all four women." Added as if the cat needed clarification, "The features were the same as in both sets of twins."

Bird stretched his forelimbs upward and let his paws drop, limp.

"So why did Polly come to see me, you ask? Excellent question. She wonders if the woman depicted in the death mask could be her great-aunt, Sybil. And if so, she wants to know if I can discover what happened to her."

Out on the lawn, a tree snapped with a dull pop. I heard a crack far overhead, then something big ratcheted across the roof.

The cat scrabbled for cover under the quilt.

We hunkered there the rest of the night, Birdie shivering, me wondering what devastation I would face in the morning.

Unaware that the storm damage would be nothing compared to that triggered by an upcoming call.

3

Wednesday, October 6

I awoke to pitch-black.

Groggy, I rose to a crouch and groped for the chain on the overhead fixture. Pulled. Nothing.

Great. Still no electricity.

Dropping back onto the improvised bed, I located my phone. The screen showed the time to be 6:22.

Morning?

I opened my hurricane-tracking app.

Inara had made landfall as a Cat 2 storm between Savannah and Charleston around nine the previous night. After a five-hour tantrum, she'd moved offshore and was now Virginia's problem.

Good news. Charlotte had caught only her western edge.

I opened the closet door. Pearl-gray light was seeping between the closed slats of the plantation shutters, throwing off-angle slashes onto the floor.

I crawled out into the hall. Birdie, ever cautious, remained huddled in the blankets.

Inside the annex, all was quiet. No humming refrigerator or

blowing AC. Outside, bird chatter high above and the staccato barking of a distant dog.

Using my iPhone for illumination, I made a quick tour of both floors. Save for a torn screen on one bedroom window, everything appeared to be intact.

Coffee was impossible, so I got a Diet Coke from the slumbering fridge, then crossed the kitchen. Despite much forceful shoving and shouldering, the back door wouldn't budge. Encountering no such impediment in front, I stepped out onto the stoop.

As is typical following hurricanes, the air seemed extraordinarily clear and crisp. The sky, slowly brightening, was unmarred by even the tiniest of clouds.

Sharon Hall looked as if a bomb had gone off. Trees were down, and debris and vegetation covered the grounds. Uprooted shrubs lay jumbled along the manor house foundation, and a trash can hung wedged between its pillars. Two concrete urns lay shattered on the porch, soil and begonias spewing from them like innards from a squashed roach.

Slowly, my neighbors began to emerge, hesitant but game, like survivors of some B-movie apocalypse. Most were already suited up for yard work. A few pushed wheelbarrows. Many carried garden tools.

I went inside, brushed my teeth, and changed into jeans and a sweatshirt. After locating a pair of old work gloves, I joined the recovery effort, doing my bit with a very questionable rake.

Shortly after nine, word spread that the power had been restored. I took a break to return to the annex to plug in my mobile. And to rejoice. I have to admit, I'm a huge fan of electricity.

Birdie had ventured forth, startled awake when the bare bulb in his haven lit up. He was calmer, but still needed two milligrams of something to restore him to normal.

I was heading back outside when my newly connected mobile warbled. The first of three calls that day. Not the one that would send my life off-kilter.

Recognizing the number, I steeled myself. Previous conversations had shown that—I'm being kind here—Lloyd Thorn lacked certain interpersonal skills.

"Good morning, Mr. Thorn."

"I wasn't sure I'd get through. A real pisser, this storm."

"We've just started to clean up the mess."

"My clients are shitting their shorts waiting for your take."

"I understand."

"Don't misread me. Tereza's death is a freakin' tragedy. But my clients did nothing wrong. It's an outrage they're sitting in jail."

"Please hold while I get my notes."

Resuming the conversation, I placed Thorn on speaker. I could hear him fidgeting impatiently, probably clicking a ballpoint pen.

"I'm somewhat limited having never examined Tereza or viewed a photo of her. But I did spend several hours with the X-rays."

"Let's cut to the chase."

"In my opinion, Tereza at the time of her death was in her early to mid-twenties. I believe she had a condition called Silver-Russell syndrome, or SRS."

"What's that?" The clicking stopped. Paper rustled.

"A congenital growth disorder tha—"

"I went to law school, not med school. For now, just the basics."

"SRS can explain the stunted growth."

"Stunted?"

"Children with SRS tend to have high foreheads, small jaws, and triangular faces. But those features become less obvious with age."

"Uh-huh."

"There's no specific radiological indicator of SRS. However, delayed bone age, clinodactyly, and fifth middle or distal phalangeal hypoplasia have been reported as suggestive of the syndrome." Speaking über-slowly and purposely using medical jargon.

"What the hell's that mean?"

"They are features that can be seen on X-rays. Which is what I had to work with and which is objective evidence. Clinodactyly refers to the abnormal curvature of a digit. Hypoplasia refers to the underdevelopment of a body part, in this case, of portions of the little finger."

"Tereza had all that?"

"She did."

"How's this relevant?"

"It can explain her extremely short stature."

"Short stature in adults?"

"Yes. Especially if growth abnormalities aren't treated post-natally."

"Like *that* would have happened in Bulgaria. How common is this SRS?"

"Stats put the occurrence somewhere between one in three thousand and one in one hundred thousand births."

"That's about as useful as a tit on a nun."

Unable to disagree, I didn't respond.

"You said congenital. This thing's inherited?"

"Yes. But the genetics are unclear. Autosomal dominant, auto-somal recessive, and X-linked inheritance models have been re-ported, but without going into—"

"Yeah, don't."

Having had my fill of Thorn's abrasive manner, I did.

"It's thought that loci—think genes—on chromosome eleven play a major role in SRS. But chromosome seven may also—"

"You're saying Tereza was a dwarf because of wonky genes."

"I wouldn't put it in quite those words." Wondering precisely where this jerk *did* go to law school.

"So she was an adult, not a kid. In her twenties."

"Yes."

"Not fuckin' fifteen."

Definitely not Harvard.

"You're gonna put all this on paper?"

"I'll send a full report."

"When?"

"When it's finished."

"You know, one time this little psycho drowned the family puppy. Another time, she set fire to the house. I could go on." Info added to spur me to quicker action? "Anyway, great stuff, doc. I'm gonna get this asshole prosecutor on the horn right now."

I didn't envy the hapless DA whose phone was about to ring.

Despite the gloves, I developed an epic assortment of blisters. At noon, I returned to the annex to treat them.

My mobile lay on the counter, fully charged at last. The little green icon showed one voice message. My best friend, Anne Turnip.

The second call of the day after Thorn's. This one not the world-tilter, either.

I listened to the directive, delivered with typical Anne melodrama.

"Call me ASAP. Like, now! As soon as you hear this."

A few words about my BFF.

Anne has emerald eyes and long blond hair, its color now maintained through the magic of chemistry. She is leggy-tall and, despite an aversion to exercise and all forms of sport, has remained as thin as the day we met. A very long time ago.

After downing a somewhat warm peach yogurt, I hit call back.

"Oh, God, Tempe! You've got to come!" Anne's tone made Birdie seem tranquil in comparison.

"Where are you?"

"At the beach house. Now that the weenie boy-cop at the connector finally let me onto the island." Vowels reflecting her Alabama birth and Mississippi schooling, broadened further by the moment's indignation. "You wouldn't believe the Gestapo—"

"How does it look?"

"Devastated! I need help!"

"Take a deep breath."

Long pause. Then, "Right. You're absolutely right. I'm sounding eighty-proof bonkers."

"The house is still standing?"

"Yes."

"Your roof is still on?"

"Most of it."

"The roads are open?"

"Yes."

"Do you have power?"

"Not yet. Jesus, Lord, nothing's working. The damn commode won't flush!"

"It'll flush. The seat just won't light up. Besides, you have six others."

"I can't charge the car. I'm trapped here!"

Sounded similar to my morning. Except for the TOTO toilet and the Tesla.

"Where is TT?" I asked.

"Who the flipping flamingo knows?"

For years, Anne was married to an attorney named Tom Turnip. Decades back, when Tom was a second-year associate, a senior partner at his firm addressed him as Ted for an entire month. We'd called him Tom-Ted ever since. TT.

The marriage eventually ended. Long, unoriginal story. Anne walked away with a handsome settlement, including property at the Isle of Palms, South Carolina, known as IOP. Despite the financial spanking, she and TT remain friends. With benefits. Apparently, post-storm restoration was not among them.

"Anne, I can't—"

"They've reversed the eastbound lanes on I-26 back to normal. You won't have any problem getting here."

"It's not that."

"Did you have much damage at your place?"

"No. But—"

"Are you working on any *humongous* cases?"

"No. But—"

"If your boss needs you, Charlotte is just three hours away."

She had me there. And were the situation reversed, I knew Anne would drop everything to rush to my aid. She had in the past. More than once.

I looked at the clock.

"Fine." Unnecessarily dramatic sigh. "It'll take me at least an hour to secure the annex and pack a few things."

"Hallelujah, Harry! The kitchen's intact so I'll mix us a whole passel of drinks with those little paper umbrellas in 'em. Virgin for you, of course. Thank God, I've got Fritos in the pantry."

I promised an infusion of provisions and disconnected.

Turning, I saw Birdie watching me intently.

"Ready for a road trip?"

Totally noncommittal stare.

A quick call to Nguyen, minimal packing, a go at the tree limb jamming the back door, then we were off.

Driving across town was an experience I don't wish to repeat. Broken branches and downed trees littered the streets, requiring U-turns and rerouting at several points. Traffic lights were malfunctioning at many intersections, forcing drivers to figure things out for themselves. Some were better at that than others.

Normally, it's twenty minutes from the annex to I-77. That morning, it took sixty. With Birdie yowling the whole way.

Three hours after leaving Charlotte, I'd exited I-26 and gone several miles along I-526 when my phone rang for the third time that day.

Area code 843.

The call that would send my life off-kilter for weeks and alter my worldview forever.

"Temperance Brennan." I answered, using speakerphone.

"Dr. Brennan. My name is Ebony Herrin." The voice was gravelly, neither high nor low. Based on pitch and cadence, I thought the caller might be black and male. Wasn't sure on either. "I'm the newly elected Charleston County coroner."

"How can I help you, Dr. Herrin?"

"No need for titles. I'm an RN."

"How can I be of help?" Sir? Madam?

"I called your office in Charlotte, got forwarded to Dr. Nguyen. She told me you were heading to Charleston."

A little backstory.

With one short and unpleasant hiatus, I've served for decades as forensic anthropologist for the Mecklenburg County Medical Examiner in Charlotte, North Carolina. The MCME is the decoder of death for the region, and I'm the specialist who analyzes remains unfit for a pathologist's scalpel: the decomposed, dismembered, burned, mummified, mutilated, and skeletal.

Throughout my career, my boss was Dr. Tim Larabee, a brilliant pathologist, amateur marathoner, and all-around good guy. Larabee ran the office until a hopped-up junkie took him out with two bullets to the gut in a mindless mugging.

After Larabee's murder, Dr. Margot Heavner was hired. In her spare time, the new chief authored tell-all books on forensics that earned her the label Dr. Morgue. To boost sales, Dr. Morgue appeared on any media platform that would have her and sensationalized her work. I didn't like many of her comments. And said so. As a result, there was history between us.

Case in point. I publicly criticized Heavner for a series of interviews she did with a tinfoil-hat blogger and conspiracy theorist named Nick Body. Heavner was incensed. And held a grudge. Thus, the hiatus. During Dr. Morgue's tenure, I was exiled from the MCME.

Fortunately, that tenure was short. Within months of assuming her duties, Heavner was exposed as corrupt and forced to resign in disgrace. Dr. Samantha Nguyen was chosen as her replacement.

Unlike Heavner, Nguyen had no trouble directing outside callers to me.

"Yes." Tires humming as I rolled across the bridge spanning the Wando River. Glancing south, I saw the quayside cranes at the Wando harbor, dark and bony against the pinks and yellows of the fading day.

"As I'm sure you're aware, we've had no resident forensic anthropologist in South Carolina for many years. But I noted from old reports that you've done consults for my predecessor."

"Yes." Wary.

"I have a situation that requires your expertise."

"I'm listening." Not wanting to.

"Last night's hurricane tossed a container ashore down near the battery. I won't burden you with details on the phone, but a couple of kayakers found the thing early this morning, pried off the lid, and spotted what they thought was a body. They called the cops, the cops called me.

"My investigator collected the container and transported it to the MUSC morgue. There are actually two people inside. Just eye-balling the bulk, it looks to be one adult and one kid."

"Any possibility of visual IDs?" Seriously, Brennan? If that were the case, why would Herrin be contacting you?

"The amount of mass tells me decomp will be too advanced."

"Any personal effects, clothing, jewelry, et cetera?"

"Both bodies were wrapped in plastic sheeting secured with electrical wire. I didn't want to do too much poking around, but I peeled back enough to see that at least the one is nude."

From nowhere, a flashback image. A woman. A child. A plastic container washed from the sea.

My gut clenched, and my mouth went dry.

I swallowed.

"Any clues to cause of death?"

"I caught a better glimpse of the one body, because of the kids pulling on the wrapping and me tugging it a bit more. Looks to be a single bullet to the head. Also, the fingers and teeth are gone."

It can't be.

"You'll need a pathologist." Sounding calmer than I felt.

"I like a guy named Klopp. I've left him a message suggesting y'all meet at the hospital tomorrow. I'll text you the time he's available."

"Fine."

"A detective named Vislosky came to the scene. Not sure about her stomach for autopsies." A brief pause, then, "Tell me what you need."

I did, and we disconnected.

Moments later, I crossed the bridge connecting Mount Pleasant to the Isle of Palms. Salt marsh stretched to the horizon on both sides, tranquil and still. Here and there, I saw a wink of white, an ibis or egret, fading into shadow along with the spartina grass in which it stood.

I turned onto Palm Boulevard, a single phrase ricocheting in my head, a mantra born of foreboding.

It can't be.

It can't be.

4

Wednesday, October 6–Thursday, October 7

Anne was four chardonnays in when I arrived. And, predictably, quite serene. Despite one downed palmetto palm that had taken out a corner of the front porch.

Birdie, not a fan of travel in any form, radiated displeasure through the mesh window of his carrier. While I set up a feline hygiene station, Anne's term, she did her best to cheer him with tidbits of a Whopper left over from her lunch.

Anne has never been a cat person, so her best wasn't great. Ditto for dogs, birds, rabbits, and fish. Sensing this aversion to pets, the cat kept his distance, despite the tempting bribes.

The power was still out, so Anne and I barbecued grouper fillets on the grill. I'd brought lettuce, tomatoes, and a somewhat sad-looking avocado that combined into a passable salad. All the chopping and tossing and grilling distracted me momentarily from the gruesome images troubling my thoughts.

We dined on the back deck, watching the ocean roll ashore and recede. Like my hostess, it was also remarkably calm.

In addition to the uprooted palm, the damage that had goosed Anne into near-panic mode included sand in the yard and loss of the board-

29

walk leading over the dunes and down to the beach. She could now see the humor in her overreaction. In everything, actually, funny or not.

We talked as we ate. Nothing serious, mostly our kids. Herrin's call had made me far too anxious to tackle anything deep.

Anne reported that her youngest, Stuart, was still a gay rights activist and currently living in Colorado. The twins, Lola and Josh, were in L.A. trying to break into film, one as a writer, one as an actor. I reported that my daughter, Katy, finishing her second deployment to Afghanistan, was due to rotate stateside in several weeks. We slapped a high five and yelled "Hot damn!"

Anne asked about Ryan. I explained that he was in Yellowknife.

"That boy's a keeper," she said, not slurry but moving that way. "Dangle him much longer, he'll slip the line."

"You've mentioned that." Ad nauseam.

"Well, it's true. What's your damn problem?"

When I danced around an answer, she didn't press.

"Anything interesting going workwise these days?"

Wishing to avoid the inquisition that would ensue should I mention Herrin's call, I told her about Polly Beecroft and the death mask.

"So who is it?" When I'd ended.

"I don't know. But here's the odd part. They all look vaguely familiar to me."

"The twin sisters and their grandmother and great-aunt?" Beyond dubious.

"And the mask."

"How can that be if you'd never laid eyes on any of them? I mean, before Polly."

"Maybe they remind me of someone I've met."

"You said Polly has a condo at Rosewood. Maybe you saw her there."

"I considered that. But Mama's only lived there a very short time. And her unit isn't anywhere near Polly's, not even in the same building. Besides, if I'd seen Polly in passing, I think I'd remember."

After a pause, Anne said, "Josh and Lola look about as much alike as a parrot and a hamster."

"They aren't monozygotic."

Blank stare.

"In their case, two little swimmers found two separate eggs."

"Right. Different genes. Chromosomes. Whatever."

Anne disappeared into the kitchen for another chardonnay fill-up. Her fifth? A text pinged in as she was coming back through the door.

I glanced at my phone. Herrin.

"Is that *monsieur le détective*?"

"No."

"Katy?"

"No."

"Brad fuckin' Pitt?" Boozy chuckle at her own joke.

Herrin's corpses were not my preferred topic of conversation. But my absence the next day would need justification.

"It's the Charleston County coroner," I said.

There are two types of people in this world: those who wish to avoid all reference to my work and those who relish every grisly detail. Like my mother, my BFF rolls with the latter.

Anne leaned forward, eyes luminous with reflected moonlight. "Dish."

"She wants my help with a case." He?

"A murder?" Entirely too enthused.

"It's no big deal. Some remains washed ashore during the storm."

Sensing I wasn't being straight with her, Anne's antennae went live.

"If it's no big deal"—hooking slightly sloppy air quotes—"why have you been tense as a bedspring all evening?"

What the hell? Herrin hadn't shared top-secret intel. And discussing my fears might ease them.

I outlined the basics. The container. The remains. The plastic wrapping and electrical wire. The trauma. Anne listened without interrupting.

When I'd finished, "Sounds grisly, but nothing you haven't seen before."

"That's the problem. It sounds exactly like a case I had in Quebec."

"When?"

"Fifteen years ago."

"Are you serious?"

"I am."

"That's a long time back and a long way from here."

I shrugged.

"Fine. What are the parallels?"

Images fired in my brain.

I began listing items using the fingers of my right hand.

Pointer. "In both cases, the bodies were stripped, wrapped in plastic, placed in a waste container, and thrown or dropped into the ocean." Technically, it was a river in Montreal, but close enough. Middle digit. "In Quebec, I estimated that one individual was a female in her thirties, the other a child between eight and ten. Herrin thinks the victims here are an adult and a kid."

"Are you certain that's true?"

Good point, Annie. "No. Herrin is an RN, not a medical doctor or anthropologist."

"Go on."

I continued, *sans* digits. "In both cases, death was due to gunshot trauma to the head. In both cases, the victims' fingers were cut off and their teeth were destroyed."

"So, no prints, no dentals." Did I mention that Anne watches a lot of crime shows?

I nodded.

"Time since death?"

"It was hard to be precise. I estimated more than one but less than five years."

"Did Ryan work the case?"

"He and I busted our asses for months. At Ryan's urging, a task force was formed. Members searched missing-persons records to hell and back. Canvassed everyone living anywhere near the site where the container washed up. Pulled marina and port records going back years. Set up special phone lines for call-in tips."

I recalled the effort as if it was yesterday.

"Ryan floated queries to every elementary school in Quebec asking if any kid had stopped attending, eventually expanded to other provinces and down into Vermont and New York. He spent endless hours checking and rechecking the RCMP, FBI, and other databases.

"I had facial approximations made from the skulls. The sketches were broadcast by a few TV stations and published in some papers. Surprisingly, the media weren't all that interested."

"And?"

"And zilch. It all led nowhere."

"The victims were never ID'd?"

"Nope."

"What happened to them?"

"Eventually, the bodies were buried." I went silent, recalling the heartbreak I'd felt at our failure.

"That's so sad."

"One of those victims was just a kid. To this day, that kid is lying in a grave marked by nothing but a number. Meanwhile, someone somewhere is wondering what happened to her, and someone else is thinking they got away with it." Said with far too much emotion.

"That case really got to you," Anne said softly.

"Child murders always do."

"Because of Kevin?" Reaching out to place her hand on mine.

When my baby brother succumbed to leukemia at age three, my entire eight-year-old universe collapsed. Though I'm not a believer in Freudian theory, I suspect that at some level, Kevin's passing is the subconscious force underlying my commitment to the dead.

"No," I mumbled. "Maybe. Hell, who knows?"

Anne knocked back the remains in her glass, set it overly carefully on the table, and stood.

"Tomorrow I get to rounding up workers to sort out this mess,"

she said, twirling an upraised hand to take in the house and yard.
"And you get to slapping names on those bodies."

In the year 2021 CE, the state of South Carolina still relies on a coroner system to oversee death within its boundaries. And on elections
to determine who that overseer will be.

To run for office, a candidate must be at least twenty-one years
old, a U.S. citizen, a county resident, a registered voter, a high-school
graduate, and free of any felony convictions. Hot damn. That excludes
Ted Bundy and the kid on that cereal commercial.

A medical examiner, on the other hand, is usually appointed and
must be a forensic pathologist, a pathologist, or, minimally, an MD.
While some coroners are very good at what they do, their roles are
limited and never involve scalpels or Y incisions.

Charleston County has an additional requirement for coroner,
met either by experience in death investigation or by varying edu-
cational achievements. One qualifying credential is a BS degree in
nursing. Thus, Ebony Herrin, RN.

Though Herrin's office is located out in the burbs, most autopsies are performed at the Medical University of South Carolina's main
hospital, a bland, multistory building in a complex of bland, multistory buildings situated a respectful hair outside Charleston's most
privileged hood, "South of Broad" on the "Peninsula." Think cobbled
streets, brick Georgians, walled gardens, carriage houses.

By nine thirty in the morning, I'd navigated the same sort of
debris field as I had in Charlotte. Lots of tree branches and Spanish
moss lying on the ground. A downed power line here and there.
Trash bins and lawn furniture dropped or washed up in odd places.
The occasional street blockage due to standing water. Already much
of the wreckage lay stacked or in large tangles along the curbs.

After parking as directed by Herrin, I made my way to Ashley
Avenue and went in through the hospital's main entrance, having

passed an armada of brightly colored food trucks along the way. *Promise to self: an empanada is in your future. Maybe a roti.*

Thanks to backup generators, the hospital was in full operation. After presenting ID at the desk, I requested directions to the morgue. The receptionist, an elderly black woman wearing an ill-fitting wig, asked me to wait. Then, moving at sloth speed, she dialed an extension and connected with someone somewhere, probably Cambodia.

Ten minutes later, a young man approached, bony arms dangling from the sleeves of scrubs at least one size too large. His skin was blotchy, his hair so thin it made the wig lady's arrangement look good.

"Dr. Brennan?" His name tag said Brian.

"Yes."

"Follow me. I'll take you to the second floor."

I did. He did.

"Ladies change in there." Hooking a thumb at one of several doors along the hall. "Scrubs are on shelves to the left." More thumb. "Autopsies there."

Thanking Brian, obviously a man of few words, I entered a small room with lockers lining the walls and forming rows in the middle. A metal bench ran down the center of each subdivided area.

The scrubs were located as promised. I found a set in size small, changed from my street clothes, and headed out.

Passing what I assumed were staff offices, I entered where Brian had indicated and found myself in the heart of the operation. Surrounding me were an elevator for direct access to the morgue one floor down, a viewing area, a main autopsy room, and a smaller autopsy room, possibly for decomp and other malodorous cases.

Stepping into the viewing area, I assessed the space in which I'd be working. Noted stainless-steel tables, roll carts, countertops, sinks, and hanging scales. Multidrawered cabinetry. Adjustable high-intensity lights. Painted concrete flooring generously outfitted with drains. The same setup I'd seen dozens of times.

In addition to Brian, two people were present, one of each gender. The woman, dressed in navy blazer, white polo, and khaki chinos, stood off by herself, thumbs hooking her belt, eyes roving the room. Roughly six feet tall, with mahogany skin and sage-green eyes, she looked like she'd emerged from preschool a cop.

The man was hunched down, observing something on a computer screen. With elephant ears, a beak nose, and bulging Adam's apple, he resembled the cartoon version of Ichabod Crane, only older, taller, and thinner.

A prebreakfast cyber search had revealed that MUSC has five pathologists on faculty, among them one Walter Carl Klopp. I assumed Ichabod was Dr. Klopp.

Klopp's scrubs suggested he'd already been cutting. Blood smeared the right half of his chest, and a kumquat-shaped splotch darkened one sleeve.

Each of the two tables held a body bag. The contents on the left looked considerably more substantial than those on the right.

Deep breath.

Odor carried outward as I pushed through the swinging stainless-steel door, an acrid-sweet mix of refrigerated flesh, putrefaction, and disinfectant. And a touch of something else. Something briny and pungent that triggered images of the sea.

Three heads swiveled my way. Klopp smiled. The cop did not.

"Dr. Brennan, I presume." Klopp's mask was off and bunched in one hand. "Herrin says we're to treat you like royalty."

"I hope I can be of use," I said.

"Walter Klopp." Doing that two-finger salute thing some men find cool. "Walt."

"Tempe," I said, pleased that Klopp hadn't offered to shake.

Klopp turned toward the woman. "Detective Vislosky is with the Charleston PD."

Vislosky nodded.

I nodded.

"Just finished a medical autopsy." Did Klopp feel compelled to explain his untidy scrubs? "A capno case."

I must have looked confused.

"Capnocytophaga." Klopp chin-cocked the screen he'd been viewing. "Have a look. You don't see it every day."

Curious, I crossed to him.

The image showed a corpse on a table identical to the pair behind us. Its trunk and skull gaped empty. Its organs lay divided between a hanging scale and a cork cutting board.

"The poor bastard was infected by his own cockapoo."

I wasn't sure what that meant but was clear on one thing. The poor bastard had met a most unpleasant end. One leg, amputated at the knee, showed surgical scarring but little healing on the stump. The surviving foot and every finger were black as creosote. Scaly patches covered the man's forehead, lips, and cheeks, and a yawning triangle was all that remained of his nose.

I made a note to myself to read up on capno. And to avoid it. Cockapoos?

"Let's start with externals on both." Klopp spoke to Brian, indicating Herrin's container victims. "Get an overall sense of the situation."

Vislosky watched as Brian, Klopp, and I gloved and masked. Added aprons and goggles for extra protection.

When we were ready, Klopp gave a thumbs-up.

Upon arrival at the morgue, each victim had been assigned a case number indicating that the autopsy was forensic in nature. Brian started with the body bag showing the larger bulge, AF21-986. The *whrrrp* of the zipper sounded like a scream in the silence.

He crossed to AF21-987.

Another scream.

Vislosky kept her distance.

I stepped close.

5

Thursday, October 7

It was déjà vu.

Same sky-blue polyethylene sheeting. Same poppy-red electrical wire. Same parrot-green Chlorophyta algae. Same stone-gray polypropylene bin bearing a faded orange label.

Same multicolored skull.

A rainbow déjà vu.

After stumbling upon the container and prying it open, the kayakers had put some effort into tugging at the plastic sheet wrapping the uppermost body. Herrin had cut some wire and a bit more plastic to confirm that the body was human. And the ocean had taken its toll.

Klopp directed Brian to further unwrap the skull of AF21-986 as much as possible without cutting. His efforts exposed half the face. The orbits stared empty and wide, as though startled at the sudden exposure to light.

Below the head, hints of algae-coated bone could be seen through tears in the plastic. A toothless section of mandible. Three proximal phalanges truncated at mid-shaft. A slimy pelvic rim.

Things had gone slightly better for AF21-987, the lower-down and smaller of the two victims. There the macabre packaging had remained largely intact.

Herrin had supplied everything I'd requested. While I arranged equipment on a countertop—I'm finicky about placement—Klopp shot video of the remains.

Bone saw. Calipers. Magnifier. Forceps. Tweezers. Dental picks. Soft bristle brushes in graduated sizes. Toothbrush. Specimen-collection vials.

Finally, I flipped through an array of charts and diagrams, chose several, and snapped them onto a clipboard.

When I turned, Klopp was setting down the camera.

"Did you get that?" I pointed to the fifty-gallon bin dripping muddy seawater onto a tarp in one corner. Brought here at my request.

Wordlessly, Klopp crossed and began recording more footage. After labeling two vials, I joined him, a hollowness blossoming in my chest.

"The lettering's toast." Klopp was hunched as before, this time for close-ups. Given his height, it was quite a hunch.

"It's a biohazard warning," I said. "For medical waste."

"I'll be damned. You can read that?"

"Film the rocks in the bottom."

"Bastard weighted the thing down to sink."

As with the Montreal vics.

I indicated several patches of encrustation on the container's inner and outer surfaces. "Shoot the barnacles, then I'll collect samples."

"Why?"

"They might be useful for determining when the container went into the water. Maybe where, if you get extraordinarily lucky."

In my peripheral vision, I sensed the first glimmer of interest from Vislosky. Unhooking her thumbs, she straightened and watched closely as I detached a number of the tiny, stalk-like crustaceans, divided the collection, and sealed each half into a separate vial.

Intent eyes followed me back to the counter. When my gaze met hers, one penciled brow cocked up ever so slightly.

"Or they might not," I said.

Vislosky said nothing.

An autopsy rarely provides the drama depicted in some crime fiction. Uncommon is the great *Aha!* moment when the microscopic scale of an extinct Patagonian reptile is tweezed from the victim's inner ear. The goals, as with any scientific endeavor, are threefold: accuracy, precision, and documentation.

The protocol is specific, the process tedious.

Klopp and I discussed strategy. Agreed. He would focus on soft tissue. I would focus on bone. My task would turn out to be more taxing than his.

Odor swelled as Brian, Klopp, and I eased each bundle from its body bag. The noxious cocktail of rotting algae, sea creatures, and human flesh burned my eyes and forced me to breathe through my mouth.

AF21-986 made a wet *thunk* sliding onto the stainless steel. AF21-987, feather-light, made almost no sound. Both corpses had been curled tight in order to stuff them into the container.

As Klopp shot more video and I made notes, Brian manned the wire cutters. Twenty minutes of snipping and peeling resulted in our first unobstructed view of the remains.

You might think that sinking deep below the waves would be a good way to avoid all that nasty postmortem decomp business. You'd be wrong. A corpse in the ocean is subjected to a variety of physical and biological forces, all committed to recycling the body's molecules back to nature. Temperature, salinity, currents, depth, and the nature of the substrate all affect how long the process takes. As on land, many creatures play a role.

Marine animals are as opportunistic as their terrestrial counterparts. Fish and eels will scavenge. Arthropods, especially the large ones like lobsters, shrimp, and crabs, are experts at opening up a body. Mollusks, many of which normally dine on algae, will happily switch to carrion. Echinoderms such as sea stars, sand dollars, sea urchins, and sea cucumbers will belly up to flesh if given the chance.

And there are the aforementioned barnacles. These and other sessile invertebrates don't so much feed on remains as attach to them.

The polypropylene bin had survived immersion better than a metal one might have but had failed in its promise of a watertight seal. Degraded and warped, the lid had allowed the inflow of salt water and invasion by a variety of species.

And that invasion had kicked the recycling circus into high gear.

I yielded first access to Klopp, waited while he surveyed each set of remains. Watching him bend to the task, I couldn't help but think of a praying mantis. Finally, he straightened and turned to me.

"Seems this will be your show, Dr. Brennan." Shaking his head. "No brain, no organs, nothing but bones. Not sure if that pleases me or not."

"Perhaps you could sift through the contents of the bin? Continue shooting video?"

"I'm happy to do that. Actually, I wouldn't mind observing while you work. Maybe I can pick up a few tricks."

"Of course." I hate having anyone look over my shoulder.

I started with AF21-986. Though completely skeletonized, due to the tightness of the plastic shroud, the major segments of the body had remained in rough anatomical position. The small bones of the hands and feet, not so much.

"Why so splotchy?" As I was disentangling and rearranging skeletal elements, Klopp was filming the red, green, and blue mottling on the skull.

"Algae."

"What's that?" Zooming in on a series of coiled carbonate tubes on the frontal and parietal bones.

"Probably some sort of sea worm."

"And the little craters?" Klopp was asking about a cluster of small, round pits on the left parietal and temporal bones.

"Snail rasping."

"Snails?" Skeptical.

"Except for the bivalves—"

"Clams, mussels, oysters, the good-eating critters?"

"Yes. Except for them, all mollusks—think whelks, periwinkles, slipper snails—have chitinous teeth that are very efficient at grating on bone. But I'm not a marine biologist."

"'Course you're not." Klopp resumed filming. "Got one bullet entrance at the back of the skull. Looks like she was shot from behind."

I didn't agree or disagree.

"Teeth are history. Suppose they fell out postmortem?"

"I doubt it." I knew I'd find microfracturing on the mandible and maxilla. Didn't say so.

"Either way, they're gone. Ditto the fingers. Maybe snipped off with pruning shears? We've had some luck nailing tool type from patterning on the cut surfaces. You done any of that, maybe with dismemberment cases?"

Focused on my task, I nodded absently.

Klopp shot a bit more footage, then moved to the other table.

I continued my reconstruction, paying particular attention to cranial and pelvic features and to the state of the long bones and clavicles. By the time I'd finished, I had a sense of the victim.

And the mantra was again battering my brain.

It can't be.

It can't be.

"Got some tissue on the foot and ankle on this one. Might yield DNA."

I crossed to AF21-987.

Klopp was right. Remnants of ligament and cartilage lingered at the major joints, and a swath of putrefied skin and muscle overlay the left tarsals and metatarsals.

"Looks like we've got some fibers stuck to the underside of the zygomatic."

Before I could respond, Klopp had picked up forceps and begun tweezing threads from the back of the right cheekbone. I marked a vial and handed it to him.

When he returned it, sealed, I held it up to the light.

"I think these are hairs," I said.

"Might be," he agreed, squinting at the vial, then shaking his head. "Don't folks do the damnedest things?"

The hairs, short and curly, were dark at the roots, cotton-candy-pink throughout the shafts.

I snapped a shot, then made a note on my form.

"This one's smaller than the one over there." Klopp stated the obvious. "Herrin had it pegged as a kid. I'm not so sure. Too bad we've got no teeth for aging."

I didn't respond. My eyes were roving over the bones. The cranial sutures. I picked up a clavicle. The skull. An innominate—one of the fused bones of the pelvis.

"Looks like the left foot got twisted backward, then held in place inside the plastic," Klopp went on.

"This one went into the container first. Then she"— I indicated AF21-986—"was forced in on top of her. That positioning provided some protection."

For the first time that day, Vislosky spoke. "She?"

I nodded.

"How do you know?" Klopp asked.

"Mostly the pelvis."

"Show me." Klopp circled the table.

Vislosky strode over to us.

Crap.

Mine was going to be a very long day. Not in the mood for an anatomy lesson, I decided to skim through it quickly.

While rotating the innominate of AF21-986, I described features, using common terminology and profoundly oversimplifying. "Broad, flaring hip area on the upper portion. Long pubic element and wide subpubic angle in front. Broad sciatic notch." I demonstrated the breadth of the last by inserting and wiggling my thumb.

"You can tell from just that bone?" Vislosky sounded grudgingly interested.

I swapped the pelvis for the cranium. "The skull's also important. Note the smooth muscle attachments, small mastoid processes and brow ridges, and sharp upper orbital margins." Pointing to each.

"Any thoughts on age?" Klopp asked.

"They're both young," I said.

"How young?" Vislosky asked.

I retrieved the innominate and pointed to the pubic symphysis, the point at which that pelvic half would have met its counterpart in life. "See how rippled this surface looks? That tells me young."

I turned the bone to show the curving upper rim of the hip blade.

"Rippled," Klopp said.

"Bingo," I said. "A crest of bone fuses onto that surface between the ages of fifteen and twenty-two in girls. These are very broad and very rough estimates. Anyway, it's not there."

I swapped the innominate for a clavicle. "This is a collarbone. See how one end is rippled?" Vislosky and Klopp nodded, never raising their eyes. "A tiny cap of bone called an epiphysis fuses onto that end during the late teens or early twenties in girls, sometimes later. It's not there."

I switched the clavicle for a femur. "This is the thigh bone." I pointed to a large knob at one end. "That's the femoral head. See that line?" Again, the nods. "That tells me that the epiphysis is in the process of fusing but hasn't finished. That fusion takes place between the ages of thirteen and seventeen for most girls."

"She was in her mid-teens." Vislosky got it.

"Probably," I said.

Thumb jab at AF21-986. "And that one?"

"A little older."

Vislosky shot me a *gimme a break* look.

As Ryan pointed out, I despise being pressured.

"I dislike drawing conclusions until I've completed my analysis."

"Do it anyway," Vislosky said.

I didn't respond.

"Nothing you say will leave this room?" Klopp said, leveling a meaningful glance at Vislosky.

"What am I, Fox News?" she snapped.

"Knowledge of descriptors will help Detective Vislosky begin her investigation," Klopp said to me, trying to defuse the tension.

I started to object. Vislosky cut me off.

"Look, some asshole capped these two, clipped their fingers, then deep-sixed them in the Atlantic. You're saying this one was a kid." Indicating the bones at her elbow. "That makes me want to net *said* asshole and put his nuts in a vise. The sooner I can float profiles and search MP files, the sooner I can figure out who these two are. Which is step one in nailing the fuckwad who killed them. *Comprendo*?"

Offensive as her tone was, she had a point.

"As I said, your vics are both female. This one was probably fifteen to seventeen." Indicating the near table. "That one was a few years older."

Vislosky pulled a notebook and pen from one pocket. "Anything else?"

"Some asshole capped both of them."

The sage eyes showed no amusement. "Race? Height? Medical history? Individual peculiarities?"

"Not at this point."

Vislosky pocketed her pad, strode to the counter, and tossed a card on it.

"I'll be waiting for your call."

I watched the WNBA frame disappear through the door.

6

Klopp lasted until six. Brian and I were there past ten.

First, I did a full skeletal inventory of the older victim. Next, I took measurements and ran them through the Fordisc 3.1 computer program that classifies adults by ancestry and sex. Then I calculated height.

Morphoscopics and metrics completed, I shot video and made casts of the bullet entrance and exit wounds. That finished, I did the same with the truncated end of each phalange. Finally, I examined every millimeter of every bone with my naked eye and under magnification.

Brian captured stills as I worked. And assisted in collecting samples for possible DNA and radioisotope testing. He also finished sifting through the muck and bagging every item that came from the container. As I was completing my notes on AF21-986, he made a stealth run to the food trucks. I'm not sure what we ate.

After dinner, I repeated the process for the younger victim.

I noticed the time as we were rolling the gurneys from the elevator back into the morgue cooler: 10:29 p.m.

And the fact that Ryan had called. More than once. No voice mail.

Anne was still awake when I got to the IOP beach house, sipping a chardonnay while viewing an old episode of *Bones* on an iPad she'd plugged into a portable charger. By candlelight.

"Hey, girlfriend. Join me." Patting the sofa. "I'm watching the one where they find a body squashed behind the gym bleachers."

"That's the last thing I want to see."

"Right." Then, tapping the bricklike object tethered to her tablet, "Pretty cool, eh? My Zeus portable jump starter and USB charger."

"You bought that?" Stunned that such a thing remained available for purchase.

"No. TT reminded me it was here."

"Doesn't this house have a backup generator?"

"It does. I sort of forgot to schedule a gas fill-up. They're coming tomorrow. Can I make you a snack?"

"I already ate."

"What?"

"Maybe chili."

"Was today just too ghastly?"

I shrugged.

"Might help to talk about it."

"I just want to shower and turn in."

"Why don't you do your toilette while I make us some nice chamomile tea?" Anne, undeterred. "It will help you relax."

"OK." Resolved not to discuss my day. "Tea sounds nice."

The shower was quick. And tepid at best. Ten minutes later, I was back in the living room, smelling and feeling considerably better.

My resolve lasted about five minutes.

"Two girls. My gut says one was around fifteen, the other closer to twenty. Each killed with a single shot to the back of the head."

"Crapsticks."

"Big ones." Sipping my herbal brew. "How did you boil the water?"

"Put the kettle on the grill."

"Genius."

"Do you still see a link to your Canada case?"

"One of the Montreal victims was in her thirties, the other was around nine or ten. Here they were both in their teens."

"And yet?"

"A medical waste container dumped into the ocean. Bodies wrapped in plastic sheeting and secured with wire. Two female victims. A single bullet to the brain. Severed fingers and smashed teeth."

"That's a shit ton of coincidence."

"It is."

Anne thought about that a long time. Then, "Why do you suppose that case went cold?"

"Duh. We never ID'd the vics." A little too sharp.

"But why?"

A question I'd wrestled with repeatedly over the years. Why hadn't we?

"Back then was a raucous time for Montreal law enforcement."

"That whole Quebec separation thing?"

I shook my head. "*La guerre des motards.*"

Anne raised one brow

"The biker war."

"What bikers?"

"Motorcycle gangs. Beginning in the mid-nineties, the Hells Angels and some local talent called the Rock Machine began slugging it out over control of the Quebec drug trade. From then until around 2002, it was unbridled killing and bombing on both sides."

"How did it end?"

"In March 2001, a joint effort by the Mounties, the Ontario provincial force, the Sûreté du Québec, and the Montreal police resulted in the arrests of Angels all over Canada. Something like one hundred thirty-eight in Quebec alone, another fifty-one in Calgary."

"Good score."

"It was. But the violence didn't stop with that. In 2006, the Bandidos, then the only possible rivals to what remained of the Angels, self-destructed with the killing of eight of their own members in Ontario. The media dubbed it the Shedden massacre."

"Judas on a trampoline. Sounds like a wild ride back then."

"It was. And a lot of the bodies ended up in my lab."

"What does all this have to do with your container case?"

"Maybe a lot. The container washed ashore in 2006, not long after the Shedden massacre. That same week, a man was shot to death shortly after his release from prison. His body was found in a burning car not far from the site where the container turned up. The guy was some gang wannabe, and torching a vehicle was a common biker MO, so it was assumed to be an Angels or Bandidos hit."

"Which generated fear that the war was about to reignite."

"Exactly."

"So that investigation got more attention than your container case."

"That's an understatement. Everyone was focused on it. The Ontario and Quebec provincial police, the Montreal city PD, what remained of the task forces. And the slaughter of the Bandidos was all anyone was talking about. Other than Ryan, myself, and his small group at Crimes contre la Personne, no one was interested in old bones washed up from the St. Lawrence. Our case was largely neglected."

Birdie chose that moment to make his entrance. Hopping onto the sofa, he stretched full length between us.

"Also, all the separate investigations created a lot of false leads," I said. "Which led to loss of time and waste of resources."

"That must have been frustrating."

"It truly sucked. Besides those committed by these asshole bikers, murders weren't that common in Montreal. Our investigation should have been given high priority. But it wasn't. And we never ID'd our vics, a woman and a child. Which meant we could never narrow our focus."

"So the case went cold."

"As an Arctic stream."

Birdie rolled to his back. I started stroking his belly. He began purring like mad.

A few moments passed.

"What happened with the guy in the burning car?" Anne asked.

"I don't think the investigation went anywhere. After I examined the remains, I gave my report to the pathologist and to some detective. Ryan didn't catch that case. I was totally focused on the container vics, so I made no effort to follow up."

"If someone was charged, wouldn't you have heard? Or gotten a subpoena or something?"

"Possibly." I made a mental note to ask Ryan.

Anne reached out to pet the cat. He didn't recoil, but he didn't exactly melt to her touch.

"So." Anne picked up the thread. "You had no dentals and no prints on your container corpses. And you were unable to get DNA."

"We tried but failed to extract enough for sequencing. The bones were pretty degraded."

Anne was quiet for a very long time.

Then she made a startling suggestion.

7

Thursday, October 7–Friday, October 8

U p in my room, I opened the sliding glass door leading onto the balcony. The tide was out, and far across the beach, the ocean drummed its sibilant beat. The smell of salt air, seaweed, and wet sand, normally soothing, conjured images of a barrel and algae-coated bones.

And of something else.

A ring set with an emerald too garishly large to be real. Worthless. Except to a child who saw beauty in the gaudy stone and the peeling silver paint.

Though I'll never know for sure, I picture the little girl, desperate, slipping her treasure into the only hiding place available to her. On her knees, a gun barrel pressed to her head.

When I found the plastic bauble wedged in what was once the tiny esophagus, my heart stopped, and a burning desire consumed me. *I will avenge you*, I'd whispered to the dead child. *I will bring you down*, I'd whispered to her killer.

That awful moment lies perpetually curled in some dark corner of my mind. Over the years, I've learned to keep the memory in its lair. But, when goaded, the image slinks free, sharp and clear as a high-def print.

As does my obsession with motive. Unlike with other crimes, the reason for murder is often unclear. Jealousy? Passion? Revenge? Financial gain?

But a woman and a child? Had the killer's victims witnessed something that threatened him? Refused a demand? For money? For information? Did the killer promise to shoot the child if the woman didn't comply? Did the child die first, the woman begging for mercy? Did the woman die first, the child watching in terror?

Stop!

Forcing my head clear, I dropped onto the bed and propped myself up with pillows. After calculating the hour in the Northwest Territories, I phoned Ryan. He answered right away.

"*Bonjour, ma chère.*"

"Hey."

"I called several times, but you didn't pick up." A note of annoyance?

"Sorry. I spent the day in a morgue."

Ryan either missed that or chose to ignore it. "Where are you now?"

"At IOP. With Anne."

Silence.

"Anne Turnip?" I prompted. "My forever best friend?"

"The one with the legs tha—"

"Yes. She had some damage to her beach house and asked for my help."

"Anything major?"

"No. The storm hit pretty far south of Charleston, not a biggie, then moved offshore."

"Is the annex OK?"

"Unscathed. Still enjoying Yellowknife?"

"I discovered a place called Bullocks Bistro. It's on Ragged Ass Road. I may move here."

"Hm."

"There's a polar bear in the airport terminal."

"Alive?"

"Stuffed."

"Probably died waiting for baggage."

"It's Yellowknife."

I stifled a yawn.

"Am I keeping you up?" Ryan asked.

"Not very well. It was a long day."

"Spent in a morgue."

I should have known. Ryan misses nothing. I told him the whole story: the container, the wrappings, the vics, the severed fingers, the gunshot wounds to the head. He listened without interrupting.

There was a pause when I'd finished. Then Ryan said, sounding more cop than lover, "You're thinking about the case back in 2006."

"Yes." Suddenly wide awake. "You see the parallels, too?"

"Could be coincidence."

"My gut's telling me different."

"South Carolina is a long way from Quebec." Precisely the same reaction as Anne.

"Those vics never got the attention they deserved."

"Whoa."

"Not because of you, of course." Jesus. Fatigue was making me say all the wrong things. "Your team did everything possible. But coming on the heels of the Shedden massacre and the guy found torched in his car, everyone was freaked by a potential flare-up with the Angels."

"Some of the higher-ups thought the container murders might be gang-related," Ryan said.

"A woman and a child?"

"You're right. Not a biker MO."

"But the biker war was just so much sexier than old bones in a barrel."

"Not as sexy as you." Definitely not cop-speak. "When do you return to Montreal?"

"Two weeks. Listen, will you do me a huge favor?"

"There might be a quid pro quo involved. You know that thing you do with your—"

"Could you pull the case file? Send me anything you find?"

"I'll do what I can." Sounding far from confident. "It's been fifteen years."

"Thanks."

"What are you thinking?"

I told him about Anne's suggestion.

"That's a long shot," he said.

"From here to Pictor and back."

"Pictor?"

"The constellation where that kid discovered the new exoplanet."

The power returned sometime during the night. I awoke to the piercing whine of a chain saw. Merely the opening volley.

By nine, the house and grounds were crawling with workers. A solo carpenter was reconstructing the front porch. Another pair was hammering shingles onto the roof. A team was pumping sludge from the pool on the back deck. A guy was trimming palms and bundling fronds in front.

I'd just finished brewing coffee when Herrin called. I went through my notes. The coroner thanked me, then asked that I brief Vislosky. I agreed.

Instead of phoning, I decided to update her in person. Any excuse to escape the chaos.

Charleston's blue-blood and lace-curtain side of the tracks is a petal-shaped hunk of land carved from the Atlantic by two rivers, the Cooper on the east and the Ashley on the west. Particularly coveted is a hive of narrow, tree-lined streets at the petal's southern tip. Though far from a majority these days, many residents of this area, known as South of Broad, or SOB, claim ancestry back to the plantation culture before the Civil War.

I wound my way from IOP to Sullivan's Island, through Mount Pleasant, over the Cooper River Bridge and across the petal to 180 Lockwood Boulevard. Though close geographically, the address is centuries removed from the quaint shops, horse-drawn carriages, and narrow street-facing Georgians of SOB. Parking is adequate, though. A nice contrast.

The Chief Reuben M. Greenberg Municipal Complex houses the courthouse, the municipal court operations offices, the department of traffic and transportation, and a DMV office. Behind the Greenberg is the much larger Chief John Conroy Law Enforcement Center, home to the Charleston Police Department.

Looking at CPD main, I suspected a similar architectural hand had been at work to that at the MUSC hospital complex. Same functional but uninspiring square lines and miles of red brick and glass. Same palms growing in orderly rows never present in nature.

Across Lockwood stretched Brittlebank Park, a swath of green space fronting the Ashley River. To the northwest was the River Dogs stadium, home to the Yankees' A-level minor league team. To the southeast, the College of Charleston and a Marriot hotel. Only a few blocks distant was the building in which I'd toiled the previous day. And the scraggy stretch of shoreline where the container had beached itself.

Before leaving my car, I pulled Vislosky's card from my purse. She was assigned to the violent-crimes division. No shocker there.

I dialed. Vislosky answered and told me to come in.

I crossed the lot, climbed the steps, and entered CPD headquarters. The lobby was standard-issue. Scuffed tile. Wooden doors. Floor-bolted seating. Glass-fronted cases displaying trophies and photos of the department's outstanding performers.

And an item that caused me to halt for a moment.

Beside one pillar stood a bright red container provided by the CVS pharmacy chain. Lettering on its front explained the container's purpose: *Medical Disposal*. After snapping a photo with my phone, I crossed to reception and spoke to the duty officer. He asked for ID. I held my driver's license to the glass. He eyed it, then called upstairs.

Moments later, the elevator arrived. Vislosky was in it. Today's blazer was charcoal, the pants pale gray. Vislosky's glossy black hair haloed her head in short, tight curls.

We rode in silence, both focused on the digits lighting up then going dark. Now and then, I sneaked a sideways peek. Vislosky had at least five inches on me. Her stance, feet spread, body tense, suggested a perpetual preference for fight over flight.

When the doors opened, she led me down a corridor to a squad room that, like the lobby, offered no surprises. Cinder-block walls held city, state, and U.S. flags. Between them, bulletin boards were layered with photos, flyers, wanted notices, and takeout menus.

Vislosky's desk was in a far corner. B+ for neatness.

Ankle-hooking a chair from an absent neighbor, Vislosky gestured me to it. Seated on the opposite side of her desk, she asked, "Whatcha got?"

"It's nice to see you, too, detective." As I dug out my notes.

No smile from Vislosky.

"Two females. One fifteen to seventeen, one eighteen to twenty, but I wouldn't rule out someone as old as twenty-two. Both Caucasoid."

"White." Grabbing pen and paper.

"Yes. The younger was sixty-one to sixty-two inches tall, the older sixty-eight to seventy inches."

"Weight? Body build?"

"No can do," I said. "Except to say that the younger one was probably slight."

Vislosky raised her brows.

"Small muscle attachment points."

"Go on." Eyes on the paper.

"The younger girl suffered a lateral condylar fracture of the right humerus, probably nine months to a year before her death." When Vislosky looked up, I indicated a bony prominence on the outer part of my elbow. "The break healed well with no distortion, suggesting she was seen by a doctor, probably wore a cast for a few weeks."

"What causes that type of injury?"

"Kids fall."

Vislosky's chin came up, and her head tipped sideways. "How common is it?"

"Elbows account for about ten percent of all fractures in children."

Vislosky wrote something.

"She may have had short, dark hair tinted pink," I added, recalling the "threads" Klopp had discovered.

I stopped, feeling the same ache as during the autopsy. The youngster had broken her arm, perhaps turning a cartwheel or tumbling from a skateboard. She'd dyed her hair an outrageous cotton-candy pink, experimenting with the image she'd present to the world. Examining her bones, I'd sensed a joie de vivre mixed with adolescent insecurity. I'd been there once, in that awkward half-child, half-woman stage. So much hope. So much to live for. So much snuffed out.

Vislosky's question brought me back.

"And the older kid?"

"She had an abscess near her upper second left molar, active when she died, so she might have been in some pain. Doubtful she was being treated by a dentist."

Two desks over, a phone rang.

"Each suffered a single gunshot wound to the occipital."

Vislosky's eyes rolled up.

"The back of the head. The trajectory suggests the victims were on their knees, the shooter standing behind them."

"Execution-style."

Flash tableau of the woman and child in Montreal. I forced it aside.

"Looks that way. I found no evidence of violence elsewhere in either skeleton, other than postmortem."

"After they'd been shot."

"Yes." The phone went silent. "Both victims had their teeth knocked out or pulled and their fingers cut off just above the knuckles."

"Cut with what?"

"An implement with a non-serrated blade. My guess would be pruning shears. Unfortunately, that's all I can say."

"What else?"

"That's it."

"How long do you think they were in that container?"

"Hard to be exact. One to five years?"

"What about all that barnacle business?"

"That will take time. And different expertise."

"Who do I contact?"

"That's on you."

"The plastic?"

"Ordinary polyethylene sheeting. Ditto the wire. Common eighteen-gauge electrical available in any hardware department."

Vislosky tossed her pen onto the desktop, leaned back, and stretched out her legs. They went a very long way. A beat of silence, then, "You got all this from the bones?"

"Except for the intel on the availability of the wire."

"I'll be damned."

Vislosky picked up and waggled the pen back and forth in her fingers. They were very long fingers. Then she reached her free hand across the desk and smiled ever so slightly.

"I maybe was abrupt at the morgue yesterday." No apology, just laying it out there. "First name's Tonia."

"Temperance Brennan. Tempe." We shook, my hand disappearing inside hers. "Tonia is unusual."

"My mama heard it somewhere, probably wrote it down wrong. What the hell. She wanted me to be a doctor. I wanted to be a cop."

"You persisted."

"It's what I do." Vislosky pistol-pointed one ET finger at me, picked up and opened a sky-blue folder.

"After leaving the autopsy yesterday, I started hunting through MP reports. Went back five years looking for kids fitting your profiles. Got nada."

"How wide did you go?"

"No hits in the Charleston area, in South Carolina, North Carolina, or Georgia. Now I can refine my search. The medical info's gold. I'll contact hospitals, have them check their records back five years for any kid presenting with a"—her eyes rolled to her notes—"lateral condylar fracture."

"They'll love that."

"I'll reach out to the FBI, float queries to schools, check with the NCMEC." Vislosky referred to the National Center for Missing and Exploited Children.

For the next ten minutes, she laid out her game plan. It all sounded sadly familiar.

When Vislosky finished, I said, "These murders may have broader ramifications than you realize."

"Meaning?"

I told her about the Montreal case.

Her reaction was what I expected.

8

Friday, October 8

Ryan called around five thirty. I was working at my laptop on the back deck. Anne was below me in the yard, arguing with a worker. Loudly.

"*Bonjour, ma chère.*"

"Hey."

"What's all the yelling?"

"One of Anne's landscapers found a snake in a clump of sea oats. He wants to kill it. She's advocating for catch and release."

"What kind of snake?" Sounding like his sympathies lay with the guy with the rake.

"A harmless little ole blacksnake." Doing my best Anne imitation, at a much lower volume.

"What are you up to?" Ryan asked.

"Creating reports for my coroner friend Herrin and that lawyer Thorn. While everything is fresh in my mind."

"And a fresh mind it is."

"Were you able to pull the file?"

"Tell me I'm a genius."

"You're a genius."

"Tell me I'm your hero."

"What did you find?"

"Babe." Faux wounded.

"You're my hero. What did you find?"

"*Toute la patente.*"

"The whole file?"

"*La totale.*"

"Ryan." A note of impatience.

"Detectives' notes and reports, anthropologist's report, photos, some news clippings, the—"

"Is the file huge?" Totally psyched.

"No."

"Can you scan and send it to me?"

"Already in the works."

"You're my hero."

"Not an easy mission."

"Am I so hard to please?"

"No comment. But this should delight you. I also pulled up info on the guy who got broiled in his car."

"You think he's relevant?"

"Mostly I was curious. It bugged me that I couldn't remember how that investigation went down."

"Weren't you on special assignment a lot back then?"

"Yes." I heard a page flip. "The victim was ultimately ID'd by dental records. Jean-Pierre Tremblay from Sorel. The trail dead-ended for five years, then the cold-case unit reopened the investigation."

"Why?"

"I don't know. Anyway, it turned out Tremblay's common-law wife, Sonja, had a lot of time to think while hubby was in the slammer. Sonja decided she was over being Jean-Pierre's punching bag. Also, she'd found a new squeeze."

"Let me guess. Sonja and her new sweetie devised a plan."

"They shot Jean-Pierre within days of his release. Torched the car to make it look like a biker hit."

"You have to give them credit for keeping up with the news."

"Indeed."

"Were Sonja and company charged?"

"Here's the mother lode of all karma. Their truck was pancaked on a railroad crossing a year after they popped Jean-Pierre."

"Both were killed?"

"Quite thoroughly." I heard a chair squeak. "You should get the file on the container vics this evening."

"Really, Ryan. I owe you."

"When might you deliver?" Voice husky and not at all subtle.

"I'm not due at the lab for a couple of weeks."

"Not sure I can wait."

"I know you'll keep busy."

"Got a call today from a guy in Vermont."

"You are one popular PI."

"It's that genius thing I've got going."

The shouting had stopped, and Anne was clumping up the stairs.

"I'll watch for your email."

"Ciao."

"Ciao."

"That moron has the brains of a blueberry pancake." Anne's hair was in the last hurrah of a hasty updo.

"He's a yard guy."

"Exactly. Which means he doesn't chair the committee on what fauna lives and what dies. Not on my property."

"Where is the serpent in question?"

"The tree trimmer helped me trap him in a seed bag. Promised to drive him over to the marsh."

"Can blacksnakes survive in salt water?"

Anne just looked at me. She had a smear of what looked like guacamole on her right cheek.

"I'm sure Señor Snake will prosper in his new home," I said. "What should we do for dinner?"

"I'm cooking."

Oh, boy.

I went back to my report.

An hour later, Anne called me inside. She'd made shrimp and pimiento cheese grits, a dish guaranteed to raise my cholesterol level.

"You got a lot done," I said, adding crustaceans to the orange carbs heaped on my plate.

"Not easy when the help has a collective IQ that suggests they need weekly watering."

"Were you outside all day?"

"A goodly part. But not all. I did some research. You're going to light right up when you hear what I found."

"What kind of research?"

"On death masks."

I must have looked puzzled.

"Polly Beecroft? The photos?" she prompted.

"Right."

"Lord a'mighty, Tempe. Did you forget about that sweet old lady?"

"Of course not." Given the hurricane and the container case, I had.

"Hold on."

Anne left the table, returned moments later with her laptop. Which she deposited on a rather large glob of grits.

"OK. The practice of preserving faces in wax or plaster, sometimes bronze, began way back in antiquity. You've seen pictures of Tutankhamen's mask, right?"

"I've seen the real thing."

"Of course you have." Rolling her eyes. "Tut's was a funerary mask. Well-heeled Romans also made masks but for different reasons. To display their ancestors, maybe even to worship them, I'm not totally clear on that."

Anne stopped to pop a shrimp into her mouth. Chewed.

"The Victorians were obsessed for a while. Far as I can tell, a lot of it had to do with something called phrenology. Ever hear of that?"

"Phrenologists claimed you could determine intellect and personality based on head shape and features. It was total bunk."

"Right. It started with this German doctor, Franz Joseph Gall. Gall came up with the theory that lumps and bumps on the head could be used to determine a person's character. Sounds wackadoo, but during phrenology's peak popularity, roughly from the 1820s into the 1840s, a potential employer could actually demand a character reference from a phrenologist."

"Seriously?"

Anne nodded. "As you say, pure rubbish, but it led to folks making copious masks. This Brit, James De Ville, collected more than two thousand of the things. Not all were created because of phrenology, of course. Some were made as templates for people wanting their portraits painted—"

"What does this have to do with Polly Beecroft?" I interrupted. A bit brusque, but we'd finished eating, and I was anxious to check my in-box for Ryan's message.

"I'm getting to that." Anne worked a key sequence, verified something on her screen. "Princeton University has a collection of death masks. So do Edinburgh University's Anatomy Museum and Scotland Yard's Crime Museum. The Victorians were obsessed with gruesome murders, so a shit ton of masks were made on executed criminals. Ever hear of William Burke?"

"Burke and his buddy, William Hare, robbed graves, then turned to murder to provide cadavers to medical schools."

"And quid for their own pockets. Anyway, his mask is out there." More keystrokes. "Some of these things have become crazy valuable. A bronze mask of Napoleon, made shortly after he died in 1821, sold in 2013 for about two hundred twenty thousand dollars."

My eyes drifted to the wall clock over Anne's shoulder. She noticed.

"Don't get your panties in a twist. I'm getting to the good part."

"I'm listening."

"Dante, Mary, Queen of Scots, John Keats, Napoleon, Oliver Cromwell, William Blake, Beethoven, John Dillinger, James Dean— you'd be amazed how many people have been masked. And not just celebs.

"For years, University College London had a collection of thirty-seven heads. No one knew who they were. For a while, they were lent out to people studying art to use as models. Then, in the 1990s, some students found a publication titled *Notes Biographical and Phrenological Illustrating a Collection of Casts* by Robert R. Noel."

"The UCL masks originally belonged to Noel?"

"Yep. Apparently, there used to be more—about forty-seven, including a bunch of skulls."

"Over the years, specimens went missing." I was getting the drift.

"Bingo. These days, a Brit named Nick Booth collects death masks. He's offering a 'skull amnesty.'"

"A what?"

"Booth is saying that if you went to the Slade School of Art in the 'eighties and pinched one of Noel's little beauties, you can return it to him, no questions asked."

Anne closed her Mac and looked at me expectantly.

"You're thinking the mask in Beecroft's photo could be one of those missing from Noel's collection?"

"Didn't you say Polly's sister was an artist?"

"Harriet. She was a painter."

"Could Harriet have studied in London in the 'eighties?"

I did some quick math.

"It's possible. But—"

"Think about this. The masks in Noel's collection were divided into two categories: intellectuals versus criminals and suicides."

"Speaks volumes about attitudes toward suicide at the time."

"What if the woman in the mask was Beecroft's great-aunt and she killed herself?"

I could think of no response.

"And here's another interesting fact I picked up. Masks weren't made only by phrenologists or as models for portraits. There was one other reason."

She left me in suspense for a moment, then unveiled her discovery.

"Sometimes they were made on unidentified bodies."

"So that relatives of missing persons could view the masks at the morgue."

Anne nodded solemnly.

"Not bad, Annie."

"I'll stay on it."

I didn't doubt she would.

Like a hound on a sirloin.

Thirty minutes later, table cleared, dishes loaded into the Bosch, Birdie and I retreated to my room. As before, I opened the sliding glass door. Drawn by the call of the wild, the cat wandered out onto the balcony.

Sitting cross-legged on the bed, I booted my Mac. The Atlantic was feeling friskier tonight, so I worked to the sound of waves crashing and foam fizzing across the sand. To the cries of gulls sharing avian gossip. Perhaps complaining about the shortage of fish.

Ryan's email had landed. I downloaded and peeked at its two attachments. One folder contained documents, the other photos.

I started with a quick inventory of the former. The items included the following: The scene report. Scores of witness interview summaries. Forms listing evidence and property recovered and analyzed. Notes made by Ryan, the lead detective, and two other members of the task force, both SQ. Ryan's overview of the investigation. A report on a snail. A report on water hydraulics in the St. Lawrence River. Reports by the pathologist, myself, and the coroner.

Leaving the documents for later, I turned to the second folder, thinking pictures might kick-start my recall more vividly than text.

Ryan had scanned collections of photos from four separate packets. One set was produced by the SQ crime-scene unit that processed the scene. One came from Pierre LaManche, the LSJML pathologist who performed the autopsy. One came from me. The fourth series I wasn't sure about. I left it for last.

I was sadly correct about the impact of visuals. Clicking through the images, the whole ugly mess came thundering back: The container gouged into a muddy beach. The algae-slimed wire and plastic sheeting. The mottled bones. The severed phalanges. The bullet holes, dark and round and lethal. The little fake emerald ring.

It was all too much to block out. I saw the woman and child down on their knees. Imagined the girl quickly palming her treasure into her mouth.

The usual wrenching questions pummeled my brain. Were the child and the woman shot together? Did they plead for their lives? Who was killed first? Did the child know she was going to die?

I thought of my daughter, Katy, at that age. Wondered. Did the child understand death? What does one know of mortality at age ten?

Banishing these unbearable thoughts, I turned to the final series. Those images were the most heartbreaking of all.

The desolate cemetery on rue Sherbrooke, Le Repos Saint-François d'Assise. The row of markers, none bearing a name. The forlorn inscriptions.

LSJML-41207 Os non identifiés d'une femme. LSJML-41208 Os non identifiés d'un enfant.

Unidentified bones of a woman. Unidentified bones of a child.

The pain felt as sharp as on the day I stood at that grave.

Brushing a tear from my cheek, I remembered Anne's suggestion. I made a decision.

9

Saturday, October 9–Sunday, October 10

Despite the calming lullaby of the waves, I slept poorly. A million images and worries ricocheted in my brain. Bones. Barrels. Beecrofts. Birdie. What to do about the cat if I followed through with my plan?

At six thirty, I gave up, donned running gear, yanked my hair into a pony, and headed outside. The tide was low, the sun barely cresting the horizon. The sea and shore glistened rosy bronze in the low, angled rays.

The beach was almost empty. Pounding along, I passed a few dog walkers playing fetch with their poodles or boxers. At one point, my right foot nearly came down on a sandpiper probing the sand, its long, spindly legs disappearing into an inverted image of itself.

At the southern tip of IOP, beneath the bridge to Sullivan's Island, a pod of dolphins executed slow, lazy loops in Breach Inlet. Their skin gleamed silvery gray each time their backs broke the surface.

The quick two-mile jog helped to clear my mind. Leaving my sandy shoes on the deck, I showered, threw on shorts and my favorite UNCC jersey, and descended for a session with the Jura X8, a coffee-brewing extravaganza that may have cost more than my car. I was working on Herrin's report, and my third cup, when my hostess stumbled through the door.

Mornings are not prime time for Anne. Even midmornings. *Disheveled* didn't capture the wild disarray of her hair. Her mascara was a war zone around her eyes.

"You look lovely," I said.

"Mm," Anne said.

"I made coffee."

Anne raised one finger in acknowledgment, then moved toward the miraculous machine. I heard a cabinet open, some rattling, then the toaster.

I was entering one final detail on AF21-986, when Anne joined me at the table. Her toast was coated with something dark and gelatinous that looked like it should never be on toast.

"What is that?"

"Vegemite. Super nutritious."

"Only if you're Australian and stranded in the Outback."

"You should try some. It's made from veggies."

"They're a dangerous breed, mate."

"What?"

"Never mind. Let me ask you something."

The black-smudged eyes rolled up to mine.

"I've been considering your suggestion."

"About the Vegemite?"

"About the open case in Montreal."

She said nothing.

"Would you mind if I left tomorrow? I'd like to head north earlier than planned."

"You're no longer needed in Charleston?"

"I'll check with Vislosky and Herrin. And my boss in Charlotte."

"I think it's a splendid idea. Lord knows you're not doing me any good here." Smeary L'Oréal wink. "And it will definitely jangle Ryan's jockeys."

I gave her an eye roll, then spent the next half hour on the phone.

Herrin said a report would be plenty. Vislosky asked a few questions, offered zero new intel. Nguyen had nothing requiring my attention, promised to phone or email should that change. Each advised me to go.

Laying aside my mobile, I felt relieved. And a bit unloved.

Until I dialed Ryan. I could hear his jockeys jangling.

After calling American Airlines, I gathered my belongings and assorted feline paraphernalia, then went in search of the cat.

Like Anne, Birdie is uncannily skilled at reading my mind. And at decoding my actions. It took forty minutes to locate him under a bed, inside the torn lining of a box spring.

The drive to Charlotte was irritatingly noisy with my back-seat passenger persistently voicing his indignation. To drown out the me-owing, I listened to the local NPR station, curious about whether Thursday's discovery might make the news.

There was no mention of the bin or the bodies, which didn't sur-prise me. Neither Herrin nor Vislosky struck me as the media-friendly sort. Or perhaps the case had already dropped from the cycle.

One story did catch my attention, a brief report on the rising number of capnocytophaga deaths in South Carolina. While listen-ing, I thought of Walter Klopp and the man he'd autopsied two days earlier.

According to the newscaster, although the CDC hadn't yet des-ignated it an official cluster, medical authorities were monitoring the regional incidence of capno. I wondered what count was needed to make the CDC scoreboard.

An interesting side note to the piece was a reported increase in gun sales in the state. Those interviewed said they'd heard capno came from pets. Apparently, Joe Citizen was arming up to blast any-one trying to impound Fluffy or Fido.

At the annex, I unpacked and did laundry. Then I phoned Archie, the twelve-year-old who looks after Birdie when I travel.

First glitch. Archie's mother said he was away at his school's fall mountain camp.

I tried my neighbor Walter.

Second glitch. Walter's niece Rhonda was visiting from Colorado. Rhonda was severely allergic to cats.

"Crap!" Belted with such vehemence, Birdie braced for flight.

I looked at the cat. He looked at me, offered no suggestion.

For the rest of that day and into the evening, I read with greater care the documents Ryan had sent.

What I found was not promising.

A word about my schizoid cross-border life.

For eons, I have taught biological and forensic anthropology at the University of North Carolina at Charlotte. Decades back, a notice about the National Faculty Exchange made the agenda at a departmental faculty meeting. The NFE, a program in which a professor from one institution changes places for an academic year with a professor from another institution, had a gentleman in Canada wanting to come to UNCC.

What fun, I thought. And off I went.

While teaching at Concordia and McGill, the two English-language universities in Montreal, I was approached by the director of the Laboratoire de Sciences Judiciaires et de Médecine Légale, the central crime and medico-legal lab for the province of Quebec. The LSJML, which went by a shorter name and acronym in those days, needed an *anthropologue judiciaire*. There were two prerequisites for the position: certification by the American Board of Forensic Anthropology and French language skills.

Though far from fluent at the time, I got the job.

Fantastique!

At the end of my NFE year, the LSJML was happy with me, and I was happy with them. Though I returned to Charlotte, we struck up an arrangement whereby I'd commute to Montreal every couple of months. With the understanding that I'd be immediately available should a disaster occur, a case prove urgent, or court testimony be needed.

That's been my life ever since.

———

At ten the next morning, Birdie and I were at the Charlotte Douglas International Airport. The flight boarded on time but took off twenty minutes late. Which did nothing to improve the cat's disposition. He was already out of sorts, and the delay goosed his protests to what may have been a personal best.

By the time we landed at Pierre Elliott Trudeau International in Dorval, I was the second least popular passenger on the plane. My under-the-seat companion took first prize.

Now for the promised intel on Andrew Ryan.

As I mentioned earlier, when he and I met, Lieutenant-Détective Ryan was assigned to the crimes-against-persons unit of the provincial police, the Sûreté du Québec. Since the SQ is headquartered in the same building as the LSJML, and my lab, it was inevitable that our paths would cross.

For years, Ryan and I investigated homicide cases together, strictly professional. Colleagues totally focused on murder.

Eventually, Ryan began sweet-talking for more. Eventually, he got it.

We dated. A long, long time.

Recently, Ryan had proposed marriage.

Whoa, boy!

I agreed to try cohabitation.

To demonstrate my commitment to this new arrangement, I built an addition to the annex in Charlotte and sold my beloved condo in Montreal's Centreville. Ryan and I purchased a unit in a spiffy new high-rise, also downtown. Though blocks from my comfortable old garden-level home, the new place is a galaxy distant in every other way.

I gave my rue Sherbrooke address to the Uber driver, André. Eyeing the cat with distaste, André muscled my suitcase into the trunk of his Maxima, and off we went.

Given the lack of rush-hour traffic on Autoroute 20, the trip into town was reasonably quick. But not quick enough for Birdie.

Arriving at our building, André couldn't get rid of us fast enough. After yanking my bag out onto the sidewalk, he scowled at the cat and gunned off, gutter gravel and dead leaves spitting from his tires.

The doorman, Sylvain, relieved me of both the pet carrier and my Buick-sized bag, then helped me into an elevator. I was too frazzled to object. Not Bird.

"*Grande paire de poumons,*" Sylvain said.

"*Oui,*" I agreed. Great pair of lungs.

We whooshed up in the sleek new elevator car, and Birdie and I entered our sleek new digs.

I had to laugh out loud.

Ryan had hung balloons, draped crepe-paper streamers, and taped a big glittery sign to one wall. *Bienvenue!*

After rolling my suitcase to the bedroom, I released my exceedingly unhappy traveling companion. Stepping from his prison, Birdie looked around, still irked but curious about the new place. Silent at last.

I was checking the contents of the refrigerator when a text pinged on my mobile.

Safely arrived?

Yes.

Cat happy?

No comment.

Relax. I'll bring dinner.

Love the balloons.

See you soon.

First off, I set up Birdie's feline hygiene station. He used it. Didn't thank me but did a superb job camouflaging his deposit by rearranging litter.

I'd just finished unpacking when I heard the front-door lock click.

"Where are you, sugar lump?" Ryan sang out.

"Call me that again, I won't be here long."

Ryan appeared at the bedroom door, a pizza in one hand, a small furry rodent in the other.

"An Angela *spécial* for us." Raising the pie. "A trinket for your friend."

"Birdie's affections can't be bought."

"The little guy already idolizes me."

After setting the toy and the pie on the nightstand, Ryan swooped in and wrapped me in a crushing bear hug. Followed the embrace with a very long, very heartfelt kiss.

Have I mentioned that Ryan is rock-solid fit and five-star good-looking? And that we hadn't seen each other for almost a month?

I felt a lurch in my stomach. Or, more precisely, somewhere to its south.

I didn't push him away.

Over pizza, grown cold during our romp in the sheets, Ryan and I discussed the container case. And the reasons the file was so slim.

"The vics had been dead for years. Without names, we couldn't contact family or known associates. There were no witnesses, no persons of interest. No one knew zip."

"Or admitted to knowing zip," I said.

Ryan angled his bottle of Moosehead to acknowledge my point.

"The container washed ashore in a trailer park in Saint-Anicet," I said.

"Correct. We interviewed the guy who found it."

"Not one of God's more intelligent creatures."

"Basically, a brain stem on two legs. We talked to all the residents of the park and to people living in town and on the neighboring farms. We canvassed every yacht club up and down the shore, ran the owner of every boat registered in the province."

"Thinking the container had been tossed overboard into the river."

"We contacted every school in the area. Hell, every school in the province, and then some."

"There were very few entries on the evidence and property forms," I said. "The polyethylene sheeting and eighteen-gauge electrical wire were identical to the materials used in Charleston."

"Here we had the kid's ring," Ryan said. "There you found no personal items."

The buried image rolled over and raised its head. I denied it entry into my higher centers.

"Yes," I agreed. Then, anticipating Ryan's question, "No prints on anything. Ditto for the container."

Ryan reached over to thumb sauce from my upper lip. Maybe cheese.

"Thanks." Not minding that his hand lingered far too long. "An analysis was done on stones found at the bottom of the container."

"I forgot about that. Any joy?"

"Common river rocks, found in a bazillion locations."

"Wasn't there a snail in there, too?"

"Black and of indeterminate species." I quoted the malacologist's summation. "The expert on river hydraulics was equally unhelpful."

"Lots of parallels to your Charleston vics?"

I laid them all out.

Together we cleared the dishes and ziplocked the leftover pizza. Ryan popped the cap on another Moosehead, and I made myself tea.

We moved to two easy chairs facing the glass wall overlooking the skyline stretching all the way down to the river. Twelve floors below, the windows along Sherbrooke winked copper in the warm rays of the waning day.

"Will you be busy while I'm here?" I asked.

"A guy in Montpelier wants me to look into an auto fatality."

"Sounds rather dull."

"Mm." Ryan's thoughts were not on a crash in Vermont. After chugging the last of his beer, he swiveled my chair, leaned forward, and started kneading my neck and shoulders.

I set down my tea. For the first time in a while, began to relax.

Ryan's hands moved lower, his thumbs working deep circles in the muscles paralleling my spine.

Full disclosure. I am a sucker for a good back rub. Or a bad back rub. Massage me properly, I will disclose the location of every nuke in the U.S. arsenal.

Ryan's hand slid inside the waistband of my jeans.

"Twice in one night? How easy do you think I am?"

"We can debate that later."

His fingers slipped lower.

Advantage Ryan.

10

Monday, October 11

I awoke to the smell of coffee. And an empty bed.

A Post-it note graced the door of the sleek, state-of-the-art Sub-Zero stainless-steel fridge. Blushing, I crumbled and tossed Ryan's art.

Birdie was glued to the living-room window, tail flicking each time a pigeon dropped into view on a downward swoop from the roof. Ryan was nowhere to be seen.

When we purchased the condo, its price alarmingly above our budget, Ryan and I decided to splurge further on a pair of in-house parking spots. Retired from the SQ, he no longer had access to a city ride and relied on the Jeep he'd owned for years. Having ponied up for a new car in Charlotte, I now kept my old Mazda in Montreal for use during my bimonthly visits.

What the hell? You only live once.

When I arrived in the garage, Ryan's slot was empty. Off to see a man about a crash, I presumed.

Emerging from the underground, I wound my way toward the Hochelaga-Maisonneuve district, a working-class hood just a bump east of Centreville. A ten-minute prowl through the maze of narrow streets brought me to a gap between cars lining one curb. With much strenuous wheel twisting and back-and-forth maneuvering, I wedged myself in, leaving a good twelve inches at each bumper.

Winded and a bit sweaty, I got out and checked the three signs listing restrictions for that side of the street on that weekday in that month for drivers lacking a resident's permit or an edict of exemption from the pan-galactic tribunal on temporary vehicular storage. Don't get me started on Montreal parking regs.

Reasonably satisfied that the spot was legal, I *wheep-wheeped* the locks and started walking. The day was chilly, the sky leaden, the air heavy with the smell of dead leaves and exhaust. Now and then, a hint of oil and dead fish was carried up from the river.

In minutes, I arrived at a T-shaped high-rise jutting inharmoniously from the warren of one- and two-story walk-ups surrounding it. The Laboratoire de Sciences Judiciaires et de Médecine Légale occupies the top two floors, the Bureau du Coroner is on eleven, and the morgue is in the basement. Since the remaining footage belongs to the provincial police, the structure, though officially named the Édifice Wilfrid-Derome, is still referred to by old-timers as the SQ building.

I swiped my security card, passed through metal gates, and entered the restricted LSJML/Coroner elevator, then swiped again and ascended with a dozen others, some of the more perky mumbling *"Bonjour"* and *"Comment ça va?"* Hi. How are you?

It was all anyone could manage early on a Monday morning.

Four of us exited on the twelfth floor. After crossing the lobby, I swiped a second security card and passed into the lab's working area. Through observation windows and open doors, I could see secretaries booting computers, techs flipping dials, scientists and analysts shrugging into lab coats.

I swiped one last time. Glass doors whooshed, admitting me to the medico-legal wing.

The board showed three of five pathologists present. The box beside Emily Santangelo's name said *Témoignage: Joliette*. Testimony in Joliette. Natalie Ayers was on *congé personnel*. Personal leave.

Continuing along the corridor, I passed pathology, histology, and anthropology/odontology labs on my left, pathologists' offices on my right. LaManche. Pelletier. Morin. Santangelo. Ayers. Mine was the last in the row.

More security. Old-school lock and key.

I'd been away two weeks. My office looked like I'd been gone since the wall went down in Berlin.

Workers, probably floor polishers, had displaced every freestanding item onto my desk. The wastebasket, my chair, the hall tree with clean lab coats still on hangers. My CSU kit and boots had been jammed onto the windowsill, along with a potted barrel cactus, DOA. But the tile at my feet shone brightly.

After muscling the furnishings back into place, I settled into my squeaky old chair.

The blotter was mounded with enough paper to have cost several trees their lives. I tossed the flyers and ads, saved the following: the latest copy of *Voir Dire*, the LSJML gossip sheet; a medical dossier from a hospital in Saint Jérôme; a packet of photos from a Section d'Identité Judiciaire photographer; a letter from an attorney in Quebec City; two *demande d'exportiso en anthropologie* forms.

Antediluvian, granted, but I keep all hard copy from my cases. In addition to the photos and final reports, which go into the system, I retain my handwritten notes and diagrams and the forms I fill out while doing an analysis.

Ignoring the survivors of my triage, I crossed to a disturbingly hefty file cabinet, which tends to lurch forward when the top two drawers are opened simultaneously, and dug out the folders for LSJML-41207 and LSJML-41208. Fifteen years old meant the bottom drawer—safe turf vis-à-vis the gravity thing.

Returning to my desk, I opened the first folder. Skimmed. Moved on to the second.

Armed with the necessary information, I began my quest. First by computer, then at a number of locations around the building.

An hour later, I was back, empty-handed. Discouraged and frustrated, I shifted from old business to new and skimmed the first request for an anthropology consult on remains recently arrived at the LSJML.

Pathologist: M. Morin. Investigating officer: L. Claudel, Service de Police de la Ville de Montréal. SPVM. Formerly known as the Service de Police de la Communauté Urbaine de Montréal, or SPCUM, the SPVM are the city boys. Same force, new handle. *Nom: Inconnu.* Name: Unknown. Skipping over the LSJML, morgue, and police incident numbers, I went straight to the summary of known facts.

A homeowner had unearthed bones while digging in his basement in Saint-Leonard. Could I determine if the remains were human? If human, the number of persons? Time since death? If recent, could I ascertain age, sex, race, and height and describe individuating characteristics for each individual? Could I establish cause of death?

Typical FA stuff.

The second form listed Pierre LaManche as the pathologist. I read that summary. The situation involved an auto accident and a missing leg bone. I read it again, baffled.

Unlike Morin's, LaManche's case fell to the SQ. The provincial cops.

One town, two agencies? Sounds complicated. It's not. And it is.

Montreal is an island, its southern tip wrapped by the Fleuve Saint-Laurent, its northern side by the Rivière des Prairies. Only fifty kilometers long, the tiny hunk of land varies from five to thirteen kilometers in width, narrowing at its extremities and thickening at its center. Its dominant feature is Mont Royal, an igneous intrusion rising a proud 231 meters above sea level. *Les Montréalais* call this modest bump *la montagne.* The mountain.

For policing purposes, Montreal is parceled out according to these particulars of geology. On the island: SPVM. Off the island: SQ. Assuming there's no local PD. Though rivalries exist, in general *ça marche*. It works.

Dr. Pierre LaManche, the director of the LSJML's medico-legal section, favors crepe soles and empty pockets and moves so quietly he can appear without a hint of warning.

He did so at that moment.

"What a fortunate turn of events." LaManche's French is Parisian and precise.

I looked up.

Le directeur was standing in my doorway, file folders pressed to his chest. A lot of them. Which was typical for a Monday morning. As in any jurisdiction, *les Québécois* find limitless ways to off themselves or others on weekends. Following a six-pack or a liter of bourbon, a half gainer into a quarry or a DIY booby trap seems like a brilliant idea.

"I heard a rumor that you had rejoined us early."

"*Bonjour.* Please come in." Hiding my surprise. It wasn't often the boss visited my humble little space.

LaManche is a big man in a Great-Uncle-Joe-was-a-linebacker sort of way. At well past sixty, his posture is beginning to suggest he should be ringing bells at Notre Dame. He looked around, hesitant.

"Sorry." Circling my desk, I gathered the lab coats, currently heaped in my sole visitor's chair, and returned them to the hall tree.

Nodding, LaManche entered and reconfigured himself from a stooped upright to a stooped seated position, brows tightly knit. Clearly, something was on his mind. I waited for him to begin.

"You know *maître* Lauzon, of course."

In Quebec, coroners are either physicians or attorneys. Odd system, but *ça marche*. It works. Hélène Lauzon was a lawyer, thus the title *maître*.

I nodded.

"Saturday, while driving home from his weekly bowling game, *maître* Lauzon's father, Alfonse Vachon, rear-ended a moving van, pinning one of two workers who were loading a sofa. The force of the impact stood M. Vachon up behind the wheel. His right lower leg and several ribs were fractured, and his face was severely lacerated."

"Was he wearing a seat belt?" Clueless where this was going. A common occurrence of late.

"No. And he had been drinking."

"Ouch."

LaManche seemed to consider the condition of the cactus. I waited for him to continue.

"M. Vachon went into surgery early this morning for repair of the broken leg. Upon dissecting and cleaning the surrounding tissue, the surgeon discovered that a portion of his patient's tibia was missing."

"Gone?" Unsure if I was translating *manquant* correctly.

"It wasn't there."

"Where was it?"

"Precisely his question."

I said nothing.

"The surgeon called *maître* Lauzon. She phoned me to explain the situation and to request a thorough search of her father's vehicle. I mentioned that you were currently in Montreal, and she asked that you be present."

"Why me?"

"You know bones."

"This sounds very bizarre."

LaManche levered a shoulder, executing one of the limitless repertoire of shrugs so perfected by the French. *Who knows? Does it matter? I need a smoke.*

"Where is the car?" I asked.

"Pierrefonds."

"When do they want me there?"

"As quickly as possible. When you phone downstairs, an SQ officer will transport you." When. Not if. Great.

"How is the worker who was pinned to the truck?"

"That gentleman is in our cooler."

"I'm on it." Resigned. It was not how I'd envisioned my first day back.

LaManche placed both palms on his knees, preparing to rise.

"If you have a moment, there's something I'd like to discuss before I head out."

"*Bien sûr.*" Of course. Settling back.

I'd prepared my pitch and was concise.

I briefed LaManche on the unidentified container corpses found in 2006. Showed him photos and my old reports. He said he vaguely remembered the case.

Then I told him about last week's Charleston vics.

It's often hard to read the old man. Not then. The lines in his face shifted into furrows of doubt.

I pressed on. "There have been advances in DNA since 2006. Improvements in techniques of extraction and amplification. Expansion of databases. The same is true for all forensic protocols. Isotope analysis—"

"What are you proposing, Temperance?" LaManche always uses my full name, emphasizing the final syllable and rhyming it with *sconce*.

"An exhumation."

"Did you not take samples back in 2006?"

"The bone was so degraded the results were inconclusive."

"Can you not use those same specimens now?"

"I can't find them. I suspect the bone plugs were destroyed during a culling of stored materials back in 2016." Without my consent. I didn't add that.

The furrows rearranged. Not in a good way.

"I'll handle all the arrangements." I forged on. "But I need your approval."

LaManche's shoulders sagged, and his head wagged slowly.

"I am sorry, Temperance. Right now, I cannot divert personnel or funds for the pursuit of such an old case. Dr. Ayers is away due to the death of her mother. Dr. Santangelo will be in Joliette for an extended period. I hope you understand."

"Of course." Not bothering to hide my disappointment.

"Should the situation change—" Shrugging, LaManche let the thought hang.

The island of Montreal is shaped like a foot with the toes pointing northeast, the heel southeast, and the ankle angling to the southwest. Hochelaga-Maisonneuve and Centreville are located down by the heel. The borough of Pierrefonds-Roxboro is on the northwest side of the shin, along the Rivière des Prairies. Which is a circuitous way of saying that M. Vachon's car wasn't exactly around the corner. By the time I got back to the condo, it was almost seven.

One of life's joys is the smell of cooking after a long workday. That's what met me when I opened the front door.

"Honey, I'm home." A *Father Knows Best* trope that always amuses us.

No response. I hung my jacket in the closet and followed the aroma of rosemary and garlic.

Ryan was in the kitchen, looking like someone on day release. His face was flushed, his hair pointing in a million directions. His untucked shirt, liberally speckled with grease, was partially covered by an apron looping his neck and tied at his waist. It said *Patron du thon.* Tuna boss. The wit of the rhyme failed to translate to English.

"Nice apron," I said.

"It belonged to my mother."

Keeping my views on Mama's castoff to myself, I crossed to kiss him. Birdie, ever hopeful, didn't budge from his vigil by the stove.

"Smells delicious," I said.

"And so it shall be, *ma chère.* Go." Shooing me with the hand not holding the spatula. "First seating is at seven thirty."

"What—"

"Go."

I went.

Forty minutes later, we were in the window-facing chairs, sipping espressos and digesting the garlic rosemary chicken breasts, mashed potatoes, and broiled asparagus. Ryan hadn't exaggerated. The meal had been superb.

"The vehicle was in an impound lot," I said, continuing our discussion of the day's events.

"Did the lot have a dog?"

"A big brown one."

"Auto-yard dogs can be prickly."

"His name was Merle. He kept a very close eye on us. Anyway, the car had mats, you know, for snowy boots or whatever."

"It's Quebec. Even Merle has mats."

I gave Ryan "the look." "The only thing evident on the driver's side was dried blood. But when I removed the mat, down by the pedals, I could see a little puckered hole in the carpeting below. After cutting out that segment of carpet, I spotted a small triangular puncture in the floorboard. Damned if there wasn't a chunk of tibia embedded in there."

"The guy's bone was driven through the mat, the carpet, and the metal floor of the car? Is that even possible?"

"The cortical portion of a tibia is thick, giving the bone impressive tensile strength. Vachon was doing forty, and the truck was at a dead stop, so the impact was powerful."

"I imagine the first responders were focusing on extracting Vachon, not worrying about leaving part of him behind."

"And the leg was an open fracture, so there would have been lots of blood." I took a sip of my coffee. "After more than forty-eight hours, the soft tissue was toast. But you could still see carpet fibers stuck to the bone."

"The guy's foot must have been flopping like a rag doll."

Now I shot Ryan a look of feigned disapproval.

"What happens with the chunk you found?" he asked.

"Bagged and tagged. Not sure what the lab will do with it."

"Can it go back into Monsieur Vachon?"

"Not a chance. What's the story on your accident vic?" Earlier, Ryan and I had commented on the irony of us both working auto mishaps.

"Not much to tell. The guy who contacted me is an insurance adjuster in Montpelier. In a nutshell, the decedent's wife insists her husband's death was a workplace accident. If true, she'll be due a hefty chunk of change."

"Sounds rather mundane."

"The weird thing is the crash happened four years ago."

"Why did the claim sit around for so long?"

"My client's question exactly."

"You think it's a scam?"

"I intend to find out."

I was about to ask a follow-up when my mobile rang. I checked caller ID.

"LaManche," I said to Ryan.

"Does he often call on your cell?"

"Never."

I clicked on.

LaManche said the last thing I expected to hear.

11

Wednesday, October 13

Stretching for more than nineteen miles, rue Sherbrooke is a major east-west artery and the second-longest street on the island of Montreal. Our Centreville condo sits toward one end. Le Repos Saint-François d'Assise lies toward the other.

At seven Wednesday morning, I was motoring east. As I had done on Tuesday.

As I had done one bleak fall day in 2010.

LaManche's call had sent me scrambling. With no explanation for the stunning reversal, he said he'd decided to greenlight the exhumation. He suggested that I contact Rémi Arbour, manager of Le Repos.

I did that. A nanosecond past Tuesday morning's opening bell. Though unenthused, Arbour had agreed to see me. Suggested we meet at his office at noon.

I'd arrived a half hour early. Arbour had rolled in ten minutes late. In his forties, wheezy, and obese, the guy had heart attack written all over him.

A recent hire, Arbour possessed no knowledge of burials older than two years. And zero interest in learning about them.

With much urging on my part, he'd agreed to help me search the archives. Then we'd set out across the grounds in Arbour's pickup. A few landmarks looked familiar to me. A statue of St. Frank. A dragon.

Eventually, we'd located the section used for the interment of unknowns back in 2010, the year LSJML-41207 and LSJML-41208 were finally laid to rest. Alighting from the truck, we'd walked the rows until we'd found their graves.

I'd checked the scene against the photos I'd brought. An old maple was gone, a stand of shrubbery greatly expanded. Otherwise, the backdrop was a match to the one from a decade earlier.

Ditto the cold hollowness filling my chest.

So. Here I was behind the wheel as I had been the day before, squinting into a saffron dawn, pulse hammering way too fast.

To allay my anxiety, I reviewed the knowledge I'd gleaned via one quick late-night Google search.

Established in 1724, Le Repos Saint-François d'Assise is one of the oldest burial grounds in Montreal. Having undergone several name changes and relocations over the years, the current cemetery offers both burial and cremation, along with three options for long-term storage: columbarium, mausoleum, or old-fashioned grave. No matter your vision for the hereafter, Saint Francis of Assisi has you covered. No pun intended.

Another fact, one not touted online. Back in the day, Le Repos was under government contract to provide plots for those making the poor decision to die penniless or nameless.

Just past rue Saint-Germain, the SUV in front of me stopped suddenly. I hit the brakes.

Work on a pipeline had half the street torn up, and traffic was at a standstill in both directions. A woman with a neon-orange vest, a rotating pole sign, and a Napoleon complex was controlling the flow. The little general was in no hurry.

I sat finger-drumming the wheel, listening to a twenty-four-hour all-talk station, CJAD, for possible mention of our little exhumation party. Heard none. The twenty-minute delay, and the day's news, did nothing to calm my agitation.

The sun was well above the horizon when I pulled through *le cimitière*'s main entrance near rue Langelier. After much winding among headstones and roller-coastering up and down knolls and depressions, I drew close to the gravesites that Arbour and I had ID'd.

And cursed. I was late to the dance.

Parked beside the narrow lane were an SQ cruiser, an SIJ crime-scene truck, a coroner's van, a golf cart, and Arbour's pickup. After adding my Mazda to the back of the line, I got out and hurried toward the group, mentally logging details.

No precautions had been taken to safeguard confidentiality. No temporary fencing. No plastic tenting. No sawhorses strung with yellow tape.

A backhoe stood ready, operator at the controls, drinking from the cap of his thermos. Plywood panels covered the ground to either side of each grave.

Nine people stood chatting in clumps of two or three. Two SQ uniforms, the van driver and his partner, two SIJ techs, Arbour. Off to one side, a pair in matching boots, jeans, windbreakers, and scowls leaned on long-handled spades.

Good call on the privacy issue. No protection was needed. Not a single journalist had turned up. Perhaps the media hadn't heard. Perhaps, as in the past, they didn't care.

"Sorry I'm late," I tossed out to no one in particular.

One of the coroner's transporters crossed to me. Gaston something. I'd done other recoveries with him.

"*Bonjour, doc.*" Gaston proffered a Styrofoam cup.

"Thanks." The cup's contents weren't quite tepid. Gaston had been here a while. The others also, I presumed.

Radiating impatience from inside his shiny polyester coat, Arbour asked, "*Nous sommes prêt? Enfin?*" Are we ready? Finally?

Christ on a cracker.

"Let's do it," I said, cool but smiling.

Arbour raised and circled one finger, fast and hard.

"Asshole probably has a stiff needs planting," Gaston mumbled. Or some Quebecois equivalent.

The backhoe operator recapped and set down his thermos. Seconds later, the big yellow brute roared to life. After much maneuvering, the machine stopped, and the front-end loader bucket dropped into position at one end of the northernmost grave.

Arbour repeated the finger thing.

The bucket's claws dragged backward, scoring the winter-brown lawn. The scent of dead grass and moist soil filled the air.

The boom rose and swung right. The bucket dropped its load, swung back, and repeated the action. Again, and again.

As the wound in the earth deepened, I observed closely, eventually spotted a handful of soggy splinters mixing with the fill.

"Stop!" Raising a hand and shouting to be heard over the grinding.

The boom froze in mid-swing.

To confirm, I squatted at the side of the pit.

"Time for shovels," I said.

"That will slow us down greatly." Arbour's annoyance was evident from ten yards off.

"I'm beginning to see fragments."

A lumpy shadow fell across the grave. I pointed. The shadow's hands shot to its hips.

"The remains will be in body bags inside pressed-wood boxes." Knees protesting the sudden reorientation, I stood. "Those are remnants of a box. We're close."

Arbour hand-signaled again. He appeared to enjoy it.

The cemetery workers jumped into the trench and manned their spades. The sun crept higher, warming the chilly air and melting the pale lens of frost tinting the lawn. Eventually, both men shed their jackets.

New sounds filled the void left by the stilled backhoe. The *thunk* of shovels gouging the earth. The *shush* of soil sliding from blades. The *crackle* of static sputtering from the cruiser's radio. Occasionally, an optimistic bird threw in a few hopeful notes.

Like autopsies, exhumations don't make for heart-thumping

drama. There, too, the process is tedious and slow. To pass the time, I intermittently checked my phone. And my surroundings.

The cemetery remained mostly deserted. Now and then, a car or groundskeeper's truck passed by. At one point, a woman drove up in a blue Hyundai, got out, and wove through the headstones across the road. She wore a black leather jacket and a long green skirt. Her hair, short and wiry, was a most unfortunate carroty orange. I watched her discreetly, wondering who it was she mourned.

Carrot Hair stopped at a pink granite marker shaped like a cross. Arms crossed, feet spread, she appeared to study the inscription.

"Yo! We can pull her up." Arbour's bellowing brought me back.

The diggers had climbed out of the pit. Both were sweating and gulping water from plastic bottles.

I walked past them and looked down.

The burial lay fully exposed. Saturated by percolating groundwater and crushed by the weight of overlying soil, the makeshift coffin had collapsed and now wrapped the body bag like a sodden diaper.

Pulling on gloves, I raised my bandanna from my neck to my mouth, grabbed a trowel, and dropped into the grave. A few minutes of scraping muddy soil exposed the tag. A little thumb action cleared the tag's surface enough to read the number.

I took a deep breath. Let it out slowly. We'd found the child.

Accepting a hand up to ground level, I gave the word.

One of the SIJ techs snapped pics while the other shot video. When they'd finished, Gaston and his partner lifted LSJML-41208 and gently placed her on a stretcher.

The backhoe cranked to life.

As the second exhumation began, I tracked the coroner's team to their van and watched them slide the stretcher inside. Saw and heard the rear doors slam shut.

Beyond our parked vehicles, Carrot Hair was still at the cross-shaped headstone, seemingly deep in thought. Prayer? Long time for a visit with the dead, I thought.

Peeling off my dirty gloves, I crossed to the cooler. Was straightening, water bottle in hand, when my eyes again drifted across the road.

My spine tensed, and my pulse spiked.

Carrot Hair's phone was pointed directly at me.

Seeing my reaction, the woman dropped the mobile into her shoulder bag, hurried to the Hyundai, and drove off.

Had Carrot Hair been filming me? Was it my imagination?

Better question: Why the hell hadn't I noted her plate?

The whole operation took six hours. I left Arbour yelling instructions about refilling the graves.

Arriving at the lab, I called downstairs. The disinterred remains were there and had been logged. I asked that both cases be brought to *salle quatre*, a space outfitted with special ventilation. While I anticipated minimal odor, I like working in the "stinky" room, the farthest down the hall of the four autopsy suites. More solitude, less interruption.

I keyed in and descended in the coroner's elevator. At morgue level, the basement, I changed into scrubs, then hurried to *salle quatre*.

Two stainless-steel gurneys sat snugged to opposite walls. Each held a mud-coated body bag. An extra gurney was parked beside the floor-bolted table at the room's center.

After filling out separate case ID cards, I unzipped each pouch and shot backup Polaroids. Lisa arrived as I was setting down the camera.

A word about Lisa Savard. Bright and self-motivated, Lisa anticipates and doesn't require direction at every step. Having worked with many morgue techs over the decades, she remains my favorite.

Blond and endowed with a legendary rack, Lisa is also a favorite with the cops. At least, with the male demographic.

"Do you want X-rays?" A Francophone, Lisa always practices her English with me.

I nodded. "If there's anything suspicious in there, I want to know about it."

Lisa was back in thirty minutes. Together we viewed the films. Spotted no surprises.

While Lisa spread sheets across the autopsy table and the empty gurney and balanced a screen on the sink, I took a paper apron from a drawer, slipped it over my head, and tied it around my waist. Then I masked, pulled on surgical gloves, and began removing skeletal elements from the bag labeled LSJML-41207.

Starting at the feet and working toward the head, I arranged the bones in anatomical order. Lisa sifted the fill, screening each handful of soil under gently running water.

Three hours later, the painstaking process was done.

One dirt-crusted skeleton lay on the table. Another much smaller one lay on the gurney.

A collection of insect casings and pebbles sat drying on the countertop, along with one plastic button and one rusted safety pin. The presence of a partial mouse skeleton solved the riddle of the man-made items, puzzling since both sets of remains had been buried nude. We couldn't guess the appeal of these objects to the late burrowing rodent.

The wall clock said nine forty-six. I was exhausted, suspected Lisa was equally tired. And hungry. We'd eaten nothing but a vending-machine sandwich around six.

I thanked Lisa and told her to go home. While she wheeled the adult victim into the morgue cooler, I quick-scanned the child. Skull. Pelvis. Long bones. It was 2006 all over again.

Charleston all over again.

Tomorrow I'd do a full inventory and confirm both bio-profiles. But I knew what my conclusion would be. We'd unearthed the right people—the woman and child found in a container near Saint-Anicet.

I lingered a moment, the skull of LSJML-41208 cradled in my palm.

"I promise you," I said softly. "I will find out who you are."

The vacant orbits stared up at me, silent in death.

I was recentering the cranium on its rubber ring when a wink of light caught my eye. A glint of reflection from the overhead fluorescents.

Curious, I dug a penlight from my bag and pointed the beam at the right orbit. Spotted nothing trapped in or behind the butterfly fissures deep in the socket. I shifted the light. The left orbit was also clean.

I illuminated the nasal opening.

My breath caught in my throat.

12

L isa, still there, spoke up.

"You look like you've seen, how do you say, *un fantôme*?"

"Ghost. Forceps, please."

She handed them to me.

Moving gingerly, I tweezed the object free of the nasal conchae.

Lisa had nailed it. A ghost. An achingly sad one.

Crossing to the sink, I ran water over my find, then set it on the counter. Lisa drew close. We both stared.

"What is it?"

I shook my head, not trusting my voice.

Lisa didn't press. Something else I like about her.

Together we placed sheeting over LSJML-41208, and she rolled the child from the room. After stripping off our gear, we changed into street clothes and left the building.

A final *adieu*, then we angled into the night in opposite directions.

———

Ryan was reading in bed.

"Long day." Allowing the book to drop to his chest.

"Which must end with a very long shower," I said.

"Need assistance?"

"I'm good."

He helped anyway. Ryan is world-class at lathering and scrubbing. And other things.

As hot water pummeled my body and Ryan worked his magic, I felt my blood pressure settle back to normal.

Thirty minutes later, we were both under the covers, smelling of grapefruit and bergamot, nibbling from a cheese plate Ryan had prepared.

"Nice soap," Ryan said.

"Old Whaling Company. What are you reading?"

"*Tess of the d'Urbervilles.*"

"Why?"

"It's a classic."

I couldn't disagree.

"The dig went smoothly?" Ryan switched topics. "No surprises?"

"Actually, there was one."

I told him about the object I'd pulled from LSJML-41208.

"How did a prayer card get into her nose?" Ryan asked.

"I put it there."

Ryan's brows shot up.

"Not in her nose," I corrected myself. "On top of her skull. Just before the burial."

"How could it slip into a nostril?"

"Seriously? That's your first question?"

Ryan shrugged.

"It was some sort of miniature. Maybe meant for a key or a neck chain."

Ryan said nothing.

"The plastic coating helped. Still, the image was almost destroyed."

"Image of who?"

"Whom." Ryan and I love to catch each using incorrect grammar.

"Point for your side."

"Mother Mary MacKillop. She's depicted wearing an old-fashioned nun's habit."

"Why her?"

"It's a long story."

"I've got all night." Ryan Groucho waggled his brows. "Perhaps you'd prefer to—"

"There was a mourner at the burial back in 2010, a parishioner named Ariel something from a nearby church. She said one member of her devotional group attends every anonymous interment."

"Committed to giving the nameless a send-off."

I nodded

"A very kind gesture."

"It is. Was. I'm not sure they still do it."

I helped myself to a hunk of cheddar.

"Anyway, Ariel asked that I slip the holy card into the child's body bag. She was very keen, and it seemed harmless, so I figured what the hell?"

"Why MacKillop?"

"She's the patron saint of abused girls."

"She's been canonized?"

"Yes. That was the other reason she was on Ariel's mind. You're familiar with Brother André, right?" I was referring to André Bessette, a Holy Cross brother and a much-loved figure in Montreal.

"Are you kidding? When those asshats snatched his heart, the whole town went berserk."

It happened before my time, but the story remained legend. For years, the brother's heart rested in a glass vessel atop a marble pedestal below the basilica of Saint Joseph's Oratory. In 1973, thieves stole it for ransom. When the organ was recovered the following year, our lab did the ID.

"According to Ariel, Brother André and Mother Mary McKillop had both become saints the previous week. On the same day."

Funny how the brain works, retaining some details and deleting others. That day was October 17. Did I recall the date because it was also my baby brother's birthday? Was that the reason I'd acted so impulsively? Had I agreed to Ariel's request because of Kevin?

"Nothing else weird?" Ryan asked. "No gawkers or journalists to lion-tame?"

"Actually, there was one odd thing. A woman visited a grave across the road from where we were working."

I paused, unsure if the incident was worth mentioning.

"And?" Ryan prompted.

"I caught her taking pics of the exhumation." Maybe.

"Morbid curiosity?"

"Who knows? Perhaps she hopes to sell the story to *Dateline*."

"What's on for tomorrow?"

"I'll do an overview of both skeletons, for the record, but the main goal is sampling."

"The quest for the golden double helix."

"Bone isn't ideal, but we could get lucky. I may also request radioisotope testing."

"I'm sure you'll explain that."

"Using bone, radioisotopes can show where a person spent the last ten years before they died. Using teeth, they can show where they spent their first five to ten."

"Where they grew up."

"Presumably. Hair can be even better. By dividing a hair into growth increments, you can track a person's actual movements during the last period of their life."

"Do you have some?"

"Teeth, no." Unsure which he was asking about. "I'll recheck for hair, but I'm not optimistic."

"Sounds like another day of giggles and laughs."

Ryan was right. It was another fun day.

I woke at seven. Again, my roommate had beaten me out the door. Damn, he was quiet in the morning.

I fed Birdie, something from a can involving chicken. He sniffed the brown glump and walked away in protest.

Note to self: stock up on the cat's preferred brand.

Quick teeth and hair. Different brushes, same level of effort. Whom would I see that I needed to impress?

After throwing on jeans and a sweater, I scooped up my mobile. Anne had phoned. And texted. Twice.

Though anxious to be off, I returned her call. Got voice mail. Left a message.

Traffic was bumper-to-bumper. By the time I'd parked and walked to the lab, it was well past eight. Leaving my purse in one of my desk drawers and my jacket on the coat tree, I hurried downstairs.

Lisa was suited up and ready to go. I threw on scrubs, and we spent the next hour and a half rechecking the bones, the body bags, and the debris from the screen. Found six stray hairs. All from the mouse.

Lisa packaged a femur from each victim while I changed. Then I rode the elevator back upstairs.

Claire Willoughby was the DNA tech doing intake. In her late twenties, tall and willowy, Willoughby carried herself like a woman who knew she was beautiful. She wasn't, due largely to her taste in makeup.

Willoughby skimmed the request form, one overplucked brow arched high above one emerald lid. Then she listened to my account.

"I'll be straight with you." British accent so strong it should have been waving a photo of the queen. "I'm not optimistic."

"Give it your best shot," I said.

We both did the thumbs-up thing.

Back in my office, I checked my contacts, then entered a number. A voice answered, perky and friendly as the Sugar Plum Fairy.

"DNA Analysis International. How may I direct you?"

"Dr. Griesser, please."

"May I ask who's calling?"

"Temperance Brennan."

"One moment, please. You have a blessed day."

A Muzak rendering of "Brown Skin Girl"—definitely not Beyoncé—was mercifully truncated by another voice, this one cigarette-rough and tinged with concern.

"Tempe. How's haps, girl?"

"Haps be good. Sorry to phone during working hours."

"Is something wrong with Mom?"

Lizzie Griesser is a molecular biologist employed by DAI, a private DNA lab headquartered in Virginia. We'd met while working the same cases in Charlotte, Lizzie for the CMPD crime lab, me for the MCME. Eventually, collegiality had morphed into friendship.

Several years after Lizzie was head-hunted away to Richmond, her mother developed dementia and required assisted living. Since the facility isn't far from my place, I promised Lizzie to visit as often as possible. I'd kept that promise for almost eight years.

"I saw her last week," I said. "She's fine."

"Thanks for looking in on her." Relief evident. "So. I hear there's a new sheriff in town."

"Samantha Nguyen."

"And?"

"I like her."

"Boo-yah! You're back in the game."

"Actually, that's why I'm calling."

"Lay it on me."

I told her about the container and the exhumation and explained that I wanted a DNA-based phenotype sketch and a probability statement concerning geographic ancestry for each victim. Lizzie did this type of analysis regularly. She didn't need me to diagram the play.

A beat. When Lizzie spoke again, there was doubt in her voice.

"Up to five years in the sea, four more in a cooler, eleven in the ground. Your folks may not be able to sequence shit."

"They're going to try," I said. "And this time, the request will be official."

During my exile from the MCME, Lizzie did a facial approximation for me, off the books.

"Meaning we'll get paid?" Throaty laugh.

"Handsomely."

"Send the form directly to me."

After promising to meet when both of us were next in Charlotte, we disconnected.

My old hard-copy files for LSJML-41207 and LSJML-41208 were still on my desk. The facial approximations I'd ordered in 2006 had been scanned into the central archives, but, pack rat that I am, I'd retained the originals.

I pulled both sketches and set them side by side on my blotter.

The images uncorked as much heartbreak as had the scene and the autopsy photos. Perhaps more. I studied them, allowing the agonizing memories to breathe in my mind.

Though facial reconstruction was never my thing, I knew what the process was back then. Affix tissue-depth markers to key anatomical points. Scan the marked skull into the computer. Input data on sex, age, and racial background if available. Select and superimpose features from the program's database.

The result was always a cartoonlike gray-scale image. Beard? Mustache? Glasses? Bangs? Bushy brows? Chubby cheeks? Anyone's guess based solely on bone. The goal was to achieve a resemblance while adding nothing distracting. If all attempts at identification failed, the cops and media would circulate the images in hopes that someone might recognize the subject.

As expected, the faces were expressionless and unnaturally symmetrical. I stared at each.

The woman's eyes were large, her nose long and narrow. Her jaw tapered sharply to a prominent chin. The artist had given her center-parted hair swept behind unremarkable ears. The slender, arched brows were pure speculation.

The child's forehead was high, her hair done in the same un-obtrusive style as the woman's. Her eyes were wide-set and angled downward toward her temples. Same brows.

Both subjects were depicted with tightly closed lips. No teeth meant no telltale dental detail to help prompt recall.

Viewing the child's face triggered the troubling memory of the ring. The heartbreaking image of her attempt to hide it from her killer. I thought of all the things she'd never experience. The Christmas trees she'd never trim. The sandcastles she'd never build. The proms she'd never attend.

Stop!

I shifted from the child's sketch to that of the woman.

Staring at her face, a bad feeling slowly took hold of me.

Those eyes.

No way. A gaggle of brain cells cautioned.

That chin.

It's not that unique. The cells reasoned.

Suddenly, I felt dread.

Pit-of-my-stomach-type dread.

13

Winter blasts into Montreal like an icy five-kiloton bomb.

On Thursday, the mercury had risen to a mild fifty-six degrees.

On Friday, I awoke to temperatures in the teens and four inches of snow.

A true daughter of Dixie, I love sandals and sundresses, the smell of Hawaiian Tropic, the sound of palm fronds scraping against my screen. It can never be too balmy or too tropical for me.

And yet I work north of the forty-ninth parallel.

Each winter, I have a pep talk with myself. *It will be cold. Very cold. There is no bad weather, only bad clothing. You will dress properly and be ready.*

I never am.

Maybe *les Quebecois* weren't ready that year, either. Depressed by the rapidly decreasing hours of daylight? Dreading another long, dark season? Pissed that it was too damn early to be so damn cold? Whatever the impetus, the locals had gotten busy culling the herd.

Giving me plenty to do while awaiting DNA results.

A farmer in Saint-Felicien strangled his wife and buried her in his barn. Two days later, he hallucinated that she'd started nagging again. A sleepless week, then hubby dug her up and phoned his priest. The missus rolled through our doors not looking her best.

A pharmacist in Trois-Rivières overdosed on product he'd pilfered from his shelves. His girlfriend found him three days gone, slippered feet propped on a space heater, quilt covering his legs. The gentleman's love of warmth hadn't worked to his benefit.

A tweaker in Val d'Or crawled into a culvert and rammed a knitting needle into her temple. Not sure on the chronology of those actions. A maintenance crew found the body while investigating a blockage.

Fishermen netted a pair of legs in Lac Saint-Jean.

You get the picture. Every day, I had to navigate to the lab and back.

Full disclosure. Hanging out with a putrefied or dismembered corpse, no sweat. But driving on snow or ice scares the crap out of me. Not totally my fault. Mention a flake, and Charlotteans dive for cover until the world thaws.

That's not how Montreal rolls. Following a blizzard, the main thoroughfares are plowed by the next morning's rush hour, and it's business as usual.

For others, at least. Me? I'd look down on the snow-covered cars lining rue Sherbrooke and weigh the merits of car versus Métro. Mass transit meant being squashed elbow to earlobe in a small, poorly ventilated space. Since the COVID-19 pandemic, not an option for me. Instead, I'd don heavy socks, boots, parka, mittens, and muffler and, ignoring Ryan's jibes about Eskimos and the Pillsbury Doughboy, trudge down to the garage.

White-knuckling the wheel, sweaty but undaunted, I'd join the army of wooly-hatted commuters puffing exhaust from their tailpipes in icy little clouds. Since the small streets in Hochelaga-Maisonneuve were passable only via tire tracks snaking down their centers, I'd pay to park in the Wilfrid-Derome lot. Then, attentive to ice, I'd step out

into the frigid air and, head down, face wrapped in cashmere, scuttle
to the building.

Weekends, I never left the condo.

The first Saturday morning, while I prepared cheesy scrambled
eggs and bacon, one of my few culinary talents, Ryan ventured forth
for a copy of the *Gazette*. After breakfast, he built a fire, and we divided the paper. I started with news and art. He went for sports and
finance.

I was on page four of the local section when a photo caught my
eye. Grainy black-and-white, below the fold. The accompanying article was one column inch, ten lines. I read it quickly.

"Sonofabitch!" I exploded.

"Atta girl." Not looking up.

"I don't believe this."

"More snow?"

"Remember that woman I told you about?"

"The one who sold you the bad Camembert?"

"The one in the cemetery the day of the exhumation."

"You didn't like her hair."

Eyes rolling, I thrust the paper at Ryan.

A quick glance at the photo, then, "That's you."

"It is."

"You look good."

I definitely did not.

"Did you speak with her?" Ryan asked.

"No way."

"The coverage seems accurate. 2006. A woman and a child.
The—"

"That's not the point."

"There's no byline credit. Do you think your carrot-headed shut-
terbug wrote the story?"

I shrugged. "Who knows?"

"Maybe Arbour acted as a source?"

"Or one of his employees."

Ryan thought a moment. Then, "No harm, no foul. Exposure might even help. You know, spur the public into thinking about the victims again."

"Maybe."

I let it go.

My mistake.

That night, Ryan walked to Le Roi du Wonton for Chinese take-out. After dinner, he watched the Canadiens play the Bruins, the Islanders play the Sharks, someone else play someone else. I took a stab at Polly Beecroft's request.

Seated at the dining-room table, I booted my laptop and pulled up the shots I'd taken of Beecroft's death mask photo. Then, unsure what else to do, I started with Anne's discovery about UCL.

As Anne said, the Robert Noel Collection of Life and Death Masks, consisting of thirty-seven specimens, was the work of an avid nineteenth-century German phrenologist. By casting the heads of both the living and the dead, Noel hoped to validate his belief that cranial lumps and bumps provided insight into a person's character.

As Anne also said, Noel's collection was displayed at various times in the past. Once at the Galton Eugenics Laboratory, once at the Slade School of Fine Art. Until recently, little else was known about it. The first breakthrough concerning its history came when one of the cast heads was offered to a group of museum studies students as their second-year collections curatorship module. The specimen chosen was the only one retaining its original documentation, the inscription *Irmscher N; 34, murderer, decapitated 1840* hand-scrawled on a label attached to its neck.

I already knew, again thanks to Anne, that the crafty students had managed to unearth an obscure volume in the British library: *Notes Biographical and Phrenological Illustrating a Collection of Casts.* Authored by Noel, the book provided background on every individual in his assemblage.

What Anne hadn't conveyed was the absolutely mesmerizing nature of Noel's undertaking. Nor had she mentioned the YouTube clips describing subjects in both of his "criminal" and "intellectual" categories.

As Ryan focused on nets and pucks, occasionally erupting with a shout or a groan, I found myself caught up in the videos. It was like wandering among old tombstones, imagining the tragedies reflected in the inscriptions.

Carl Gottlob Irmscher drowned his two-year-old son in a stream, then returned the dead child's body to his bed. Later, fearful of discovery, Irmscher sent his wife to the cellar for potatoes and killed her with an ax as she descended the stairs. He was executed by decapitation with a sword. Irmscher's mask shows a man with lips parted, eyebrow hairs embedded in the plaster.

Christian Gottlieb Meyer murdered his children by throwing them down a mine shaft. He was convicted and died in prison. Interestingly, Noel's take on Meyer differed sharply from his assessment of Irmscher. According to Noel's notes, the region of Meyer's head reflecting love of children was quite prominent, and nothing on his skull indicated a tendency toward violence. Meyer's actions, Noel concluded, derived from overuse of alcohol and fear of institutionalization of his kids. Despite the infanticide, Noel classified Meyer as "nonviolent." A little fudging of the data, doc?

The only female in the Noel collection was Johanne Rehn. Wishing to avoid rejection by a new lover, Rehn threw her daughter into a cesspit headfirst. An autopsy showed that the child had survived the fall but drowned in the filth. Noel categorized Rehn as criminal, noting that her frontal region was small compared to the "hinder part of the crown," rendering Rehn "deficient in her faculty of love of children." Rehn was beheaded in front of a crowd of twenty thousand. The executioner missed twice, and the false starts, sutured postmortem, were evident in her death mask.

On and on, I looped through videos and written accounts, fascinated by the faces and the stories behind them. Not just Noel's subjects but hundreds of others, some famous, some not. I discovered nothing pertinent to Polly Beecroft's missing great-aunt.

When I looked up, the TV was silent, and Ryan was poking the fire.

I spent most of Sunday in further death mask exploration. Again, learned nothing germane to Beecroft.

The following week and weekend were rinse and repeat. Cold cycle.

DNA turnaround isn't flash-bang as depicted on TV. Results take time. I knew that. Still, the wait made me edgy.

I phoned Vislosky twice. Got identical feedback in both conversations. Using my profiles, she was pursuing multiple lines of inquiry: MP reports, schools, hospitals, old Amber alerts, juvenile arrest records. So far, she was coming up blank.

I got the call the second Monday out, an hour after arriving at the lab. Ten days after submitting the femora for DNA testing. Willoughby's preliminary report was finally available. I hurried to see her.

Willoughby was visible through one of the corridor windows, at the control panel of a complicated-looking machine. When I tapped on the glass, she buzzed me in.

"*Bonjour*, hi." Today Willoughby's lids were teal. At least, the one I could see. Her hair, now shaved on the left, was streaked with purple and draping her forehead on the right.

"Hi," I said, searching the tech's face for a hint. Good news? Bad news?

"Let's go to my desk," she said.

We did. Without sitting, or smiling, Willoughby scooped up and handed me two printouts.

I skimmed the top of the first page, translating as I read. *Name; Offense; Case number; Priority; Date requested; Date completed; Date reported; Requested by; Completed by.*

Below that, *Evidence received: 1 right femur in sealed container labeled LSJML-41207.*

My gaze fired to the bottom of the form, to the data that interested me.

Results: Human DNA was recovered and quantified from the femur.

Yes!

The recovered DNA was characterized through polymerase chain reaction (PCR) with analysis of the amelogenin locus for sex determination and the following short tandem repeat (STR) loci.

A paragraph listed the loci.

Heart banging, I read the second printout.

My eyes flew up. Willoughby was watching me, arms crossed on her chest.

"Awesome!" I almost high-fived her.

She shrugged.

"You managed to profile both."

"Did you doubt me?" The crimson lips hitched up slightly at one corner.

"Never. How did you do it?"

"Purify and amplify, baby." A DNA catchphrase?

"I imagine techniques have come a long way since 2006."

"And equipment."

"You ranked my request as top priority. I owe you."

"Wouldn't turn down a bottle of Jimmy B."

"Done."

"This report is just between us," Willoughby said. "A prelim."

"Understood. How come you bumped me up?"

"Rumor has it you can be a real pain in the arse."

"Thanks." I think.

"The whole kit will appear as attachments to the official reports."

I nodded.

"You do know this tells you naught about who your vics were."

"Granted. But now I'm certain the child is female."

"She is."

"And I now have profiles to run through every database on the planet."

"A bit of an overreach, I'd say. But that part's up to the cops."

"You get what I mean."

"My super says I'm to send the report to a guy named Trout over at SQ."

The name wasn't familiar. "Is it OK if I give Detective Ryan a heads up, too?"

"I thought he'd retired."

"Never from this case."

"That bloke really knows how to fill out a shirt."

"When can we expect full profiles?"

"I won't be faffing around."

Willoughby's unlikely blend of Queenly pronunciation and rough street slang always amused me. I took that to mean she'd stay on it.

"There's one other thing," Willoughby said.

Though not a stunner, her observation was definitely useful.

14

Back in my office, yet another *demande d'expertise* form lay on my blotter. LaManche wanted my opinion on "suspicious body parts" found in a building under construction on rue Verreau.

Ignoring the request, I phoned Ryan. He answered right away. Background noise suggested he was on the road.

Supernova pumped, I launched right in.

"*S'il te plaît, ma chère. Lentement.*"

"Willoughby did it." Slowly, as Ryan had requested. "She sequenced DNA."

"From the exhumed bones?"

"Yes."

"I'll be damned. Has the reopened case been assigned to someone at SQ?"

"A guy named Trout."

"I know Trout." I sensed words left unsaid. Uncomplimentary ones. "Let me see what I can do."

"Really?"

"I'm a genius, remember."

"If I send the official report, can you run the profiles through

115

NDDB, CODIS, the DNA Gateway, whatever?" I was referring to the Canadian national DNA database and the U.S. and Interpol equivalents. And suchlike.

I waited out an interlude of impatient honking. Then, "Can do."

"I'll update our entries on NamUS and the Canadian sites for missing persons and unidentified remains," I added.

"Don't get your hopes up. We tried this in 2006."

"We didn't have DNA in 2006."

"True."

"Willoughby did share a couple of interesting things. The child is definitely female."

"You knew that."

"I strongly suspected that."

"She did have that ring."

"That's hardly proof. DNA is. Also, the woman and the child are related."

"Mother and daughter?"

"Maybe."

"That's something."

"It is. Where are you?"

"Driving to Burlington."

"Vermont?"

"As I told you, my dead guy's wife is claiming her husband's car crash was a workplace-related death. She says she's owed two hundred thousand big ones."

"The policy pays that much?"

"If she's right about the circumstances."

"Why did she wait four years to file?"

"That's what the adjuster would like to know."

Sudden guilty realization. I'd been so focused on my own concerns I'd shown no interest in Ryan's.

"I'm sorry," I said. "Bring me up to speed."

"I spent last week poking around down here, learned that the guy's coworkers never heard of the wife. Her name is Agnes, by the way. His is Rupert. Also, I found out that the accident happened more than a hundred kilometers from the plant where Rupert worked."

"A bit odd."

"I also tracked down some of Rupert's former colleagues. Most barely remembered him."

"That's sad."

"When you're dead, you're dead."

"Now what?"

"During the workweek, Rupert stayed at a trailer park called Idle Acres."

"Sounds idyllic."

"They allow pets under twenty-five pounds. I'm heading there now."

"To continue detecting."

"It's what I do. How about you?"

"I'm looking at something for LaManche." Sort of.

"I should be home by five," Ryan said.

"Take care," I said.

"Beware the shih tzus and Yorkies?"

"A pissed-off bichon mangled my grandfather's toe."

When we'd disconnected, I thumbed in another number. Eight-four-three area code.

A robotic voice apologized with all the warmth of a DMV clerk. Asked for a message. Annoyed, I left one.

One glance at LaManche's "suspicious parts" was all I needed. A carpenter or roofer had enjoyed a pork shank in the empty house, then tossed the bones.

I was finishing a one-line report, thinking about whether I could summon the energy to make osso buco later, when my mobile rang.

"Thanks for getting back to me so promptly," I said.

"This'll have to be quick. It's bonkers here."

"Oh?"

"Remember Klopp's *rare* capno autopsy?" Herrin's adjective was bloated with sarcasm.

"He told you about that?"

"He did."

"Go on." Recalling the disfigured corpse on the pathologist's screen. And my failure to follow through on my intent to research the pathogen.

"South Carolina is exploding with cases."

"I heard something about that on a local news broadcast."

"COVID-19 knocked Charleston on its ass. Now this. Could be the death blow for my budget. No pun intended." Despite the joke, stress was evident in Herrin's tone.

"I didn't think capno was contagious."

"It's not. But suddenly, we're the epi-freaking-center of a major outbreak. Look, I have to run. What do you need?"

"I'll keep it short. I'm in Montreal. The LSJML was able to pull DNA from the woman and child found in the container in Saint-Anicet in 2006."

"You're still thinking your Quebec vics are linked to the kids found here?"

"I'm thinking it's a possibility."

"Uh-huh." So skeptical it had both hands on its hips

"During my analysis, I separated out bones to be submitted for DNA testing. I'm wondering if you've done that."

"Sweet Mother of God! The whole friggin' world has DNA on the brain. The media's got folks so scared of capno they're spitting in vials."

That piqued my curiosity. "There's a test for it?"

"These yokels think there's a gene makes some folks immune, others susceptible."

A voice spoke in the background. The line went thick, probably Herrin covering the phone with a hand.

"Sorry about that."

"The container cases?" I said, steering the conversation back on track.

"This isn't my first parlor game, doc. The state lab worked its magic."

"They got DNA?"

"They did."

"On both girls?"

"Yep. Surprised you haven't heard from Vislosky. My office forwarded the report to her last Thursday."

"Could you please forward it to me? And to a microbiologist named Lizzie Griesser?"

"Sure. Send me her contact info."

"I will."

"Probably should have done it earlier. Things are batshit here."

"Thanks."

Three beeps told me Herrin had moved on.

I sat a moment, tamping my anger back down to earth. I'd talked to Vislosky on Wednesday. She knew how invested I was in these container cases. She'd gotten DNA info the next day and hadn't bothered to tell me?

Deep calming breath. Another. Then I entered another number.

"Vislosky." Familiar hubbub suggested she was in the squad room.

"Tempe here."

"I do have caller ID."

"Herrin tells me her office sent you DNA results."

"They did."

"And?"

"I'm running them."

"And?"

"And nothing. So far, no hits, local, state, or national. Still zero reports of missing kids matching the descriptors you gave me."

"You went back five years?"

"We've been over this."

"Anything else I should know?"

"Since Wednesday?"

You sat on the DNA. I didn't say it. "I have profiles on my vics up here."

Vislosky didn't respond to that.

"The woman and the child are related."

"To each other?"

"Yes."

"Big whoop."

"Big whoop?" Working very hard not to lose my temper.

"What did you expect? Your perp grabbed some random chick and some random kid and stuffed them into a barrel together? No shit they're related."

I couldn't disagree. But I detested Vislosky's arrogance. And her Lone Ranger act.

"Did you follow through on the barnacles?"

"There's a marine biologist at the College of Charleston says he'll take a run at simulations."

"Narrowing time since death could help."

"Could."

"Or knowing where the container spent time."

"The guy's not optimistic."

"Keep me in the loop."

"Uh-huh."

And then I waited again.

Willoughby sent me her full report late Tuesday afternoon. As she'd pointed out, forensic labs can legally profile designated portions of an individual's genome. But only law enforcement can run those profiles through the various DNA databases that exist.

After talking to Willoughby, I'd dialed a familiar number at SQ headquarters. Detective Yves Trout listened to me, clearly impatient, then promised action on my container case only when and if time allowed.

Infuriated at the brush-off, I'd phoned Ryan. He'd explained that Trout, newly assigned to the Crimes contre la Personne squad, had a reputation for pursuing only those matters that would enhance his career. And that cold cases typically didn't make the cut.

Wednesday morning, recognizing that I'd probably be a "pain in the arse," as Willoughby had tagged me, Ryan took a break from Rupert and Agnes to swing by his old digs at SQ headquarters. Trout explained that he was focused on a domestic homicide investigation and told him to do whatever he wanted with regard to the Saint-Anicet vics. Ryan didn't really need Trout's approval. Though retired, he still had pull.

Since I had paperwork to complete and needed access to materials at the LSJML, we rode to Wilfrid-Derome together. Awaiting our separate elevators, we agreed to meet in the lobby at four thirty.

At two p.m., as I was completing a report on the farmer's wife from Saint-Felicien, my mobile chirped. Reminding myself that I needed a new ringtone, I checked the screen.

Vislosky.

Surprised, I answered.

"Good morning, detective."

"It's raining like hell here."

"I hope you're calling with good news."

"I may have a lead on the younger vic." Underscored by an ambient mix similar to the one I'd heard with Ryan on Monday. Engine. Wiper blades. The AC was a new addition.

"No shit."

"No shit. In 2017, the ER at Beaufort Memorial treated a kid for, what was that break?"

"A lateral condylar fracture of the right humerus."

"For that. Jessica Gray Jeben. White female, DOB July 1, 2002."

Quick math. "Age fifteen. That tracks."

"Jeben never returned to have the cast removed. About that same time, she stopped attending school."

"Sonofabitch."

"The mother's still at the same address in Yemassee."

"Where's Yemassee?"

"Beaufort County. I'm leaving there now. The area's rural, and Mama's definitely not cum laude."

"How does she explain her daughter's broken arm?"

"They've got one of those homemade rope-and-tire swings hanging from a tree in the front yard. She says the kid fell from the swing."

"Do you believe her?"

"Who knows?"

"Has Jessica reappeared?"

"No."

"What does she say about that?"

"The kid split with her boyfriend."

"I don't suppose she filed an MP report?"

"This chick couldn't manage to file her own nails."

"Did you get a DNA sample?"

"Got a Coors can in a ziplock on the seat beside me."

"Well done."

"Serve and protect, baby."

"Keep me—"

"Yeah. Yeah. Looped in."

Though Ryan was just a few floors below me, our paths didn't cross all day. I arrived in the lobby before he did. One look at his face, and I knew he'd struck out.

"No hits?" I asked as he exited the elevator.

Ryan shook his head.

"Not surprising for the child," I said. "But I thought we might get lucky with the woman."

"I guess she kept her nose clean."

"And never enlisted in the military."

"You're taking it well," Ryan said. "I thought you'd be gutted."

I told him about Vislosky's lead.

"No shit," he said.

We both needed to expand our vocabularies.

Conversation stopped when we left the building. In the sharp, biting wind, breathing almost did. I kept my head bent, my mouth closed, hoping the tears wouldn't freeze on my face.

Once in the Jeep, Ryan fiddled with the heater, which was often tetchy. I curled and uncurled my fingers, hoping to reintroduce circulation.

"You need heavier mittens," Ryan said.

"I do."

"It's unusual to be this cold in October."

"Hm." How many times had I heard that?

"I looked up your paparazzo." As Ryan pulled from the curb and slid into traffic.

"Sorry?" The quick segue left me in the dust.

"The glamour shot in Saturday's paper."

"It was hardly a glamour shot."

"I gave a call over to the *Gazette*. The journalist is a freelancer named Laura Bianchi. Word is she's young and ambitious, monitors police frequencies looking for scoops."

"That's how she learned about the exhumation?"

"It was a quiet news cycle, so she figured digging up bodies was better than nothing. Snapped the pic, sold the piece to some wire service, the *Gazette* ran it. End of story. Nothing creepy."

"You didn't see the woman's hair."

It was *l'heure de pointe*, rush hour, though rushing anywhere was impossible. Still, we diverted to rue Saint-Laurent for smoked meat. While Ryan ran into Schwartz's deli, I checked my email, fingers at last warm enough to work the keys.

Herrin's DNA reports had arrived.

I opened and skimmed both documents. Casual, convinced we'd soon have the younger vic ID'd. That her name would lead to the identity of her companion.

As I squinted at the data on the tiny screen, something far down in my psyche said, *Huh?*

What?

Hard as I tried, I couldn't budge the thought from the subliminal cranny in which it was wedged. Was still trying when Ryan opened the door and slid behind the wheel. The car filled with the contradictory scents of wintry air, wet wool, and warm spiced meat.

Not sure why, I forwarded Herrin's reports to Willoughby. Expected no reaction.

How wrong I was.

15

M y mobile rang at midmorning Friday with a significant development.

"The older girl in Charleston is related to the woman here."

Willoughby's words sent a jolt of adrenaline through my body.

"You're sure?" I asked, momentarily taken aback.

"Yes."

"What about the child here?"

"Her sample was too degraded."

I knew just enough to understand that Willoughby and her counterpart in South Carolina had looked at gene variations in short repeat sequences of DNA at specific loci on the chromosomes. Willoughby had been able to amplify enough from the Montreal woman for comparison to the two teens in Charleston. That had not been possible for the Montreal child.

"—catch these tossers."

Willoughby's words brought me back.

"But you were able to determine that the child here is related to the woman in the container with her." More question than statement.

"Yes. But that comparison was based on fewer loci. It's complicated. Do you want me to walk you through it?"

"Not right now." My mind was racing to process. "So, if the Montreal woman and child are related, presumably both are related to the older girl in Charleston."

"Presumably."

"Wow." I'd started to say *No shit.*

"Your hunch was spot-on."

"What prompted you to try the comparisons?" I hadn't asked her to do that.

"Something in the genomes caught my eye, so I figured, why not have a punt?"

"Ryan ran your profiles here and in the States. Came up empty."

"Not surprising."

I debated telling Willoughby about Jessica Jeben. For some reason, held back. Instead, "Again, I owe you."

"Just admit it. I'm a ledge."

"You are." Unsure of Willoughby's meaning.

"Anything else comes up, give us a bell."

My mobile beeped an incoming call.

Ryan. Perfect.

I clicked over, the exhilaration making me so clumsy I almost dropped the phone.

"Good morning, detective." *Lentement.* Slowly.

Ryan wasn't fooled. "What's up?"

"What?" Faux defensive.

"You sound like a junkie with an eight-ball."

I shared what I'd just learned from Willoughby.

Ryan said nothing.

"I was right. The cases here are connected to those in Charleston."

"Any word on the Jeben lead?"

"Vislosky asked for a rush. Even if they bump her request to the front of the line, results will still take a few days.

A moment, then, "We should celebrate."

"It's a little early to dig out the party hats."

"True. But we can enjoy a nice dinner for no reason."

"Tonight?"

"Why not."

"Where?"

"I'll surprise you. Be ready at seven."

I sat a moment, talking myself down. Eyes on the landscape beyond the window by my desk.

Overnight, a gentler front had bullied out the Arctic cold, and twelve floors below, the melting snow was sending glistening black rivulets across the asphalt surface of the parking lot. In the distance, bloated clouds hung low over the Fleuve Saint-Laurent stretching dark and silent along the horizon.

When my pulse was again normal, I phoned Vislosky.

She answered right away. "Vislosky."

While relaying Willoughby's shocker, I could imagine that one cynical eyebrow lifting.

"Could be a major break," I said after a long moment when Vislosky hadn't responded.

"So now there are four."

Always were, I thought. "Any word on Jeben?"

"The boyfriend's a guy named Thomas Slinger. Age twenty-six. Went by Slick."

"Slick Slinger?"

"Tells you all you need to know about the little worm."

"That and the fact he was dating a fifteen-year-old kid."

"And that."

"What's his story?"

"Guy's a walking charm school."

"Meaning?"

"His juvie sheet is long and uncreative. Mostly petty stuff—DUIs, disturbing the peace, vandalism, shoplifting. The Marines bounced him with a dishonorable in 2015."

"Why?"

"The gentleman has a fondness for blow. My personal favorite: the Beaufort County sheriff busted him in 2016 for feeding live chickens to pit bulls he was training for the ring. Record ends there."

"Jesus. Have you talked to him?"

"Ex-Private Slinger is currently in the wind."

"Let me guess. He vanished about the time Jessica Jeben went missing."

"Bingo. Look, I've got some door-to-doors to wrap up and a shit-load of ass-in-the-chair follow-ups to do."

Dead air.

Again, all I could do was wait.

Three thirty p.m. Outside, the clouds were now so low they seemed to be kissing the river. Dark and swollen, they promised delivery soon.

I'd just finished another report. The tweaker in the culvert was, indeed, Marie Cloutier, the suspected mental case. Though I couldn't state cause of death, I could say that Marie's knitting needle had inflicted impressive damage to her temporal lobe.

The instant I hit send, my mind toggled back to the woman and the child washed ashore in Saint-Anicet. I pulled the file up on my computer and stared at the crude renderings of both faces.

The two stared back. A woman with a narrow nose and a prominent chin. A child with a high forehead and wide-set eyes.

I was assaulted by the usual tumult of thoughts. While I attempted to sort through them, a cluster of neurons issued a provocative *psst!*

What?

I tried coaxing the subliminal synapse to the surface.

The neurons remained hunkered down.

Studying the features on my screen, I asked myself, what minutiae had my lower centers noticed that I was missing?

Unexpectedly, my mind flashed an image of Polly Beecroft.

Was this synaptic alert similar to the one I'd received as I viewed Beecroft's mask? What had triggered the alarmist cells then?

I closed my eyes and tried to reconstruct my pre-hurricane meeting with Beecroft.

The mental gears refused to mesh.

Frustrated, I reduced the two sketches and opened the file containing my shots of Beecroft's photos.

A few reluctant neurons yielded, admitting that the source of my disquiet was the feeling that the women, long dead, were somehow familiar.

But before her visit to the MCME, I'd never met Polly Beecroft. And definitely not her mysterious death mask ancestor. *Maybe* ancestor.

Brain snap. Was that it? Was Beecroft's journey what the cells were urging me to consider?

I sat back, mind slipstreaming in a zillion different directions.

Out of the morass of ideas, one seemed a possibility.

I looped over to the American Academy of Forensic Sciences website, logged in as an AAFS member, and pulled up the *Journal of Forensic Sciences*. Found the article I was seeking and read it through.

I picked up my phone.

Ryan had reserved at one of my favorite bistros, Leméac, on avenue Laurier Ouest in a part of the city known as the Outremont. He insisted we drive, not a great idea on a Friday night. We ended up parking several light-years away. Fortunately, the rain hadn't started. But the heavy, moist air promised that wouldn't last.

Melting snowdrifts, blackened by oil and car exhaust, oozed murky runoff into the gutters and onto the sidewalks. Our heels clicked wet tattoos as we hurried along the pavement.

The small restaurant was packed, but we were seated quickly. I ordered the arugula and fennel salad to start. Ryan chose the butternut squash soup. We both went with the *moules et frites* for our mains. Mussels and fries.

While waiting to be served, I made a point to ask Ryan about Agnes and Rupert. The noise level was such that we had to lean close to converse.

"How was Idle Acres?"

"Met a rottweiler named Jose."

"A rottweiler under twenty-five pounds?"

"I didn't query Jose's weight. He didn't query the purpose of my call."

"Fair enough."

"Turns out the park has a new owner. Arnie Kim. Kim said the place had changed hands several times. He bought it two years back and didn't know Rupert or Agnes.

"Did Kim have any old records?"

"It's a trailer park."

"Did he know the former owner's name?"

"He did. Jimmie Gardner."

"Did he know Gardner's whereabouts?"

"He did not."

Our starters arrived. Ryan and I spent time with salt and pepper. I ordered another Perrier with lime. He ordered another Moosehead, then picked up the thread.

"Undaunted, I phoned every Jimmie and James Gardner in every phone directory in Vermont."

"Sounds daunting."

"I always get my man."

"Seriously?"

"Would I kid about something like that?" Ryan's eyes sparked like sapphires in the flickering candlelight. "Gardner remembered Rupert, vaguely recalled Agnes and their son, Zeke, from the few times the two had stopped by. Their last name is Schultz, by the way. He didn't care for Zeke."

"Why not?"

"Jimmie's reasoning was unclear." Ryan finished his soup and laid his spoon on the table. "Weekdays, Rupert stayed at Idle Acres because it was closer to the plant where he worked. Weekends, he drove home to a spit-on-the-map town called Ferdinand."

Downing a slug of beer, Ryan leaned back in his chair.

"And?" I prompted.

"I did some detecting in Ferdinand."

Ryan's account was terminated by the arrival of our food.

My selection was all I'd hoped it would be. The dessert, a tall concoction involving chocolate mousse, cherries, and whipped cream, was even better. By the time we finished and Ryan paid the bill, over my protests, it was half past ten.

Ornery after a day of restraint, the storm was finally letting loose. Ryan offered to go for the car, but I insisted we both make a run for it. A brief argument, in two languages, he agreed.

Hand in hand, we jogged up Laurier, largely deserted except for cars forced to both curbs. The deluge pounded their windshields, hoods, and roofs. The wind, gusting now, spun dead leaves in circles around our feet. Buildings, trees, and utility poles appeared as peachy blurs in the muffled radiance of the sodium lights.

We were sprinting, hunched, water streaking our hair and faces, when the street was illuminated from behind. I saw Ryan glance over his shoulder, followed his sight line to a set of headlights half a block back.

I could see little through the veil of rain. But two things registered. The paired orbs were enlarging. A fog light, glowing amber on the left, was dark on the right.

A few seconds, then the headlights winged left and disappeared onto avenue Durocher. Ryan quickened our pace. Uneasy?

Moments later, a vehicle turned onto Laurier from avenue Querbes, ahead and coming our way. As before, I couldn't make out the model, the plate, the driver, or the number of passengers. But a single detail was clear. One fog light was dead.

"That's the same car!" I shouted to be heard.

Not needed. Ryan's grip on my hand had tightened, and his body had tensed.

Before he or I could react, an engine growled, and the headlights swelled in a rush.

The car was barreling straight at us.

16

Friday, October 29–Saturday, October 30

The next sequence of events seemed to last a lifetime. In reality, it played out in seconds.

The headlights drilled through the downpour, expanding and separating with terrifying speed.

Ryan's years of training kicked in. Grabbing my shoulders, he spun me and shoved with both hands.

I flew sideways. One foot caught the curb, and I crashed to my knees.

Raising myself up on my palms, I twisted for a view of the street.

Ryan was a black silhouette in the blinding glare of the double beams.

Words flashed in my mind. From some long-ago passage on threat assessment. *A vehicle's first pass is to confirm. Its second pass is to kill.*

No! A voice screamed.

Mine?

Unbidden, my mind logged data. The vehicle was low and sleek and sounded like the *Millennium Falcon*. The driver was a blur behind the wheel. When he floored it, the rear tires spun on the wet pavement. The car fishtailed and arrowed straight for Ryan.

And closed in fast.

Ten feet.

Five.

Then sounds that will forever haunt my dreams.

The dull *boom* as the grille slammed Ryan's flesh. The sharp *crack* as his skull struck sheet metal. The *shss-thud* as his body slid downward and hit the ground.

The car roared off. I squinted to read the plate. Saw only taillights shrinking to red dots, then vanishing into the night.

Heart thundering, I scrambled to my feet and, ignoring the pain in my knee, hobble-scurried to Ryan's still body.

After he was thrown high by the impact, Ryan's forward motion had been stopped by one corner of a bus shelter. He lay at its base, motionless, limbs twisted all wrong. Blood smeared the shelter's street-facing wall in a streak that ended at his head.

Chest heaving, I fumbled my phone from my pocket. Blinded by a mix of rain and tears, it took me two tries to punch 911.

That done, I dropped beside Ryan. Ever so gently, fearful of causing further damage, I tested his carotid for a pulse.

Felt a timorous trembling?

In the distance, a siren wailed.

Around me, dead leaves swirled in a vortex.

"I love you, Andrew Ryan," I sobbed to the rain-scented air.

Then I waited.

Watching Ryan's blood washing from the dingy glass.

Seven hours later, I sat slumped in a chair drawn close to Ryan's bed, a frenzy of emotions battling inside me. Anger. Fear. Regret. Ryan had taken the hit trying to protect me.

Fear dominated. An icy burning in my chest.

Muted sounds drifted through the open door. An elevator chiming. A cart rattling. A robotic voice paging a code.

My mind kept flashing back to the ambulance ride. To Ryan's bloody face pulsing red, then going dark. To the brace on his neck. The mask on his mouth.

To the mantra throbbing in my brain. *He is breathing. His heart is beating.*

At the hospital, while Ryan was rushed away for X-rays, or a CT scan, or an MRI, maybe surgery, I'd been examined, under protest, in the ER. I'd wrenched one knee and scraped one elbow. Otherwise, I'd escaped unhurt.

Once released from the ER, I'd waited in the lobby. The chair was molded plastic. One edge was chipped, the gap shaped like a unicorn's head.

Funny, the things you remember.

As word spread, law enforcement descended on the hospital, both SPVM and SQ. Leaving their cruisers and unmarked Impalas and Crown Vics jammed at odd angles outside the main entrance, they'd swarmed the atrium. Furious, powerless, showing support by their presence.

The case fell to the SPVM, the city cops. Two detectives questioned me, one apologetic, the other with his usual bully approach, each determined to nail the bastard who'd injured one of their own. Luc Claudel and Michel Charbonneau. I'd worked with both.

Still high on adrenaline and crazy with worry for Ryan, I'd tried to provide as detailed an account as possible. It wasn't very detailed. Charbonneau was sympathetic. Claudel was peeved.

I'd described our path up Laurier. Shared my impression of the vehicle. Told them I'd been unable to see the driver or the plate. Looked blank when Claudel asked if the assault was intentional or a hit-and-run.

Eventually, they'd all gone.

Now we were in this room with its overcomplicated bed and beeping machines. Gauze protected the right side of Ryan's head. A sheet covered his body from the neck down, leaving only his arms exposed. A pronged tube sent oxygen into his nose. A needle infused liquids into a vein in his wrist. The IV arm lay tucked to his torso. The other lay loosely flexed across his chest.

For hours, I'd watched the lines on the screens trace their erratic mountains and valleys. For hours, I'd listened to the rhythmic pinging of the sensors.

Though exhausted, I'd refused to allow myself sleep. Irrational, I know. But I needed to stay awake to will the tracing and pinging to continue. I'd been told that the films hadn't shown any cranial fracture. Probably because the plexiglass bus shelter had kept him from slamming directly against the concrete.

I got up and crossed to the window. Overnight, the rain and clouds had departed. The sun was sending its first tentative feelers above the horizon, lighting the multicolored buildings of the Montreal General. Beyond the complex, the hills of Westmount shimmered hazy blue-gray, like the colors and textures of a Monet painting.

I recalled the surgeon's words. Good news and bad. Though there was no fracture, a CT scan had picked up an epidural hematoma. Immediate surgery was needed.

An eon later, she'd returned, eyes caring, voice calm through the fatigue. She'd made a tiny burr hole in Ryan's skull to drain the pooled blood and relieve the pressure. All had gone well. Now we must be patient.

So, I was waiting.

I thought of the many years Ryan and I had spent together. The joys and sorrows. The shared challenges. The shared sense of accomplishment when we'd solved a case. The mutual frustration and disappointment when we hadn't.

Ryan and I had seen much death together. Lives ended in every imaginable way. Male, female, old, young. Throughout our careers, we'd often been the bearers of life-changing news. Informed anxious next of kin that their loved ones were dead. Given comfort by reporting that a killer had been found.

Death was a constant in our work. We'd had our ups and downs, and Ryan hadn't always been there. But when we were together, he'd listen as I unburdened myself, and he'd offer comfort and support.

I felt a tremor in my chest. Was fighting it down when a nurse appeared, rubber soles noiseless on the immaculate tile. She was silver-haired and hefty, probably looking at retirement in the next few years. A badge on her scrubs said *S. Beauvais*.

"*Bonjour.*" S. Beauvais gave a quick dip of her chin.

"*Bonjour,*" I said.

S. Beauvais began checking fluid levels and dials and tracings, hair gleaming aqua-green in the monitor's reflected light. "My night-shift colleagues tell me you have been here throughout."

"Yes," I said.

"You must be exhausted."

"I'm good." I watched S. Beauvais, impressed with the fluidity and efficiency of her movements. And with her perceptive abilities. I was, indeed, *épuisée*.

"He will sleep a while. This is normal. You might use this opportunity to do the same?"

"I don't wan—"

"We will call if there is any change in his condition."

I said nothing,

"To be of value, a caregiver must be fit and alert."

I stared at Nurse S. Beauvais's broad back as it disappeared through the door. She was right. Which annoyed the hell out of me.

Agitated, I pulled my phone from my pocket to check for messages. No signal. I knew that. I'd repeated the ritual a thousand times.

I resumed my vigil.

In the eerie cast-off light from the monitor, Ryan's face looked gaunt, his eyes more deeply set than normal. Each showed the beginning of a spectacular shiner.

I watched Ryan's sheet-clad chest rise and fall. Rise and fall. Rise and fall.

The sensors pinged.

My lids drew together. My chin dropped.

My head snapped up. I was losing the battle.

I rose from my chair.

I'd worn a silk dress for our "date" at Leméac. The fabric was as wrinkled as the face of a mountain apple doll, the bright red mottled by raindrops and smeared with blood.

I brushed both hands over the skirt and tugged the sleeves down to my wrists. Pointless. No one I saw would care how I looked. I dug Ryan's keys from the plastic bag holding his belongings, grabbed my coat, and left.

Out on the street, my mobile offered five full bars. I flipped screens and clicked on an icon.

It was rush hour. The Uber would take twenty minutes.

To pass the time, I checked my messages. No texts, one voice mail. A number in Charleston, South Carolina.

I clicked on. Listened.

"Vislosky here. Thought you'd want to know. Jessica Jeben is alive and shacking with her man Sling in Myrtle Beach. So we're back to base zero. You have questions, you know where to reach me."

It was too early to return Vislosky's call. And I was too shattered.

Behind me, dawn was lighting the empty spaces between the hospital's many buildings and gleaming off the meltwater-crusted snow. Above me, the branches of a maple shifted stiffly in a breeze.

The Uber arrived after thirty minutes, a green Dodge Dart with a driver named Farid. Farid drove me to Ryan's Jeep. I drove the Jeep to the condo.

After feeding Birdie, I stripped off and tossed the devastated dress. Then I showered for a very long time. Before dropping into bed, I lowered the window shades and set the alarm for noon.

Birdie joined me, nonjudgmental over his night spent solo. Perhaps sensing my distress, he pressed close and set to purring in earnest.

Though comforting, the cat wasn't enough. At that moment, I needed human solace.

I dialed Anne. Her voice mail answered.

Of course, it did. The clock said 7:22 a.m. I left a message. Call me.

Mama was incommunicado on one of her spiritual retreats.

Katy was in Afghanistan.

Pete? Nope. My ex had problems of his own.

The bed was so big. So empty.

I felt utterly alone.

And for the first time in my life, I felt true hatred and rage.

Lying there, I was overcome with a loathing so intense I could taste it in my mouth. I burned with a primal yearning to hunt down the person who'd injured Ryan.

But who was that person? A man, I assumed.

Why?

Was Ryan the target? Was I? Were we both?

I knew what I had to do.

17

Saturday, October 30

C langing church bells jarred me awake.
    It took several seconds to orient.

Leméac. The incident on Laurier. Ryan.

I grabbed my phone. It showed no missed calls.

I threw on slacks and a sweater, then did a half-hearted job with my morning toilette. After feeding Birdie, who eyed me with disbelief, I gathered items I thought Ryan might want. Then, avoiding eye contact with the cat, I grabbed my jacket and purse and bolted.

Saturday afternoon. Traffic was light. Even with a stop for coffee and a croissant, I was at the hospital by one forty-five.

The nicely permed lady at reception was named Veronique. I told Veronique I was there for Andrew Ryan. Her red-lacquered nails clacked on a keyboard. Lots of keys, lots of clacks. Then she looked up and informed me that the patient was in room 1807.

I crossed to the elevators, pleased that Ryan had progressed from the ICU. Irked that I hadn't been called as promised.

Everyone around me had flowers, balloons, or stuffed creatures. I was debating a trip to the gift shop when the elevator doors whooshed open. I boarded and ascended with the gaggle of gift bearers.

The room was a single with a standard-issue bed, swivel-arm table, chair, and narrow wardrobe. Bad floral curtains were open, allowing a pretty good view of the complex.

The patient was propped on pillows eating Jell-O from a small plastic cup.

Big Ryan smile as I came through the door. *"Bonjour, ma chère."*

"Nice digs," I said.

"Exquisite," he said.

"You look like someone beat the snot out of you." Low-keying it, feeling tears threatening at the sight of his face.

"You should see the other guy."

I crossed to Ryan. He put the Jell-O on hold to receive my kiss.

"I brought you some things." Holding up the overnighter. "PJs, dopp kit, phone, the Stephen King you were reading. I wasn't sure what you'd want."

"You're the best."

"That's why they pay me the mediocre bucks." I placed the bag on a shelf in the wardrobe.

"How's the Birdcat?" Ryan asked.

"Annoyed at being left alone so much."

"He'll get over it."

"He will."

As Ryan finished the Jell-O, with far more enthusiasm than the green goop warranted, I dragged the chair to his bedside.

"You're really rocking the new look." Ryan's hair was spiking in clumps around the bandage taped to his head.

"Below this dressing is manly bare bone." Pointing with the spoon to his right parietal.

"You could tattoo it."

"There's also a wee hole."

"Work it into the design."

"I'll give it some thought."

"You seem extraordinarily chipper," I said.

"Could be some pharmaceuticals involved." Now the spoon indicated the drip line running into his arm.

"Better living through chemistry," I said.

"How's the weather?"

"Winter is back and appears to be planning an extended stay." I relieved him of the empty Jell-O cup and spoon. "How long have you been awake?"

"A couple of hours."

"How do you feel?"

"Thirsty."

I filled and passed him his water tumbler.

"How much do you remember?" I asked when he'd finished sucking on the flexible straw.

"The red dress." Groucho-flicking his eyebrows, then wincing at the effort.

"Sadly, it was DOA."

Ryan pulled a face. With the black eyes and prickly hair, he looked like a B-movie serial-killer clown. Which reminded me of the date.

"Tomorrow is Halloween. I'll bring you jelly beans."

"I'll be out of here by then."

"In your dreams."

"The doc says I'm making remarkable progress"

"For a guy with a wee hole in his head."

Ryan ignored that. "Claudel and Charbonneau came by earlier."

"Itchy and Scratchy. They questioned me last night."

"Charbonneau's a good guy."

I said nothing.

"Claudel's solid."

"Right. *Deadline Hollywood* described him as zany."

"Dead-on."

Now I made the face. "They shouldn't be bothering you so soon."

"You know the old cliché."

"The first forty-eight," I said.

"Time is the enemy."

"Another good one. Still."

"It was fine. Though I couldn't tell them dick."

"You don't remember?"

"Bits and pieces. I'll jot things down as they come to me."

"Did you get any sense of the car?"

"Something fast. Maybe a Porsche."

"That was my impression, too."

"And hard."

"All cars are hard."

"Very, very hard."

I rolled my eyes.

"Whatever the model, the psycho driving it needs his head ripped off and shoved up his ass," Ryan said.

"You really mustn't hold back on your feelings."

"I'll work on it. Any developments on your container cases?"

"You really want to hear about that?"

"I do."

I told him about Vislosky's call.

An odd look crossed Ryan's face. Before he could respond, a nurse entered. Not S. Beauvais. This one was tall and bony, with oversize black-framed glasses. She went through the drill with charts and monitors and tracings.

Then, turning to me, "We have had a very full morning. We mustn't overtax the patient."

When she'd gone, I asked Ryan, "Seriously. How do *we* feel?" Imitating the nurse-speak.

"Like someone who's had the snot beat out of him." This time, the smile didn't make it to the purple-rimmed eyes.

I stood and took Ryan's hand. "Call me when you're rested. I'll be here in a flash."

"What will you do without me?" Groggy.

I had a plan.

———

My mobile rang as I was exiting I-20 onto rue Guy.

"Annie Fanny!" Summoning a cheeriness I didn't feel.

"What the sweet baby Jesus is going on?"

"What?"

"You sounded like death on that voice mail."

I unloaded all the way to the condo. When I stopped talking, the line was silent for so long I thought we'd been disconnected.

"Anne?"

"I'm here. How's the little buckaroo doing?"

"He's hurting but out of danger. And already antsy. He thinks they'll discharge him tomorrow."

"Is he planning a Halloween costume?"

"Trust me, he doesn't need one."

"He looks that bad?"

"Worse."

"Will they?"

"Will they what?"

"Discharge him."

"No."

"Is he on painkillers?"

"Oh, yeah."

"What do *you* think happened? Accident or attack?"

"A deliberate hit, but I have no idea why."

Another long pause, then, "Need a distraction?"

"Sure. But I'm about to enter the garage and may lose signal."

"I might have a lead on Beecroft's mask."

"I'm listening."

Anne launched into a dialogue on ancestry and descent and family resemblances, cut off when I dove underground.

Upstairs, I coaxed Birdie from beneath the bed with his favorite Greenies treats. Too many for his own good. Or for that of the white carpet. A guilty conscience is a powerful force.

Next, I made myself peanut butter toast and washed it down with a Diet Coke, all the while thinking about one of Anne's comments.

Kicking back in a living-room chair, I hit redial, idly observing the bundled figures below on rue Sherbrooke. Shoppers, tourists, mothers or nannies pushing strollers. Everyone more tolerant of cold than *moi*.

"Sorry." When Anne answered. "Lost signal in the garage."

"I figured."

"Listen, can I roll something by you?" Not sure why I was bouncing the idea off Anne. To see how plausible it sounded when spoken aloud?

"Rock and roll."

"You said your research on Beecroft's mask led you to some genealogy web pages."

"Not on purpose. It's like falling down rabbit holes. One leads to another, then another. I stumbled onto a boatload of sites offering to profile my genes."

Anne was right. In the past decade, a vast array of companies had sprung up offering users the opportunity to test their own DNA. Purchase the kit, mail us your spit. We'll tell you where Great-great-grandma and -grandpa were born. Easy-peasy. Some of them, such as AncestryDNA, were geared mostly toward family-tree building. Others, such as 23andMe, were more medically focused.

Not long after the appearance of these direct-to-consumer DNA services, amateur cyber-sleuths began to explore whether they might be of value as investigative tools for law enforcement. Specifically, could their databases be used to identify unknown crime victims and suspects? To put names to unknown dead?

It turned out the answer was yes. But indirectly. The forensic application relied on the use of another type of open-source database. And on users' willingness to upload the DNA results they'd obtained in hopes of locating relatives.

"Did you come across any mention of forensic genetic genealogy?" I asked.

"Give me a hint."

"The Golden State Killer?"

"Sure did. Some genealogist helped the cops nail that turd."

"GEDmatch was the name of the site used to ID the guy," I said. "GEDmatch doesn't offer DNA testing but allows users to upload results from companies like 23andMe or AncestryDNA. They claim to be able to identify a third cousin or closer for more than ninety percent of the population."

"So how does it work?" Anne asked through the crinkle of cellophane. I wondered what she was eating.

"It's not so different from, say, an adoptee looking for a birth parent. You do your DNA test—"

"By mailing off a swab."

"You then upload your DNA results to an open-source database like GEDmatch. In most cases, the matches they find will be distant cousins. That's where the genealogists come in. They piece together family trees by cross-referencing shared bits of DNA with things like gender, age, place of residence, obituaries, public records, social-media profiles, et cetera. In criminal cases, law enforcement might actually go out and contact family members for additional info or more DNA."

"To narrow down the possible hits."

"Yes."

"You said a database *like* GEDmatch. There are others?"

"Many. FamilyTreeDNA, for example."

"Wait." Loud syrupy swallow. "I've seen their ad. The one with the father of that kid who escaped her kidnapper."

"Elizabeth Smart."

"That's her. The dad urges viewers to submit their DNA to help catch offenders."

"A good spokesman helps create demand, and there's a lot of money to be made. I think I read that FamilyTreeDNA recently raised its price to law enforcement from one hundred to seven hundred dollars a pop. And they're hiring like crazy."

More cellophane. "Go on."

"What are you eating?"

"Snickers. I bought a bag for trick-or-treaters."

God, that sounded good.

"So . . ." I was searching for the right way to frame it.

"Let me guess. Even with DNA, you've run into a wall with your container victims. So you're thinking you might try forensic genealogy."

"I am."

"It's a long shot."

"From here to the outer rim."

"Go for it."

18

Saturday, October 30–Friday, November 5

Next, I phoned Claire Willoughby on her mobile.

She answered right away. Sounds of traffic and children shouting suggested she was outside. Panting suggested she might be running.

"I'm sorry to bother you on a weekend."

"No worries. I'm jogging. I hate jogging." Her words came out in short little bursts.

I got straight to it, didn't mention Ryan. "Have you heard of forensic genetic genealogy?"

"Are you joking?"

"No."

"Of course, I've heard of it. Those blokes are on *fuego*, claiming to be cracking a cold case a week."

"Could it be done on the bones I exhumed?"

"The container woman and kid?"

"Yes."

She didn't hesitate. "Not a chance."

"Why not?" Fighting to hide my disappointment.

"First off, our lab doesn't do SNP testing. Only STR."

149

"Short tandem repeat."

"Yes." I heard her pausing to take a breath. "The kind of profile that goes into a database like CODIS to search for possible matches. Forensic genetic genealogy uses SNP genotype data."

"Single nucleotide polymorphism."

Based on the meager knowledge I'd acquired from reading and from colleagues in molecular biology, I understood that an SNP involved a substitution of a single one of four possible bases, A, T, C, or G, at a particular location on the DNA molecule.

I ran my distilled definition by Willoughby.

"Basically, that's it. In layman's terms, at a specific position along the double helix, where most folks have one gene, a minority have another." Despite the labored breathing, Willoughby's footfalls sounded rapid and steady. "And such polymorphisms, as we call them, are responsible for individual variations, things like differences in susceptibility to diseases like sickle-cell anemia and cystic fibrosis."

The footfalls slowed, stopped. I heard rattling, then gulping.

"Look, Tempe, I live for this shit. But no can do. Even if we performed SNP at our lab, which we don't, the bone you recovered was too degraded. I used up most of the sample for the STR."

"Who does SNP testing?"

"As far as I know, mostly private labs."

"Thanks."

"I did nothing."

"You took my call on a Saturday."

"Did I mention I hate jogging?"

"Run, Forrest, run."

"What?"

"Never mind."

I gazed out the window at the street below. A light snow was falling. People were still streaming in both directions along rue Sherbrooke. A van was pulling from the curb on rue Crescent beside the Musée des Beaux-Arts. A car was waiting, eager to claim the spot.

A Porsche Panamera. Sleek and low to the ground.

Sudden flashback to avenue Laurier.

All my senses jolted awake.

Body tense, I watched the Porsche lurch back and forth, the driver clearly struggling with the steep downhill incline. After six or seven passes, the ragged maneuvering stopped. A door opened, and a woman got out. She wore a brown overcoat that hung below the tops of her boots, a plaid muffler, and a red tuque rimmed by curly white hair.

I settled back in my chair, embarrassed by the melodrama that had taken hold of my brain.

On to plan B.

Scrolling through my contacts, I thumbed in another number. Far off in Virginia, a receptionist asked my name, then connected me to Lizzie Griesser.

"You're pissed that I haven't sent your sketches." Lizzie blew out a breath. "My bad. But we've been—"

"That's not why I'm calling." Though there was some truth to what she said.

Lizzie waited.

"Does your lab do SNP genotyping?"

"Yes."

"Forensic genealogy?"

"Oh, my God. Lately, we're doing a shit ton. So much that we've contracted with a forensic genealogist. That's part of the reason—"

"If I have the Charleston coroner provide additional samples—"

"I never received samples from Charleston."

"Seriously?"

"All I got were the ones from your Montreal vics."

Herrin hadn't followed through on my request. That *did* piss me off.

"If I have samples sent, can you do SNP genotyping on the two kids found in the container down there?"

"How degraded is the bone?"

"The state lab was able to sequence STR."

"Doesn't mean diddly-squat. But I can try."

"Thanks."

"And I *will* get those phenotype sketches to you."

"Right on."

To his dismay, Ryan spent Halloween in his exquisite room, 1807. I brought him a trick-or-treat bag filled with his faves, Hershey's, Twix, and Kit Kat bars. Actually, my faves. Ryan thanked me, face looking like a Merriam-Webster illustration beside the definition of *cranky*.

Though Ryan argued, neither his physician nor the surgeon would budge. Concussion. Burr hole. The patient was staying put. I sided with the docs.

First thing Monday, I phoned the office of the Charleston County coroner. Got voice mail. Left a message.

Herrin returned my call two hours later. The conversation made our last one seem downright effusive.

Sounding exhausted, Herrin apologized for not following through with Griesser. Explained that the samples had been collected but not sent. Same excuse. An explosion in the number of capno cases.

Herrin promised a FedEx shipment would go out by day's end.

Lizzie's email hit my in-box at five p.m. on Tuesday. According to her phenotype report, the woman and the child were both of western European ancestry, with pale skin, blue or green eyes, dark brown to black hair, and no freckles. All predictions were at confidence levels above ninety percent. No surprises there.

I dug out my facial approximations from 2006 and placed them beside my laptop. Then I opened Lizzie's composite profiles.

The woman's eyes were large, her nose long and narrow, her jaw tapering to a prominent chin. The child's forehead was high, her eyes wide-set and slanted obliquely toward her temples.

Both sets of images shared those features. But beyond these vague similarities, I might have been viewing different women and children, those on my screen more realistic than those on the tabletop.

My old facial approximations had been based solely on bone. I've never been a fan of the technique. This comparison confirmed that skepticism. And explained why our sketches had produced no results back in 2006.

Lizzie's reproductions had been generated by digitally combining the lab's DNA predictions with detailed cranial photos and measurements that I'd provided.

I stared at the images. The faces were so vivid, so real. So young. I felt the old heartbreak rekindle anew.

Ignoring the black hole burning in my chest, I forwarded Lizzie's attachment to Ryan. He could view the report while convalescing.

Ryan was released midmorning on Wednesday. The shaved patch of scalp was now covered with tape, and the shiners were morphing from purple to sickly yellow-green.

After driving Ryan home, I made grilled cheese sandwiches and served them with root beer, Ryan's choice of beverage. The phone rang before I'd cleared the table.

Charbonneau and Claudel were in the lobby. They'd been busting ass trying to find the guy who'd run us down and wanted to do some follow-up with Ryan. Reluctantly, I buzzed them in.

As I made coffee, Claudel scanned the decor, a look of disdain wrinkling his parrot nose. Fortunately for him, he kept his critique to himself.

We all took our mugs to the dining-room table. When we'd settled, Charbonneau began the interview.

Ryan still remembered little about the attack. I filled in gaps in his timeline. It was just rehash. We'd been over these details.

Then Claudel switched gears, picking up on a thread from a hospital meeting from which I'd been absent.

"We spent yesterday in Ferdinand."

"Where Rupert and Agnes Schultz lived." I was playing catch-up. Apparently, Claudel and Charbonneau were talking to people involved in Ryan's auto death case. Because Ryan was laid up? Unofficially, since the parties all lived in Vermont? Or because they suspected a connection to the attack?

Claudel ignored me. "The town is the size of my left nut."

"Place must be pretty damn small," I mumbled, irritated at being dismissed.

Claudel ignored that, too.

"Agnes wasn't at any address you gave us and didn't answer any number you provided." Claudel was directing all his comments to Ryan. "We asked around, finally found this dimwit clerk at the Circle-K who thought maybe she might know the old lady. There's one chick won't be getting any invite to Mensa."

"She directed us to a house," Charbonneau jumped in.

Claudel mimicked, I assumed, the unfortunate clerk. "Down t' end of Broadberry. The green one wif t' white shutters needs painting."

No one laughed.

"Turned out the house belonged to Agnes's mother, Mary Gertrude. Lady must have been in her nineties," Charbonneau said. "Mary Gertrude phoned Agnes, she came, they both had a big cry, then the two of them started pulling out albums to show us photos of Rupert."

"Guy looked like a hemorrhoid gone bad." Claudel's smirk made me want to smack it from his face.

"It's nice to know someone is grieving for Rupert," I said, recalling the cavalier attitude of his coworkers.

"Heartwarming."

I glared at Claudel.

"The ladies told us Rupert died on a Monday morning on his way to work." Charbonneau, the peacemaker. "Normally, he'd return to the trailer park Sunday night, but it was Easter, so he stayed over."

"What do they say happened?" Ryan asked.

"Same as the police report. The old man swerved off the road and hit a tree."

"So Agnes will probably get the insurance money." Ryan ran a hand down the good side of his face. Sighed. "But why the four-year delay in asking for it?"

Seeing that Ryan was fading, I tried to move the conversation along. "How is all this relevant to finding the jerk who blasted Ryan?"

"Breaking news." Claudel waggled both hands in the air. "Rupert got the policy through work, and Agnes had no idea."

"No shit?" Ryan perked up. "Who filed?"

"Sonny boy."

"Zeke?"

"Ezekiel Hoag. Agnes's pride and joy from a previous marriage."

"Zeke found out about the coverage and filed the claim without telling his mother?" Ryan sounded incredulous.

"He did."

"That was wishful thinking. Zeke wasn't a named beneficiary and not a relative of Rupert. No way he could collect. Still, why wait four years?"

"I've only started looking into this shitbird. But when we ran Zeke's name, a very hefty sheet came back. Listing, among other achievements, a nickel bump for vehicular homicide."

"Holy crap," I said.

"Holy crap," Ryan said.

"At the Northwest State Correctional Facility," Charbonneau added. "In Swanton, Vermont."

"Let me guess," I said. "The claim was filed after Zeke got out?"

Claudel and Charbonneau both nodded.

"*Tabarnac!*" Ryan was struggling to wrap his battered head around this development. Frankly, so was I.

"Was Zeke into white-collar crime?" I asked.

"No. But his cellmate in Swanton was a guy named Roger Carnegie. Carnegie was doing time for embezzlement and money laundering."

Everyone took a moment to digest that. Ryan spoke first.

"You think Zeke saw me as an impediment to profiting from his stepfather's death? He learned I was sniffing around and decided to take me out?"

"That's our current thinking."

"That plays," Ryan said, nodding slowly.

"Like a hooker on a stroll," Claudel agreed.

Lizzie Griesser called two days later. I thanked her for the DNA phenotypes and reproductions. Then, barely breathing, I listened to her latest report.

"I received a sample for each of your Charleston vics."

"Yes."

"A femur from the older kid, a femur and some tissue from the younger."

I didn't interrupt.

"Despite the lengthy immersion in salt water, each was in pretty good condition. And you won't believe this."

"Try me."

"Seems impossible, but traces of dried blood were preserved deep within the medullary cavity of the younger victim's bone."

"Enough to do an SNP genotype?"

"Damn tooting."

"Enough to do a forensic genealogy analysis?"

"Enough to try."

"Do it."

Long silence. When Lizzie spoke again, she was clearly uncomfortable.

"Much as I'd like to, Tempe. I can't slip another one through off the books."

"I understand. How much?"

She quoted a price. A high one.

I didn't hesitate.

"If the coroner won't authorize funding, I'll pay for the testing."

"Good enough for me."

Over the next few days, temperatures in Quebec went polar. Everyone commented on the unseasonable cold. In both languages. The French were particularly creative. *Un froid de canard*. Duck cold. *Un vent à écorner les bœufs*. A wind to dehorn the oxen.

Ryan and I stayed home and ordered a lot of takeout.

The world slowly rotated on its axis.

He healed.

I waited.

19

D r. Aubrey Sullivan Huger.
It had been so long I'd stopped counting the days. And now there it was. A name. A link.

"Repeat that." Grabbing pen and paper from the counter.

Lizzie did. "Dr. Aubrey Sullivan Huger."

"The younger Charleston vic is related to Huger?"

"Don't have a thrombo."

Lizzie was right. Her news had me wired to the next galaxy and back.

"Sorry."

"She is," Lizzie said.

"What about the older vic?"

"There was too little DNA to do an SNP genotype. Also, forget about radioisotope testing on either."

"Damn."

Silence.

"Don't get me wrong. I'm thrilled."

"Could have fooled me." Prickly.

"It's just that the older girl is related to my Montreal vics, so info on her could have blown the whole thing wide open."

"It is what it is," Lizzie said, a little edge to her voice.

"What do you know about Huger?"

"Nada."

"He's alive?"

"I don't have the genealogist's report in front of me. I called with the name knowing you'd be eager to hear."

Eager was an understatement. "How is Huger related? Father? Brother? Cousin?"

"I think the genealogist said third cousin at the closest. Or something. But you'll have to talk to him."

"Where does Huger live?"

"Genealogist."

"Is Huger a physician? What does he do for a living?"

"Are you listening to me?"

I drew a deep, calming breath. Exhaled. Poised pen over paper.

"What's the genealogist's name."

"Bando Slug."

"You're kidding."

"I'm not."

"How do I contact him?" Jotting Slug's name below Huger's.

Lizzie gave me a number. "Don't expect a warm reception."

"Meaning?"

"The guy's personality tallies with his name."

"Thank you thank you thank you," I said.

"You are welcome. Thrice."

As soon as we'd disconnected, I punched in Slug's number.

"Hello. You're hearing this because I'm probably trying to avoid you. Leave as brief a communication as possible."

A beep sounded. Another followed shortly after the first, truncating most of my message.

I called back and, speaking shotgun, left only my name and number.

I was dialing Vislosky when Ryan wandered into the kitchen. He was featuring a retro crew cut, and it didn't look bad.

I disconnected.

"What was that all about?" Ryan asked.

"Lizzie's genealogist got a hit. Or whatever they call it."

"Calm down." Noting my agitation.

"A man named Huger," I said. "A distant cousin."

"No shit."

"No shit."

"What do you know about him?"

"His full name is Aubrey Sullivan Huger. He's a doctor of some sort."

"That's it?"

"That's it."

"You should speak to the genealogist."

"He's not taking calls."

Ryan inclined his head toward my laptop. "Do what you do so well, buttercup."

"Don't call me that."

"Meanwhile, I'll run the name. Shot in the dark, but maybe he's in some database."

I raised a hand. Ryan high-fived it.

Within two hours, I had a sketchy picture of Dr. Aubrey Sullivan Huger. Or, more correctly, of his public persona as reflected on Google and the other search engines I used.

I was still at it when Ryan reappeared. Not sure where he'd been.

"Anything pop?" I asked.

"Nada. The guy's clean. At least, in Canada. Did Vislosky run him?"

"I was so caught up here I forgot to call her."

"She won't like that."

"Nope," I agreed, feeling a bit guilty.

"Did you find him?"

"Oh, yeah."

Joining me at the table, Ryan leaned back and assumed a listening expression.

"Huger goes by Sullie."

"Of course he does."

"I found quite a few articles about him. Most include the words 'genius' and 'brilliant' somewhere in the text."

"Genius at what?"

Picking up my semi-shorthand notes, I cherry-picked highlights.

"Huger was born in 1964. Earned two PhDs from UNC–Chapel Hill in 1990 and 1991."

"At the ripe old age of twenty-six."

"Yep."

"In what?"

"Biochemistry and software engineering."

"So the guy's no dummy."

"I told you. He's a genius."

"And brilliant."

"Right out of grad school, Huger went to work for the Human Genome Project, which was just starting up."

Ryan looked a question at me.

"You've not heard of it?"

"Heard, yes. Taken notes, no."

"The goal was to sequence the whole human genome and identify all the genes it contains."

"Ambitious."

"It was."

"Who ran it?"

"The National Institutes of Health and the U.S. Department of Energy coordinated, but the effort was international in scope."

"Did they succeed?"

"The project finished in 2003, two years ahead of schedule."

"A blueprint to build a human being. I'd score that as a win."

I hadn't thought of it quite that way. "A big one. Better understanding of the functions of genes and proteins is having an enormous impact on medicine and biotechnology."

"But we digress."

"We do." More triaging. "Huger left the project in 1995 to take a position at GlaxoSmithKline, also known as GSK."

"Big pharma. Suppose he was lured by the bucks?"

"Who knows? But given that Huger was a biochemistry wunderkind, I suspect the offer was substantial."

"Can one still qualify as a wunderkind at age thirty-one?"

"I think so." Skimming. "Huger was also an entrepreneur. In 1999, he launched a company called GeneMe."

"Purveyors of blue jeans?" Ryan deadpanned.

After giving Ryan "the look," "GeneMe was one of the very earliest DTC genetic testing companies." Even as the words left my lips, I sensed I was coming across as a genetics know-it-all. How did *that* happen? A month ago, I couldn't have cited more than a few facts on the topic.

"DTC?"

"Direct-to-consumer. In the early days, they did paternity testing and such. In 2000, the company won some sort of invention of the year award. Looks like users were supposed to submit DNA to trace their ancestors."

"Mine would arrow straight back to one of the Louises. Maybe all of them."

My eyes rolled without input from me.

"Is GeneMe still operating?" Ryan asked.

"No. At some point, it morphed to GeneFree."

"*Tabarnac!* The jeans are free?"

"The GeneFree website is still active."

"Where does the boy genius live?"

"I found almost zilch on his personal life. And not that."

"Doesn't everyone on the planet have a Facebook page?"

"You don't."

"Because I have you." Choirboy grin.

"Huger has zero presence on social media. No personal website. No Facebook, Instagram, or Twitter account. Though he could tweet using any handle."

Ryan thought a moment. "Huger earned his doctorates at the University of North Carolina?"

"He did."

"GlaxoSmithKline has facilities all over the country. Where did Huger work for them?"

I checked my notes.

"Zebulon, North Carolina."

"And where is GeneFree based?"

It took me another few seconds on Google.

"Charleston."

Ryan and I looked at each other.

"Looks like Sullie may be a Carolina boy."

"Time to call Vislosky?" Ryan asked.

"Past time," I said.

Before dialing, I sat a moment studying one of the many images the World Wide Web had happily supplied. In the shot, Huger sat at a microscope, test tube held high in his gloved left hand. A blue lanyard looped his neck, its ID badge tucked into a lab-coat pocket, unreadable.

Huger looked like half the fifty-something men in Dixie, with standard-issue gray hair sweeping his forehead and curling behind his ears. A trim build suggesting hours in a gym. A deep tan suggesting days on beaches, ski slopes, or golf courses.

Bottom line. Huger resembled a gracefully aging tennis coach rather than a lab rat.

I hit speed dial. Vislosky answered in her usual brusque manner.

"Vislosky."

"It's Temp—"

"I know."

I told her about Lizzie's call.

"Bando Slug?"

"That's his name. And Aubrey Sullivan Huger."

"Gimme a few."

The line went dead.

An hour and a half later, Vislosky called back.

"Other than traffic tickets, Huger's clean. He's involved in some philanthropy, donates to about a half dozen charities."

"Does Huger live in Charleston?"

"I found an address on James Island. A local number, possibly a mobile."

"Where does he work?"

"He's self-employed, runs his own internet companies."

"GeneFree?"

"Yeah, that's one. And others. One's some sort of bullshit holistic food operation."

"What now?"

"I'll drive out there, ask about the kid."

"I have a better idea. Invite him to the station."

"Why?"

"I can observe via Zoom."

A hitch, then, "I might consider it, seeing as you found the guy."

"What reason will you give him?"

"I'll think of one."

"And if he won't come to you?"

"He will."

I didn't doubt that for a second.

"Could be the breakthrough we need," I said.

"If not a breakthrough, at least it's a crack."

20

Vislosky had placed a laptop on the far side of a two-way mirror. Before joining Huger, she'd emailed me a Zoom link. Not sure of the legality of that, but I didn't ask.

The image was shadowed, the sound hollow and staticky. Still, the feed was good enough to provide a sense of Huger and to follow the conversation.

The interview room resembled scores of others I'd seen over the years. Cinder-block walls. Tile floor. Scarred gray metal table, three metal chairs. Wall phone. Recording equipment high up in one corner.

Huger was seated at the table wearing an ecru linen blazer over a pink knit shirt with a perky palm tree emblem on his left chest pocket, tan chinos, and loafers. No socks. Passing time with his iPhone, he seemed surprisingly relaxed for a guy called into a cop shop.

Huger looked up when the door opened. Even with the lousy feed, I could tell that his tanned face was far too smooth for a man of fifty-seven. He'd obviously had work done. And done well. Groomed and plucked brows curved above very blue eyes. I couldn't tell if the startling turquoise was the real deal or courtesy of tinted contact lenses.

"Thank you so much for coming in." Vislosky was uncharacteristically pleasant. "Sorry to keep you waiting."

"It's no problem at all, detective." Huger's vowels were as thick as day-old grits. "Though I must admit I'm baffled." Baffled smile.

"Would you like something to drink?"

"No, ma'am. Thank you for offering."

Huger watched Vislosky cross the room, take the chair opposite his, and place a mug and a file folder on the table. Then his eyes rose to the video camera.

"Will you be recording our conversation?"

"Would you prefer that I do?"

Huger flapped a hand, the gesture balletic in its fluidity. "What's all this about? Safety at my place of business?"

"No, sir. It's nothing like that." Vislosky sipped her coffee, then cocked her head in satisfaction. "Gotta have that jolt in the morning. Are you certain you don't want a cup?"

Huger shook his head. Certain.

"It's doctor, right?"

"It is. But there's no need for formalities."

"Doctor of what?"

"Biochemistry and software engineering."

"Impressive."

Huger gave a small, humble shrug.

"Did you know, doctor"—she raised her mug in tribute to the titles—"that the number of hate crimes in our state has skyrocketed recently? That several transgender women of color have actually been killed?"

"That's mighty sad." Huger's friendly expression rearranged into one of concern. "But how does that involve me?"

"The CPD is launching a safe-place initiative. No points for originality. The idea originated with the Seattle PD."

"I see."

"We're asking local business owners to display stickers indicating that they offer safe havens for LGBTQ residents who might feel threatened."

"You're referencing my plant on the Maybank Highway?"

"Yes, sir."

Firm nod. "It sounds like an admirable endeavor. Don't understand the lifestyle, but you can count me in."

"Thank you, Dr. Huger." More caffeine, then Vislosky switched tack. "I'm thinking of buying property on James Island. Do you like living out there?"

"I do, indeed." A note of surprise that Vislosky had researched his home address.

"Why?"

"I've got acreage, a fine water view, and my own fishing dock. What more could a man ask?"

"Is there a Mrs. Huger?" Casual.

Huger laughed, as though nothing could be more amusing. "No, detective. There is no Mrs. Huger."

"I understand you own a company called GeneFree."

"Among others."

"What's the pitch?"

"Sorry, ma'am?"

"What do you sell?"

"Online DNA testing."

"Testing for what?"

"We analyze a user's genetic code to offer optimal dietary choices."

"Quick tune-up, then soak 'em for protein powder and dried seaweed."

"The process is far more complex than that."

"I'm sure it is."

"I'm beginning to suspect this is not about stickers."

Vislosky set down her mug. "Did you sustain much damage from Hurricane Inara?"

"Lost part of my pier."

"Not too bad."

"No. Why am I here, detective?"

"The storm tossed a container ashore down by the battery."

"Storms do that." Smile holding but a little less warm. "They're famous for it."

"The container held two bodies."

I watched Huger for signs of agitation. Muscle tensing. Flushing. A twitching lower lid. Saw nothing beyond the normal repugnance one would expect when faced with such news.

"Two kids," Vislosky continued, giving minimal detail. "Both murdered."

The balletic hand rose to Huger's throat. "Sweet baby Jesus in heaven. What brand of monster kills children?"

Vislosky opened the folder. Took a moment to read something. Or to pretend to do so.

"I'm sure you've heard of forensic genealogy."

Huger nodded, expression now somber and serious.

"We did that, sir. It turns out one of the victims is related to you."

"What? That's impossible! How?" Huger looked and sounded genuinely appalled.

"You know how it works, you being fluent in double helixes and all."

"That wasn't my meaning."

"We extracted DNA from the victims' bones—"

"Bones?"

"Yes."

"How long were they dead?"

"I can't reveal details of the investigation."

"How did they die?"

"Same answer."

"What can I do?" Huger's aquamarine frown level on Vislosky.

"A critical first step in any homicide investigation is to ID the victims."

"I have no idea who these poor dead children might be." Huger looked and sounded sincerely mystified. If he was faking it, his performance was Oscar-level.

"Your DNA was in GEDmatch. Why?"

The manicured brows arced up, puzzled. "I had myself sequenced years ago. Of course. It's what I do. I must have authorized use of my profile by that database."

"Let's talk family."

"I'll be honest with you, detective. It may seem cold, but family has never been important in my life."

"You didn't hatch from an egg."

Huger's chin dipped in acknowledgment of her point. He let out a small sigh. Then, "My parents are both dead. I have no living siblings. No offspring."

Vislosky said nothing, hoping Huger would keep talking. He did.

"My father was an only child."

"His name?" Sliding a pen and tablet from her pocket.

"Jordan Sullivan Huger."

"J. S. Huger?"

Huger nodded.

"There's a building named for him at the College of Charleston?"

"Daddy made a rather large contribution to the school." A hint of bitterness leaking through. "Then proceeded to lose everything via ill-advised investments in fast-food franchises."

"I had a buddy got stung that way."

Huger said nothing.

"Your mother's name?"

"Cheryl Leigh Hinkes." He spelled the names. "She had one brother, Farley. Farley died in Vietnam."

"I'm sorry to hear that. You said you had no living siblings." Stated as a question.

"My older brother, Shelby, drowned when he was eight. Just about destroyed my parents. I remember little about him."

There was a long moment of silence. Vislosky broke it.

"Let's spread out, Dr. Huger. Grandparents? Second cousins?"

"I'm afraid we're not a prolific clan, detective. My grandmother— my mama's mama—had one sister, Zara. She married a man named Eden France. They had one son, Digby."

"Did Digby have kids?"

"Maybe one daughter. I'm unsure."

"Her name?"

"I've no earthly idea."

"Where can we find this relative of yours, Digby?"

"I don't know."

"What *do* you know?"

"I may have met Digby once as a very small child. I think he may have come to Shelby's funeral. The memory is vague. I recall a large man with whiskey breath and frightening facial hair. According to my mother, who clearly didn't care for her cousin, Digby was a musician of some sort."

"Anything else?"

Huger spread his hands, fingers splayed. "I wish I could be more helpful."

"So do I."

Huger didn't reply

"The younger victim could be your cousin."

"That thought breaks my heart."

"She was shot and then dumped like garbage."

"I will pray for her soul."

"You do that. In the meantime, please leave me your current contact information."

"I am an open book, detective."

Vislosky slid the pen and the tablet to Huger. He scribbled, returned them.

"May I go now?"

Vislosky handed Huger a card. "If you think of anything, call."

"Of course."

Both rose.

Huger headed for the door.

"And, doc?"

Huger turned.

"You can sign for that sticker at reception."

———

An hour after cutting Huger loose, Vislosky and I were at our laptops twelve hundred miles apart, discussing Uncle Digby via FaceTime. Though France's cyber footprint was smaller and less current than that of his nephew, like everyone alive today, he had one.

"The Digger France Band." To the phone propped beside my Mac.

"Never heard of them," Vislosky said.

"Are you into country and western?"

"Yeah." Derisive snort. "Like I'm into hippo sweat sunscreen."

"That's a real thing?"

"It is."

"I like some C-and-W." Actually, I like a lot of it, but given Vislosky's negative attitude, I didn't share that.

"Looks like the group was big from the late 'sixties until the early 'nineties," Vislosky said.

"Mostly in the Southeast."

"Mostly in a five-mile radius of Nashville." Vislosky snorted again. She really had it down.

"They made one album."

"Christ in a cornfield. Do you believe these song titles? 'Hungover with Love for Jesus.' 'Hand Me a Beer and Tie Up the Dog.' 'All I Need Is the Lord and My Refried Jeans.'"

"Poetry of the people," I said.

"What the hell are refried jeans?"

"Run France? See what pops?"

"Roger that, when I get a break. The town's going apeshit with some kinda outbreak involving dogs."

"Capnocytophaga?" I recalled Herrin's frazzled comments.

"Sounds right. Got the public arming themselves to the teeth."

"Why?"

"Half want to shoot every hound they see. Half swear they'll defend Old Yeller to the death."

"It's that bad?"

"People are dying."

"And nerves are still raw since COVID-19."

"Nothing an AK-47 can't fix." Dripping with sarcasm.

And she was gone.

It took an eon for Vislosky's next call.

"France has a sheet but nothing major. Drunk and disorderly, pissing in public, typical macho shit."

"Anything recent?"

"His last bump was in 'ninety-seven."

"Think he's still alive?"

"I found a car registration in the name of Digby Nelson France listing a Nashville address."

"Did you find a phone number?"

"Yes."

"You're a very gifted detective."

"I used the Nashville white pages. The listing was dropped five years ago."

"Time to give Mr. France a ring?"

"I did. The number is disconnected."

"That's not good."

"No."

Late that afternoon, despite my disapproval, Ryan insisted on walking to his favorite grocery, Fou d'Ici, roughly a mile to the east on boulevard de Maisonneuve. The store's inventory is eclectic, and its takeout menu changes daily, so I couldn't imagine what he'd bring home.

Ryan had barely left when Claudel called from the lobby.

"Ryan's gone, but he should be back in an hour."

"I prefer to speak with you."

"It might be better—"

"Now, *s'il vous plaît*."

Fearing Detective Delightful might take a bite out of Sylvain, the doorman, I buzzed him up.

Claudel's nose and cheeks were red from the cold. The cant of his brows suggested bad news.

"May I take your coat?" I asked, extending a hand.

"I will not stay long."

"Would you like to sit down?"

A tight shake of the head, then he launched in with typical Claudel brusqueness. "The driver of the car was not Zeke Hoag."

"Really." That surprised me.

"Hoag was in the hospital at the time of the assault."

"Might he have—"

"Hoag has stage-four colon cancer. He is dying. His intent was not to defraud his mother. He'd arranged for the insurance money to go directly into her account."

"Why not say so?"

"He wanted the payment to be a surprise."

"Now what?"

"Detective Charbonneau and I are reconsidering our approach."

Cop-speak for *we were on the wrong track*. I waited.

"We can think of no motive for an attack on Detective Ryan."

"Former detective."

"*Précisément*. Ryan is involved in nothing that might prompt such a violent threat to his person."

I waited.

Claudel's eyes drilled into mine

"We believe the intended target was you."

21

To keep my mind off Claudel's bombshell, I got online and did some digging on capno. I learned the following.

Capnocytophaga canimorsus is a bacterial pathogen found in the saliva of healthy dogs and cats. Though rare, the organism can cause illness in humans. Transmission occurs via bites, scratches, or licks.

A capno infection can lead to severe sepsis and fatal septic shock, gangrene of the digits or extremities, high-grade bacteremia, meningitis, endocarditis, and thoroughly messed-up eyes.

At increased risk of serious illness are persons who have undergone a splenectomy, persons who abuse alcohol, and persons with weakened immune systems, including those with HIV.

Online images of mottled and swollen limbs, inflamed eyes, blackened digits, and pus-oozing abscesses confirmed that the capno organism is a supremely nasty little bugger.

The case-fatality rate of the disease is roughly twenty-six percent.

My romp through the medical literature triggered flashbacks of the corpse Klopp had autopsied the day of our skeletal analyses at the hospital in Charleston. And sparked questions about the situation there. Primary among them, why the sudden spike in capno cases?

I glanced up from my laptop to find Birdie stretched full length on the table beside me. When I shifted in my chair, he raised his head and fixed me with a look I couldn't interpret. Apprehension? Annoyance? Or maybe the cat was still half asleep.

"It's mostly from dog bites," I said, a bit defensively.

Birdie said nothing.

"And capno is very uncommon."

Still no response.

"Fine. There's some sort of outbreak in Charleston. But I'm not worried."

Birdie repositioned his chin on his paws. Satisfied with my explanation, I assumed.

Ryan returned with poke bowls, one tuna and one salmon, each with enough toppings to sink a passenger ferry. I could identify beets, carrots, mangoes, and avocados. The rest, not so much.

As we ate, I told Ryan what Claudel had said. I saw his jaw muscles bulge and his eyes light up in anger. An instant later, he seemed to be grimly calm.

"What's their thinking?" he asked, voice flat.

"You know what I know."

"What's *your* thinking?"

"I undertipped an Uber driver?"

"Hilarious." Ryan speared and ate what might have been an edamame bean. "What have you been working lately?"

"Seriously?"

Ryan nodded.

I listed all my recent LSJML files. The farmer in Saint-Felicien. The pharmacist in Trois-Rivières. The tweaker in the culvert in Val d'Or. The legs from Lac Saint-Jean. "But my involvement in those cases isn't public knowledge."

"What else?"

"Before leaving Charlotte, I did a couple of private client consults."

"The Silver-Russell syndrome adoptee."

"You have an excellent memory, detective. Yes. Tereza Deacon.

I also agreed to look into Polly Beecroft's missing ancestor, but I haven't really followed through on that."

"Unlikely someone would try to off you because of an old death mask."

"Very. Besides, those are North Carolina issues."

Ryan and I had the same thought at the same moment. He voiced it.

"The container cases. The older Charleston girl is related to the Montreal vics."

"Vislosky has been pushing hard on the South Carolina end. But that's a thousand miles from here. And the Quebec murders took place at least fifteen years ago."

We finished our meal in silence. Ryan got up and began to clear the table, his face a stone mask that frightened me.

"Claudel and Charbonneau are on it, Ryan. They'll find the guy. If there *is* a guy."

Ryan set down the empty bowls and took my hands, his smile of reassurance forced and unconvincing. "I have no doubt about that. But until they do, you need to be cautious."

"I'm always cautious."

"This asswipe's going to wish he'd never been born."

Vislosky still hadn't phoned by nine. I wondered if she'd been side-tracked by the capno situation. Or if she'd hit a wall tracking cousin Digger.

I worked my laptop, searching for mention of a missing kid with the surname France. Found nothing.

Antsy and unable to relax, I decided to construct a kinship chart based on the info Vislosky had obtained during her interview. Using circles for females, squares for males, and solid lines to indicate blood relationships, I started with Aubrey Sullivan Huger, then moved back a generation to his parents, J. S. Huger and Cheryl Leigh Hinkes, then further back to Cheryl Leigh's mother. Moving sideways to Cheryl

Leigh's mother's sister, who'd apparently married a man named France, I then worked downward to Digger.

When finished, I studied my crude diagram, puzzled. If Digger had a daughter, as Huger thought, she'd be too old to be the girl in the container. If he had a granddaughter, would she be a second cousin to Huger? Third? Something once removed?

I gave up in frustration, hating the exercise as much as I had when forced to take ethnology classes in grad school.

Ryan reappeared at ten thirty to say he was turning in. I joined him but sat propped against the bed pillows, iPhone in hand, wasting time with social media.

By eleven, I was resigned to the fact that Vislosky wouldn't call that night. After turning off the lamp, I pulled the covers to my chin and snuggled against Ryan. Did I mention that he keeps the bedroom thermostat on the polar ice cap setting?

My brain was a maelstrom of visuals. Suppurating lesions. Algae-coated bones. Blinding headlights. Blue polypropylene sheeting. A child's plastic ring.

A half hour of tossing and turning, then I gave up. I quietly closed the bedroom door behind me, went to the kitchen, and made myself a cup of chamomile tea. Again seated at the dining-room table, I opened my Mac and entered the name Digger France.

The Digger France Band came right up. Active from the 'sixties into the 'nineties, the group performed mostly Christian country and cover renditions of classic C&W and bluegrass songs. Digger France played guitar and was the lead singer throughout the group's existence. Otherwise, membership fluctuated. The sole female vocalist changed often. One named Joy Sparrow seemed to have lasted the longest.

The band's single recording was with MCA Records. I found a link and listened to the first cut on the album, called "All I Need Is the Lord and My Refried Jeans," one of the titles that had so delighted Vislosky. Lots of banjo, harmonica, washboard, and multipart vocal harmony. A style I could only describe as twangy.

The images I found were fuzzy and dated. Some were promo shots. Others were candids snapped during live performances, most of which seemed to have taken place in bars. Digger always wore a T-shirt, jeans, boots, and round wire-rimmed shades. His hair and beard were long and auburn, the former ponytailed, the latter cinched with bright elastic binders at two levels.

By midnight, my tea was cold, and a headache was tickling my frontal lobe. I was about to call it quits when I stumbled onto a shot of the Digger France Band playing in a place called Shady Sam's. A banner behind the stage announced that the night's show was part of a reunion tour and gave the year as 2015.

Folks hadn't aged well. Digger and his beard were thinner. No more binders. His hair, faded to salmon, appeared to be losing ground to male-pattern baldness.

Patrons sat below the crude stage, their faces obscured by poor lighting and the rear-facing camera angle. What caught my interest was a small form at a front-row table. A girl with short, spiky hair dyed cotton-candy pink.

I tried zooming in. The scene went blurry.

Could the pink-haired kid be Digger France's granddaughter? Is that why the child was taken to a saloon? To see Gramps play?

A person sat to the kid's right, but only one arm and shoulder were visible. The limb looked fairly slim but not definitively so. Was her companion a woman? Her mother?

Reenergized, I plunged back into the game, this time using keyword combos related to the reunion tour and to Shady Sam's. Minutes later, I found the girl again, this time perched on a stool offstage at a place called the Dirty Rabbit.

The camera, focused on the band, had caught the kid in profile. She sat with chin on knuckles, elbows on knees. Her nose was long and straight, her eyes mere shadows. Her hair sparked like rosy dandelion froth in the cast-off glow of the stage lights.

The girl looked about thirteen years old. I ran the numbers. That tracked.

Like Digger, the kid was wearing a tee. Zooming in, I was able to read the lettering: *Amity House*. Underneath those words was a stylized graphic of people holding hands. Below the graphic, a smaller font looped in a semicircle: *Harmony. Hugs. Help.*

A quick search revealed that Amity House was a youth shelter in Nashville. I navigated to its website.

Operating since 1979, Amity House described itself as a crisis center providing support for homeless and runaway children ages seven to seventeen. The facility was able to house twelve kids. Youth could stay as long as three weeks while they and their families worked on resolving issues. Residents were expected to take care of the shelter and one another. Additional services included a twenty-four-hour crisis hotline and walk-in crisis support.

I linked back to the photo taken in the Dirty Rabbit. Studied the girl in the wings, pulse humming.

Did I finally have a lead? Had the kid with the candy-floss hair stayed at Amity House? Called their hotline? Was she a volunteer at the shelter? Would they have her name?

Was she Digger France's granddaughter?

Sullie Huger's distant cousin?

The younger vic in the Charleston container?

Should I phone Amity House?

Big no there. Selfish to tie up staff in the wee hours should a kid need help.

One thing was certain.

I couldn't wait to talk to Vislosky.

I sent the image to the printer. Was about to collect it when my mobile indicated an incoming text.

At one in the morning?

I checked the screen.

Anne.

I read her message.

Are you awake?

I am.

You're going to love this.
?????
I found her.
Amelia Earhart?
The mask lady.
No way.
Can you get online?
It's where I live.

I set down the phone and poised my fingers over the keys.

Anne provided a link. I navigated to the website.

And stared.

Shocked.

Not shocked.

22

Thursday, November 11

A didgeridoo blasted me awake.

Cursing my new choice of ringtone, I fumbled to answer. "Temperance Brennan."

"I know." Background noise suggested Vislosky was again in her car. "My dime."

"I was expecting to hear from you last night." *Jesus, Brennan. Don't antagonize her!*

"Things were happening here."

"Did you find France?"

"I did. Dammit. Hang on."

Vislosky put me on hold for a lifetime.

I was alone in bed. Clicking to speakerphone, I noticed that the digits on my screen said 7:14.

"France owns property outside Nashville," Vislosky said after reconnecting. "A house with a couple of acres off Highway Two Fifty-One."

"Is he living there?"

"My contact in the Nashville PD says utilities are in France's name. No phone. No internet."

"But is he actually *there*?"

185

After a brief, censoring pause, "My buddy did a drive-by. Ran the plate on a truck parked in the drive. The vehicle is registered to France."

"Hot damn."

"Fucking A."

I told Vislosky about the girl with the cotton-candy hair. About the tee pointing to Nashville.

"You're liking this kid for our vic?"

"She ticks a lot of boxes."

"Seems so."

I heard a honking horn.

"Are you in your car?" I asked.

"I like face-to-facers. Allows me a good read."

It took me a second. "You're driving to Nashville?"

"Ye olde Music City."

"I want to be there." *What the hell?* Did I?

"How's that work?"

"I book the next flight out."

After a pause, "When?"

"Give me ten minutes."

I threw back the covers and hurried to the kitchen. Ryan was eating toast with cream cheese, raisins, and granola on top. Bird hadn't quite emptied his bowl.

I asked if they'd mind playing bachelor for a few days. Both were good with the idea.

It took seven minutes to make a reservation.

Ryan offered to drive me to YUL.

Vislosky said she'd meet me at BNA.

Aviation miracle. Both legs went well. I made my connection in Detroit, no sprint, no sweat. Landed in Nashville early at 4:07.

Vislosky was parked in the cell-phone lot when I texted.

We set out, following directions provided by Waze. I use Jane's voice. Vislosky had chosen some dude who sounded like a ballet student in London. No telling taste.

The programmed address was on a narrow, unmarked stretch of asphalt off a little-used two-lane blacktop cutting east from Tennessee Highway 251, in an area known as Bullfrog Hollow. Five minutes after making the final turn, the ballet dude reported that our destination was on the left. A rusty mailbox agreed. Painted on one side was the name *France*.

Vislosky rolled to a stop, and we both scanned our surroundings.

It was one of those rural places that is neither farm nor country estate. No barn, shed, or outbuilding of any kind. No chickens or cows. No John Deere waiting to plant or sow. Just a modest house surrounded by fields.

The one-story bungalow had lime-green siding, white trim, and a canary-yellow front door. The porch was wood and permitted to do what it liked.

A gravel path bisected a discouraged-looking swath of grass in front. A matching driveway bordered the lawn to the east. An old red pickup sat at its far end.

I looked to Vislosky. She nodded. We both got out.

Weeds crawled the shoulder and ditch flanking the asphalt. To either side of the home, barbed wire enclosed something dry and brown with very tall stalks. Stunted pines disrupted the evenly planted rows, too stubborn to die or too deeply rooted to justify the effort required for removal.

We paused, listening.

Wind feathered the crops with a soft rustling sound. Somewhere out of sight, a crow cawed. Far off, water gurgled. Otherwise, all was quiet.

"That a river we're hearing?" I asked.

"The Cumberland's just yonder." Nodding toward the fields.

"Did you say yonder?"

"It's Tennessee. Ready?"

I nodded.

"Let's go meet Digger."

The crow went silent at the sound of our slamming doors.

Vislosky strode up the gravel path, boots crunching, eyes roving, watching for signs of life and taking in detail. I followed, doing the same.

The air smelled faintly of pine, wet rocks, smoke, and autumn leaves. Gnats dive-bombed my face, surprising given the coolness of the day.

Vislosky and I stopped at the bottom of the stairs, swatting at bugs.

"Hello?" she called out.

No answer.

"Mr. France?"

Same response.

We climbed to the porch and stepped to either side of the door. Vislosky knocked. Hard.

A dog went berserk.

A moment, then a voice spoke over the frenzied yapping. "Goddammit, Axel. I'm gonna kick your scrawny butt from here to tomorrow." Then, louder, "Hold on out there."

The dog squealed, then began to whimper. After its cries receded, locks rattled, and the door opened.

Though even older and thinner, Digger France lived up to his online image. He wore jeans and a faded tee featuring an American flag. No shades, and the beard was now a scruffy goatee.

"Yes?" Scraggly brows raised in question.

"Digby France?"

"Ain't heard that handle in years."

"Digger?"

"That's me. But you be looking for autographs, I don't do that no more." Not unfriendly but not offering a hand.

"I'm Detective Vislosky." Flashing her badge.

France glanced at the shield, then his eyes lifted to me.

"Dr. Temperance Brennan," I said, flashing nothing.

France crossed bony arms on his bony chest. "That jerklord Jensen send you?"

"No, sir."

"I haven't had a drop in over five years, so he can kiss my skinny patootie."

"Very commendable, sir," Vislosky said. "But that's not the purpose of our visit."

"Oh?"

"May we come inside?"

"Don't normally have callers."

"Do you have a granddaughter, Mr. France?"

I watched his face closely. Noticed a twitch in his right lower lid. "Why you askin' that?"

Vislosky kept her gaze steady on France.

A beat, then Digger sighed and stepped back. "Don't mind Axel. He's all holler and no foller through."

A short, dim hall made a right midway down its length and opened onto a small living room. The decor was startling.

The walls were apple-green. Chartreuse pillows accessorized a poppy-red couch flanked by orange leather recliners. The coffee and end tables were teal. A rainbow braided rug covered the floor.

The art consisted mostly of posters featuring the Digger France Band, each inside a garishly bright plastic frame. Interspersed with the posters were pictures of Jesus.

An aquarium the size of the Great Barrier Reef stretched the length of one wall. I recognized a spotted clown fish, a bicolor blenny, a lot of purple tangs.

A fuchsia guitar hung over a fireplace at the far end of the room. The hearth and bricks were painted a shocking carnation-pink.

The kaleidoscopic onslaught was almost overwhelming.

"Your home is stunning," I said.

"Always had a hankering for color but don't see it so well."

Somewhere farther back in the house, a dog whined and scratched frenetically.

"Might as well turn Axel loose. If not, he'll just keep up his carping."

"Of course," I said. *No*, I thought.

France gestured Vislosky and me onto the couch. As we settled, he disappeared through the door by which we'd entered. I heard hinges squeak, then claws scrabbling on wood.

A nanosecond later, Axel fired into the room. If pressed to guess the dog's parentage, I'd say chihuahua and wolverine. A round of hysterical barking and yelling, then France dropped into a recliner. Axel hopped onto his master's lap, circled, then sat and eyed us with trembling contempt.

"What's this about my granddaughter?"

I'd printed the photo taken at Shady Sam's. Vislosky indicated that I should lay it on the table.

"Is that her?" she asked.

France glanced at the picture, then did an angled jerk of his chin. "This about me taking a minor to a tavern?"

As per Vislosky's directive, I remained silent while she did the questioning.

"Can you tell us about your granddaughter, sir?"

"What are you wantin' to know?" Guarded.

"Perhaps we could start with her name?"

"Harmony."

"Do you mind if I record our conversation?"

Before France could object, Vislosky pulled out her mobile, thumbed the screen, and centered the device between us.

"First off, are you acquainted with a man named Aubrey Huger? Goes by Sullie?"

"Never heard of him."

"Thank you. Your granddaughter's name is Harmony France?"

"Harmony Wren Boatwright."

"That is a truly lovely name," I said.

France didn't acknowledge my comment.

"Is she your only grandchild?" Vislosky asked.

"She is."

"Harmony is your daughter's child?" I noted Vislosky's use of the present tense.

"Her mama's long gone." Leaning toward the phone and speaking slowly. "That'd be Bonnie Bird Boatwright."

"Is Bonnie still living in Nashville?"

"Bonnie Bird," France corrected. "Not likely. No one's seen her since Harmony turned thirteen."

"Your daughter's whereabouts are unknown to you?"

"Don't make me happy, but that's a fact." France crossed one scarecrow leg over the other. Axel popped to his feet, yipped in annoyance, then resettled. "Best this way. Bible says it's abomination for man to lie with man. Goes for women, too."

"Is that a fact." Vislosky's tone was suddenly cooler.

"Leviticus eighteen twenty-two."

"You sent your daughter away?"

"Did it to protect Harmony, she being at an impressionable age by then. Had some regrets later. Bonnie Bird's leaving really tore the girl up."

"How so?"

"After Bonnie Bird left, the child couldn't focus on nothing but finding her mama."

"Did *you* try to find your daughter?"

"I eventually reported her missing. The cops give it a look-see. But that was Bonnie Bird's way. She got to feeling pissy, she just took off. Cops figured motherhood wasn't her thing."

"And there was that ugly lesbian thing." Glacial.

France said nothing,

"When was the last time you saw Bonnie Bird?"

"Summer of 2015."

"Who raised Harmony after you threw her mother out?" Vislosky asked.

"That weren't how it was."

"Uh-huh."

"Harmony's upbringin' fell to me," France said. "The Boatwrights, that'd be her other granny and grandpa, was dead, and her daddy got himself killed in prison."

Sensing Vislosky's hostility, I joined in, "good cop" style: "That must have been hard."

"I got some help from a lady friend used to sing with the band."

"Joy Sparrow?"

"Yes, ma'am." With an edge of surprise.

"Is Joy Sparrow Bonnie Bird's mother?"

"No, ma'am. Not that my personal life's any of your business."

"Did Harmony grow up in this house?" Vislosky asked, eyes cutting sideways to remind me of my vow of silence.

When France shook his head, the tip of his goatee grazed Axel's ears. "We was living in town back then."

"Where is Harmony now?"

"Guess the apple don't fall far from the tree."

"Explain that."

France raised his chin and ran a hand down his throat. When he spoke again, the wispy triangle of hair bobbed in the air.

"The young-un took off, just like her mama."

"Do you know where she went?"

"No."

"Does she keep in touch?"

"No." A pause, then, "I'll be honest, ma'am. Harmony was a handful after her mama left. And I'll admit, I was drinking some then."

"How was she a handful?"

"Had a temper like a hornet. We'd argue, usually about her schooling and such, she'd run off, sometimes stay away for weeks. Then she'd turn up and carry on like nothing happened. That was her way. She'd come and go. The last time she went, she didn't come back."

"Did she have a boyfriend?"

"Beats me. Like I said, me and the hooch was in a relationship."

France's nostrils blanched on a quick intake of air.

Afraid we might lose his cooperation, I asked gently, "Did Harmony ever break her arm?"

"Yes, ma'am. That she did." Same note of surprise. "Fell off a skateboard. I took her to the ER. They fixed her up with a cast and all. She didn't like it none, but she wore it."

"Did she frequent a youth shelter called Amity House?"

France nodded, apparently no longer astonished at the amount of personal info I had. "That's the reason I didn't fret none. I always reckoned that's where she'd go."

"When was the last time you saw your granddaughter?"

Again, the uplifted chin. This time, the liver-spotted hand stroked the dog, not his throat.

"February the fifth, two thousand and eighteen." Pronounced Feb-you-wary.

"Your memory is very precise," I said.

"It was the day after her sixteenth birthday. I give her a regulation Army backpack that year, the kind with lots of zippers and compartments. Thought maybe we'd go fishing together."

"You haven't seen or heard from her since?"

"She was sixteen." Defensive. "State of Tennessee says that's old enough to get married. She didn't want to be here, what was I gonna do?"

"How did Harmony get around?" Vislosky asked.

France waggled an upraised thumb to indicate hitchhiking.

Vislosky's eyes dropped to her hands. I saw the tension in her neck and shoulders. Despite her distaste for France, I knew the anguish she was feeling at what she was about to say.

A subtle squaring of the broad shoulders, then, "I'm afraid I may have bad news."

France continued stroking Axel's back.

"A girl was found dead in Charleston, South Carolina, last month." Choosing her words ever so carefully. "We have reason to believe that girl may be your granddaughter."

France remained impassive, not understanding, or not certain how to reply.

"The victim was in her mid-teens and had short, dark hair dyed pink. She stood between five-one and five-two."

France's right lower lid began kicking again. "She OD on something?"

"There's no indication of that."

"How'd she pass?"

"I'm not at liberty to discuss details of the investigation."

"You said victim. That mean someone killed her?"

Vislosky said nothing.

"Could be it's not Harmony." France's utterance was barely audible over the burbling fish tank.

"It's possible." Vislosky cleared her throat. "We need a saliva sample for DNA testing."

France nodded, looking somewhat dazed.

I got a kit from my bag and, ignoring Axel's growling, swabbed France's cheek, then sealed and initialed the vial.

"Do you know if Harmony owned a cell phone or laptop?" Vislosky asked when I'd finished.

"'Course she had a phone. This is Nashville, not the backside of Hooterville."

"Do you know what happened to it?"

"Gotta think she took it with her. What kid would be without a phone these days? Besides, I haven't seen it nowheres."

"Do you pay the bill for that?"

"No."

"Do you know what carrier she used?"

France shook his head, then stood. "It's Axel's time to eat. I don't feed him, he gets fractious."

Vislosky scooped up her mobile, then laid a card on the table. We both rose.

"If you think of anything, please call," she said.

"Harmony left a few belongings. Not much. I boxed and hauled some of the stuff when I moved out here." The devastating possibility of his granddaughter's death was at last sinking in. "Guess I kept thinking one day she'd turn up, maybe want her things."

"Any items you have would be useful to our investigation."

France disappeared, Axel close on his heels, returned a few minutes later with a large cardboard box in his arms.

"I wrote a song about Harmony, not long after she come to live
with me. 'Motherless Little Wren.' Thought it might make her feel
less cross."

"I'm sure she appreciated it," I said.

France shook his head slowly. "Riled her something fierce."

France's grief was evident now. It coated his words and deepened
the creases lining his face. I felt like a ghoul in this act that was forever changing his life. Yet I participated, knowing it was necessary to
gain justice for two murdered girls.

"Harmony was always yearning for her mama." Wistful. "I figured maybe she found her somewheres."

"We'll keep you updated," Vislosky said.

France nodded, arms clasping the stored pieces of a life.

At the door, Vislosky turned.

"You know what else the Bible says is abomination, sir?"

France just looked at her.

"Trimming your goddamn beard."

We took the box and left.

23

Vislosky placed the box in the trunk, and we climbed into her car.

"Is that true?" I asked as we buckled our belts.

"What?"

"The Bible forbidding a man to cut his beard?"

"Yeah."

"Old Testament?"

"Hell if I know."

"Why did you say it?"

"The guy's a bigoted wanker."

I didn't pursue it. But I was curious about the source of Vislosky's antipathy toward France. His cavalier attitude toward Harmony's disappearance? His rejection of Bonnie Bird's lesbian lifestyle? His twangy musical style?

"Amity House?" I asked,

"Can't hurt," she said.

I programmed the Waze dude. His directions took us to a tree-shaded street hosting a mix of private residences and large homes converted for genteel commercial use. An architectural firm. A law office. A children's theater.

Our destination was a two-story red brick number with a tile-roofed veranda spanning the entire street side. An enormous live oak spread its branches above most of the sloping front yard. Below the oak, a sign declared, *Amity House: A Youth Crisis Center.*

Three concrete steps rose from a short walkway to the front porch. We climbed them. Vislosky thumbed the buzzer. A moment, then a voice spoke through a perforated brass plaque.

Vislosky explained who we were and dropped the name Harmony Boatwright.

A short wait, then the door was opened by a woman doing a look-alike for the sheriff's elderly aunt in Mayberry. Short and stout, plump cheeks, gray hair swept into a poofy updo. She could have been friendlier but only with the aid of powerful pharmaceuticals.

"Dear, dear Harmony." Chirrupy with anticipation. "Do tell how she is."

"May we come inside?" Vislosky asked. I wondered if Nashville protocol required a request.

"Ooh." Aunt Bee quavery. "Of course. Please, excuse my bad manners."

The door gave directly onto a large rectangular living room. One end contained a mishmash of battered upholstered and wooden furniture arranged in conversational groupings. The other end was filled with tables and chairs, most of the former stacked with boxed games. I recognized Scrabble, Monopoly, Chutes and Ladders. A sideboard held a partially completed jigsaw puzzle, loose pieces scattered around the incomplete center.

Aunt Bee led us to one of the groupings. "Would you like some cookies? Lemonade?"

"No, thank you." Vislosky and I declined in unison.

Out of habit, we took the couch. Aunt Bee sat in an armchair with ankles crossed, knees splayed but modestly covered by her print housedress and long butcher-style apron.

"Do you mind if I record our conversation?" Again, Vislosky activated her phone without awaiting permission.

Aunt Bee looked dubious but didn't object.

"May I ask your name and role with Amity House?" Vislosky began.

"Gertrude Pickle. I know. Both are terrible." Giggly chuckle. "The kids call me Mama Gertie."

"Your role here?"

"House mother."

"Do you live on-site?"

"I have an apartment downstairs. It's small but has everything I need."

"How long have you worked here?"

"Oh, my goodness. Since I was widowed, nineteen years next month. How time does fly. Can't imagine what I'd do if I had to live alone."

As before, I laid the Shady Sam's photo on the table.

"You remember Harmony Boatwright?" Vislosky asked.

"I surely do. Harmony stayed with us often. I love hearing about our young people, especially when they've been away for so long. How is she? Do tell me everything."

Vislosky and I exchanged discreet glances.

"When was Harmony last here?" she continued.

"Well . . ." Straining to remember. "It has been a while."

"A while?"

"Our policy is that young people aren't obliged to sign in or out. The administration feels that requiring formal registration might—"

"One year? Five?"

Pickle closed her eyes and canted her head sideways in thought. It felt as if a full minute passed.

"Yes." Pickle nodded slowly, doubling her chin count. "I'd say it's been five years."

"Why did Harmony come here?"

"For the same reason many young people do. To escape conflict at home. Oh, dear. What's all this about?" Her brows furrowed as the significance of a police visit finally dawned. "Has something bad happened?"

As Vislosky gave a brief account of the dead girl in Charleston, Pickle's whole body seemed to curl inward.

"Do you know Digger France?" Vislosky asked.

"We met once or twice." All chirpiness gone.

"Your impression?"

"Harmless and hopeless."

"Hopeless?"

"May I see ID?"

Vislosky badged her. Pickle studied the info for so long I thought she was memorizing it. Then, "You're a police officer. And poor, dear Harmony is, I mean, may be"—her voice trailed off, leaving the awful thought unspoken—"so I suppose it's permissible to share what I know."

Vislosky waited.

"In my opinion, Harmony Boatwright was a very troubled girl."

"Troubled?"

"After her mother left, the child bounced from relative to relative. The family is, well, what doesn't need saying. Her granddaddy tried, but he was a drinker. And ill-equipped to handle a teenage girl. I'm sure you know that Harmony's mother disappeared when the child was twelve or thirteen. All Harmony wanted in life was to find her. In my view, she was obsessed with the idea."

"What makes you say that?"

"We provide Wi-Fi here. Otherwise, some of the children would have no access to the internet. But we don't just turn them loose. That would be foolish. We make it clear upfront that the browser history on each and every machine is reviewed each and every day. That's one of my tasks. If any user does anything that breaks house rules, they lose their internet privilege." Pickle cupped her mouth and spoke in a low, conspiratorial whisper. "You know, like looking at porn and such."

"What if a kid connects using a private device?" I asked.

"We can't control that."

"Did Harmony have her own laptop?"

"I don't believe so. She used one of the house PCs. That's how I know she frequented sites devoted to finding missing persons. That poor, sweet lamb ran endless searches on her mother's name."

"Can you recall which sites she visited?"

"I'm sorry. It was a long time ago." Pickle looked genuinely regretful, then her face brightened. "Wait. There was one called MMM. I'm partial to the candy, you know, the little round chocolates? M&M's? Melt in your mouth, not—"

"Yes." Vislosky flicked impatient fingers.

"That's why the name stuck with me." A bit pouty due to the brusqueness.

"That's very helpful," I said, not sure that it was but wanting to placate.

"Harmony mentioned making a friend that way, in some kind of chat room." Pickle raised a pudgy hand to me, palm out. "But please don't ask. She never shared a name. Just that this other person was also looking for her mother."

"Do you recall anything about this cyber-friend?"

Pickle's response sent adrenaline firing through me.

"Missing and Murdered Moms dot com." Vislosky was at the wheel. I was Google searching with my iPhone. "It's a site for the children of—"

"Missing and murdered moms." Vislosky cut me off.

"Do you want to hear this?"

Vislosky shrugged. We were both cranky. I was regretting my decision to ride the nine hours with her to Charleston. But Anne had phoned, adamant. She was in crisis mode again and wanted me back ASAP. She'd explained the latest drama, something involving her ex-husband, but I hadn't really listened.

"The site has a chat room, so Pickle's intel tracks," I said.

"Can anyone join in the lively banter?" Disdainful.

"Participation is free, and users don't have to register for an account. It's like Zobe or Teen-Chat."

"Zobe?"

"Never mind. All one does is create a username and sign in."

"So there's no way to identify participants."

"Correct."

"Can you spot any handles to suggest the far northland?"

Vislosky referred to Pickle's parting comment, the words that had gotten my adrenals pumping. Harmony Boatwright had told Mama Gertie that she'd befriended a Canadian girl in the MMM.com chat room.

"Not yet," I mumbled, attention focused on usernames and messages.

diggitydog appeared to be in New Haven. *violetdawn* posted that s/he was pressing the Albuquerque PD to dig up the neighbor's garden. *foreversearching* and *neverletgo* were arguing the merits of cadaver versus tracker dogs. *neverforget* and *alwayslooking* were discussing decomposition rates in water. *leftbehind* was suicidal, and *babysnowflake* and *uptheanty* were talking him or her down.

I was still concentrating when I felt the car turn, then stop. I looked up. Vislosky had pulled into a Burger King.

"Don't know about you, but this bad girl needs fuel."

"What time is it?" I asked.

"Eight forty-five."

I hadn't eaten since downing a quick bagel at the Montreal airport. Suddenly, I was starving.

My fries were cold and greasy. The Whopper was a Whopper. But delivery was quick, and we were out in twenty minutes.

"How do you feel about driving through the night?" Vislosky asked.

"Not enthused."

"Motel?"

"You don't need to be back?"

"It's Veterans Day, you know."

I'd totally forgotten.

"And I took another twenty-four off."

"You made this trip on personal time?"

"You got a problem with that?"

"No." Thinking that despite the snippiness and sarcasm, maybe Vislosky wasn't so bad after all.

The next exit offered a place called the Music City Inn. The sign featured red neon letters and a blue musical staff with green treble clef and orange notes. Digger would have approved.

The office was nondescript, with dingy glass facing the parking lot and knotty pine behind the counter. The kid who checked us in was at least twelve years old and in need of a dermatologist.

Vislosky and I took our keys, which were attached to guitar-shaped wooden plaques, and followed a walkway to our rooms. My Rollaboard didn't appreciate its bumpy ride over the cracked cement.

Despite my exhaustion, sleep took its time coming. My over-wrought neurons offered up images of bedbugs. Of luminol-lit crime-scene pics, bedspreads and mattresses glowing with bodily fluids.

Full disclosure. As a result of my job, I am motel-phobic.

The neurons also offered up zillions of questions.

Was the younger victim in the Charleston container Harmony Boatwright?

Could Boatwright's cyber-pal be her companion in death? The girl whose DNA linked her to the 2006 Montreal vics?

According to Pickle, Boatwright connected with the Canadian girl through MMM. Did the two ever meet in person? Communicate directly, perhaps by email, text, or phone?

Like Boatwright, the Canadian girl was searching for a missing mom. Was her mother the woman in the Montreal container?

Who was she?

Who was the child with her?

Who killed them?

Who killed the girls in Charleston?

Were they all killed by the same person, though many years and many miles apart?

24

My eyes flew open.
     Dim room. Rough sheets smelling of harsh detergent.
Muted traffic sounds.
     Insistent banging.
     I looked around. A pale gray rectangle framed what had to be a
window.
     Then a barrage of synapses. Digger France. The box. Amity
House. Gertrude Pickle. The Whopper. The neon notes.
     The zillion questions.
     More banging.
     I leaped out of bed. Nearly tripped over the coverlet I'd jettisoned
onto the floor.
     Gingerly barefooting across a prickly shag carpet, I put my eye to
the peephole. Vislosky was standing outside, balancing a cardboard
tray in one hand while pounding with the other.
     I cracked the door.
     "You sleeping all day, princess?"
     "What time is it?"
     "Six twenty."

"Give me ten."

Vislosky wiggled free a Styrofoam cup. Thanking her, I took it and withdrew.

After donning clean undies and yesterday's jeans and top, I threw back the drapes. And noticed there was nothing to notice about the beige-on-beige decor.

While performing a quick toilette, I thought about motel rooms. Wondered who mandated the universal lack of charm and originality.

When I got to the car, Vislosky was slamming the trunk.

"Did you go through the box Digger gave us?" As I tossed my overnighter into the back seat.

"I only pocketed the good stuff."

"Hilarious." Wondering what Vislosky would classify as good.

"Of course, I didn't go through the box. Just kept it with me to maintain chain of possession."

"Should we have a quick look?"

"At headquarters. I want to dot all the i's. Follow protocol."

Though anxious to see what France had saved, I couldn't disagree. We both got in and buckled our belts.

Vislosky indicated a white paper bag on the center console. "Doughnuts."

"Aren't you the early bird," I said, looking over the assortment.

Vislosky said nothing

"They're all plain glazed," I said.

"I prefer plain glazed."

I took a doughnut and washed it down with the tepid remains of my coffee.

"I like your ride." I did. It was a Ford Mustang GT. Red. "What year is it?"

"A 2019."

"Do you get good mileage?"

Vislosky did a one-shoulder shrug.

A few miles of silence, then I took another stab at conversation. "Did you ever play basketball?"

"You asking because I'm black?"

"I'm asking because you're tall." Jesus. What was her problem? Nothing.

One more try. "Fun fact," I said. "I don't know a single black person named Vislosky."

"You know a single white person named Vislosky?"

Fine. No small talk. Suited me.

I went for more pastry, then spent the next fifty miles working through the MMM menu and lurking in the site's chat room. I'd chosen the username *bigbirdie*.

No surprise that nothing helpful popped up. It had been half a decade since Harmony had connected with her Canadian friend. If, in fact, the friend existed. And if Harmony and the Canadian girl actually were the Charleston vics, neither had visited MMM in a very long time.

I was searching for similar sites when the didgeridoo shattered the silence.

"What the fuck?" Vislosky burst out.

I clicked on.

"When do you arrive?" Anne asked without preamble.

"I'm on my way now."

A beat, then, "You're in a car. Are you driving? From Montreal?"

"Nashville."

"Tell me you're not banging Toby Keith."

"I'm not banging Toby Keith."

Vislosky's head whipped my way, brows floating high above the gold rims of her shades.

"So. I've busted this death mask mother wide open, eh?"

"I'm sorry, Anne. I haven't had time to follow up."

"Seriously?"

"I was urgently needed on an investigation."

Vislosky snorted.

"Who's that?"

"A detective. Listen, I'll be in Charleston late this afternoon. We can discuss the death mask tonight."

Chilly silence.

"I'll bring dinner."

"I sure as sugar don't feel the love coming my way."

Three beeps.

Anne was gone.

"Want to listen to some music?" I asked, tossing my iPhone onto the dash.

"No," Vislosky said.

"Let me know if you'd like me to drive."

"I won't."

Alrighty, then.

I focused on the world streaming by my window. We'd left the mountains and entered a landscape of rolling hills. Now and then, we passed a small factory, and once what looked like a massive salvage yard. Otherwise, it was nothing but fields and trees and cows.

Eventually, the monotony made me drowsy. Not sure how long I'd been dozing when Vislosky startled me awake.

"Point guard."

I struggled to connect the dots. "Are you talking b'ball?"

"Do I look like a hockey player?"

"What does a hockey player look like?"

"A dentist's dream."

"Hilarious."

"At six foot nothing, I wasn't tall enough to be up front."

"Where did you play?"

"Wake Forest. My unmatched agility won me a four-year ride."

"Not to mention your humility."

"And that."

"Impressive." It was.

"What's this about a death mask?"

"What?" The quick segue surprised me.

"Your abrasive caller is working on some kind of death mask?"

"Anne is not abrasive."

"OK. Your loud caller."

"You really want to hear about the mask?"

"Beats listening to you snoring."

"I don't snore."

Vislosky did that guffaw thing again, a sort of choking gurgle in her throat.

I provided a brief overview. Polly Beecroft's odd request. The three photos. The uncanny resemblance between Beecroft and her twin sister, Harriet, and between the Beecroft twins and their grandmother and great-aunt, Susanne and Sybil Bouvier. The mysterious disappearance of Sybil in Paris in 1888. The resemblance of all four women to the death mask found in Harriet Beecroft's home.

"So what's Annie Abrasive's world-shattering breakthrough?"

"She found the mask on the web."

"Everything in creation is on the web."

"Do you want the full story?"

"What the hell. We've got another four hours to kill."

"It turns out this girl's death mask isn't all that rare. During the early years of the twentieth century, hundreds of copies were made and sold, primarily in France and Germany. People hung her face on the walls of their homes as decorative art."

"That's morbid."

"She was known as L'Inconnue de la Seine. The Unknown Woman of the—"

"I've heard of the river."

"Apparently, people were enchanted with the 'sublimity of the young lady's smile.'" Hooking air quotes.

"The chick was dead."

"Sincerely so. According to most accounts, in the late nineteenth century, probably during the eighteen-seventies or eighteen-eighties, the woman's body was recovered from the Seine near the quai du Louvre and taken to the Paris morgue for identification. Hold on."

I snatched up my phone and scrolled to Anne's email.

"At that time, the Paris morgue was located behind Notre-Dame, at the eastern tip of the Île de la Cité, quai de l'Archevêché." Going full French to annoy Vislosky? "Unknown bodies were displayed for public viewing in the hopes someone might recognize a deceased."

"Maybe we should try that."

"The Paris morgue was a big deal back then. I've read that thousands visited every day."

"Nothing like corpses to bring out a crowd."

"As the story goes, a morgue pathologist was so smitten by the girl's beauty that he called in a *mouleur*—a molder—to preserve her face in a death mask. Some versions have him as a medical assistant. Either way, that first plaster cast became the source of all the mass-produced masks later sold as art."

"Was the chick ever ID'd?"

"No. There's endless conjecture as to who she might have been. A prostitute. A beggar. An orphan seduced by a nobleman."

"Manner of death?"

"Again, lots of speculation. Because the girl's body showed no trauma, she was presumed to have committed suicide. Others claim she must have been murdered."

"Based on what?"

"Skeptics say she couldn't have drowned because her features were too perfect."

"That's lame."

"It is. For one thing, it was common practice back then to re-sculpt death masks."

"Like retouching with Photoshop."

I scrolled through my pictures to the shot I'd taken of Beecroft's mask. I had to admit, the girl did look serene. Her cheeks were full, her hair demurely drawn back behind her neck. Her eyelashes, oddly matted, still looked wet. Though pleasant-looking, the girl wasn't classically beautiful. I estimated her age at late teens.

"What happened to the body?" Vislosky asked.

"No one knows."

"You're thinking this unknown woman could be Polly Beecroft's missing great-aunt?"

"The resemblance is striking. The girl's age tallies. The time period fits."

"How could you ever prove that she is?"

An excellent question, detective.

We got to Charleston a little past three and headed directly to the law enforcement center. The scene on Lockwood Boulevard was chaos. People crammed the walks on both sides, some holding signs, a few shouting at passing cars.

Along one curb, the sentiment seemed to be pro-canine. *Don't pinch my pooch! Back off my beagle! My dog is my best friend. Dog = God spelled backward.*

Along the opposite curb, the protesters were advocating animal control. *Don't let the hounds out! Woof! Woof! Leash it or lose it! Contagious Canines!* I wasn't sure about *Bite Me!*

"What the hell?" I asked, watching a guy wave a placard showing a dog with a baby's head in its open mouth.

"Don't get me started. The media's been on this capno shit twenty-four seven, broadcasting gore shots and citing infection rates and death counts. It's like the mask insanity of the COVID pandemic. People have turned the situation political and chosen up sides."

"Sides?" As Vislosky entered the garage.

"Some think the government's out to confiscate their precious pooch. Others want every dog shot on sight."

"Jesus."

"And here's a good one. Your boy Huger's been fanning the flames."

"He's not my boy. What do you mean?"

"Huger's running ads claiming there's a gene makes some people more susceptible to the virus than others. Says if they mail their spit to his website, he'll diagnose where they stand."

"GeneFree?"

"One and the same."

"What's his game?"

"What do you mean?"

"Do you think he's in it to score some bucks? Or to provide a valid medical service?"

"How should I know the fucknozzle's motive?"

Though tempted to retort, I held my tongue.

The silence continued as Vislosky and I entered PD headquarters, rode the elevator, and walked to the violent-crimes unit. After placing the box on her desk, Vislosky punched digits on her phone and spoke to someone in the forensic-sciences division.

A staff photographer showed up a half hour later. He was small and dark and may have weighed less than his equipment. His name badge said *Denton*.

We all moved to a counter running along the back wall of the squad room. Vislosky and I pulled on latex gloves. My pulse hummed as I watched her disengage and lay back the flaps loosely sealing the box.

Denton shot video and stills as each object came out. Vislosky entered everything on an evidence sheet.

The contents included the following: a hinged plastic case holding an assortment of cheap costume jewelry; a frayed pet collar with a tag that said *Missy*; a snow globe housing a village that would have blended well in Zermatt; a stuffed lamb missing most of the fur on its belly; and a faux-leather diary with a tiny brass lock, broken.

The final article caused a frisson of pain to sweep through me. At the very bottom of the box was a framed print of a Ralph Waldo Emerson poem: "This Is My Wish for You." I knew the words, had given a copy to Katy when she was a very little girl.

Had Bonnie Bird chosen the same gift for her daughter? If she loved Harmony, how could she have abandoned her? Had Harmony left willingly or under duress? Had Bonnie Bird also come to harm?

"Am I done here?"

Denton's voice snapped me back to the present.

"You got everything?" Vislosky chin-cocked the objects spread out on the counter.

Denton nodded. "I'll shoot the e-file to you right away. Get you hard copy by tomorrow."

"Thanks."

As Denton collected his cameras, Vislosky picked up the diary. It looked very small in her oversize hands.

She moved to her desk. I followed. Watched as she randomly flipped pages.

I was reaching for my purse when Vislosky muttered, "Hot fucking damn."

I looked a question at her.

She slid the diary across the desktop, opened to the page that had triggered the expletive.

I read the entry.

25

Friday, November 12

The handwriting was cramped, the ink faded in spots. I had to struggle to make out some lines.

It was the diary's final page that had caught Vislosky's attention.

February 5, 2018

Dear Di,

Off to Charleston this aft. Wish me luck. Thumbing it.
Hope I don't get picked up by cannibal cultists. Ha! 😊
   Feel bad about Paps, not that he'll notice I'm gone. (Like the $40 I snagged from his pants!)
   Hope Lena turns out to be cool, not a salty noob.
   OMG! We've been emailing and texting for almost a year. I'm sure she's totally lit.
   Backpack stuffed!
   Thumb cocked!

*I'll take a cannibal cultist over this snotrag we're dogging
any old day.*

YOLO!

                                                    HWB

My eyes flew to Vislosky's. "Harmony wrote this the day France
remembers her leaving."
"Heading to Charleston."
"To meet a kid named Lena."
"Maybe a kid."
I gestured that Vislosky had a valid point. "Lena could be Mama
Gertie's Canadian contact."
The other murdered girl. Neither of us voiced the dreadful
thought.
I riffled through the pages. Each one was filled with the same girl-
ish scrawl.
"May I take this with me overnight?"
When I looked up, Vislosky seemed to be wrestling with it.
"I'll sign it out," I assured. "Dot all your bloody i's."
Vislosky's desk phone rang. She ignored it.
"Be honest." I waggled the little book. "With all this capno
hysteria, will you have time to read this?"
"Fine." Green eyes narrowing. "But—"
"Yeah, yeah. I know."

Anne was at the stove doing Joplin and stirring a large pot. Hearing my
footsteps, she sang the next line into her spoon: "Windshield wipers
slappin' time . . ."
She extended the spoon-mic toward me: "I was holdin' Bobby's
hand in mine . . ." I added.

In reasonable sync: "We sang every song that driver knew."

We both laughed. My first in a long time.

I set my purse and a bag on the counter.

"The wanderer returns bearing food," Anne said.

"Fried shrimp and oysters. I called ahead to the Long Island Café."

"An excellent choice. Which my chowder will complement nicely."

While Anne ladled soup into bowls, I set places and divvied up the seafood. As we ate, I half-listened to her tale of woe featuring a horse and her ex-husband and one of her twins. Made comforting noises at all the right spots.

"So," I said, eager to move things along. "Tell me everything you've discovered about the death mask."

Finished venting, Anne retrieved a downloaded photo of L'Inconnue and her copy of Beecroft's print and laid both on the table. We agreed. There was absolutely no doubt. It was the same face.

Anne launched into an excruciatingly detailed account of her death mask quest. Though I nodded approvingly and asked a question now and then, my heart wasn't in it. Every few minutes, I discreetly checked the time, anxious to get to Harmony's diary.

When Anne finished, I granted that she had, indeed, made a major breakthrough. Assured her that Polly Beecroft would be thrilled.

"But how could you ever prove that Sybil Bouvier was the lady in the Seine?" she asked, tone wistful.

"That would be tough," I said.

"Or figure out how she ended up in the river?"

"Even tougher."

As we chewed on that, and on the last of the shrimp, my eyes drifted to the photos.

Again, I felt that soft elbow nudge from my id. What? The woman couldn't possibly look familiar. No matter her name or fate, she'd died almost a century before I was born. Our paths could never have crossed.

"How's Ryan doing?" Anne and I had discussed the hit-and-run incident by phone.

"Sketchy haircut but nimble as ever."

"Why would some dickwad run you down?"

"That question is currently under investigation." Not mentioning Claudel's theory as to which of us was the real target.

"Did you make progress on your cold case?"

I gave a very brief accounting. Exhumation. DNA. Genetic genealogy. Dr. Aubrey Sullivan Huger.

"Why the trip to Nashville?"

Again, quick and succinct. Digger France. Harmony Boatwright. Amity House. MMM. The online Canadian friend. The diary.

"How did you get here from Nashville?"

"Caught a ride with the lead detective on the Charleston case."

"How long did the drive take?"

"A millennium and a half."

By the time I made my escape, it was nine fifteen.

Up in my room, I took a quick shower, climbed into bed, and phoned Ryan.

Got voice mail. Left a brief message.

Beyond the French doors, the ocean was calm. Inside my chest, the situation was anything but. Opening the diary, I felt my heart beating double time.

The first page was dated January 2, 2017. The entry was short and direct. Harmony explained that the diary was a gift, that she'd give journaling a shot but wasn't sure writing was her thing. She named the little book Di.

For a while, she penned only brief narrative accounts listing the day's activities. Eventually, her entries became more frequent. And more creative.

And, to my dismay, more cryptic.

Her style, one of direct conversation with her fictional confidante

Di, evolved into a hodgepodge of kid lingo and texting abbreviations. Devolved?

Some acronyms I knew. *BFF. TBH. OMG. YOLO. LMAO. WTF.* Others I hadn't a clue.

Lacking a bubble-gummer to translate, I found a teen slang dictionary online.

MMD: Made my day. *AFAIK*: As far as I know. *ROTFL*: Rolling on the floor laughing. *4YEO*: For your eyes only.

Page by page, Harmony's personality materialized through her words. She wrote: *School is way basic.* Read: boring. *dm told me something that was totally cap.* Read: untrue. *st was flexing again today.* Read: showing off. *es went full on emo in the caf.* Read: emotional/drama queen in the cafeteria.

Individuals were referenced by lowercase initials. Opening a Word document, I started a list. *dm. st. es.*

P911 appeared a lot. Parent alert. I wondered. If Digger was taking no notice of his granddaughter, who was this hovering authority figure?

As my fluency in teenage-ese improved, the process went faster. I skimmed through days and weeks of typical adolescent angst. *Is the hair too rad? Paps is such a dick!* And the perennially popular: *I think ak is into me!*

But some of the anguish was not so typical. It was apparent that Harmony desperately missed her mother. Bonnie Bird's name, the only one never abbreviated, appeared often.

Reference to MMM.com first occurred on March 4, 2017, during a stay at Amity House. Mention of the site continued at irregular intervals thereafter, interspersed with normal day-to-day chatter.

Occasionally, Harmony described her interactions with other visitors to MMM, the passages sometimes buoyant with hope, sometimes dark with despair. From time to time, she cited specific usernames: *kerrydo. maplehope. safarisam. nowimfound.*

maplehope? The Canadian girl?

maplehope began to appear regularly by late March. Harmony gave little detail, other than to write that *maplehope* was also search-ing for her mother.

The script was small and cramped, the ink faded and smeary. By page forty, my eyes felt like gravel, and my frontal bone was thrumming.

The clock said 11:50.

Still no call from Ryan.

Given my remark to Vislosky about having free time that she didn't have, no way I could quit.

I got up, downed two aspirin, then returned to the diary.

The initials *lc* first appeared on April 10, 2017. Harmony had gone offline with *maplehope*, and they'd exchanged names.

lc?

Lena C.?

It took another fifty minutes. Then I sat bolt upright, the ocular gravel and headache forgotten.

May 14, 2017. Harmony and *lc* had been texting and emailing regularly for a month. Harmony devoted a full page to her new cyber-friend, *lc*.

Lena Chalamet.

"Holy shitballs!"

I froze, listening for signs that my outburst had awakened Anne. The house was silent.

As I read the brief passage, my pulse spiked.

Lena Chalamet told Harmony that she was eighteen years old. That she lived in Laval, a town not far from Montreal. Lena said that in 2002, when she was two years old, her mother, Mélanie, and her sister, Ella, vanished without a trace. Mélanie was thirty-two, and Ella was ten. Lena had dedicated her life to learning what happened to them.

On May 27, 2017, Harmony wrote that Lena's passion was totally *wig*. Awesome. That she and Lena had made a pact to support each other *no matter what*. That they'd sworn to maintain secrecy *to the death*.

On July 17, 2017, Harmony hinted at a discovery that Lena had made. Apologized that she was not at liberty to share the *deets*. Details.

Sweet Jesus in a jumpsuit!

Everything fit. The ages. The time of disappearance. The location.

Were Mélanie and Ella Chalamet the vics in the Montreal container? Was Lena Mélanie's other daughter?

Were Lena Chalamet and Harmony Boatwright the vics in the Charleston container?

Was I finally going to put names to their bones?

It was 2:14 a.m. Way too late to phone anyone.

I hurried to my laptop and fired off an email to Ryan. Another to Vislosky.

Then I fell back into bed.

And lay awake, mind in hyperdrive.

Polly Beecroft.

Sybil Bouvier.

Bouvier had disappeared almost a century ago. Yet Beecroft was still searching for answers.

Mélanie, Ella, and Lena Chalamet. Harmony Boatwright.

Why had no one kept searching for them?

26

Saturday, November 13

The didgeridoo had to go.

Before answering, I checked caller ID. And the time: 8:15 a.m.

"Tell me you found her." Not bothering to hide my drowsiness.

"I found her."

"Really?" Instantly wide awake.

"I'm tip-top. How are you this morning, *ma chère?*"

"Terrific." Bunching and leaning against the pillows. "You found Lena Chalamet?"

"Birdie seems a little under the weather."

"Oh, no. What's wrong with him?"

"Partly my fault. We walked over to Hurley's for a beer last night. He knocked back three pints of Guinness before I noticed."

"ROFL," I said, eyes doing a three-sixty. Pointless, since Ryan couldn't see me.

"Sorry?"

"Rolling on the floor laughing."

"What are you, twelve?"

"Tell me about Lena?"

"The kid had a tough go of it."

"Start at the beginning."

223

"I don't know the beginning."

"Ryan, it's too early—"

"There's no birth certificate for a Lena Chalamet in Quebec or in any other province, at least none that I've been able to locate. I suspect she may not have been born in Canada."

"Any immigration record?"

"No."

"What about Mélanie and Ella?"

"Same for them. No paper trail at all."

"That's weird."

"It is."

"So, what *do* you know?"

"In 2002, a Lena Chalamet went under the care of Direction de la Protection de la Jeunesse."

"Child protective services."

"*Oui*. She was placed in the *famille d'accueil* system."

"Foster care."

"*Oui*, again."

"How old was she?"

"Two."

Born in 1999. That tracked with my estimated age for the older vic in Charleston.

"A quick scan of Lena's DPJ file—"

"How did you get access without a warrant?"

"My charm and boyish good looks."

Again, my eyes rolled.

"Seems the kid was a chronic runaway, bounced from family to family, eventually dropped off the radar."

"When?"

"Around 2015."

"DPJ just quit checking on her?"

"In Quebec, social workers are overwhelmed and underpaid."

True everywhere. Still. She was only sixteen.

I held my tongue.

"The dossier just stops after that," Ryan said.

"Keep digging."

"I will."

The didgeridoo warbled again at 9:07. I was in the kitchen, drinking coffee and toasting a bagel. I assumed Anne was still sleeping.

Vislosky.

I briefed her on the diary. On Lena Chalamet.

She didn't interrupt. I had to admit, she was an outstanding listener.

"I submitted France's swab to the lab," Vislosky said when I'd finished.

"Good," I replied, hoping the process would happen quickly. "I've got people working Chalamet on the Montreal end."

"The marine biologist at College of Charleston finally sent a report. Not the speediest toad in the pond."

"What does it say?"

"He can't tell shit."

"Shoot it to me?"

"Will do."

Ryan called again around ten.

"Looks like Lena took to living rough, as the Brits say."

"Not easy, given Montreal winters."

"These street kids aren't all that obliging, and most weren't around back then. But one brave little Einstein vaguely recalls a Lena with bad-looking teeth."

"Where?"

"He says she was a regular in Centreville for a while. Rue Crescent, Bishop, Sainte-Catherine, boulevard de Maisonneuve."

"The area around Concordia University."

"Yes."

"When did he last see her?"

"He thinks it was about three years ago."

"What else?"

"He says she used to sneak into the Concordia library to use the computers."

"Don't they have security to prevent outsiders doing that?"

"She'd swiped a student ID."

"Anything else?"

"She was really tall."

"Sonofabitch!"

"Well put."

"Did you find any record of Lena entering the U.S. around 2018?"

"Still working that angle. But I doubt the kid crossed the border legally, since she had no passport."

"I really appreciate your help with this, Ryan."

"Saint-Anicet was my case, too. Besides, I've got some free time right now."

Disconnecting, I wondered. Was failure to find closure for the container vics the real explanation? Or did Ryan suspect a link to the hit-and-run on Laurier?

I returned to the diary.

Twenty pages in, hit gold.

Despite her oath of secrecy, Harmony couldn't contain her elation over a newly acquired deet. Apparently, she considered Di a safe confidante.

I had to go over the line several times to be sure I was reading it correctly. Once with a magnifying glass.

WTFH? lc's mo worked for big pharma???? I can't even!!! We will def peep that!!!

The entry was dated August 25, 2017.

I dialed Ryan.

He picked up right away.

I read him the line.

"She can't even what?"

"She's amazed."

"Does peep mean they intended to check the deet out?"

"I assume so."

We both thought about that.

"When Lena went into DPJ care in 2002, where was she living?"
I asked.

"Hold on."

Not sure what Ryan did, but it took him forever.

"Laval."

"Aren't there scads of biotech firms there?"

"Indeed, there are."

Ryan's next call came around noon. The ringtone was now Unified
Theory. Chris Shinn's "A.M. Radio" definitely beat the didgeridoo.

"Laval is lousy with biotech and big pharma. Roche. Corealis
Pharma. Biodextris. A lot of companies are located in a research-
and-development center called La Cité de la Biotech."

"Biotech City. Catchy."

"Probably paid some marketing prodigy a million bucks for that
handle."

"What goes on there?"

"Manufacturing. Testing. R and D. Anything health-technology
related. Get this. Biotech City covers about a million square meters."

"That's big."

"Very big. So big that—"

"I get the picture."

"La Cité is located within the Laval Science and High Technology
Park, which opened in 'eighty-six. In—"

"Do I need the full history?" Grumpy, I know. But I wanted to
hear about Lena Chalamet.

"Stick with me, butter bean. Later came a two-hundred-fifty-
million-dollar influx, part from government funding, part from the private sector. The result was major expansion and a surge of new hiring."

"Did—"

"That surge began around 2000, 2001."

I realized where Ryan was going.

"One of those companies hired Mélanie Chalamet," I guessed.

"Yes, ma'am."

"Which one?"

"InovoVax."

"Never heard of it."

"They're not Merck or Pfizer, but they're big enough."

"What do they do?"

"Manufacture vaccines." I heard pages flip. "Apparently, they're testing some newfangled method using mRNA."

"Did you say newfangled? Is this 1920?"

"Cutting-edge."

"Better. You found someone who remembers Mélanie?"

"I found someone willing to pull up old personnel records."

"How long was she employed there?"

"Are you ready for this?"

I waited.

"Mélanie Chalamet was terminated less than two years after she was hired."

"Why?"

"The file doesn't say."

"This was in 2002?"

"It was."

"The year Lena went into foster care."

"The very one."

"Holy shit."

"Holy shit."

"What next?"

"Monday morning, I head to Laval."

"I want to go with you." The same knee-jerk response that had landed me in Nashville.

"What about Anne?"

"I'll buy her a pricey chardonnay."

"Birdie will be delighted to see you."

"Where is he?"

"On the couch with a cold rag on his head."

27

Monday, November 15

Lying just minutes away from Montreal, across the Rivière des Prairies, Laval is the city's largest burb. The town occupies the Île Jésus and the Îles Laval. The Rivière des Milles Îles borders it on the north.

Lots of isles. Lots of rivers.

Ryan and I rolled into Laval at nine fifteen Monday morning. Were at Biotech City shortly thereafter.

InovoVax was headquartered in a twelve-story street-facing tower with a low, rectangular wing jutting off in back. The tower involved a lot of glass and steel. The wing was a windowless concrete box. Surrounding the whole was a half acre of thoughtfully landscaped grounds. Probably lovely in summer, the picnic tables were empty now, the trees bare and black, the dead brown lawn coated with frost.

Walking from Ryan's Jeep to the building's entrance, I feared the loss of digits to frostbite. The temperature was a breath-stopping minus fourteen Celsius, and a wet wind coming off all those rivers was scything my skin.

Ryan had phoned ahead. As per instructions, we passed through security and checked in with reception. After presenting ID and receiving temporary passes, we waited on a green leather sofa flanked by potted palms at one side of the lobby.

The woman sent to collect us was small and grim. She wore wireless specs, a white lab coat, and eerily quiet crepe-soled shoes. A lanyard-hanging badge gave her name as Mariette Plourde. So did she.

In the 2016 census, roughly twenty percent of Laval's population self-classified as Anglophone. English-speaking. Mariette Plourde was not among them. And her French was so strongly accented I barely understood a word she said. I guessed her origins were far up-river.

Plourde led us past a bank of elevators and down a spotlessly clean first-floor corridor that would have made any OR proud. Twenty yards, then we entered a spacious office, also incandescently pristine. A plaque beside the door said *Personnel et resources humaines*/Personnel and Human Resources.

Shiny gray tile winked up from the floor. White vinyl shelves covered three walls, all filled with industry publications. *The Journal of Pharmaceutical Analysis. BioPharm International. BioWorld. Applied Clinical Trials.*

A blond-oak table-and-chair set filled most of the room's far end. Scandinavian sleek and angular, the chairs promised unrelenting discomfort. Chosen for that reason? My mind flashed an image of a nervous job applicant trying not to fidget.

A blond-oak desk occupied space to the left of the door, its design exuding a similar lack of warmth. The woman at it was trying to appear focused on papers she was sorting. With minimal success. An engraved acrylic block introduced her as *Dora Eisenberg*.

"*Attendez ici.*" Plourde gestured to the table. "*Docteur Murray sera avec vous dans un instant.*" Wait here. Dr. Murray will be with you in a moment. *Très* efficient. *Très* cold.

Ryan and I took side-by-side chairs. Mine faced Dora Eisenberg— I assumed some sort of HR administrative assistant—allowing me to observe her while appearing not to.

Eisenberg was bosom-heavy, round-shouldered, and upper-arm-jiggly. Her hair was brown and curly, her eyes enormous behind Hubble-thick lenses.

Perhaps sensing my curiosity, Eisenberg glanced up. Color spread across her cheeks like blood on snow. I smiled. Flushing even more flamboyantly, she finger-waggle-waved and returned to her papers.

It was a bit longer than *un instant* until Murray appeared.

"Please accept my apology for making you wait." Murray spoke in English while striding across the room, hand extended.

As Murray closed in, my brain took a snapshot.

The man wasn't big, but his body was lean and toned, his spine straight enough to stand in for a flagpole. Though showing some mileage, his jawline was good, his silver-gray hair professionally styled. Colored? A gold chain heavy enough to moor the *Queen Mary* looped his neck, and a bagel-sized sapphire graced one finger. I put his age at somewhere north of fifty.

Ryan and I rose and took turns shaking. Murray's grip was pretentiously heavy-duty.

"Dr. Arlo Murray." We knew that. "I'm the director here." We didn't know that.

Ryan and I introduced ourselves.

"Please." Murray pulled out a chair. "Make yourselves comfortable." As if.

"SQ, eh?" To Ryan as we both dropped back into place.

"Many years." Leaving out the bit about being retired.

Murray didn't ask to see Ryan's badge or query my credentials. "I understand you have questions about a former employee. May I inquire why?"

"No," Ryan said.

Murray's brows rose, but he said nothing.

"Mélanie Chalamet," Ryan said.

"So I was told."

Noting that Murray had completely ignored Eisenberg—not so much as a nod—I wondered if that was his manner with every subordinate.

"I did pull her file," Murray said. "But there's not much I can tell you. Ms. Chalamet came on board in 2000, stayed with us less than two years."

"In what position?"

"She was just a lab technician." As if referring to a slug under an upturned rock.

"What background does that job require?"

"I think she may have had an undergraduate degree." Similar tone of disdain.

"*De quel institution?*" Ryan, testing.

"I'm sorry. I do not speak French."

"Did Mélanie?" With a sharp edge of disgust. Irritating to Fran-cophones are longtime Quebec residents who haven't bothered to learn the language.

"*Oui.*" Sarcastic.

"Do you know where she earned her degree?"

"Some school in the States?" Half question, half statement. "I'm not sure. It's been so long. And it's not in her file."

"Was she American?"

"I don't know."

Beyond Ryan, I noticed Eisenberg's face pop up, heavy brows angled down below the bridge of her glasses.

A beat, then Ryan circled a hand and asked, "What goes on here?"

Murray launched into what sounded like a well-practiced pitch. "InovoVax focuses on the development and manufacture of vaccines for infectious diseases. We're at the cutting edge of research, one of very few labs exploring an mRNA mechanism. Are you knowledge-able concerning vaccine manufacture?"

"Knowledgeable enough."

"I'm certain you are." Tone suggesting the opposite. "Some of our products include Influvax, Penivax-B, Inov-3607, VGGX-2812—"

"What's *your* background, doc?"

"I hold a doctorate in molecular biology."

"Impressive."

"Thank you."

"How long have you been with InovoVax?"

"Twenty-one years."

"So you started the same time as Ms. Chalamet?"

"I suppose that's true."

"I assume you weren't director back then."

"I was a researcher."

"Was Ms. Chalamet one of your techs?"

"She and I worked in separate divisions."

"What can you tell me about her?"

"I've already answered that." Condescending smile. "It's a big facility, and she was far below my pay grade."

Eisenberg's frown deepened.

"You formed no impression at all?"

"Based on the very few conversations that we had, I'd have to say she was a bitter and unhappy woman."

"Why?"

Murray shrugged. "It's my understanding, and I may be completely wrong, Ms. Chalamet was to begin an MA program and had to drop out due to pregnancy. I believe she resented those of us who completed our studies and, as a consequence, were enjoying more responsibility and more generous compensation."

"Why did she quit?"

"She didn't quit. She was fired."

"Why?"

"The usual. A young woman, too many distractions—"

"What distractions?" Cool. Ryan wasn't digging Murray's arrogance.

"It's been a very long time, detective."

"Dig deep."

"I'm certain she was terminated for failure to carry out her duties."

"What does that mean?" Ryan pressed.

"She was incompetent. Is that what you want to hear?"

"You the one who canned her?" Low and hard.

Murray drew back in his chair, playing the role of insulted inno-cent. "I didn't agree to this meeting in order to be badgered."

"Why *did* you? Surely an underling could have handled some-thing this mundane."

"What division did you say you're with, detective?"

"I didn't."

"I'm afraid I must request ID." Stiff.

"Damn. Tendered my badge last year."

"You're no longer officially employed by law enforcement?" A flush crept up Murray's neck. Embarrassment? Anger?

Ryan smiled, oh so unperturbed.

Murray stood, every vertebra aligning perfectly. "We're done here."

"One last question, doc." As Ryan and I rose. "You being a good corporate citizen and all."

Murray glared but didn't walk away.

"When Ms. Chalamet stopped working here, where did she go?"

"I've no earthly clue."

Eisenberg's chin came up again, and her eyes sought mine.

Her head wagged slowly.

Crossing to the parking lot, I described Eisenberg's odd reaction, not an easy task, given my wind-numbed lips and cheeks.

Ryan was silent behind his muffler.

"I slipped her my card." Frosty vapor puffing from my mouth.

"Think she'll call?"

I shrugged. "Who knows?"

Once in the Jeep, Ryan asked, "Want to give her a few minutes?"

"Sure."

"What did you think of Murray?"

"Pompous prick."

"Nice alliteration."

"Thanks."

"Anything else?" Ryan ventured.

"He and Chalamet worked in different divisions back in the day, yet he seemed to know quite a bit about her. The reason she dropped out of grad school, for instance."

"My reaction, too."

"Otherwise, the guy was spectacularly unhelpful."

"Exactly. But why?"

"It *has* been almost twenty years. And InovoVax *is* huge. Maybe he genuinely doesn't remember much about Chalamet." The engine was running, the heater doing its best, but still it was frigid. "What did *you* think?"

"I've heard a lot of end runs, but Murray's was exceptional. What I don't get is why the need to be so evasive over minor matters."

"I could sense you didn't like the guy."

"Not at all."

"Why?"

"My gut tells me something's off."

I looked at Ryan. His cheeks were red from the cold, his eyes laser-blue. It was a good combination.

"I don't know where Murray fits in, if at all." I flexed my fingers to encourage circulation—or maybe just to redirect nervous energy. "But I'm convinced Mélanie and Ella Chalamet are the Montreal container vics."

Ryan was about to respond when a text pinged in on my phone.

"Eisenberg?" he asked

"Yes."

I read her message aloud, then my replies as I keyed them in.

DE: *I have something to tell you but I can't talk here.*

TB: *Shall we meet?*

DE: *Yes.*

TB: *When? Where?*

DE: *Tim Hortons. Boulevard Chomedy. Noon.*

I glanced at Ryan.

He was already shifting gears.
TB: *We'll be there.*

Tim Hortons coffee shops are like dental offices. Predictable, reliable, and unimaginative. This one was situated on a corner, at one end of an uninspired strip mall.

A red awning topped by Tim's familiar signature overhung the entrance. Inside, a lighted wall menu behind a long vinyl counter listed selections. Below the counter, a glass case offered an array of sandwiches and pastries.

Tables filled the floor. Three were occupied. A mother with a chocolate-smeared toddler in a stroller. A trio of workers wearing boots, parkas, and earflap hats. Two women in scrubs, both looking exhausted and probably fresh off a graveyard shift.

While Ryan got coffee and doughnuts, I chose a spot as far from the other patrons as possible. Eisenberg had seemed nervous. I didn't want her spooked.

Ryan arrived with three lidded red cups and a bag. He was placing the coffee on the table when Eisenberg pushed through the door dressed like a trapper returning from the Klondike. Mercifully, the hat, gloves, and ankle-length coat were all imitation. Not a single animal had been killed in their making.

A birdlike scan of her surroundings, then Eisenberg scurried toward us, bootheels clicking like corn in a popper.

"Thank you so much for meeting with us." Ryan and I had agreed that I'd steer the conversation.

"It's not right." Eisenberg was clearly agitated.

"I hope you drink coffee, Dora." I gestured at the cups. "May we call you Dora?"

"I can't stay long."

Eisenberg lowered herself into one of the empty chairs. As she shrugged from the acres of fake fur, a tsunami of odor wafted my way. Doing my best not to react, I opened the bag and offered the doughnuts. She chose an apple fritter and a honey cruller.

Ryan and I waited while Eisenberg pried off the lid and added sugar to her coffee. Stirred. Tested. Added more. Replaced the lid. Ate the cruller.

Finally, I asked, "You work in human resources at InovoVax?"

Eisenberg nodded. Took a bite of the fritter. A big one.

"Have you been with the company long?"

"Twenty-five years." Through a mouthful of sugar and dough. "Since before the move to Laval."

"Did you know Mélanie Chalamet?"

"He's not really a policeman?" Eyes flicking to Ryan. "I'm not sure I should be talking to you."

"Detective Ryan is a licensed investigator," I said, taking some liberty with the title.

"What about you?"

"I'm also an investigator." Not wanting to alarm her by mentioning the lab or the coroner.

"Did something happen to Mélanie? Are you doing some kind of cold-case investigation? I've seen shows about that on TV."

"Mm. What can you tell us about Mélanie?"

"I can tell you that Dr. Murray was lying just now. He knew Mélanie, knew her well. Toward the end, he made her life miserable."

"Oh?"

"And Mélanie wasn't fired." Head again wagging, which caused the hide hat to shift. "Uh-uh. No way. I'll swear to that on a stack of Bibles."

Sudden thought. "You have access to the company's personnel files, don't you, Dora?"

Eisenberg licked a finger and began picking sugar particles from the tabletop.

"You retrieved Mélanie's file?" I guessed.

Eisenberg's finger froze. A moment of indecision, then she lowered her voice to ensure that her words were for our ears only.

"It's gone."

"What's gone?" I was lost.

"Mélanie's file has been deleted from the system."

28

"When?"
      "Last night."
"Do you know who deleted it?"
"No."
"Who has access to the system?"
"A lot of people."
"Is it routine practice to remove files? Say, after a certain period of time?"
"I don't think so. I don't know. I've never noticed that."
As Eisenberg finished the fritter, Ryan and I exchanged glances. I sensed that he felt as psyched as I did.
"What can you tell us about Mélanie?" I asked, after a brief pause.
"She was a really nice person."
"Not unhappy and bitter as Dr. Murray described her?"
A slight hesitation, then, "Mélanie didn't like that we were paid so little."
"Did she resent people with higher degrees?"
Eisenberg gave a slow, noncommittal shrug of one shoulder.
"Were you friends?"

"Yes. Well, mostly work friends. But not totally. Our lives were kind of similar."

"How so?"

"I was unmarried. Still am." As before, her cheeks blossomed red. "Mélanie was a single mom. We were both young and poor."

"How did you meet?"

"Neither of us could afford the cafeteria, so we'd bring bag lunches from home and eat in the first-floor break room. I still do that. Now it's because of colitis, not money. I have to watch my diet."

"How old was Mélanie when she left InovoVax?"

"Thirty-two. Same as me."

"How old were her kids?"

"Ella was nine or ten. An absolutely precious little girl. The baby was just a toddler."

"The baby's name?"

"Oh, my. I only met the little ones a couple of times. But Mélanie talked about them a lot, so I should remember."

I was actually holding my breath.

"I'm sorry. I just—"

"It's OK. Do you know who the father was?"

"Mélanie never said. But I think he was American."

"Why?"

"Because Mélanie was American. And Dr. Murray knows that." The last added with a vehement finger jab to the table.

"Is that why you say he lied?"

"That's part of it." Eisenberg seemed to draw inward, perhaps returning to another time in her mind.

"Go on," I urged gently.

"Oh, dear. I hope this won't get back. I just can't lose my job. Most companies want young people with lots of tech skills these days."

"We won't let that happen." An impossible promise?

"Dr. Murray really rode Mélanie hard. Not at first but later."

"How?"

"He was always harassing her. Not sexually. Don't take me wrong."

Again, the pale cheeks flamed. "Just saying mean things, criticizing her. Being finicky, you know."

"More so than with the other techs?"

"Seemed that way to us."

"Why?"

"I'm not sure. Maybe because she spoke French and he couldn't. She studied it in college, you know. Maybe because Dr. Murray is a maniac when it comes to work."

I floated a brow.

"I've never been in the building when he wasn't there. Well, practically never. And talk about micromanaging. He's everywhere. The R-and-D labs. The manufacturing line. The business office. The shipping dock. And I'm talking all hours of the day and night."

"He works long hours?"

"When the company first moved to Laval, I had to put in a lot of overtime migrating data from the old system to the new one. I frequently stayed very late. Dr. Murray was often there. After Mélanie left, he was *always* there."

"Do you think Mélanie was fired for not working enthusiastically enough? Maybe refusing to put in overtime?"

"Mélanie was a really hard worker. And she *wasn't* fired. Well, I suppose technically she was. Eventually."

"I don't understand."

"She just stopped showing up."

"When?"

"The summer of 2002. Late July, maybe early August. It made absolutely no sense."

"Why do you say that?"

"Mélanie would have told me if she was planning to leave. We confided in each other. Besides—" A long, hesitant pause. "Her options were even more limited than mine."

"How so?"

"I don't want to make trouble for her."

"You won't." A promise easily kept.

Eisenberg leaned forward and whispered, "Mélanie was in Canada illegally."

"How did she manage to work without a visa?" Matching Eisenberg, sotto voce.

"I don't know all the details. I wouldn't say she was living off the grid, but she was definitely lying low, using a false name."

"What was her real name?" Calm, though my heart was thumping. The thick lenses swiveled left, then right. "Melanie Chalmers."

"How was she lying low?"

"She had an aunt who owned a building here in Laval, or a great-aunt or something. Family, anyway. She was renting from her."

"Do you recall the aunt's name?"

"No. Sorry."

Crap!

Eisenberg looked truly glum. Then, "But I remember the house. It was on avenue Voltaire, brick with green shutters, right across from the entrance to a small park."

"Do you know who got Mélanie the job at InovoVax?"

"She made it clear that topic was off-limits. Super hush-hush." Eisenberg leaned back and began wriggling into the malodorous outerwear. "I've probably said too much."

"Just a couple of more questions, please?"

Eisenberg went still.

"Back then, why did you think Mélanie quit?"

"I assumed she couldn't take Dr. Murray's badgering any longer."

"Where did you think she'd gone?"

Eisenberg looked down at the gloves clutched in her sausage fingers. Sighed. When her eyes came up, they were moist with emotion.

"Mélanie loved her kids above all else in this world. She would never have done anything to put them at risk. I assumed she took them back to the States."

"Why leave so abruptly?"

"I had no idea."

Eisenberg's description took us to a two-story four-flat near the intersection of rue Vallières and avenue Voltaire. The brick box was one of an armada of boxes, each featureless save for some slap-dash patches of siding, shutters, or paired balconies jutting from first- and second-floor windows.

Ryan pulled to the curb. We scoped out the scene.

"Grim," Ryan said.

"It's not so bad," I said.

"All the appeal of an outlet mall in Ipswich."

"Have you ever been to an outlet mall in Ipswich?"

"I just like to say Ipswich."

"The trees are nice."

"Right out of *Architectural Digest*."

But I had to admit Ryan's point was valid. The block had none of the charm of older Montreal *quartiers*. No gabled roofs. No weathered brownstone facades. No iron staircases whimsically sweeping front elevations. Here the leitmotif was function over fashion.

We got out and hurried up a walkway bisecting a swatch of concrete that should have been lawn. Not far off, vehicles droned steadily, probably traffic on Autoroute 440.

The door was unpainted steel and unlocked. Ryan and I passed through into a tiny lobby, flavorless in keeping with the building's exterior. The left hand wall hosted four mailboxes, three with names displayed behind yellowed rectangles of plastic.

"T. Sadoul. F. Sorg. T. Y. Chou," I read aloud.

"My money's on Sorg," Ryan said.

"Here's hoping Auntie hasn't moved on up," as I pressed the button.

I expected a voice warbling through a speaker. Instead, a buzzer sounded, and the lock behind us clicked. Ryan pulled the door wide, and we climbed a set of metal stairs.

There were two units per floor. Number 2B was on the right, bright plastic flowers affixed to the door.

Ryan knocked. We heard movement, but no one answered.

Ryan knocked again.

Still nothing.

The garish bouquet made my eyeballs want to bleed. Purple asters. Orange marigolds. Black and yellow sunflowers.

Between the stems and leaves, a bright blue iris in a sea of venous pink.

Hiding my surprise, I said, "Madame Sorg?"

The eyeball drew closer to the peephole.

"My name is Temperance Brennan. I'm here with Detective Andrew Ryan. We wish to speak to you concerning Mélanie Chalamet."

"Piss off."

I tried French.

"*Va chier, mon tabarnac.*"

Rough translation: go shit, asshole. Awesome. I'd been disparaged in two languages.

Hiding a smile, Ryan raised his brows and pointed to his chest. I yielded center stage at the bouquet.

"Madame Sorg, we're so very sorry to call unannounced." Oozing gentlemanly charm.

The eye in the peephole blinked.

"We wish only a few moments of your time." So honeyed that I feared an onslaught of cavities.

"I'm naked in here."

"We're happy to wait." Ryan didn't miss a beat. I admired that.

Immediately, a bolt turned, followed by another.

I cast a bemused glance at Ryan. He shrugged.

The door opened.

In her youth, F. Sorg's height may have been equal to mine, but postural kyphosis had bent her spine, lowering her sight line to midchest on me. Thus, the ladder at her side.

"Thank you so much for talking with us." Despite his nonchalance, Ryan appeared relieved to see the old woman's piss-yellow housecoat. To see *any* attire, I suspected.

"You gotta speak loud. My ears are shit."

Ryan pumped up the volume. "Thank you so much f—"

"Christ almighty. I'm hard of hearing, not deaf."

Sorg twisted her head sideways in order to take in our faces. Lingered on Ryan. "Aren't you a good-looking stud."

"Madam Sorg—"

"Name's Florence."

I observed as Ryan smooth-talked Florence. The old woman had astonishingly wrinkled skin and blue-tinted white hair that allowed a good view of her scalp. But the intensity of her gaze suggested a scalpel-sharp mind.

"You checking me out, handsome?"

"We'd like to discuss Mélanie Chalamet." Ryan stayed on topic. "I believe you are her aunt?"

"Who told you that?"

"Dora Eisenberg."

"Don't miss seeing that cow waddling up my walk."

"Twenty years ago, Mélanie was working at InovoVax, is that correct?"

"Might be."

"She and her children lived in this building?"

"Maybe."

"They left suddenly in the summer of 2002?"

"*Mon esti de tabarnac*, are you stupid?" Sorg's head swiveled while maintaining its sixty-degree angle as she shifted her focus from Ryan to me and back. Made me think of a turtle.

"I don't understand," Ryan said.

"That girl didn't leave."

"She didn't?"

"Of course not."

"Then—" Ryan began.

"Some sonofabitch murdered her ass."

29

S org was a hoarder.

Tupperware bins, cardboard cartons, and bundled newspapers and magazines lined both sides of the hall. The living room, small to begin with, was reduced to just enough open space for an upholstered grouping, a coffee table, and an ancient TV.

Sorg waddle-swayed to the sofa and winged an elbow at it. Easing into one of the chairs, she craned her head up and regarded us with cerulean eyes.

"Do you know who killed Mélanie?" Ryan asked as we sat.

"What? Do I look like the Great Karnak?"

"You said—"

"I know what I said. I *meant* the girl wouldn't just up and leave one of her kids. Someone musta whacked her."

One of her kids? Lena? My pulse quickened.

"This is just your theory?" Ryan asked.

"You got a better one?"

Sadly, we didn't.

As Ryan interviewed Sorg, I did a visual sweep of the room. Boxes, tubs, and freestanding articles of all kinds took up most of

247

the square footage—books, picture frames, cushions, folded clothing, dolls, stuffed animals, small appliances. I counted four ironing boards, six blenders, and eleven brooms. Fortunately, due to Sorg's limited reach, the stacks surrounding us weren't perilously high.

"You were Mélanie's aunt?"

"I'm ninety-four years old, sonny."

"You certainly don't look it." Ryan flashed a charm-your-knickers-off grin.

"'Course I do. And I earned every damn wrinkle. And the hump."

"Perhaps her *great*-aunt?"

"Sounds right. I came north so long ago the good Lord was still thinking up rocks. Right after the war. The big one. Never took to French, but I learned all the cuss words. I like Quebecois cuss words. They're churchy."

"Came north from where?"

"Vermont. Married a Montrealer. Stayed that way forty-one years. Then the big C took him."

Ryan nodded sadly. "We understand Mélanie was also American, that she was in Canada illegally, and that her actual name was Melanie Chalmers."

"I'm noting your verb tense. That mean I was right about her being dead?"

"Dr. Brennan and I are looking into—"

"Took you dumbasses two decades to get around to investigating?"

Ryan ignored that. "What can you tell us about Melanie?"

Sorg closed her eyes and dug through memories hoarded in her mind. "She wasn't no dummy, had a degree in biology from some uni in the States. Don't recall which one." A pause for more excavation. "Before coming here, she worked for some outfit called HGP."

"Do you know how she got the job at InovoVax?"

"Some hotshot colleague helped her. That's all she'd say."

"Do you know who?"

"Are you the one with the hearing deficit?"

"Did she ever mention a man named Arlo Murray?"

"*Esti*. That bastard was a pain in her tushy."

"How so?"

"Constantly badgered her at work. Guy had the balls to come here once. I heard them arguing about someone named Christian. No." A gnarled finger shot up. "Christopher. All the shouting gave me the collywobbles. Not that I was listening on purpose."

"What did you mean, she wouldn't have abandoned one of her kids?" I asked.

"Meant exactly that. She wouldn't have split without that baby."

"Lena?" Pulse humming.

"No. Shirley Temple."

I just looked at her.

"Hell, yeah, Lena. Poor little thing, left all alone."

"Can you tell me what happened?"

"Not much to tell. She dropped Lena with the sitter and went shopping with Ella. I think the kid needed shoes. Maybe it was shorts."

"And?"

"And she never came back."

"Who was the sitter?"

"Sabine Esnault. I knew her from my canasta group. Stubborn as a bucket of mud. Don't matter. She's dead now. Got the big C, too. Gone in six months. Cancer's a mean bastard."

"It was Esnault who turned Lena over to child services?"

"You implying I should have stepped up? I was seventy-five years old, *tabarnac*."

"Not at all. I'm just trying to verify facts."

Sorg glared at me. She looked like an angry turtle in a housecoat.

"I understand Lena moved frequently while in foster care. Did you follow her progress?"

"I wasn't so good at keeping up. Gotta admit, I feel bad about that."

"Did you ever see her again?"

"She came by twice. The first time five, maybe six years ago. She'd learned we're related. I guess when you turn sixteen, you get to look at your own file. Or maybe she hacked it. I don't know. But there she was, sitting where you are now."

"What did she want?"

"What do you think? My recipe for poutine?" Air puffed through the crenellated lips. "She was asking about her mother and sister, of course. Wasn't much I could tell her. The three of 'em was only here a year or so. The second visit was a couple years later. She'd tried to get info from that buttwipe from Melanie's work."

"Arlo Murray?"

"He shut her down. Now, why in bloody hell would he do that?"

Good question, Florence.

"I'll tell you why." Again, a knobby finger shot up to emphasize her point. "I'll bet my ass he's the one killed her."

I decided to switch tacks. "Did Melanie leave any belongings in her apartment?"

"Not much. Clothing, some toys, a bike, a camera. She rented furnished, ya know. I own the building, so I had to clean the place out."

"What did you do with her things?"

"They're here somewhere."

"Do you think you could find them?"

"'Course I could. I'm not daft."

Sorg grunt-shoved to her feet and shuffled to one of two closed doors at the rear of the apartment. When she opened the left one, we could see a narrow path cutting through lofty mounds of junk.

"There." Pointing at a collection of boxes piled two deep and six high between a heaped bed and the easternmost wall. "Bottom three, second stack in."

"May we move—" Ryan began, with little enthusiasm.

"Knock yourself out."

We did. For forty minutes, my claustrophobia sensors at DEFCON 1.

The boxes produced a single item of potential interest: a corrugated file labeled *InovoVax*.

We found Sorg in the living room watching a rerun of *Cheers*, the volume cranked to a thousand decibels.

"May we keep this?" I shouted, holding up the file.

"Whatever." Focused on an exchange between Norm and Cliff.

"There was an old camcorder in one of the boxes, but we saw no videotapes."

The thunderous laugh track obliterated her answer.

"I'm sorry?"

The network cut to commercial.

Sorg swiveled to face us. "Tapes?"

I nodded.

"They were in a kitchen drawer."

"And?"

"Second time she come, I give 'em to Lena."

"What's a collywobble?" I asked when we were again in the Jeep.

"It's *your* mother tongue."

"Crotchety old biddy."

"But not daft."

As Ryan drove, I started thinking out loud, summarizing what we knew and, more important, what we didn't.

"In 2000, Melanie Chalmers is using the alias Mélanie Chalamet. She and her children are living, if not off the grid, at least in its outer reaches. Other than Sorg, maybe Eisenberg, they have no family or close friends."

"Which explains why no one reports them missing," Ryan said. "And why they turn up in none of our searches."

"Who do you suppose this Christopher is?"

"First time that name's come up."

"What got Murray so steamed that he visited Melanie at home to argue about Christopher?"

Ryan offered no speculation.

I returned to my timeline.

"Melanie disappears in 2002. People believe she's left Canada, but she hasn't. She and her daughter Ella have been murdered, their bodies stuffed into a polypropylene bin. Lena enters foster care. In 2006, the bin washes ashore in Saint-Anicet."

Questions bubbled in my brain like lotto balls.

"Why did Melanie relocate to Quebec? Where did she come from? Vermont? Who got her the job at InovoVax?"

"I'll look into all of that."

"According to Sorg and Eisenberg, there were bad feelings between Melanie and Murray."

"Maybe over this dude Christopher?"

"Whoever the hell he is. Funny Eisenberg didn't mention him."

"I'll request employee records at InovoVax going back to 2000."

"I'm sure Murray will hop right on that."

"If he stonewalls, I'll have Claudel get a subpoena."

I picked up the narrative.

"In 2015, when Lena turns sixteen and accesses her records, she tracks Sorg and demands information about her mother and sister. Sorg tells her about InovoVax, Murray, and Christopher and gives her videotapes. Lena goes to Murray, but he refuses to help her. Why?"

"Because he's an arrogant tool, or because there's stuff he doesn't want her to know?"

"Around this same time, Lena tells Harmony Boatwright that she's made a breakthrough in her search. She goes to Charleston, and Harmony joins her there."

"Why Charleston?"

"I don't know."

I'd asked myself that question a million times. What linked Montreal and Charleston?

"Lena and Harmony are shot in the head, the same MO as with Melanie and Ella," I continued. "This year, during the hurricane, their bodies wash ashore."

Sudden thought. I twisted toward Ryan.

"All four victims were dumped in medical-waste containers. Such containers would be common at a place like InovoVax."

"Yes." Noncommittal.

"Eisenberg said Melanie's file was deleted from the InovoVax system. Why?"

"Maybe it's routine."

"Or maybe it was done to cover someone's tracks."

"Whose?"

"I don't know." I was saying that a lot. "Do you think Sorg could be right about Murray?"

"Being an arrogant tool doesn't make the guy a murderer."

"No," I agreed. "It doesn't."

Still.

I settled back in my seat. As we rode in silence, new images joined the balls bubbling in my mind. Headlights on a rainy street. A body slamming a bus stop upright.

"Can you check out what model car Murray drives?" I asked. "Or have Claudel do it?"

Our eyes met. Ryan's looked dubious.

"Humor me," I said.

"OK." Then, "Where to?"

"I'm ninety-nine percent certain the remains at the morgue are those of Melanie and Ella, but I want to take one final look."

"That thorny one percent."

"When I'm finished with the bones, I'll start going through Melanie's papers."

Two hours later, the skeletons lay articulated on their stainless-steel gurneys, one adult, one juvenile. Brown and weathered, they looked like macabre Halloween props.

I'd been over every bone and tooth. Checked every measurement, reviewed every morphological detail, reassessed all trauma. Though confirmation by DNA was still lacking, there was no doubt in my mind.

I looked at my clipboard. At the form I'd completed fifteen years earlier.

LSJML-41207 Os non identifiés d'une femme. The unidentified woman was Melanie Chalmers/Mélanie Chalamet.

I flipped the page.

LSJML-41208 Os non identifiés d'un enfant. The unidentified child was Ella Chalmers/Chalamet.

A mother dead at age thirty-two. Her child dead at age ten.

Silence echoed in the empty morgue. Expectant?

"Who are you, Mélanie Chalamet?" I whispered. "Where did you come from? Why did you move to Canada and change your name? Whom did you fill with such rage or so seriously threaten that they took your life? And why your daughter's?"

I lifted the ziplock lying beside the small, unfinished skull. Stared at the garish plastic ring only a child could love.

My eyes drifted to the little orbits, sightless forever.

"I am so sorry, Ella. I promise—"

Tears threatened. I blinked them away.

"I will never stop looking."

30

Tuesday, November 16

Claudel phoned at eight the next morning. He'd wasted no time. And was his usual surly self.

"My first sweep is suggesting that Arlo Murray is as clean as a urinal in a convent."

"No arrests?"

"I dislike repeating myself."

"What kind of car does he drive?"

"A Lexus LC 500."

"What do they look like?" Automotive detail is not my thing.

"The one that ran you down."

"Does it have fog lights?"

"All cars have fog lights. In case of fog."

Easy, Brennan.

"Is Murray's right fog light broken?" Enunciating each word.

"I'll be checking that out. And I'll be canvassing body shops to see if any Lexus 500 was brought in recently for repairs."

"Find out everything you can about him."

"I intend to know the nature of the gentleman's polyps. But one question, *s'il vous plaît*. Why are you so certain Murray is dirty?"

"He and Melanie started working at InovoVax at the same time, both having come from the States. Two witnesses say there was friction between them, yet Murray lied about knowing Melanie. Years later, when Melanie's daughter Lena showed up asking questions about her mother, Murray refused to help her."

"*Oui, mais—*"

"Think about this. The day after Ryan phoned to request an interview, Melanie's file is deleted from the InovoVax system."

"Murray would have had access, but undoubtedly others as well."

"I have a bad feeling about this guy. He should be under surveillance."

"Couldn't do my job without you, Dr. Brennan."

Beep. Beep. Beep.

Ryan was gone, as usual. How could a human being be that stealthy that early? Most mornings, I scrabbled around like a squirrel in a feeder.

Ryan had made coffee. Without clanging a cup or banging a cabinet door.

After filling a mug, I took Melanie's file to the dining-room table. I was spending so much time there lately that Birdie hopped up, Pavlovian, and curled beside me.

The file's contents were disappointingly meager. Six sheets of paper. I skimmed the first. It seemed to be a schedule, but out of context, the dates, abbreviations, and series of numbers were meaningless.

The rest of the pages, all blue-lined and torn from a spiral notebook, were written in some sort of shorthand or code. I began culling recognizable words and phrases and entering them into a Word document.

antigen; antibody; replicated; inactivated; attenuated; purified; surface proteins

These terms were self-evident and suggested that the notes had to do with vaccine production. Made sense. The file was labeled *InovoVax*.

The remainder of the text was much more cryptic.

EBFV; CBFV; RFV; WHOGIS&RS; CVV; LAIV; FDA; CDC; HAs; CRISPR; baculovirus; neuraminidase; M2 ion channel; RNP

Might *CDC* stand for Centers for Disease Control and Prevention? And *FDA* be Food and Drug Administration?

Now I was getting somewhere.

I knew that a baculovirus is a virus that infects invertebrates. Had Melanie been concerned about the health of worms?

I was turning to the web when my phone rang. Sang.

"I have a somewhat more enlightening rundown on Monsieur Murray." The timbre of Claudel's voice suggested a morning not going as planned.

"Docteur," I corrected.

"As I mentioned earlier, *le docteur* has no dossier, though his traffic record is long and sullied. Apparently, the man has quite the leaden foot."

I didn't correct his misuse of the idiom.

"Murray was born here in 'sixty-seven, grew up in NDG." Claudel used the nickname for Notre-Dame-de-Grâce, a middle-class residential neighborhood in Montreal's predominantly English-speaking West End. "He attended public for primary, Loyola for secondary school. Then, apparently having higher aspirations, he went to study in the States."

"Where?"

"Some place called Grinnell. I've never heard of it."

"I have."

"*Félicitations*," said Claudel. "He was awarded a doctorate at MIT in '95, something to do with genes and immune systems. I phoned down there. The biology department has some eighty faculty members, but no one remembers a boy genius from Quebec. At least, no one with whom I connected."

"Who was his PhD adviser?"

"A brainbox by the name of"—I heard rustling, pictured pages flipping—"Hao Jianghong. I think it was a male. *Sacre bleu.* Who knows with these—"

"Did you talk to him?"

"He died in 2012."

"What did Murray do after leaving MIT?"

"He went to work at"—more rustling—"The Whitehead Institute at the MIT Center for Genome Research. In Cambridge, Massachusetts."

"Doing what?"

"Call me crazy, but I'm thinking genome research."

Easy.

"Five years in Cambridge, then Murray returned to Canada to take the job with InovoVax," I said.

"*Oui.*" In Quebecois, it sounded like *why*.

"Where does he live now?"

"Laval."

"Any joy on the Lexus?"

"No. But the province has many *travail au noir* garages. I'm unsure how to say that in English."

Claudel was referring to businesses in which the customer pays cash, is charged no tax, and the operator pockets the money.

"Black market," I said. "Will you stake out Murray's home? Get eyes on his car?"

Claudel made a noise in his throat, noncommittal. Taking this as encouragement, I described my efforts with Melanie's notes. When I'd finished, Detective Delightful did something quite out of character. Without Taser prodding from me, he volunteered a suggestion. A good one.

As before, I heard no goodbye, only the three abrupt beeps.

I looked at the name I'd written. Figured what the hell? After googling, I dialed a 617 area code.

"Department of Biology." Clipped and efficient.

"Dr. Alika Bangoboshe."

"Of course. But in future, you might find it more convenient to phone her direct line." She provided a number. "One moment, please."

Two rings, then my call was answered.

"Dr. Bangoboshe."

"Good morning." I introduced myself, explained that I'd gotten her name from a Montreal PD detective and that I worked as a forensic anthropologist for the main medico-legal lab in Quebec.

"Forensic anthropology involves the skeleton, does it not?" High and pure, with a musical lilt that made me think of a flute.

"I promise I won't ask you about bones."

"Might be a welcome diversion from host-microbe and host-pathogen interactions." She laughed. Yep. Flute all the way.

Without going into detail on the container cases, I explained that I had a matter involving vaccines, maybe, and requested help in interpreting a document.

"It sounds intriguing, but in ten minutes, I must teach a class."

"May I send you excerpts from a set of notes? Perhaps you could give the material a quick read, then ring me back?"

A beat, then, "I'll do what I can."

I spent time copying portions of Melanie's notes into a Word document. Sent it off as an email attachment.

Bangoboshe was true to her word. She phoned back shortly after three.

"I apologize for taking so long. Are you on faculty at a university, Dr. Brennan?"

"UNC–Charlotte."

"Then you understand that students can sometimes be—" She searched for a descriptor.

"They can," I agreed.

"And it took a while to get through your document."

"I apologize for that."

"I agree, the excerpts have to do with vaccines. Mostly."

I readied paper and pen. "Go on."

"Where to begin?"

"Wherever you like."

"What do you know about vaccine production?"

"Let's assume nothing."

"First off, all commercially available vaccines in the U.S. are made by private-sector manufacturers. For influenza vaccines, each company uses one of three production technologies. I believe EBFV refers to egg-based flu vaccine, CBFV to cell-based flu vaccine, and RFV to recombinant vaccine. Do you understand the difference?

"No." Scribbling like mad.

"The EBFV method has been around for more than seventy years and is currently the most frequently employed. It's used to make the common flu shot, an inactivated or killed vaccine, and the live attenuated or weakened vaccine used in nasal sprays."

"How does it work?"

"The process begins with the CDC or some accredited partner laboratory providing a private-sector company with what's called a CVV, a candidate vaccine virus. The company injects these CVVs into fertilized hen's eggs, then incubates them to allow time for replication. They then harvest fluid from the eggs, inactivate the viruses, and purify the antigen. Do you know what an antigen is?"

"A protein that triggers the production of an antibody."

"Yes. So that's the process for flu shots. For nasal sprays, the live attenuated influenza vaccines—"

"LAIVs?"

"Yes. The viruses are alive but weakened. Are you still with me?"

"I am."

"You understand that I am greatly oversimplifying."

"I appreciate that."

A beat to appraise my response. Then, "The cell-based method is also used to make inactivated flu vaccines."

"The flu shot again."

"Yes."

"As with EBFV, CBFV production is multiphased. First, the CDC provides influenza viruses that have been grown in cells, not eggs.

The manufacturer then injects the CVVs into cultured mammalian cells and allows them to replicate. The liquid is then collected, and the antigen is purified."

"The difference is the use of animal cells versus chicken eggs."

"Exactly. Recombinant flu vaccines are made synthetically and do not require a CVV. First, scientists obtain DNA, meaning genetic instructions, for making something called hemagglutinin, HA in your notes. HA is an antigen found on the surface of influenza viruses. It triggers the human immune system to create antibodies that specifically target that virus. Do you follow?"

"I do." I actually did.

"The DNA for making the flu virus HA antigen is then combined with baculovirus, a virus that infects invertebrates. The result is an RFV."

"A recombinant flu vaccine."

"Yes."

"Why baculovirus?"

"Its role is to transport the DNA instructions for making the flu virus HA antigen into the host cell." When I didn't reply, "Once the recombinant virus enters an approved FDA host cell line, it gives instructions to produce HA. The antigen is grown in bulk, collected, purified, then packaged as flu vaccine."

"People get the flu shot, produce antibodies, and voilà! Immunity."

"Basically."

"Is there an advantage to the RFV method?"

"Speed."

"Because it isn't limited by the selection of viruses adapted for growth in eggs or by the time needed for the development of cell-based viruses."

"You are very astute, Dr. Brennan."

I scanned Melanie's notes. Bangoboshe had clarified virtually every coded reference.

"Can you comment on the terms *neuraminidase, M2 ion channel*, and *RNP*?"

"They are parts of an influenza virus. Would you like me to explain?"

"I don't want to take up too much of your time," I said. *Definitely* not, I meant.

For a moment, the line went silent, then I thought of something I remained curious about.

"What is *WHOGIS&RS*?"

"Probably an abbreviation for the World Health Organization Global Influenza Surveillance and Response System. It is they, their partner labs, more precisely, who provide private-sector manufacturers with CVVs."

I was about to thank Bangoboshe when I recalled her earlier modifier.

"What did you mean by 'mostly'?"

"I'm sorry?"

"You said the notes were mostly about vaccines."

"There was one term whose presence puzzled me."

That term had puzzled me, too.

31

Tuesday, November 16–Wednesday, November 17

"CRISPR."

"Why does that one term seem out of place to you?"

"I don't see its direct relevance to vaccine production."

I heard a voice in the background. The flute muffled as she responded, then was back.

"I'm afraid I must go."

"Of course. I apologize for taking so much of your time."

I thanked Banguboshe and asked that she keep our conversation confidential. She gave me her assurance, and we disconnected.

I sat a while, assessing what I'd learned.

Melanie was keeping a file on vaccine production. Nothing sinister, given her job at InovoVax. But why was she interested in CRISPR?

I spent time surfing the web. My usual fallback when I could think of no other path forward.

Flash thought. Do people still say "surfing" these days? If not, would Harmony Boatwright mock my use of outdated lingo? Would Katy?

Suddenly, I missed my daughter terribly. Opening the Photos

app, I brought up Katy's most recent pic. How long ago had she sent it? Two weeks? Three? An eon?

Wearing head-to-toe camo, Katy sat on a rock, endless blue sky brilliant overhead, arid desert stretching forever at her back. Her M4 carbine lay dark and deadly across her knees. Her helmet rested upside down by her boots.

"Stay safe, baby girl," I said to the empty room.

Birdie rolled over.

I wrote a long reply describing Hurricane Inara, Anne's quest to crack the mystery of Polly Beecroft's death mask, my ping-pong travels between Charleston, Charlotte, Nashville, and Montreal. I kept it light, mentioned nothing about the hit-and-run or Ryan's injuries. Nothing about three women—two still teenagers—and a child slaughtered and stuffed into bins.

After hitting send, I checked my in-box.

There were ads from every business at which I'd ever made an online purchase. From charities soliciting donations. From people seeking my friendship on Facebook. From my neurosurgeon. From the MCME.

After deleting the junk mail, I opened the message from my boss in Charlotte. Bones had turned up in a suitcase behind a Chinese restaurant in Gastonia. Nguyen wanted my take. Said the case wasn't urgent. I composed a brief response, explaining that I was in Montreal and that I'd be back in town soon.

I turned to Dr. Bernard's message, certain of its contents. Yep. He wanted to schedule an MRI. Since my surgery for an unruptured cerebral aneurysm, I'd had to submit to the scans at regular intervals. Not my idea of a rollicking good time but a minor inconvenience given the alternative.

When I'd finished with email, lacking a more creative idea, I returned to the web and began visiting sites devoted to influenzas, vaccines, and baculoviruses. Panning for gold?

I googled InovoVax, Mélanie Chalamet, Melanie Chalmers, Arlo Murray. Learned nothing I didn't already know.

I was about to type in CRISPR when Birdie stretched, hopped from the table, and padded to the kitchen.

The screen digits said six thirty, and the condo was dark.

"You're right, Bird. It's my turn to cook."

After checking the larder, I decided on linguine with clam sauce, a green salad, and a warmed baguette. One of my old reliables. Plus, we had the ingredients. Things went reasonably well.

Over dinner, Ryan described what he'd unearthed on Melanie Chalmers, in some cases using sources available only to law enforcement. I didn't query his means of finagling access.

"Did you find anything surprising?" I asked.

"I did."

Ryan took a bite of salad. Chewed. Downed a long slug of Moosehead. Twirled a generous helping of pasta.

I watched him.

"This is delicious," he said.

I refused to be baited.

Two more forkfuls, then, "The Massachusetts Department of Vital Statistics has a birth certificate on file for a Melanie Judith Chalmers. Born in Boston on March 22, 1969, the baby is described as a white female. The parents are entered as Verner and Patrice Chalmers."

My butter knife froze in midair.

"A 1986 piece in the *Boston Globe* lists a Melanie Chalmers as one of that year's honor graduates of the Boston Technical High School. In an online version of the yearbook, Melanie's bio states her career goal as biochemist."

I was too stunned to respond.

"Your mouth is open."

I closed it. Opened it to ask, "Is there a student pic?"

"Apparently, Melanie skipped the bothersome senior photo bit."

"Does the bio say where she planned to attend university?"

"No."

"Arlo Murray thought she had a degree. So did Florence Sorg."

"Am I the most talented and beguiling man you've ever laid eyes on?"

I rolled those eyes.

"In the fall of 1986, a Melanie Judith Chalmers enrolled on full scholarship at American University in Washington, D.C. She graduated in 1990 with a BS in biology and was accepted into a graduate program at—"

Ryan slowly and carefully finished his pasta, laid down his fork, and dabbed his lips with his napkin.

"I could hurt you," I said.

"In the fall of 1990, a Melanie Chalmers began graduate studies in molecular biology and genetics at Tufts University."

"That's impressive."

"Sadly, she dropped out after two semesters."

"Poor grades?" I asked.

"Her transcript says otherwise."

I gave that some thought.

"Ella must have been born in 1991. Perhaps the pregnancy forced Melanie to quit. Maybe the demands of motherhood."

"Perhaps the academic disappointment was what left her 'bitter and unhappy.'" Ryan hooked quotes around the two adjectives.

"If she was."

"Murray described her that way. Eisenberg didn't refute it."

Unable to disagree, I let it go.

Instead, I asked, "Did you find anything on Melanie's children, Ella and Lena? Their father's name? Did they have the same father? Did she marry the guy? Guys? Is he still around?"

"Take a deep breath."

I did.

"Tomorrow I'll float more queries for government documents, school registrations, whatever."

"Lena would have been born in 1999, maybe as late as 2000. If it was 2000, Melanie may already have been living in Canada. You found no birth certificate here."

"None. I'll start with Massachusetts and D.C., but Melanie could have gone anywhere after dropping out of Tufts. Not knowing for sure the city or even the state, it may take a while."

We sat in silence for a few moments. I thought about Ryan's findings.

"Didn't Sorg say Melanie worked for an outfit called HGP?"

"Could start with that," Ryan said. "Eat."

I did.

"There's more."

I stopped.

"Verner and Patrice Chalmers died in 1992. Both death certificates bear the same date, and both categorize manner of death as undetermined. An obit in the *Globe* provides no detail concerning the circumstances of their passing."

"That's not uncommon."

"No." I heard an unvoiced *but*. Didn't ask.

"You found her, Ryan. I'm sure of it. Melanie Judith Chalmers must be our Melanie Chalmers. Mélanie Chalamet."

"One bitsy detail I haven't mentioned. Melanie's birth certificate provides her mother's maiden name. Are you ready for it?"

"I'm warning you, bucko."

"Patrice Sorg Chalmers."

"Holy hell! Everything fits."

"Like an Armani suit. Your food's getting cold."

I ate some more linguine, my mind pinwheeling. I returned to Ryan's opening comment.

"You said something surprised you."

"In 2000, the screen fades to black."

"Meaning?" I asked.

"Melanie Chalmers has absolutely no footprint after 2000."

"Nothing?"

"Zero. Zip. Nada. *Rien*. There was no social media back then. Nevertheless, though meager, her early life left a trail. Her birth certificate, her parents' death certificates, record of her high school graduation, the yearbook, the files at American University and Tufts. Once Melanie moved north, it's as if she ceased to exist."

"She did change her name and go underground," I said.

"In today's cyber age, it's almost impossible to disappear completely."

"Melanie's file disappeared from the InovoVax system."

"That it did," Ryan agreed.

I walked toward a building with the letters HGP above the entrance. It was dark. A sense of dread overcame me. As I drew close, doors slowly opened. I tried to turn away, but an unseen force pulled me forward. I tumbled over the threshold and plummeted into a tunnel dark as a crypt. I screamed. No sound left my throat.

I lay encased in a shiny white tube, pinpoints of light twinkling around me. I couldn't move my head. I reached up. My hands were bound at my sides.

"Don't move," a tinny voice commanded.

"Why?"

"You'll ruin everything."

"I want out."

"You know too much."

I struggled to free myself.

The tube's lid flew open.

I was on a shore, squinting and blinking into bright sunlight. Waves crashed against a rocky cliff to my left, receded with a sinuous hissing into the sea to my right. Spotting an irregularity far up the beach, I began running toward it. With each step, the sand closed around my boots. Black boots. Army boots. I leaned into my stride and pumped my arms. My feet dug deeper, but I made no progress.

Hearing a scream, I looked up. A seabird glided on the wind overhead. I tracked its flight. Noticed a figure high up on the cliffside. Dressed like a monk in a long, hooded cape, the figure was painting graffiti. Its incomplete message stretched across three rocks. I read it.

Four letters. CRIS—

The monk's head swiveled my way, the floppy hood concealing all but his eyes. His gaze raked me like a Death Star laser. The sand around my boots began to dissolve. I sank to my knees. My waist. My chest.

I stood beside a morgue cooler. The room was cold, and I was shivering. I opened a compartment. Lena Chalmers was on the gurney, her body naked and fully fleshed.

I heard a meow. Turned. Saw no cat

A corpse lay on an autopsy table behind me. Though frightened, I felt compelled to approach. Took a step.

The corpse sat up. Melanie Chalmers Her nose was gone, her body covered with festering lesions.

I took another step.

Melanie's hand rose. Her fingers were blackened stumps. One pointed at me.

The finger, elongated and spiderlike, snagged my hair and pulled. I screamed and tried to bat it away.

A silhouette stood flanked by two intensely brilliant beams of light. Behind the silhouette, a wall. As I watched, the beams drew together and brightened even more, revealing the silhouette's face.

Ryan!

The beams congealed into one impossibly white-hot oval on Ryan's chest. He staggered back and was pinned to the wall. His face constricted in agony, and his hands clawed the air.

God. Oh, God, no!

I tried to run to Ryan. Was again fixed in place. I looked down. Water gurgled and eddied around my feet.

I called out.

A figure materialized beside Ryan, features oddly clear in the blinding glare.

Arlo Murray.

No! Goddammit, no!

I awoke to find Ryan restraining me with a palm to each shoulder, his features taut with concern.

"Wake up, cupcake."

"Don't call me that." Mind still struggling to reconnect with the topside world.

"Feisty out the door." Ryan's face relaxed. "A good sign."

"I must have been dreaming."

"Ya think?" Ryan's hair was wet, and he wore only a towel. "Nightmare on Elm Street?"

"It wasn't Peter Cottontail's tea party."

"Don't you mean the Mad Hatter?"

"They share the same guest list." Though going for breezy, I still felt shaky.

Perching on the bed, Ryan took both my hands in his and kissed me lightly on the lips. "It wasn't real."

"I know. I think I was aware of that even as I was dreaming. It was just so vivid."

Ryan gently brushed sweat-soaked hair from my face. Waited.

"A car was running you down, Ryan. Just like on Laurier."

"And we saw how that went. I'm indestructible."

"Uh-huh."

"You want to talk about the rest?"

"Maybe later. Sorry to ruin your shower."

"I'd just finished when I heard you shrieking."

"I don't shriek."

"Birdie did a half gainer." Ryan unwrapped the towel to dry his hair. "Stuck the landing nicely."

"Are you trying to distract me?" I asked.

"How am I doing?"

"Hit the road, cowboy."

"You're sure?"

"Happy trails."

I watched him dress in jeans, a long-sleeved waffle tee, leather jacket, and muffler. Moments later, the front door opened, then closed.

Ignoring the issues troubling my id, I yanked on a robe and headed to the kitchen for coffee.

Beyond the window wall, the sky was charcoal all the way to the horizon. Sleet pelted the glass with a steady *tic-tic-tic*.

I phoned the lab. *Skippy damn!* No bones requiring my discerning eye. I could cocoon for the day.

Birdie was already lying belly-up on the table, looking like taxidermy gone wrong. Or roadkill.

I'd just booted my Mac when a message bonged into my mailbox. Katy.

My daughter's unit was heading out on a mission. She couldn't give details. Of course, she couldn't. Not comforting. She was well and looking forward to rotating home. A bit more reassuring.

I was typing a response when my phone did a little "A.M. Radio." I checked caller ID. Claudel.

In my hurry to answer, I upended my coffee. In one fluid move, the cat went vertical, flew from the tabletop, and shot from the room, leaving a trail of brown pawprints in his wake.

I cleaned up the mess, cursing the whole time, then called Claudel back.

"Detective Charbonneau has Docteur Murray under surveillance."

"And?"

"He is not enjoying it."

Claudel was in one of his moods. Pressing him would do no good.

"The subject rose at six this morning and went directly to Inovo-Vax. He likes to drive very fast."

"Did he do anything suspicious?" Unable to remain quiet.

"Before alighting, the gentleman poured a dark liquid onto the asphalt from the car's open door."

"The remains of his coffee."

Claudel paused, to annoy or chastise me.

"Charbonneau observed a broken fog light above the Lexus's right bumper and fresh paint on its left front panel."

I felt my heart spiking.

"He also noted a windshield sticker indicating membership in the Royal St. Lawrence Yacht Club."

"Holy freakin' hell! Murray has a boat. Are you going to arrest him?"

"Based on what, Dr. Brennan? Poor auto maintenance and a fondness for sailing?"

"Melanie and Ella may have been dumped from a boat!"

"Or a bridge, a ramp, a dock, or a cliff."

Claudel was right. I was overreacting. And making a gargantuan leap. I calmed my voice and dragged my thoughts back onto track.

"Didn't SIJ collect paint chips at the bus stop on Laurier? Record skid marks? Get *something* to match to a suspect car?"

"As you may recall, the street was wet from the rain."

"What now?"

"My partner will keep eyes on Murray. I'll visit the Royal St. Lawrence in Dorval."

"Back in 2006, Ryan canvassed every marina and yacht club within fifty miles of the spot the container washed ashore in Saint-Anicet."

"I'm sure he did."

Vislosky was "A.M. Radio's" next announcement.

She opened with, "You still got that book?"

"I—what?"

"The kid's journal."

"Harmony Boatwright's diary?"

"Journal, diary. Whatever."

Crap. I did.

"Yes."

"I need it back in the file."

"When?"

"Yesterday."

Shit.

Before I could respond, Vislosky said, "You're gonna like this."

"What?"

"You ready?"

"Just say it." After Claudel, I wasn't in the mood for suspense.

"I found the hostel where Lena Chalamet and Harmony Boatwright crashed."

"During their visit to Charleston?"

"No. I discovered they'd also done a Grand Canyon tour."

Why was everyone around me turning into a comedian? "When did they stay in Charleston?"

"February of 2018."

"That plays with the date in Harmony's diary."

"It surely does."

"You plan to question the—"

"I surely do."

I briefed Vislosky on Ryan's background info on Melanie Chalmers and on the videotapes given to Lena by her great aunt, Florence Sorg. "The recordings were probably made by Lena's mother."

"Mélanie Chalamet, aka Melanie Chalmers."

I nodded. Realized how pointless that was.

"Claudel just phoned me."

"The Montreal detective who's such a dick."

I told Vislosky about Murray's car and yacht club membership.

"But did this creep have access to boats when your vics vanished back in 2002?"

"I'm sure Claudel will query that."

"If Murray is dirty, why would he wait so long, then kill again in Charleston?"

I had no answer to that.

"We've ID'd our vics, Tonia. Murray might be their killer, or he might not. Either way, we're still clueless about motive. And about the link between Montreal and Charleston."

"Gotta be the Chalamets." Not remarking on my use of her first name.

"Lena was living on the streets when she got the videotapes from Sorg. I'm thinking she might have taken them with her when she went south."

"And that they might still be stashed at that hostel."

"They could nail our perp."

"Or they could be videos of baby's first steps."

There was a very long stretch of very dead air.

"You still there?" I asked.

"I am."

I thought about Nguyen's case. The damn MRI. The tapes. Harmony Boatwright's diary. It was time to migrate again.

"Can you hold off a day on the hostel?" I asked.

"How did I know that was coming?"

32

Wednesday, November 17

Early the next morning, I was winging my way south. Ignoring the howls of my cat. And the scowls of those around me.

I'd been apologetic until the lady beside me in 12E offered to chuck Bird down the loo and the guy in 12F agreed to help. After that, I ceased giving a shit.

Having risen well before dawn, I lacked the energy to attempt any serious work, so I sat back, closed my eyes, and let my mind go where it chose.

It chose the recent trip down nightmare alley.

My dreams fall into one of two categories. Either A, my subconscious is blocking me from completing some seemingly mundane task. Or B, the id boys are rehashing current events, often throwing in macabre twists of their own.

Tuesday night's extravaganza had been a fragmented mirror-in-mirror fun-house affair with one scene cartwheeling crazily into the next. At least, that's how I remembered it. Definitely a selection from drawer B. And rife with Freudian symbolism. Or not.

The army boots stemmed from my worry for Katy. The white tube reflected my lingering anxiety over the aneurysm. Or maybe it was simply a heads-up to schedule an MRI. Not sure the meaning of the tinny voice. *I want out. You know too much.* Sounded like dialogue from a cheesy spy novel.

HGP was Melanie Chalmers's employer after she dropped out of Tufts and before moving to Canada. OK. Fair enough. Melanie and her kids were on my mind. That also explained Lena's cameo in the morgue cooler and her mother's solo on the autopsy table.

I grew drowsy.

Melanie's lesions and eroded fingers? Perhaps a reference to capno? That was a stretch.

The cliff-climbing monk? *Was* he a monk? Why a monk? What was the meaning of his unfinished message? *CRIS*— Christ? Christopher? Melanie's Christopher?

The plane lurched. My head bobbed, and I startled awake. Half awake. Undeterred by the turbulence, my sleepy mind drifted back to the dream.

The vignette with Ryan, though terrifying, was self-explanatory. But why the walk-on by Arlo Murray? *Because the arrogant bastard is guilty*, my lower centers tossed out.

Guilty of what? Murdering Melanie and her daughter? Maybe. But why? Jealousy over Christopher? Who the hell *was* Christopher?

Christopher.

CRISPR.

When spoken aloud, the words sound similar.

Suddenly, my subconscious was fully alert.

Had Sorg overheard Melanie and Murray arguing about CRISPR, not Christopher? The term's presence in Melanie's notes had puzzled Bangoboshe. What was its relevance to vaccine production?

The plane bucked again, and I was wide awake.

Before going to InovoVax, Murray worked at the Whitehead Institute at the MIT Center for Genome Research. I decided to have a quick look-see.

Reaching under the seat, I furtively teased my laptop from the shoulder bag snugged beside the cat carrier. Birdie woke and unleashed a new volley of thunderous protest. 12E gave an audible groan.

After ponying up for Gogo Inflight, I googled "Whitehead Institute" and started with Wikipedia. I know. But I was tired.

The outfit's full name was the Whitehead Institute for Biomedical Research. A line halfway down the entry grabbed my attention. It cited the Center for Genome Research as the single largest contributor to the Human Genome Project.

I'm an eyeball person. Meaning my brain works best with visual input. Like the printed word.

The gray cells snapped a synapse.

HGP.

Human Genome Project.

Is that what Murray did at the Whitehead Institute? Did Melanie go there after dropping out at Tufts? Did she and Murray both work for the Human Genome Project? If so, was that fact significant?

Follow-up snap.

A couple of weeks back, I'd discussed the HGP with Ryan. Why? Right. Sullie Huger had worked there briefly. Probably no big deal. The project was massive, involving researchers from twenty institutions in six countries including France, Germany, Japan, China, the U.K., and the U.S.

MIT was in Cambridge, Massachusetts. Melanie was from Boston, and Tufts was in Medford, Massachusetts. Did Melanie stay close to home after leaving graduate school? If she *had* worked at the Whitehead, it would have been between 1991 and 2000. Did she overlap with Murray?

My fingers flew over the keys.

Just as we were ordered to close our devices, I found the answer.

After dropping Birdie at the annex, I went straight to the MCME.

The chap in the suitcase had been dead a very long time. His skull suggested South Asian ancestry. Tiny drill holes in his bones suggested a lengthy postmortem career as a teaching specimen. His journey to the dumpster would be a job for the cops.

I composed a brief report and headed out. While driving back to the annex, I phoned Vislosky.

"Yo." Her usual.

"Murray lied."

She took a moment to gear in, then, "Chalmers's boss at InovoVax."

"He claimed to barely know Melanie. But they were coworkers for eight years."

"Where?"

"A lab at MIT."

"Doing what?"

"Researching the human genome." I explained the HGP. The Whitehead Institute.

"How do you know they were there at the same time?"

"I found Murray's curriculum vitae online."

"His what?"

"Academic résumé."

"Thank the galloping Lord for egghead egos." A pause, then, "You're positive my older container vic is this Chalamet kid."

"Lena."

"Where are you?"

"Charlotte."

"You've got four hours, then I hit that hostel. My plate's full, and the chance of anything still being there is one in a million."

I blew off scheduling the MRI.

The galloping Lord was kind, and traffic was light. By seven that evening I'd offloaded one ferociously peeved cat, set up his litter box, scribbled a note to Anne, and raced into downtown Charleston.

On the way to the hostel, Vislosky explained how she'd found it. Nothing special, just dogged perseverance and rad hair. She'd called almost every low-end hotel and B&B in the city. Then, bingo, a clerk remembered a kid with a spiky pink do.

Ten minutes after leaving headquarters, Vislosky pulled to the curb outside a three-story frame residence that had definitely seen better days. Perhaps during the Mesolithic era. Narrow along the street, the building ran deep into the lot, a classic Charleston design. Its yellow paint was faded and peeling. Its shutters, once white, were weathered and dingy gray. Some lacked slats; others hung at angles suggesting hinges well past their shelf lives.

As we took in detail grudgingly revealed by the block's single streetlamp, the radio spit static.

A side yard bordered the home's long south-facing wall. Once a garden, the space was now an overgrown tangle of nightshade, chickweed, foxtail, and wild cane.

Overlooking the *jardin* jungle was a second-story balcony enclosed in scrolly black wrought iron. A saggy porch ran below the balcony, two steps up from ground level.

An ornate wood and glass door sat midway along the porch, with a half dozen ratty wicker chairs positioned helter-skelter to either side. Not terribly inviting, given the perpetual shadow cast by neglected magnolias and live oaks overhanging the property.

"Nothing menacing," I said.

"Just creepy as hell."

"Not when you're young and poor. A stay here costs, what? Ninety bucks a night?"

"Forty-two, Wi-Fi and breakfast included, fleas and bedbugs thrown in gratis. I'm sure customers are busting walls to get in."

Vislosky disengaged her seat belt. I did the same. We got out and walked a flagstone path to the side steps and climbed to the entrance. A tiny sign said *Garden Hotel*. A tinier one asked visitors to ring the bell. With a smiley face. Vislosky did. Without one.

"You wantin' to check in?" Tinny, like the voice in my dream.

"Detective Vislosky, Charleston PD. I have some questions about one of your boarders."

"I ain't sure what I do here."

"What you do is open the door."

Locks rattled, and the heavy panel swung inward.

The woman, making a point of blocking the doorway, looked like a house in polyester sweats. Her face was cocoa, her hair black and slicked sideways with a product that made it look waxy. Her plump lips were fire-alarm-red. Hoops the size of pizzas dangled from her ears.

Vislosky badged her. Sweats looked at the shield, back up at us.

"Your name?" Vislosky asked.

"Sondra Tong." Tong's lashes were sharply curled and stiff with mascara.

"You own this place?"

"Uh-uh. I jus' run it."

"For how long?"

"All day."

"How long have you managed the hotel?"

Tong shifted her weight. It was a lot to shift. "'Bout four years. I ain't big on calendars."

Vislosky slapped her forearm. Scratched. "We can do this here, Sondra, let the mosquitoes keep snacking. Or maybe we could talk inside?"

Tong looked confused. When Vislosky moved forward, she stepped back.

We entered a small foyer, most of which Tong filled. A counter paralleled its right wall. Looked like IKEA, modern and jarringly out of place.

Ahead, a narrow staircase curved to a second floor. Wooden banister. Threadbare runner. Beside the staircase, a hallway stretched to the back of the building. Off one side, a dining room, off the other, a parlor, both entered through pocket doors that appeared to be stuck in place. As in the foyer, tarnished brass chandeliers turned every interior an anemic yellow.

Tong led us to the parlor, and we all sat. Vislosky got right to it.

"Two young women stayed here in February of 2018. Lena Chalamet and Harmony Boatwright."

"You the one called?"

"Yes."

"Askin' 'bout the two white girls? One had bodacious hair?"

"Yes."

"Yeah." Nodding slowly. "They was here."

"For how long?"

"I ain't good with calendars."

As Vislosky pumped Tong, I took in what looked like a silent-movie set. Floral paper covered the walls, faded now but once gaudy bright. Lots of carved mahogany pieces. Acres of dark plum fabric. Lamps with tasseled shades, turned on but having little impact. A ratty Persian underfoot, which had long since given up trying to look real.

"Do you have a guest book?" Vislosky was speaking slowly, a teacher to a dull pupil.

"Yeah. We got that."

"Could you get it, please?"

"I don't know if I'm allowed."

"You're allowed."

Crimped brows, then Tong pushed to her feet and lumbered off. Vislosky and I waited.

Time passed. I forced myself not to think about Vislosky's flea and bedbug remark. Didn't fully succeed.

Antsy, I got up and began checking drawers and compartments in sideboards and end tables. Vislosky didn't join in but didn't order me to stop.

Footsteps clumped down the stairs, then a kid with a mullet and pimples passed by in the hall. After slowing to gawk through the open parlor door, he continued on his way, looking like an ad for a posture-control brace.

My illegal search turned up no tapes. I returned to the sofa.

Ten minutes after leaving, Tong was back, a red and gray ledger pressed to her bounteous bosom.

"I called my boss. He says you can't have this."

"If we need to confiscate your register, I'll return with a warrant. For now, I just want to verify that the girls were here."

The red lips pooched out in indecision. Apparently, the boss hadn't ruled on that possibility.

"Or I bring you downtown and we do this at headquarters." Mildly threatening.

Tong handed the ledger to the big bad cop.

Vislosky flipped pages. Not many. Seemed business wasn't brisk at ye olde Garden.

A few more flips, then Vislosky looked to me and nodded.

"Chalamet and Boatwright were here for eight days in February of 2018. Show me their room."

"I'm not 'sposed—"

Vislosky turned the ledger toward Tong and finger-jabbed a notation.

"D Two." Sharp. "Show me."

"No call to be rude."

"I haven't even begun."

Tong led us to a gloomy second-floor dorm with two sets of bunks and two mismatched twin beds. Double-tiered metal lockers lined the rear wall, only one with a padlock.

"Where did they sleep?"

"What boarders choose ain't my bidness."

Arms crossed, feet spread, Tong watched us search. Not a good stance given the tight polyester.

The lockers were empty. Nothing was wedged behind or hidden under either of the bunks. Ditto for the twins.

Vislosky and I stood a moment, eyeing the single beds. The one farthest from the door had a high wooden headboard.

We had the same thought. Vislosky voiced it.

"Let's pull this sucker out."

Easier said than done.

But well worth the effort.

33

Thursday, November 18–Friday, November 19

Behind the headboard was a makeshift hole in the plaster. Tucked in the hole was a plastic-wrapped package.

I dug surgical gloves from my purse and handed them to Vislosky. As I shot video with my phone, she removed and unwrapped the package.

"What's Jean Coutu?" she asked, reading the logo and pronouncing the name Gene Cow-too.

"A pharmacy chain in Quebec."

Inside the bag was a single videocassette tape.

"Jesus, take the wheel!" I'd never seen Vislosky so animated. "This baby goes with me." Side glance to Tong.

Tong started to object. Rethought the impulse and closed her mouth. Stood mute as the rude cop and I hurried down the stairs and out into the night.

Vislosky was silent on the trip downtown. Suited me. I was exhausted from my long day of air and highway travel.

We were turning onto Lockwood when her mobile buzzed. She answered. Listened. Responded curtly, saying she'd be there.

"Goddammit."

"What?" In case the expletive was for my benefit.

283

"Herrin's parking portable morgues outside the hospital. My LT says they need extra security."

"Because?"

"The lookie-loos are getting rowdy."

"Why?"

"They know what's in the reefers."

"Capno cases?"

Vislosky nodded, her faced patterned with neon from nearby store window signs.

"The death count is that high?"

"Through the roof."

"COVID-19 is still a fresh memory, and people are frightened."

"Whatever. It means my ass won't be going home anytime soon."

Approaching headquarters, she spoke again. "I'm guessing the tape was made with some sort of video camera."

"Florence Sorg had a camcorder."

"Pretty common item twenty years ago."

"Sony sold kajillions."

"Sounds like a lot."

"Every proud dad had to capture his adorable progeny."

"Why?"

"To bore his friends."

"Mine didn't."

"Were you adorable?"

"Did Sony make many models?"

"Kajillions."

"Hopefully, the e-geeks can lay hands on the right one."

Anne had left her own scribbled note.

Off to see Josh. He landed a part in a soap, and they're

shooting in Savannah. Back Monday.
Ciao!

I wasn't sure if I was relieved or disappointed.

After feeding Birdie, I grilled a Havarti and Swiss sandwich and warmed a can of tomato soup. Not gourmet, but comfort food appealed.

For diversion, I found the remote and clicked to WCSC, the "Low Country's News Leader." Half-watched while I ate.

A gunman had robbed a Dollar General and shot the clerk. An overturned eighteen-wheeler was causing a traffic mess on I-526. Deputies were looking for a van whose driver was allegedly trying to lure kids. The spike in capno cases was placing a strain on medical resources in Charleston and elsewhere in South Carolina. Columbia, Florence, Georgetown, Greenville, Aiken, Spartanburg.

The station went to a commercial break. A twenty-something with a body-fat index below twelve percent hawked a diet plan guaranteed to change my life. Subway tried to entice me with a deal on the classic foot-long. A gecko urged me to switch insurance carriers.

Then an ad that caused me to go ruler-straight in my chair.

An actor sat at a microscope wearing a lab coat and a look of forty-karat concern. Sullie Huger's company logo hovered above and behind him, a partially uncoiled double helix topped by *GeneFree* in bold green letters.

The screen filled with a tight shot on the would-be scientist's face. Looking right into the camera, he asked a series of rhetorical questions.

"Do you worry about the current pandemic in our state? Do you fear that you or a family member may be susceptible to this menace? That your beloved pet may be threatened? Listen to what the experts are saying."

A white-coated woman appeared, a stethoscope looping her neck. She said a few words about capnocytophaga and explained that immunity to the infection was a matter of genetics. Disturbing im-

ages of capno sufferers and caged dogs scrolled beside her. Then the
original actor reclaimed the spotlight.

"Take no chances. Protect yourself and your loved ones and
reduce unnecessary stress. It's quick and easy to order our kit online.
Send us a swab, and we'll tell you what's in your genes."

The logo expanded to full screen, and a male voiceover gave the
GeneFree web address and a phone number. Both appeared in large
print. Then, "Don't delay! Act today! Blah blah blah!" The usual info-
mercial hard sell.

As I copied the contact information, a gaggle of cells in my lower
centers did their annoying elbow nudge.

What?

The anchor returned with a report on the upcoming Holiday
Festival of Lights at James Island County Park. I'd taken Katy every
Christmas season when she was little. She'd loved the meandering
drive through the electric fantasy-land displays.

I finished my soup, carried my dishes to the sink, then climbed to
my room. Birdie joined me in bed.

So did the vigilant gaggle in my hindbrain. Shifting tactics, the
cells launched their rehash routine.

At last, I knew the names of the container vics on both sides of the
border. And I understood how, in this age of the FBI, RCMP, IAFIS,
CODIS, WWW, and DNA, all four had vanished without leaving a
ripple.

Each had fallen through a different crack in the system. Melanie
and Ella Chalmers/Chalamet had been hiding out as illegals in Canada, using aliases. Harmony Boatwright had lacked any meaningful familial support structure. Ditto Lena Chalamet, who'd bounced
from foster home to foster home and eventually ended up on the
streets.

No one had made an inquiry or raised an alarm. No one had
entered a police station to fill out a form.

All had been murdered, and their killer had gone undetected.

Killers?

Was my gut right? Was that killer Arlo Murray?

If so, what had motivated him?

Melanie Chalmers and Arlo Murray had both worked for the Human Genome Project. Same place, same time, but he'd lied about knowing her. Why?

Sullie Huger had also worked for the HGP. Was that fact relevant? Where had he been employed? Doing what? His expertise was in chemistry and computer systems. Might Huger have useful information concerning Lena or Murray?

Lena had gone to Charleston apparently pursuing a lead concerning her mother. Harmony had met her there.

Had Murray traveled south to strike again a decade and a half after killing Melanie and Ella in Montreal?

Unified Theory jarred me awake.

The French doors showed a limbo mix of grays and pinks, a sky not finished with dawn but not quite ready for morning.

I fumbled for my phone.

Seeing Ryan's name lifted my spirits. Hearing his voice did not.

"There was an explosion at InovoVax last night." Brisk and clipped. "Murray may have been inside the building."

"Seriously?"

"A security guard thinks he saw him go in around ten, never saw him come out. The place blew around midnight."

I was too stunned to answer.

"The fire was massive. When the rubble cools, firefighters will go in to search for bodies."

"Sonofabitch."

"Well put."

"What caused the explosion?"

"The arson boys suspect a bomb."

"Sonofa—"

"Yeah."

"Keep me looped in?"

"Like you kept me looped in on your arrival last night?" Note of reproach.

"Sorry."

"Roger that."

I spent the next few hours engaged in mundane tasks. Groceries at the Harris Teeter. Flounder at Simmons Seafood. Scheduling the damn MRI. Then I pounded out three miles on the beach. Took a very long shower.

My mobile sang again at eleven. I'd changed to War. "All Day Music."

Caller ID suggested a "maybe" that surprised me. The name wasn't in my contacts. How did the bloody phone know?

"Good morning, Dr. Bangoboshe."

"Good morning, Dr. Brennan. Is this a good time?"

"Of course."

"I took another look at that second page of notes. The one with the coded entries."

"Yes?"

"I think each line incorporates a date and a batch number."

I didn't respond.

"Every batch of vaccine is numbered."

"Of course."

I waited.

"That's all. The rest meant nothing to me."

"This is very helpful."

"I doubt it's anything worrying. Batch numbers make sense, given your subject's interest in vaccine production."

"Thank you so much for taking the time."

"My pleasure."

I sat a while contemplating the significance of Bangoboshe's insight.

Ryan called again at one.

"*Les pompiers* retrieved a body." When exhausted, or agitated, Ryan often jumbles French and English. I knew he meant firefighters.

"Badly burned?"

"A crisper."

I waited.

"It's Murray."

"Beyond a doubt?"

"LaManche rousted a forensic dentist. She confirmed ID."

"Any theory on the cause of the explosion?"

"The arson boys are finding traces of explosives. I forget which ones."

"They're thinking IED?"

"They're not sharing their thinking with me."

"Is Murray being viewed as a victim or as a suspect?"

"Same answer."

"Talk to Claudel?"

"My next call."

Again, I sat pondering the significance of Ryan's news. Hadn't worked with Bangoboshe. Didn't work now.

Frustrated, I glanced through the living room toward the floor-to-ceiling glass wall. Outside, a cloudless blue dome wrapped the island and the sea beyond, and a warm autumn sun sparked pinpoints of radiance off the zen-calm waves.

The window was similar to that in the Montreal condo, the views like scenes from different planets.

I got iced tea from the fridge and went out onto the deck. As on the plane, I closed my eyes and let my thoughts roam free, the afternoon rays warm my face.

They roamed among newly acquired data bytes.

The explosion at InovoVax. Ryan's crisper, Arlo Murray. CRISPR. The tape left at the hostel by Harmony and Lena. Capnocytophaga. HGP. The television ad for GeneFree.

My eyes flew open.

Bytes were colliding in my brain.

34

Sullie Huger had worked for the Human Genome Project. So had Arlo Murray. And Melanie Chalmers.

More relevant than I thought?

I dug out my notes. Huger went to work for the HGP immediately after getting his first doctorate at UNC in '90, left in '95 to take a position with GlaxoSmithKline.

So Huger, Murray, and Chalmers *were* all with the HGP at the same time. Murray and Chalmers were at MIT. Was Huger there also?

I hit my laptop. Found no answer.

Almost immediately, another data byte clicked in, triggering an avalanche of new questions.

Florence Sorg said a "hotshot colleague" got Melanie her job at InovoVax. Was Huger that hotshot? Had he also arranged a position for Murray?

More bytes.

The genetic genealogist determined that Sullie Huger and Harmony Boatwright were distant cousins.

Had Harmony and Lena come to Charleston to see Huger?

I hopped back online and found an address. God bless the internet.

Quick call to Vislosky. Voice mail. I left a brief message. It was time for some follow-up.

The Maybank Highway is a schizoid two-lane meandering across James, Johns, and Wadmalaw Islands. Parts are home to gas stations, strip malls, and fast-food joints. Parts are residential. Parts are unrelentingly rural.

Huger's business was located on one of James Island's busier commercial stretches. Set off from the pavement by Palmetto palms and artificial turf impersonating grass, the brick three-story structure could have been anything—a medical plaza, an office building, a mail order center. No sign hinted at the nature of the enterprise housed within.

I added my car to a half dozen others parked on a rectangle of crushed oyster shells and entered through the unmarked glass door. The lobby was small, with a speckled tile floor waxed to a gleam, a single elevator to the right, and a glass and steel A-frame desk to the left.

The lady at the desk had silver hair swept high and fixed with copious spray. Harry Potter glasses hung from a chain around her neck. Hearing the door, she glanced up from filing one lilac nail.

"Good afternoon," I added to be sociable. "It's so beautiful out today."

"Hasn't the good Lord blessed us with the most glorious weather?" The drawl was so thick you could have poured it over Dixie Bell ice cream.

"I'm here to see Dr. Huger." Wording chosen to imply a prearranged meeting.

Face furrowing into gullies of distress, Dixie Bell set down her emery board, slipped on the Harry Potters, and began tapping keys. "Do you have an appointment?"

"I don't." Smiling so apologetically my face hurt. "But I was hoping—"

A hand flew to Dixie Bell's chest. "Oh, my zip-a-dee-doo-dah! You scared the tar out of me. I thought I'd made a boo-boo."

"Perhaps I—"

"I'm sorry. But Dr. Huger is away for a few days."

Crap. I said nothing.

"Perhaps I can be of help?" Eyes enormous behind the thick round lenses.

"My name is Temperance Brennan." I crossed to the desk.

Dixie Bell grabbed a plastic bottle, sprayed both her palms, wiped each with a Kleenex.

"A girl can never be too careful."

"Never," I agreed.

"Abilene Monger." One sanitized hand shot my way. "Very pleased."

"Have you worked here long, Abilene?" We shook, her grip as strong as the discarded tissue.

"Since before Jesus raised up Lazarus." Not quite a giggle but close.

"This is a little embarrassing," I said, going hard for embarrassed.

"Oh, darlin'. What is it?"

"I'm looking for my niece."

"She's missing?"

I nodded. "For a while now. I think she and a friend may have come here a few years ago. She had short dark hair streaked pink. Her friend was quite tall."

"The pink porcupine!"

"I'm sorry?"

"I make up rhymes and jingles to help my visual recall. It's a memory trick I learned on *Oprah*. Mnemonics."

"I do that all the time."

"I use it for faces and cars and things, not so much for voices or conversations. I have what doctors call an echoic memory. Ever heard of that?"

I shook my head.

"I hear a speech or a song or such, I can remember every single word. I'm so good at it a psychologist studied me back in high school."

"I'm impressed."

"So was he. Sit your sweet self down." Indicating one of two gray velvet armchairs facing the desk.

I sat.

"Her hair. It was all spiky. Like a porcupine. And peony-pink."

"Very clever." Tone absolutely neutral, though my pulse was humming.

"Do you think the pink porcupine was your niece?"

I pulled the Shady Sam's pic from my purse and laid it on the glass. Monger repositioned the Harry Potters, leaned forward, and studied the girl seated below the stage.

"Yes, ma'am," she said finally. "What's the poor lamb's name?"

"Harmony."

"How utterly charming."

"Thank you."

"What's the child doing in a bar?"

"It's a long story."

Reproachful pause. Then, "Your niece and her friend were working on a science project for school. They hadn't called ahead, but Dr. Huger very graciously agreed to see them. I was in his office catching up on filing, so I overheard most of what was said. Good gracious, I hate filing. That's why I let it pile up."

"What was their project?"

"I'm not totally clear on that. But they had lots of questions about genomes and DNA sequencing and genetic testing and such. And about GeneFree, of course."

Monger stopped talking, distracted by the unfinished nail.

"Anything else?" I encouraged.

"They asked about pharmaceutical manufacturing. They knew that Dr. Huger had worked in that industry. They'd certainly done research, bless their hearts. They were particularly interested in vaccines. How they're made. How they're tested. Quality control, that sort of thing. They asked about a process called mRNA. I've no idea what that is."

The cells in my id sat up. *Huh?*

Monger's brows dipped toward her nasal bridge.

"Yes?" I urged.

"They also asked about viruses. I found that curious, since it's not Dr. Huger's bailiwick. But about then, I completed my chore and left the room. Are y'all worried your niece may have stumbled upon trouble?"

"I hope not."

"It's a dangerous world out there."

"It is. Did Harmony mention a family connection to Dr. Huger?"

Monger's brows now shot up in surprise. "What a very strange question."

"I know." Cursing myself for posing it so bluntly. "I'm just at a loss for what my niece's thinking might have been."

Monger shook her head firmly, sending the chains swinging to either side of her face. "I'd most assuredly have remembered her asking about that. As far as I know, the poor man has no kin at all."

"Do you know when Dr. Huger will return?"

"I do not. This trip was last-minute and not on his schedule." Miffed?

"Is that unusual?"

"Not really."

"Do you know where he went?"

"I do not."

I dug a card from my purse and handed it to her. She studied it.

"Charlotte, eh? Where y'all staying while here in Charleston?"

I told her.

"I love, love, *love* Isle of Palms." Breathy with delight. "Where abouts on the island?"

I told her, in vague terms.

"Not that absolutely gorgeous house with the little spiral staircase going up to the roof?"

"Mm." Apparently, my terms weren't vague enough.

"When I go to the beach out there, I always take a spin around to check out the homes. That one is my tip-top favorite."

I thanked her for the compliment and split.

While crunching across the oyster shells, I dialed Ryan. He answered as I was unlocking my car. Without any preamble, I shared what I'd just learned from Abilene Monger.

A moment of stunned nothing came from his end. Or maybe he was distracted. Either way, I filled the silence.

"Harmony and Lena met with Sullie Huger."

"The GeneFree guy."

"Yes."

"Harmony's distant cousin?"

"According to the genetic genealogist."

"They were asking about his DTC DNA-testing business?"

"Yes. But they also had questions about vaccines and viruses and pharmaceutical production. The school science project was obviously a cover story. Why do you suppose they were interested in those topics? Why do you suppose they were interested in Huger?"

"Lena's mother worked for a pharmaceutical company. Maybe they were just sniffing out that lead?"

"Why go to Huger?"

"Hit up a relative?"

"Monger said a family connection was never mentioned."

"She also said the girls had obviously done their research. Maybe they stumbled on the GeneFree website, saw that Huger operated out of Charleston, figured he'd be a good source."

"Maybe." I didn't really buy it. Lot of hassle involved. Travel to Charleston in the hope of meeting him without an appointment. And there was the suspicious coincidence of Harmony and Huger being related, even if distantly.

After a brief pause, "Claudel's been busting ass."

"On his charm-school application?"

"He's not that bad."

I said nothing.

"Claudel's been pursuing the yacht club lead. Turns out some marinas are inordinately fond of record keeping."

I waited.

"Murray joined the Royal St. Lawrence Yacht Club in 2009. From then until 2012, he docked a 2006 Wellcraft Scarab Sport there."

"That's a boat."

"A fast one. In 2012, he replaced the used Scarab with a spanking-new Fountain 42 Lightning."

"Atmospheric voltage sounds faster than a bug."

"What?"

"A scarab is a beetle. Lightning implies—"

"Your thought processes never cease to amaze me. In 2018, Murray upgraded to a 2016 Cigarette Maximus 45."

"Buying an older boat is an upgrade?"

"That Cigarette would leave any Scarab or Fountain in the dust. Spray. Probably cost him half a mil."

"Does he still have it?"

"He does. Did."

"What about back in 2002? That's the significant time frame."

"There's no record of Murray owning a boat back then."

"Did Claudel check—"

"Everywhere."

"Your voice tells me that's not the end of the story."

"Claudel dropped by the Royal St. Lawrence and found an old-timer who's very free with the gab. Balsé Piché. Goes by Ballsey. Ballsey, it turns out, allows short-term rental of his watercraft. Has for years."

"And Ballsey keeps inordinately good records?"

"Am I the most beguiling and—"

"What did Ballsey tell Claudel?"

"Ballsey leased his eighteen-foot Ranger Cherokee to one A. Murray from July 28 through August 4, 2002."

"Precisely when Melanie and Ella went missing!" Almost a shriek.

"Reel it in, honeybear."

"Don't call me that." Deep breath. "Could Murray have gone by boat from Dorval to where that container showed up in Saint-Anicet?"

"Yes. But it would have been a bitch of a journey, west along the Saint Lawrence River, through the Beauharnois locks, then along the Beauharnois canal for about fifteen miles. The canal has two lift bridges—"

"Pont Saint-Louis-de-Gonzague and Pont Laroque."

"Very good, captain."

"I like maps."

"Past the bridges, he'd have continued west into Lac Saint-François, which is actually just a widening of the river. A trip of about thirty miles in all."

I'd started to comment when Ryan added, "But he didn't do that."

"He didn't?"

"In 2002, Ballsey belonged to the Valleyfield Yacht Club."

"That's on Lac Saint-François, right up the shore from Saint-Anicet. But you canvassed every marina and yacht club in the area back then. Those rental dates would have raised a flag."

"Ballsey has a cottage on Lac Saint-François. With a dock."

"Where he kept the Cherokee. Private rental, private records."

"Voilà."

"Murray did it, Ryan. He killed Melanie and her daughter."

"It plays."

"Like a hymn on Sunday. But why?"

Ryan offered no suggestion.

"What's the thinking on the explosion at InovoVax?" I shifted topics. But not much.

"Some douche nozzle blew the place sky-high."

"Why was Murray there in the middle of the night?"

"Eisenberg said that was his habit."

"But why?"

Ryan started to reply. I cut him off.

"My guess is he was involved in something shady. Skimming? Cooking the books? Jacking with production? Stealing drugs? Maybe he was out there trying to cover his ass. Maybe he'd planned to set a fire, destroy records or data or whatever. Maybe things went south, and boom!"

I was on a roll.

"Maybe," I continued, "that's the reason Murray killed Melanie. Maybe she'd discovered what he was up to and had threatened to expose him. Maybe that's what her notes were all about. But why her daughter?"

"Deep inhale."

"You sound like a masseuse."

The oxygen intake helped some.

Not for long.

Way too many maybes. Way too much speculation.

35

My mind spent the drive back to Anne's spinning those maybes. Mixing them with unexplained references and unanswered questions.

Turning from the connector onto IOP, the mental turbulence ran aground on two specific items. A name popped to the foreground.

Off to my right, the late-afternoon sun was tinting the marsh and the waterway tangerine. I checked the time: 4:37 p.m. Not too late, I hoped.

I arrived at Anne's house, rushed inside, and dug my mobile, a pen, and a tablet from my shoulder bag. After locating a number recently added to my contacts, I dialed.

"Alika Bangoboshe." The flute.

"It's Temperance Brennan. Tempe. I hope I haven't caught you at a bad time?"

"Not at all. I am grading exams."

"I don't want—"

"I am ready for a break."

I liked this woman.

"I wondered if I could roll a few more questions by you."

"Of course."

"When we last spoke about the materials that I sent, you said the presence of the term *CRISPR* surprised you."

"Given that the notations appeared to focus on vaccine production."

"It's my understanding that CRISPR is a gene-editing tool."

"That's correct. The acronym stands for clustered regularly interspaced short palindromic repeats." When I didn't respond, she added, "Repeats of genetic information."

"Right."

"The full name is actually CRISPR/Cas9. Emmanuelle Charpentier and Jennifer Doudna were awarded the Nobel Prize in chemistry last year for their work with it. Two women. Isn't that absolutely marvelous?"

"It definitely is. Can you tell me how it works?"

As Bangoboshe elaborated, I scrawled like mad. When she paused, I summarized what I'd written, leaving out the technical bits.

"So Cas9 acts as a molecular scissors to snip a DNA strand at a precise location."

"Yes."

"Snip it for what purpose?"

"To delete a segment, perhaps to insert a new gene. Gods above, my colleagues would be appalled at my oversimplification." The flute whooped in laughter. Made me think of the clarinet glissando at the opening of Gershwin's *Rhapsody in Blue*.

"So CRISPR/Cas9 is basically a genetic cut-and-paste technique," I said.

"I suppose you could view it that way."

"Is it used for people?"

"The first human study took place in 2016 in a clinical trial at China's Sichuan University. So the application of CRISPR/Cas9 to humans is relatively new."

"I assume its primary function is to fix defects and cure disease?"

"Scientists are exploring the use of CRISPR/Cas9 in correcting a wide variety of conditions, including single-gene disorders like cystic fibrosis, hemophilia, and sickle cell. The technique also holds promise for the treatment and prevention of more complex ailments such as cancer, heart disease, mental illness, and human immunodeficiency virus, HIV."

"Didn't I read an article not long ago about a doctor in China altering the genomes of unborn babies?"

"He Jiankui." Coated with disdain. "He revealed at a conference in Hong Kong in 2018 that he'd created the world's first genetically edited infants—twin girls. The announcement sent the scientific community into an uproar. Exactly the effect Dr. He wanted."

"I'm sensing you don't approve."

"He and his colleagues violated internationally agreed-upon rules and crossed a line on medical ethics. Their goal is fame and fortune."

"What did they do, exactly?"

"He used the CRISPR/Cas9 technique to disable a gene called CCR_5. CCR_5 is used to make a protein needed by HIV to enter cells."

"He and his colleagues created babies immune to HIV? Why is that so bad?"

"The subject is so very complicated." The flute paused, I assumed to simplify for my benefit. "Most changes introduced via genome-editing technologies such as CRISPR/Cas9 are limited to somatic cells. Do you understa—"

"Cells other than egg or sperm."

"Correct. Changes in somatic cells affect only certain tissues in an individual and are not passed from one generation to the next. Not so with alterations made to genes in egg or sperm cells or in the genes of an embryo. Those alterations *could* be passed to future generations. So making such changes prompts serious ethical questions, including whether it's permissible to enhance normal human traits."

"Things like eye color, height, intelligence."

"Exactly. Based on ethical as well as safety concerns, cell and embryo genome editing are currently illegal in many countries. Some governments, including that of the United States, have banned such work, fearing its misuse to create designer babies."

"What happened to He?"

"A Chinese court sentenced him and two of his coworkers to prison time and heavy fines."

I glanced at my tablet. Put a check beside CRISPR.

"Can you explain the relevance of mRNA to vaccine manufacture?" The term used by Abilene Monger. The term that had roused the diligent cells in my hindbrain.

After a pause, "We've discussed traditional production methods."

"Egg-based, cell-based, and recombinant."

"Unfortunately, those approaches have not been as effective as hoped against rapidly evolving pathogens like influenza or against emerging disease threats such as Ebola or Zika viruses. Some researchers believe mRNA vaccines may prove superior."

"How so?"

"By introducing an mRNA sequence—"

"Messenger RNA. A molecule that tells cells what to build."

Bangoboshe ignored my interruption.

"Before injection, the mRNA is coated in lipid nanoparticles that allow the molecule to gain access to the interior of the recipient's cells. Once inside, the mRNA codes for a disease-specific antigen."

"A protein used by the pathogen to cause disease." I knew I should shut up and listen, but I wanted to be sure I understood. "The idea being that the recipient's immune system will recognize the protein and begin setting up a defense."

"Yes. As with its counterparts, the mRNA vaccine enables the body to mimic an infection and elicit an immune response without causing actual disease."

"What's the advantage?"

"Quicker, cheaper, safer. So the proponents claim."

"Is the technique in use now?"

"Several are in the pipeline for FDA approval. And, of course, there is the situation with the COVID vaccine."

I juggled everything Bangoboshe had said. Not sure what she did during the gap. Then, "This has been enormously helpful, Dr. Bangoboshe."

"Now it's back to grading for me. Would that my students were as keen as you. Or as apt."

"Thanks so much for your time."

"You are most welcome."

Feeling keen and apt, I disconnected.

The sun had wrapped up its cycle, leaving the room in shadow. I was turning on lights when my phone sang a few bars about all day music.

The screen showed only an unfamiliar number. I was about to hit ignore when something caused me to hesitate. For some reason, I accepted the call.

"Temperance Brennan."

"It's Abilene. Abilene Monger. I work for Dr. Huger."

"Of course, Abilene. How nice to hear from you." Not sure that it would be.

"I, well, you said any little thing could be useful." In case she wasn't being clear, she added, "In finding your niece, I mean."

"Yes."

"I probably shouldn't be talking to you. Could get me fired. But, well, your niece seemed like such a sweet little girl. It's been tearing me up thinking about her lost somewhere and maybe needing help. I read all these dreadful stories about sex trafficking and such."

I waited for her to go on. She didn't.

"I promise anything you say will stay between us," I encouraged.

"I consulted my pastor, and he said I should phone you."

"You've thought of something else the girls said?"

"They asked about a Canadian pharmaceutical company."

"Do you recall which one?"

"In over jacks."

I was lost.

"InovoVax. Do you hear the rhyme? It makes sense to me because I play poker."

"I do. Very clever."

Several seconds passed. In the silence, I feared she might hear the banging of my heart.

"But I must be honest," Abilene said at last. "I made up the rhyme because I also saw the name in print."

"In print."

"Well, in pixels or whatever. On caller ID."

"Someone at InovoVax phoned someone at GeneFree?"

"Many times."

"Do you know who?"

I heard a soft clicking. Pictured Abilene shaking her head, the swinging eyeglass chains connecting with the phone.

"Good Lord, that was a knuckle-brained move. I was wagging my noggin, but you can't see me."

"You don't know who called?"

"With the new system, the party comes up on my screen, then the call rolls automatically to the proper extension."

"When was the last time you noted a call from InovoVax?"

"Earlier this week."

"Would the number remain in the system?"

"Huh. Mighty fine question. No reason I can't have a little look-see." I heard keys click. A lot of them.

"Yes. Here it is. Oh, my. With all those zeros, I'm sure it must be the number for the main switchboard."

"Can you dial it?"

She did. It was. A mechanical voice apologized that InovoVax was closed for the day, instructed that messages could be left only on individual extensions.

"It's after five," Abilene said. "Still, doesn't that just suck pickles?"

"It does. Do you know who the caller was trying to reach?"

"Nope. I used to make every outgoing connection and take every incoming message. Now it's all autodial and voice mail. Before long, I'll lose my job to Roxie the Robot. I swear, the world's going to hell in a hand basket. Soon folks won't engage in even the tiniest smidgen of personal interaction."

After listening to further lamentations and emitting a series of sympathetic sounds, I thanked Abilene and disconnected.

I sat in the dark, adrenaline firing through me like shot from a twelve-gauge. Fresh questions swirling.

Other than Lena, the calls from InovoVax to GeneFree were the first concrete tie between Montreal and Charleston. What was their purpose?

Was Sullie Huger in contact with someone at the pharmaceutical company in Laval? Arlo Murray?

Huger and Murray were employed by the HGP at the same time. Had they met at MIT?

Huger was the more senior of the two scientists. Had he arranged for Murray's position at InovoVax?

Mélanie Chalamet/Melanie Chalmers was with the HGP at MIT. Was Huger or Murray the "hotshot colleague" who'd gotten her hired at InovoVax?

Lena went to Murray to gain information about her mother and sister. He'd shut down her efforts. Had Lena then approached Huger?

Was Huger involved in Murray's misconduct at InovoVax? What *was* that misconduct? Had Mélanie Chalamet/Melanie Chalmers discovered what Murray was up to? Were she and Ella murdered because of that discovery? Silenced by bullets?

Fired by whom?

Did that same shooter kill Lena and Harmony fifteen years later? Were they getting too close to the same secret?

Silence hummed around me. Suddenly, Anne's house seemed very big. And very unpeopled.

I opened the glass doors and stepped onto the deck. *Note to self: remind Anne that the lock still doesn't engage properly.*

Out beyond the aqua glow of the pool, the tide was high and boisterously slamming the beach. Gulls were engaged in heated conversation. Though normally an effective tranq, the Low Country concert failed to calm.

Closing the panels behind me, I moved to the kitchen and turned on the tiny countertop TV. A local news channel came to life. Whatever. At that moment, talking heads trumped no company at all.

I was opening a Kraft dinner when one of the heads snagged my attention. A familiar voice. I turned.

The actor-scientist was again hawking GeneFree, his expression sincere as a prayer-meeting preacher's.

While I listened to the pitch, several flyaway bytes collided in my brain, casting off the first murky particles of an idea.

Ah, Jesus.

I felt a sudden coldness at the base of my skull.

No way.

But the theory would explain so much.

I guzzled my mac and cheese and opened my laptop, aware that it would be an internet night.

Unaware of the horror lying in wait.

36

Vaccines. Viruses. CRISPR. mRNA. GeneFree. InovoVax. Murray. Huger. Chalamet/Chalmers.

I started with GeneFree.

Huger's first online venture launched in August 1999. Named GeneMe, the service relied on Y-chromosome DNA, and, since that part of the genome is passed only from father to son, was limited mostly to paternity testing. Eventually, GeneMe added mitochondrial DNA, carried by both males and females. Since mtDNA is passed only from mother to offspring, its testing allowed tracing through female lines.

By 2000, GeneMe's capabilities had expanded. Users could order DNA profiles, enter results from other testing companies, search the site's DNA database, create online family trees, and connect with relatives. No ancestry, yet.

Huger charged nothing for a GeneMe account.

That puzzled me. Was free access a public service? If not, how did he make money?

I quickly found the answer. GeneMe offered online consultations to help customers understand their test results. For a fee.

In October 2006, GeneMe.com acquired GlobalGeneLink.com,

307

a rival company located in Provo, Utah. GGL's genealogy database was large, allowing GeneMe to expand into the area of multigenerational ancestry tracing. Huger shut down GeneMe and relaunched as GeneFree. From then on, users had to pony up for access to services.

Ironic, I thought. Given the new name.

In April 2018, GeneFree announced that it was in talks to acquire a Cincinnati-based company called Rasmussen Genetic Ancestry Foundation. RGAF had three elements that appealed to Huger: an advanced DNA-testing capability, an immense repository of genealogy data, and a sophisticated media-sharing strategy.

RGAF.com closed on July 1, 2018, and its assets were transferred to GeneFree.com. GeneFree could now perform SNP whole-genome testing, and it owned a monstrous database.

The date triggered another cerebral collision.

Holy freaking crap!

Was that it? Had Lena and Harmony unearthed dirt that would have jeopardized the GeneFree acquisition of RGAF?

The timing fit. The girls vanished in February 2018.

The realization sparked a fusillade of new questions.

Was the girls' dirt the same dirt Lena's mother had discovered?

Was that dirt damaging enough to trigger four murders?

What was the dirt?

Remembering the old adage—follow the money—I logged on to GeneFree.com. The site's home page featured side-by-side smiling families, one in vivid color with Mom, Dad, Junior, and Sis in modern dress, one in sepia tones showing Mama, Papa, and six young-uns in nineteenth-century garb. Reminded me of the portrait of Polly Beecroft's grandmother and great-aunt.

Above the photos, tabs offered choices: *Biological Parentage. DNA. Genealogy. Health.*

Below the tabs, a pulsating red headline warned of the dangers of capnocytophaga. Below the headline, text stated that immunity to capno was genetically determined and that GeneFree could provide diagnostics and thus peace of mind.

A link took me to a page dedicated to capno. For a hefty price, I could obtain a specialized DNA-testing kit, a personalized health report, and support from medical and genetic-counseling resources.

I returned to the home page and took a whirl through the rest of the site. Was constantly bombarded by sidebar and pop-up ads linking to online sources for health foods and homeopathic remedies and to pages for those whose DNA indicated they were capno-vulnerable.

I was still whirling when Ryan phoned. I briefed him on the calls connecting the switchboard at InovoVax with the GeneFree offices, on Abilene Monger's account of Lena and Harmony's visit with Huger, and on my visit to GeneFree.com. I avoided mention of my theory, still in the embryonic scattered-particle stage.

"How much profit could there be in testing spit and selling hemp?" I asked, as much to myself as to him.

"Ask Vislosky to pull GeneFree's financials? Maybe try for Huger's tax returns?"

"Good idea."

"Not likely she'll get them without a warrant."

"I can feel it in my gut, Ryan. The calls were between Arlo Murray and Sullie Huger. I know there's a connection between those two."

"The lady wins a Kewpie doll!" Faux exultation.

"What does that mean?"

"Claudel's been on a roll."

"What's he got?"

"Raging heartburn, I suspect. The guy looks like he hasn't slept in days."

"What did he find?" Enunciating each word.

"I don't want to steal Claudel's thunder."

"No issue. He has plenty to spare."

"He'll phone you shortly."

"Ryan, I'd rather you—"

"Patience, buttercup."

"Don't call me that." Overly theatrical sigh. "In the meantime, will you do me a favor?"

"Anything."

"Can you find out if Huger has traveled to Canada recently?"

"*Aucun problème.* Oh, and one other development. SIJ dug a mobile phone from the debris at InovoVax."

"Wow."

"They think the explosion blasted it through a window out onto the grass."

"Flukey good luck."

"That, plus the thing had a metal case, a screen protector, and an impact band."

"It's Murray's?"

"That's the thinking. Who leaves their mobile at the office overnight?"

"Does it still work?"

"Can't answer that."

"Can the e-geeks get into it?"

"Or that."

"Ryan, can't you just tell me what Claud—"

Call-waiting beeped.

"Never mind. The sleepless wonder is on the line now."

"*Je t'aime, ma chère.*"

"I love you, too."

"Ciao."

"Ciao."

I disconnected from Ryan and answered the incoming call.

"*Bonsoir, détective.*"

Claudel wasted no time on pleasantries.

"I went to InovoVax and found an employee who had been with the company since the gray dawn of history. A man quite aggrieved at having been passed over for the position of director. A man very free with his views concerning the boss."

A huskiness in Claudel's voice attested to the exhaustion Ryan had mentioned.

"It is a long and decidedly tedious story, the bottom line being this: the man confirmed that around 2000, Dr. Aubrey Sullivan Huger arranged for the hiring of Dr. Arlo Murray and Mademoiselle Mélanie Chalamet."

"How?" I asked. "Why?"

"The gentleman was vague on those points. Apparently, Huger knew someone at InovoVax. And it helped that Chalamet spoke French."

I briefed Claudel as I had Ryan. He listened without interrupting, then, "I must be off."

And he was.

I sat frozen, brain integrating new bytes. Particles whipping like electrons circling a nucleus.

Ten minutes, then I snapped to and dialed Vislosky. Doubted she'd pick up after hours.

I was wrong.

"You're like a hound on a T-bone."

"Thanks," I said.

I shared everything I'd told Ryan and everything he and Claudel had told me since Vislosky and I had last talked, ending with Ryan's suggestion about Huger's financials.

"Dig into his personal finances and those of his online companies?"

"Yes."

"That would require a warrant. And *that* would require probable cause."

"You're creative."

"Not that creative."

"I know Huger's involved in all this."

"All what?"

"This whole cock-up."

"Based on what?"

"My gut."

"Problem solved. That should sway any judge."

"Can you at least try?"

"Not without something more than your innards."

Silence hummed across the line.

"Why did you call my investigation a cock-up?" Vislosky finally asked.

"Clusterfuck wasn't strong enough."

Again, I was treated to dead air.

Quick shower, then I thumbed off my ringer and crawled into bed. Birdie was already there.

"Up for some late-breaking news?" Knowing I was still too agitated to sleep.

The cat was good with it.

I turned on CNN. Don Lemon was discussing yet another congressman indicted for yet another form of misconduct. Bored, I grabbed my phone and started scrolling through Twitter. Learned it was National Princess Day.

I was wondering the whereabouts of my tiara—yeah, I have one—when Lemon's next story snapped my eyes back to the screen.

South Carolina's capno crisis was making the national news. Symptoms. Cause. Morbidity and mortality rates. Strained resources. CDC. Herrin was interviewed standing beside one of her portable morgue units. It sounded like COVID all over again.

"Why do you suppose this is just now entering their radar?" I asked the cat. "The outbreak seemed too limited in scope?" I recalled the piece I'd heard on the local NPR station more than a month earlier. "Or has there been national coverage that we missed?"

I was waiting for Birdie's answer when the device buzzed in my hand. I answered. Why not? I'd only handled a bazillion calls that day.

"I may have a clusterfuck breaker."

I offered no comment on Vislosky's sarcasm.

"Huger and his lawyers spent the early months of 2018 finalizing terms for the sale of GeneFree to an outfit called Universal Genomics."

"I've heard of them. They're huge."

"Would've been megabucks if the deal went through."

"How mega?"

"Seven zeros mega. To the left of the decimal."

"Would have?"

"Negotiations fell apart sometime in the fall of 2018 or early winter of 2019."

"Why?"

"My source wasn't privy to that detail."

We both considered the implications.

"So the stakes were even higher than I thought." Stream of consciousness, out loud. "Huger acquires RGAF, hoping to cash in with GeneFree's sale to Universal Genomics. Lena and Harmony show up, threatening to put the deal in jeopardy. Huger sees the golden wad slipping through his fingers, panics, and kills them."

Vislosky didn't agree or disagree.

"What do you suppose they had on him?"

"I don't know." Stony. "But I'm going to net this fucker and drag his ass to the bag."

"Monger said he was out of town."

"She say when he's due back?"

"No. I've asked Ryan to see if Huger entered Canada recently."

"You're thinking the prick might also be good for Murray?"

"I don't know what I think."

"By the way, the e-nerds got into that tape we found at the hostel. Most of the footage was toast, but they managed to salvage and digitize parts."

"Was the recording made by Melanie Chalmers?"

"Yeah. I had them transfer a copy onto a thumb drive. I want you to take a look at it."

That surprised me. "Of course."

"I'll be in Mount Pleasant tomorrow."

That also surprised me, since the town has its own police department.

"There's a protest at city hall because of this capno crap. I'm doing freakin' crowd control. You're on IOP, right?"

"Yes."

"You know the Sea Biscuit?"

"I do."

"Meet me at noon?"

"I'll be there."

Vislosky disconnected.

After killing the light and the TV, I lay back and closed my eyes. Birdie molded his body to my rib cage.

The ocean boomed its relentless rhythm, muted by the glass. The empty house hummed hollow around me.

Images danced on the backs of my lids, specters raised by my incipient theory.

It's impossible. No one could be that evil.

I rolled to my side.

The cat relocated.

I punched the pillow. Rolled to my other side.

Tomorrow I'd be viewing what may have been Melanie Chalmers's final communiqué.

Thinking about it made my stomach pitch.

37

Saturday, November 20

I opened my eyes to a room that was strangely silent and dim.

After disentangling from the bedding—I'd slept fitfully—I crossed to the French doors. Beyond the glass, the fog was thick enough to make snow angels.

Sliding open one panel, I stepped onto the deck. The air felt velvety damp on my skin, the wood slippery cool on the soles of my feet.

The seabirds were mute, perhaps disoriented by the hazy gray blanket enveloping their world. Not a single palm frond rustled.

I breathed in the mix of seaweed, wet sand, and salt air. Listened to the acres of silence. Felt momentarily comforted.

Then, goose bumps. Maybe the morning chill. Maybe thoughts of the dead woman who'd speak to me later that day.

I went back inside. Birdie was gone, no doubt miffed that his breakfast order would arrive later than his requested time. I checked the bedside clock.

8:17 a.m. Hours until my meeting with Vislosky.

Caffeine? Exercise?

Strongly preferring the former, I nevertheless donned running shorts and a hoodie and laced on my Nikes. After feeding the feline,

I set out in the direction of the Front Beach pier, a route of roughly three miles round trip. Plenty, given that I'd barely had a nodding acquaintance with exercise of late.

The tide was high, leaving only a narrow ribbon of hard-packed sand skimming the shore. My footfalls pounded to the rhythm of the shrouded Atlantic sucking in, then spitting out the surf.

At the halfway point, I slapped my usual barnacle-studded pylon—an OCD ritual, I know—and hooked a U-ey. On the homeward leg, the sun began poking encouraging rays at the mist. The heavy veil grudgingly started to lift. Ghostly figures materialized. Walkers. Shell collectors. Dogs chasing balls or Frisbees, then racing back to their owners.

My breathing was steady, my muscles finally loose. I kicked into high. For the first time in days, it felt good to be alive.

I showered, then pulled on yoga pants and my favorite long-sleeved jersey from Skagway. Was indulging in the deferred coffee and a side of Cheerios when Ryan called.

"*Bonjour, mon cowboy*." Close to a line by Mitsou, a Quebecoise singer.

"*Tabarnac.* Don't we sound perky."

"I just ran on the beach."

"Are you all hot and sweaty?"

"I took a shower."

"Are you still naked?"

"I'm in the kitchen eating breakfast."

"I don't suppose you'd want to *get* nake—"

"What's the haps?" Through the crunch of Os.

"What are you, twelve?"

"Blame the endorphins."

"The haps are twofold. First, traces of Semtex were found at InovoVax."

"A plastic explosive."

"That very thing."

"The one that brought down Pan Am flight one-oh-three over Lockerbie, Scotland."

"Eight ounces in a Samsonite suitcase."

"Jesus in a pear tree."

"It's powerful stuff. And easy to use. Stick a couple of ounces behind the crapper, hide in the alley, detonate with a call from your cell phone."

"Is it hard to get?"

"Ehhh. Semtex is used in commercial blasting, demolition, mining, that sort of thing. Access is regulated, but with a good source, you can score a hunk."

Ryan paused, thinking about Semtex, I supposed. Or good sources.

"Back in the day, Semtex was a bitch to detect. Now a taggant is added."

"Which does what?"

"Produces a distinctive vapor signature that helps sniff the stuff out."

"The cops are thinking Murray botched what he was doing and blew himself up?"

"They're considering all options."

"The guy's a snake, Ryan. He'd rake Disneyland with an AK if he felt threatened."

I sensed Ryan shrug, unwilling to speculate. Or not fully convinced.

"And the second hap?" I asked.

"Huger's a fan of the Great White North."

"He's been to Canada? When?"

"Many times, his last trip being this past week."

"Seriously?"

"According to customs and border patrol, Huger arrived Wednesday, left yesterday. His points of entry and departure were our very own Pierre Elliott Trudeau Airport."

"He was in Montreal at the time of the explosion at InovoVax."

"He was."

Something rolled over in a murky corner of my mind. *What?*

"That changes the picture," I said.

"It does."

We rode out quite a long moment of silence.

"Listen, Tempe." Ryan uses my first name only when deadly serious. "I want you to be careful."

"I'm always careful."

"I mean it." Ryan put steel in his voice.

"So do I."

"This guy Huger is bad news."

"What's his motive to kill?" Though I didn't disagree.

Ryan had no answer to that.

The Sea Biscuit Café is an island tradition. The main room seats maybe twenty, the screened porch a few more. Cash or check only. Nothing matches. The waitresses are local and wear unstylish Levi's or cutoffs.

When I arrived, every inside table was taken. Vislosky was at one, drinking coffee and looking generally pissed. First time I'd seen her in uniform.

"How's it going," I asked, hooking my shoulder bag onto a ladderback chair.

"Folks are having a whale of a time out there. My humble opinion? We tear-gas the whole lot."

I forced my best imitation of a smile.

"Can't tell if these assholes are in a lather for themselves or their dogs."

"Capno made the national news last night."

Vislosky glowered at me.

"According to CNN, the outbreak isn't confined to Charleston. There are clusters in Greenville, Columbia, Beaufort—"

"I'd say that misery loves company, but I don't wish this crap on anyone."

A waitress came and poised pen over pad. Shyla. Shyla had worked at the Biscuit since Sherman set off for Savannah.

I ordered a grilled crab cake sandwich. Vislosky chose tomato pie. She spoke again when Shyla had gone.

"We're briefed daily on capno, but I still don't get it. The CDC says the disease isn't contagious. It's not like COVID. People can't pass it to each other."

"It's my understanding that human infections almost always come from dogs or cats."

"Right. So one schmuck gets bitten and he's fine, another gets scratched and he's totally screwed."

"I'm not an expert, but I believe I read that a person's level of immunity is genetically determined."

"Then how come all of a sudden everyone's catching this shit?"

I had no answer to that.

Shaking her head, Vislosky pulled a thumb drive from a hip pocket and set it between us. Added a folded sheet of paper.

I reached for the drive. She blocked my move with one NBA hand.

"I'm letting you view this for one reason and one reason alone."

I cocked a brow.

"She's speaking fucking French."

"Melanie?"

"No. Brigitte Bardot."

I let it slide. I had more important things to deal with than Vislosky's attitude.

"I'm happy to translate," I said.

"The quality's shit. The e-geeks patched together the portions they could salvage. So it's not exactly Steven Spielberg."

Vislosky withdrew her hand and hooked a thumb at the paper. "That's a photocopy of a page we found wadded up inside the video-cassette case. Maybe you can translate that, too."

I took the thumb drive and paper and placed both in my bag.

While eating, I updated Vislosky on Ryan's two haps: the Semtex and Huger's recent cross-border sortie. She responded with a series of guttural noises.

When I'd finished, Vislosky said, "So the bastard went to Montreal."

I nodded.

"Why?"

"I don't know."

"What's his connection to Murray?"

"I don't know."

"Border patrol find any record of Murray coming down here?"

"I didn't ask."

"The Montreal cops thinking Huger might have done Murray?"

"They're considering many options." Quoting Ryan.

We ate in silence for a while. Vislosky spoke first.

"You must live right, doc."

"Meaning?" I was lost. Doc? That was a first.

"You realize how many breaks we've caught on this case?"

I raised a questioning palm, still not following.

"So many witnesses staying put for so long? Never happens."

Actually, I had thought about that. "Dora Eisenberg is convinced she's unemployable should she leave InovoVax," I said. "Florence Sorg is in her nineties and has owned her building for decades. Gertrude Pickle is a widow and fearful of living alone. Digger France has retired to the city that made him famous."

Bunching and tossing her napkin, Vislosky shook her head. "The only one with wanderlust seems to be Huger. The bastard up and hauled ass to Canada."

"He's back in town now."

"You can take this to the bank. I'm gonna net this knuckle dragger, shove him into a cave, and roll a big fuckin' stone over the entrance."

Sounded good to me.

"Have a nice day," I said in parting.

"Yeah. Blue skies and butterflies."

I drove home, not anticipating the calamity awaiting me there. The first of two that night.

Birdie didn't greet me at the front door. He didn't answer my calls. Not normal, especially since we were staying in a strange house.

I dumped my purse on the sideboard and searched the first floor. No cat.

In the kitchen, my heart catapulted into my throat. Bloody pawprints tracked from the deck doors to the back stairs. I followed them up to my bedroom, calling Bird's name. Inside, red trails crisscrossed the floor.

"Birdie?" Struggling to hide the panic.

No response.

I dropped to all fours to check under the bed. Two round yellow eyes peered from the shadows.

"Come here, big guy." Low and soothing, though my heart was hammering.

The cat didn't move. Reaching in, I hooked him under his forelimbs and gently slid him out.

The fur on Birdie's right rear leg was a matted red mess.

"What happened, sweet boy?"

Of course, he didn't answer.

I glanced at the French doors. One was slightly ajar.

Bolting to the bathroom, I grabbed a towel, wrapped the cat, dug his carrier from the closet, and eased him in. Not an easy ease, given his agitated state. Then I raced for the car.

The Sandy Cove Veterinary Clinic was minutes away on Palm Boulevard. I'd passed it a dozen times when driving to the Harris Teeter. I burned every speed reg getting there. Screw it. If an island cop took issue, I'd outrun him and swallow the fine.

The lobby was packed with owners holding leashes and owners pacifying pets. They all followed my progress from the entrance to the desk, smiling sportingly, secretly hoping my emergency wouldn't prolong their wait.

The receptionist wore a name badge ID'ing her as Brooke. Brooke whisked Bird into the bowels of the clinic. Returned and presented me with a stack of forms.

I sat down to fill them out. Realized that in my rush, I'd left my bag at Anne's house. Entering all but my credit-card information, I returned the paperwork to Brooke and joined the waiters.

For almost an hour. Then the vet appeared to report that my cat had deep lacerations on his right rear leg. No shit, Sherlock. Birdie had been anesthetized for suturing and now needed X-rays.

While signing yet another form, I asked if I'd be taking Birdie home with me. That depended on the X-rays. I queried how long that process would take. My pet was the next one up.

I resumed my vigil.

Animals and masters came and went. Mostly dogs and cats. One cockatiel. One pig.

Another wasted hour. I wished I'd brought my purse. And my laptop. And Vislosky's thumb drive. After another, I wished I'd brought strychnine.

Eventually, word came. No broken bones.

It was past five when Brooke finally delivered my pet. The patient was now totally cool with the carrier.

Back home, I settled Bird on my bed. The cat looked mellow as a toked-out pothead.

Puzzled about how Bird had hurt himself, I returned to the kitchen. Spotted traces of blood and fur low down on one of the deck doors.

Had I left it open a crack? Had Birdie tried to squeeze through and become wedged? Security lapses weren't my habit, but honestly, I couldn't be sure.

A quick ham and cheese sandwich, then I dug out Vislosky's

photocopy and thumb drive, collected my laptop, and clomped back upstairs. Sitting cross-legged on the bed, I decided to start with the folded paper.

I've no idea what I was expecting.

It wasn't what I read.

And, to my horror, it was.

38

I opened the paper. Intersecting dark lines suggested the original had been folded many times.

A quick scan revealed disturbingly familiar features. On two levels.

First, the script was small and cramped, the language a type of adolescent shorthand.

Like the entries in Harmony Boatwright's diary.

Second, certain acronyms recurred throughout. *mRNA. CRISPR.*

The same acronyms recorded by Melanie Chalmers in 2002.

Melanie had been interested in vaccine production. So had her daughter Lena, fifteen years later.

My appalling theory elbowed toward my forebrain.

Impossible.

I continued deciphering the girlish scrawl. Spotted names. InovoVax. Arlo Murray. GeneFree. Sullie Huger.

Not surprising that the girls knew of Murray and InovoVax. Lena had visited the director at the pharmaceutical plant in Laval. Ditto for Huger. Lena and Harmony had interviewed him at his office on James Island.

I plowed on. Spotted words and phrases that hadn't appeared in Melanie's notes.

Capnocytophaga canimorsus. TLR4.

The theory finger-tapped a cerebral mic.

Could I actually be right? Could any human really be that evil?

I booted my laptop, hopped online, and went to the Human Gene Database.

The TLR4 gene codes for a protein that is a member of the toll-like receptor family.

The more I read, the more the theory demanded attention.

TLRs play an important role in pathogen recognition and in the activation of immunity against infectious agents.

God almighty!

I went to the bathroom for a drink of cold water. Checked Birdie. Returned to Vislosky's photocopy.

Six lines from the bottom, there it was. Confirmation in two short paragraphs.

"Holy freakin' shit!" Grabbing my mobile.

Bird raised his lids to half-mast. A long, bleary look, then he lowered them.

"You're right, Bird." Forcing myself calm. "We both know Ryan's motto. Cautious, composed, completely cognizant."

After tossing my phone onto the comforter, I inserted Vislosky's thumb drive into the USB port. The tiny device contained a single file. *Chalmervideo.mpv.*

I downloaded then dragged the MPV file into my File Viewer app. Deep breath.

It was clear the opening portion had not been salvaged. The action started in mid-scene.

My first thought was that Lizzie Griesser's facial approximation had been remarkably accurate. The woman speaking had large green eyes, a long, narrow nose, and a tapering jaw. But the phenotype sketch hadn't captured how striking Melanie was. Only an overly prominent chin had kept her from being truly beautiful.

My second thought was that the setup looked like your typical hostage video. Melanie sat squarely facing the camera. She wore no makeup, and her hair was knotted on top of her head. There was nothing behind her but bare wall.

"—this is working now. Hopefully take three is the winner. I'm not sure if this part recorded on my first try, but it's January 15, 2002. My name is Melanie Chalmers."

She spoke with proper Parisian grammar and an American, not Quebecois, accent. What I think of as textbook French. Her voice was somber, her expression grim.

"I'm living in Laval, Quebec, under the alias Mélanie Chalamet. I'm employed—"

The tape jumped abruptly.

"—been just the three of us for so long. But should something happen to me, my kids deserve to know about their fathers. Not that sweet Ella ever will." Melanie looked down, I presumed, at her hands. "The sad truth is, I haven't a clue who Ella's daddy is. I was pretty much out of control my final year in college."

"Lena's father was a man named Jeff Russo. Jeff was in the Navy. We were going to get married, but the year Lena was born, he was killed in Iraq. Some of his family may still live in the—"

Again, the tape skipped.

"—unbearable at work. Arlo rides me constantly. I'm making this tape in French in case he gets his hands on it. The dolt doesn't know a word unless it's on a menu."

There was another disjointed cut-and-paste transition.

"—thought the idea would help me. Help my kids. Score us some money. But I just can't go through with it. So many people would be hurt. That's why I want everything on record. In case—"

Another break.

"—met in the early 'nineties while we were working for the Human Genome Project at MIT. I was a lowly data analyst. Zero advanced degree, you know." With a note of bitterness. "Arlo and Sullie were bigwig scientists, earning huge coin. I could barely scrape by."

Another downward glance. Another disconnect.

"—were totally different animals. Arlo was flashy, the macho daredevil always bragging about riding his bike going ninety without a helmet. Sullie was an introvert, a whiner, always moaning about how his father ignored him when he was a kid. But from the get-go, they bonded. Both had PhDs and very lofty views of themselves. Both were into genomics, boating, hair products." The last punctuated with a disparaging eye roll. "Maybe they were lovers, maybe not. I didn't know, didn't care."

The tape hopped again. Altered shadowing suggested a light source off to the left. I guessed some time had passed.

"—not sure why the great doctors deigned to slum with me, but the three of us got into the habit of having a few beers after work." Pause. "It all began as a joke. No, not a joke. A game. We'd construct these elaborate scenarios involving genome editing. At first, it was all hypothetical. What if this? What if that? Eventually, Sullie—"

An icy chill took hold of my chest.

"—chance to make big bucks. The plan was complicated, but in a nutshell, we'd edit a gene that controls immunity to some noninfec-tious condition. The mutation wouldn't be harmful, since it couldn't spread throughout the population. We'd introduce it through some pharmaceutical channel, maybe a vaccine or—"

Holy, Christ!

"—couldn't put my finger on exactly when things changed, but after a point, it wasn't mind play anymore. It got real. It was going to happen. Sullie launched a website in 'ninety-nine. GeneMe. In 2000, he got Arlo and me jobs at InovoVax through some friend of his father who's on the board. Arlo is from Montreal. My role—"

And that was it. The rest had been lost.

The chill traveled along my spine. I grabbed my mobile.

Ryan answered right away.

"I was right, Ryan. Holy Mother of God, I was right."

"Right about what?"

"Huger."

"Calm down. Then hit me with the two-minute elevator version."

"Huger and Murray figured out a way to manipulate a vaccine in order to alter a person's genome."

A beat of silence.

"Maybe a *little* more detail?" Ryan urged.

I provided a crash course, including both old and new info. CRISPR/Cas9. mRNA vaccine production. TLR4. *Capnocytophaga canimorsus.*

"TLR4 is a gene that gives an early shout-out when foreign bacteria enter the body," Ryan clarified when I'd finished. "CRISPR/Cas9 is a genetic cut-and-paste tool."

"Exactly. Huger and Murray were using CRISPR to replace a person's *good* copy of the TLR4 gene with a *bad* copy. A mutation that makes the person's immune system partially blind to infection by capno."

"So Huger could hawk his genetic-testing service and homeopathic cures online."

"The stakes would be far bigger than online sales. Huger hoped to create real panic and sell his websites for tens, maybe hundreds, of millions."

Ryan took a moment to digest what I was saying. Then, "Murray and Chalmers were planted at InovoVax with the idea that they'd contaminate specific batches of flu vaccine."

"Yes. Melanie's notes contained what Bangoboshe thought were batch numbers. I'm sure they'll confirm it."

"Melanie got cold feet and threatened to blow the whistle."

"It's all on her tape," I said.

"Murray or Huger capped her to make sure that didn't happen. Ella was collateral damage."

A sudden confirmation. "Sorg didn't overhear Melanie and Murray arguing about Christopher," I said. "They were arguing about CRISPR."

"Fifteen years later, all the hard work is about to pay off." Ryan continued the thread. "Out of the blue, Lena and Harmony show up at Huger's office with information that would expose the whole bloody scheme."

Birdie's ears shot up. He lifted his chin and sniffed the air. I stroked his head.

"Here's something that's been troubling me," I said. "Why such a long gap following the murders in Montreal?"

"Maybe Murray and Huger were spooked. Maybe they were still tinkering with how to contaminate the mRNA process."

"Maybe they were waiting for the right moment," I speculated. "The pandemic provided it."

"COVID-19 scared the whole world shitless."

I'd started to agree when a horrendous possibility broadsided me.

"Or maybe they didn't stop at all. Maybe the capno scheme is just the latest in a series."

Ryan got my meaning right away. "Maybe they've made other strikes, perhaps in other places, and capno is the first to succeed. Think about it. Avian flu. Swine flu. H1N1. West Nile virus. SARS. Legionnaire's disease. Those are just a few that come to mind."

"But those are infectious. Melanie said on the tape that the plan was to stick to noninfectious diseases."

"OK. What about the periodic salmonella and E. coli outbreaks? Or the mad cow scare? When was that?"

"I think the first confirmed case in an American cow was in 2003."

We both went silent recalling various CDC alerts over the past two decades. A full minute, then I switched tack, too horrified to continue.

"Do you suppose Huger killed Murray?" I asked.

"There's some new intel on Murray, *grâce à* Claudel. The good doctor liked his cars and boats fast. And expensive. He was in hock up to his eyeballs."

"Maybe Huger viewed Murray's financial woes as a threat. For years, their MO was to keep a very low profile."

"Or maybe Murray felt the hounds snapping, got tired of waiting, and decided to cash in early."

"By blackmailing Huger?"

Something went *thunk* somewhere in the house.

I drew a breath. Listened. Nothing. Only one possibility made sense.

"I should go. I think Anne may be home."

"You'll call Vislosky?"

"I will."

"This asshole Huger could be your Disneyland AK psycho."

"Believe me. Vislosky is doing her damnedest to find him."

"I'll rest easier when she does. Let me know?"

"Will do."

"I'm off to the shower."

"Rinse well."

We disconnected.

I sat for a long moment, phone pressed to my chest.

No movement downstairs.

Then, close by and unmistakable.

The sound of a pistol slide ratcheting back.

39

Saturday, November 20

I listened with every cell in my being.

Silence.

No way the solo *thunk* was Anne. She'd have announced her arrival with all the subtlety of Hurricane Inara.

Had I imagined the sound?

Then, from beyond my door, a whispered *shhsssh*.

A forgotten ceiling fan?

The AC kicking on?

A serial killer brushing a wall?

I eased from the bed and secured Birdie in the bathroom. Then, feeling a bit foolish, I dialed Vislosky.

Voice mail.

Leaving the line open, I placed the device on the bedside table. Moving as quietly as possible, I crept to the door and peeked out.

The figure was cloaked in the shadowy darkness of the hall. And wearing a black tracksuit. White stripes running along one sleeve indicated a forearm flexed to waist level.

My heart spiked hard.

An intruder! With a gun!

My mind splintered. Lock myself in the bathroom with Birdie? Bad idea. If the guy breached the door, I'd be trapped. Slip out onto the deck? Worse idea. The distance to the ground was a leg-breaking twenty-five feet.

I tiptoed toward my mobile to try Vislosky again. As I was half-way there, a voice froze me in place.

"Take another step, and I *will* shoot you." Vowels as honeyed as pecan pie. Male. Familiar.

"How did you get into this house?" Sounding light-years more confident than I felt.

"You really must fix that back door."

"You were here earlier."

"I'd be foolish not to acquaint myself with the lay of the land. Don't you agree, Dr. Brennan?"

"You hurt my cat!"

"I don't hate cats. But yours definitely needs to acquire some manners."

"What do you want?" Seething inside.

"Right now, I want you to lace your fingers on top of your head and turn around slowly."

I did as instructed.

Sullie Huger had me in the crosshairs of a Glock 19.

"Don't be afraid," he said.

"I'm not." I was terrified. When a gun is pointed at you, it's all you see. "How did you find me?"

"You're a very intelligent woman. You should know better than to share personal details with the clerical staff."

Abilene Monger. I said nothing.

"It's such a shame this has to happen." Huger's tone was reptilian cold.

Advice from a long-ago self-defense course managed to penetrate my fear. *Stay calm. Be cooperative. Keep your assailant talking.*

"Your scheme was brilliant," I said, eyes glued to the cold steel cylinder aimed at my chest. "I know everything."

"So I just overheard."

"Do I have it right?"

"Mostly." Huger's eyes had the glow of too much booze. Of too much something.

Keep him talking.

"Melanie's job would have been to spike designated batches of vaccine, right?"

"Poor, weak Melanie. Such an error in judgment."

"When she threatened to blow the whistle, who killed her? You or Murray?"

"Arlo was another unfortunate error."

"But Murray was your wingman."

"My *wingman*"—sarcastic—"grew reckless. And greedy."

"No choice but to take him out."

Huger said nothing.

"Ella was ten years old. Why kill her?"

"Wrong place, wrong time."

"And she could have identified you."

"And that."

"Same for Harmony and Lena?" I knew I should rein it in, massage his ego. But my revulsion was in control. "Wrong place, wrong time?"

Huger shrugged.

"Did the girls threaten to expose you? Or did they simply know too much for you to take a chance?"

"Truth be told, I found them impudent."

"You'd gotten away with murdering Melanie and Ella, so you used the old tried-and-true. Bullet to the head, mutilate and strip the bodies, wrap the corpses in plastic, toss them into the sea."

"In Quebec, it was actually a river. But you know that."

I wanted to reach out and smash the arrogant grin from his face. Instead, I continued the exchange, hands clasped so tightly my finger bones ached.

"Did you know that Harmony was your cousin?"

"I truly did not. It was quite an embarrassment to learn I was related to white trash."

"That white trash almost succeeded in bringing you down. That and a hurricane."

A beat, then, "A pity your boyfriend is so very far away."

Suddenly, my mouth felt coated with ash. I swallowed.

"Enough of this." Huger's face morphed into a look that chilled me.

More advice trickled back from the long-ago course.

Be compliant only to a point.

Had we reached that point?

Before I could decide, Huger lunged, pressed himself to me, and jammed the gun muzzle into the side of my neck.

"Move."

Molded like a pair of conjoined twins, we lockstepped into the hall, down the stairs, through the kitchen, and out onto the deck. Huger was mashed so close I could smell his sweat and cologne and the curry he'd eaten for dinner. Feel the coiled tension in his muscles.

Once outside, Huger dug the Glock even deeper into my flesh. I felt his head rotate left, then right. Pictured his eyes scanning the pool. Maybe the ocean.

Kick up and back into Huger's balls, then make a run for it? A run *at* him? Again, he took the decision out of my hands.

In one fast move, Huger shoved my shoulders while simultaneously leg-sweeping the front of my ankles. I pitched forward, and my head cracked the travertine coping rimming the pool. The world dissolved in a white mist of pain.

Before I could collect my wits, Huger pounced with a quickness I wouldn't have thought possible in a man his age. Pinning me with his full weight, he forced my head over the pool's edge and underwater.

Adrenaline flooded through me.

I tried to twist free, but Huger managed to immobilize my arms and legs.

My chest began to burn.

How long can a person survive without oxygen? One minute? Three?

A rational fragment of my spiraling mind reached out.

Don't panic!

Futile. Terror was overriding all logic.

I couldn't breathe. Couldn't scream. Couldn't thrash. Nothing existed but a desperate need to pull air into my lungs.

How long had I been under? A minute? Ninety seconds?

Bizarre images flared. My body in a blue plastic shroud inside a polypropylene bin. A confused fisherman reeling me in.

I lost all sense of time

Two minutes?

Black clouds began gathering behind my closed lids. Coalescing. I was slipping over the brink into unconsciousness.

Then the instinct to survive won out. Turning my dread inward, I bucked ferociously with my upper body. An arm popped free. I thrust it into the pool, oblivious to the pain of skin lost to stone.

Huger pushed my head deeper under the surface.

Feeling around blindly with my semi-numb fingers, I located an indentation six inches below the coping. The skimmer. Planting my palm on the box's horizontal surface, I thrust upward with all the strength I could muster.

This time, the element of surprise was mine. Caught off guard by the re-angling of my torso, Huger relaxed the pressure on the back of my skull. Taking advantage, I drove upward, twisted my limbs, and jerked my head wildly. The sudden movement pitched my attacker sideways onto the decking.

I raised my head above the water and sucked air into my throat. Desperate for breath. Desperate for life.

Huger grabbed my hair and tried clawing me back. Gasping and blinking water, I lashed out and caught him with a thumb to one eye. He recoiled, yelping in pain.

Forcing down a wave of nausea, I levered myself up onto all fours and scrabbled backward.

Far off, a siren wailed. Or was it an auditory illusion, the product of oxygen deprivation?

One gaggle of neurons was still receiving and processing input.

The gun! Where's the gun?

My eyes swept the deck. No Glock.

I struggled to my feet and, legs rubber, bent to search under the closest of the chaises. No gun.

Realizing what I was after, Huger sprang up, bore down, and head-butted me in the gut. Arms pinwheeling, lungs in spasm, I stumbled backward, Huger again clinging like a leech. A flailing hand brushed one of Anne's potted ferns. I wrapped my fingers around the stem, roundhouse-swung the plant, and clocked Huger on the temple.

He cried out but held tight. We both went down. My head took dual blows, front and back. As my occipital smacked travertine, Huger sledgehammered his forehead into my frontal.

My vision blurred. Shards of pain sliced through every lobe of my brain.

Conjoined as before, Huger and I rolled in a turbulent mess of broken terra-cotta, scattered soil, and torn fronds. I was in good shape. But he outweighed me by a good fifty pounds. And, though older, was fit.

After much sweating and grunting and thrashing, Huger muscled himself topside, planted a knee on each of my arms, and wrapped my throat in a viselike grip. I looked up into his face. A vein snaked one brow, bloated and throbbing. Below the vein, his eyes were dead and soulless. Not human eyes. Malevolent eyes. Black hole eyes.

Desperate, I clamped both hands onto Huger's wrists. He wriggled one arm loose and brought the side of his hand down on my larynx. I elbowed him in the gut, then, pumping my arm viciously, forced him off with a series of fist blows. Wheezing and trembling, I rolled sideways, then scuttled away.

The gun!

My gaze darted wildly.

Sirens screaming in hot. Real sirens.

Again, Huger came at me. Again, I dodged.

Borrow from the bastard's own playbook! the neurons screamed.

Drawing a lungful of air, I launched myself forward and, using my head as a pile driver, slammed Huger's face with the crown of my skull. I heard the sickening crunch of his nasal bones. A furious shriek. A dull thud as his body flew backward and landed.

In the driveway, car doors opening. Not slamming.

Cops!

I looked toward Huger. Blood was gushing from his shattered nose and split lower lip.

A shouted order outside. A clipped response.

Huger spit bloody saliva and broken teeth. Backhanded his mouth.

Footsteps clomping up the back stairs. Others thundering through the house.

"You've ruined everything," Huger snarled, defeated.

"My pleasure," I said.

As a uniform appeared on the top step, Vislosky came charging through the kitchen. Both had their weapons grasped two-handed at their jawlines.

Vislosky halted at the open French doors. Tense. Ready. Then a slight easing of her spine.

"You good?" she asked me, while keeping her gaze and her gun on Huger.

I nodded. "There's a Glock out here somewhere."

"Stand down," Vislosky shouted to her backup. "Weapon in the area. But first, slap some bracelets on the guy with the dental issues."

The uniform cuffed Huger and handed him off to his partner.

"You need an ambulance?" Vislosky asked me.

"No."

"I think you do."

"You've been wrong before."

"I'm calling a bus anyway."

She did, then supported me as I limped into the kitchen.

"You look like shit," she said once I was settled as comfortably as possible.

I nodded. It hurt. "How'd you get here so fast?"

"I was just over the bridge in Mount Pleasant when you phoned. Good timing."

"Thanks."

I turned and hurled into Anne's Murano glass bowl.

40

Neither Vislosky nor I had been overwhelmed with invitations. Being Canadian, Ryan had no plans. And to say Anne was insistent would be like saying the Allies dropped by at Normandy.

Once we'd all accepted, she outdid herself transforming the entire first floor. Harvest-themed kitsch covered the walls. Gourds stuck with mums and Shasta daisies, cardboard *Mayflower* pop-ups, ceramic pumpkins and turkeys, and figurines of banqueting Pilgrims and Native Americans filled every horizontal surface. Spiced candles and apple pie diffusers scented the air.

We took our places at five, every millimeter of tabletop crammed with platters and bowls overflowing with seasonal favorites. Turkey. Stuffing. Cranberry. Marshmallow-topped yams. Molded Jell-O. You know the drill.

Anne reigned at the table's head. I was seated to her left, next to Ryan. Vislosky was opposite me, an empty chair to her right. No amount of cajoling could get our jolly hostess to reveal the identity of the missing guest.

We'd just filled our plates when Anne suggested a variation on an exercise Mama often forced on my sister Harry and me at mealtimes, a game that involved sharing our "warm fuzzies" and "cold pricklies" as she called them. I wasn't a callous kid. But I hated laying out my feelings for the benefit of an audience. Still do.

"I'll start," Anne said. "This Thanksgiving Day, I am grateful for such glorious weather, for being in the most beautiful place on God's earth, and for the company of dear friends, old and new."

Anne raised her wineglass in Ryan's direction.

"I am thankful for the lovely and brilliant lady to my right. I hope she will always be a part of my life."

The lovely and brilliant lady kept her eyes on the plastic turkey beside her placemat. Wondered what it had to smile about.

"Tempe?" Anne urged.

"I am thankful that no one has teased me about my face. Except for Ryan's Darth Vader quip."

"And Anne's reference to Wile E. Coyote and the rake," Vislosky said.

"And that."

"Tonia?" Anne prompted after casting a withering look my way.

"I'm thankful to have Huger's ass in the bag." Gruff. "Pass the cranberry."

Clearly, Vislosky's enthusiasm matched mine.

Nothing from the empty chair.

"Well, then. I guess that's it for gratitude." Dramatic Anne sigh. "Fine. Let's talk about Huger."

Not the divergent path I'd have chosen.

"Let me get this straight." Anne pointed one lacquered nail at me. "Huger was spiking vaccine with a virus that attacked *what*, now?"

"Epithelial cells."

Anne stared, wide-eyed. Chardonnay-eyed. I wasn't judging. It was Thanksgiving, and she'd been cooking all week.

"Blood vessels," I clarified.

"How'd that work again?" One corner of Vislosky's mouth was hitching up. I suspected her question arose out of a wish to bait Anne rather than a desire for more detail.

"The virus delivered the CRISPR/Cas9, which snipped the DNA and replaced the gene that would normally prevent infection from capno."

I pantomimed scissors with one hand. Then, calling Vislosky's bluff, elaborated further.

"Specifically, the blood cells were altered to make an adhesion molecule that allowed the bacteria to attach and grow."

"After an animal bite or scratch," Anne said.

"Yep."

"Once the vessels were modified, could they be changed back?" Ryan asked.

"No. Since Huger's virus targeted stem cells, the changes were permanent." I narrowed my eyes to indicate he should change the subject. He didn't.

"That's where GeneFree came in?"

"Yes." Spearing an olive a little too forcefully.

"How?"

"Yeah, how?" Anne echoed.

"Huger's testing could determine where you and your pet stood."

"And?"

"If Lassie was infected with capno, one of Huger's other websites could provide the secret potion to cure her." Resigned to the fact that, despite my disapproval, we would talk about this. "And if testing determined that you carried the gene making you susceptible, GeneFree had the magic wand to block adhesion of the nasty little molecule."

"Huger hoped all that would make his sites worth millions to some large corporation," Anne said.

"Payday." Vislosky's tone was coated with disgust.

"Melanie's role would have been to spike certain batches of vaccine. When she got cold feet and threatened to blow the whistle, Murray and Huger took her out." Anne's revulsion was as palpable as Vislosky's. "And poor little Ella just happened to be with her mother that day."

"Who fixed the system so Melanie could work in Canada without a visa?" Vislosky asked.

"Unless Huger talks, we may never know that. Though it appears he arranged for the jobs at InovoVax through some family connection." Ryan turned to me. "Didn't Melanie say that in the video?"

"Yes. And she alluded to a strange bond between Huger and Murray. She said it was as if the two fed off each other. Murray was flashy, an attention seeker, a big spender, addicted to fast cars and boats. Huger was an introvert, bitter at being ignored by his parents following the death of his brother."

"Right." Vislosky snorted. "Blame the parents."

"After Melanie was killed, Murray must have altered the batches himself," I added. "Dora Eisenberg said he was at InovoVax practically twenty-four seven."

Anne voiced the question that Ryan and I had considered.

"Do you suppose they made other attempts during the fifteen years between the murders in Montreal and those here in Charleston?"

"Again, unless Huger talks, we may never know," I said.

"How could someone *do* something so diabolical?" Far too much emotion from Anne.

"Maybe the scheme evolved as Melanie implied." I was thinking aloud in stream of consciousness. "Both men were brilliant, talented. Murray craved money and adulation. Huger was driven by a need to prove himself in general and to his parents in particular. He resented that his father had lost the family fortune and wanted to show that he could get it back. Perhaps alone, neither would have acted as they did. But together, the catalysts of need and greed led to murder."

"How do you say shitbag in all caps?" Anne asked.

"Lethal injection." Vislosky forked a hunk of turkey the size of Kansas into her mouth.

"Huger must be facing godzillion charges?" Anne directed this to Ryan.

"Adulterating or misbranding a food or drug. Placing an adulterated substance into interstate commerce. Kidnapping. Attempted murder. Murder. Canada will push hard for extradition."

"Ain't gonna happen," Vislosky snapped. "Huger's staying right here in the U S of A. In South Carolina, a death-penalty state."

"Any way to connect Huger to the explosion at InovoVax? Other than the fact that he was conveniently in *Montréal*—Anne exaggerated the French pronunciation—at the time?"

"Claudel's hoping to tie him to the purchase of the Semtex," Ryan said.

"Here's to *le détective*." Anne raised her glass.

We all drank to Claudel.

"Is he talking at all?" Anne was on a roll. "Huger, not Claudel."

Vislosky levered one shoulder. "Under advice of counsel, the bastard's being very cagey. His lawyer has pointed out, and unfortunately the guy's right, that we have very little physical evidence linking Huger to any of the homicides. Or to the tampering, for that matter. It may be that our best case is the assault and attempted murder by drowning of Tempe. Those are solid."

"Why didn't he just shoot her, like the others?"

"A lot of people knew what Tempe was investigating," Vislosky said. "This time he had to make it look accidental."

"Don't quit on the murders of the women."

We all looked at Ryan.

"An IT tech in Montreal managed to recover a few voice mails from the Samsung Galaxy found in the rubble at InovoVax."

"Murray's mobile?" I asked.

"Yep. One of the messages was left by a caller with an eight-four-three exchange."

"Had to be Huger. We can trace the number and probably identify the voice."

"According to the tech, the caller sounded *furieux*." No translation needed.

We waited as Ryan pulled out his own phone, scrolled, and read. "I quote: 'Charleston harbor two. St. Lawrence two. Laurier zero. Balanced score, asshole?'"

"Holy crap. When was that left?" I asked.

"November first."

"Three days after the hit-and-run."

Ryan nodded.

"Murray must have told Huger I was reopening the investigation into the container vics. Huger ordered him either to scare me off or to take me out. But how did he know?" I asked.

"Carrot Hair."

Eight eyes again swiveled to Ryan.

"Laura Bianchi. The journalist who showed up at the exhumation."

"Of course!" I said. Which compelled a brief explanation of the pic and the article in the *Gazette*. When I'd finished, I said, more resolute now, "So. Bears or Panthers?"

The others looked at me as if I'd spoken ancient Sumerian.

"Chicago is playing Carolina this weekend. Who's your pick?"

"Oh, dear Lord." Eyes in full orbit, Anne got to her feet. "Almost time for dessert, but first, I have something that may jolt the fillings right out of your teeth."

With that dramatic declaration, she disappeared through the swinging doors, returned moments later, butt first, with something substantial wrapped in her arms.

Turning, she announced, "Y'all, meet Anne. Same name, no relation."

No Relation Anne was a female mannequin, consisting only of torso, neck, and head. As we watched, our Anne placed No Relation Anne in the vacant chair and snugged her up to the table.

The sight of the new arrival generated an odd uneasiness.

I studied the dummy's features, and the uneasiness intensified. A sensation similar to the one I'd experienced when first viewing Polly Beecroft's photos.

Snap!

"Resusci Annie!" I exclaimed.

"Aka Rescue Annie." Anne beamed. "More folks have locked lips with this lady than have kissed the Blarney Stone."

Ryan and Vislosky looked lost.

"It's a CPR doll," I explained. "But what—?"

Anne cut me off. "We all know about L'Inconnue, right?"

"The unknown subject dragged from the Seine a century ago," Vislosky said.

"Unfortunately, I didn't manage to score a name or determine the woman's manner of death, but I did learn an interesting factoid about her death mask."

No one interrupted.

"About sixty years ago, an Austrian doctor named Peter Safar developed the basics of CPR. Long story short, Safar asked a Norwegian toymaker named Asmund Laerdal to design a life-size mannequin for use as a training tool. Figuring men would be grossed out doing mouth-to-mouth on a male dummy, Laerdal decided the doll should be female. As the story goes, he saw a L'Inconnue on a wall, thought her face was beautiful, and used the mask as his model."

Anne patted the mannequin's head.

"Since then, millions have learned CPR on this little gal."

"I was one of them." I now realized why Polly and her relatives had looked vaguely familiar. "Where did you get her?"

"As you know, I went to Savannah last week to see Josh filming." To the others, "Josh is my son. He's an actor and was playing a doc in a soap. The scene was taking place in an ER, and there was a CPR dummy tucked into one corner. I'd just learned about Resusci Annie, so when the crew broke set, I asked if I could have her. They said hell yes. One less prop to deal with."

Anne circled to her place for a sip of wine.

"I'm not giving up, mind you. But for now, I hope Polly will be pleased to know that her maybe ancestor has helped save the lives of beaucoup people."

"I'm sure she will," I said.

We all pitched in clearing dishes and wrapping leftovers. Then Anne served pumpkin pie, and we poured coffee and moved out onto the deck.

The shattered planter was gone, the furniture back in proper alignment. Not a single sign remained of the life-and-death struggle that had taken place there just five days earlier.

Except for my Anakin Skywalker face.

I settled into one of the Pawleys Island rockers. Ryan took the one next to mine.

The moon hung low and full and was the same orange hue as Anne's designer pumpkins. An amber triangle sparked the water's surface from its lower border at the horizon all the way to the shore.

Inevitably, the conversation drifted back to Huger's scheme to profit off the misery of others. To the monstrous misuse of his knowledge of human genomics.

We discussed the wonder and the power of the double-helix molecule.

We marveled at how a shared sequencing of base pairs had given Polly and Harriet and their great-aunt and grandmother identical features.

At how a malevolent chromosome had saddled Tereza Deacon with Silver-Russell syndrome, a condition that had altered her body and shaped her short life.

At the irony of the single biggest breakthrough in the container-case investigations.

Genetic genealogy had linked Aubrey Sullivan Huger to his youngest victim, Harmony Boatwright.

The man's own DNA had brought him down.

Epilogue

The earth revolved and rotated.
A new year began.

January 3

I was eating leftover Chinese takeout, thinking about booking a haircut, when footsteps sounded on the back steps. Heavy ones.

I rose from the table to peek outside.

Katy stood on my porch wearing desert camo fatigues and cover, combat boots, and aviator shades. An Army-issue duffel lay at her feet. A backpack hung from her left shoulder.

Katy looked lean and tanned. Confident. A different person from the troubled kid who'd enlisted four long years ago.

Fighting back tears of joy, I opened the door.

"Sergeant Petersons reporting for duty." Smiling broadly, Katy whipped off the aviators and pointed them at me. "You'd better have chocolate chip cookies, soldier."

I threw my arms around my daughter, lumpy pack and all.

"I love you, sweetheart," I whispered. "I am so very proud of you."

I said the words then. Repeated them often throughout her stay.

Katy's return brought me greater happiness than I can begin to describe. But her presence prompted thoughts of other daughters. Other mothers.

I'd taken a break from death. A holiday reprieve.

Now I was ready.

I made two calls.

January 10

Early morning, my phone rang. The update was better than I'd hoped.

Vislosky's efforts had produced an address for Bonnie Bird Boatwright. For the past six years, Harmony's mother had been living in a women's commune in northern Minnesota.

Bonnie Bird had asked that her daughter's remains be transferred from the Charleston morgue to a funeral home in Nashville. She'd purchased two gravestones and side-by-side plots. One for herself. One for Harmony.

January 22

My mobile rang as I was returning from dropping Katy at the airport. This time, the news was mixed.

Grudgingly, cemetery manager Rémi Arbour had followed through on my request to contact Ariel, the woman I'd met at Le Repos Saint-François d'Assise—the one who'd given me that tiny prayer card to slip into what turned out to be Ella's body bag. Hearing Arbour's wheezy, nasal French triggered a flood of memories of that day in 2010. The graveyard. The markers with their forlorn inscriptions.

LSJML-41207 Os non identifiés d'une femme.

LSJML-41208 Os non identifiés d'un enfant.

He had good news and bad.

The good. Ariel Caldrea was still an active member of the church on rue Sherbrooke. Parishioners still attended anonymous interments at Saint-François.

The bad. Florence Sorg wanted nothing to do with reburying Melanie and Ella. Though she'd tried, Ariel had been unable to locate any other Chalamet/Chalmers kin.

Counterbalancing good. Since Melanie and Ella were from Massachusetts, and U.S. citizens, Ariel had found a Boston cemetery willing to donate a plot and marker and a church that would volunteer a priest's services.

Pending my approval, Pierre LaManche would release the remains in Quebec. Ebony Herrin would release those in Charleston. At long last, Melanie, Ella, and Lena would have a memorial bearing their names.

When I spoke to Ariel, she attributed the happy ending to Mother Mary MacKillop, patron saint of abused girls.

I wasn't so sure.

It didn't matter.

Three daughters would lie with their mothers for eternity.

ACKNOWLEDGMENTS

A s usual, many people generously gave input that helped me keep this book accurate.

Dr. Andrew Rasmussen, who is at the Department of Biology, Mount St. Joseph University in Cincinnati, shared invaluable insights into molecular genetics and genome editing. Dr. Susan Erin Presnell provided information on the layout of the morgue and the functioning of the Pathology Department at the Medical University of South Carolina Medical Center in Charleston. Isabelle Comtois, *technicienne d'autopsie* extraordinaire, was infinitely patient with my questions concerning updates in procedure at the Bureau du coroner and the Laboratoire de sciences judiciaires et de médecine légale in Montreal.

My BFFs in forensic anthropology, Drs. Leslie Eisenberg, Diane France, Madeleine Hinkes, Elizabeth Murray, and Marcella Sorg, answered endless queries about bones and fractures and decomp. Dr. William Rodriguez shared his knowledge of barnacles, snails, and other creatures from the deep.

My BFFs to the north, Dorothée Berryman, Melanie Kau, Pauline Normand, and Suzanne Vachon (the five of us were once dubbed in print *L'equip de choc!*), steered me straight on all things Québécois.

Denmar Dixon offered tips concerning fast boats. Bill Hurley navigated me along the water route from Dorval to Saint-Anicet.

My assistant, Melissa Fish, performed too many tasks to enumerate.

I owe a huge thank-you to my editors, Rick Horgan in the US, Laurie Grassi in Canada, and Bethan Jones in the UK. Y'all are awesome.

I also want to acknowledge all those who work so very hard on my behalf. At home in the US: Nan Graham, Roz Lippel, Jaya Miceli, Brian Belfiglio, Abigail Novak, Brianna Yamashita, and Katie Rizzo. On the other side of the pond: Ian Chapman, Suzanne Baboneau, Harriett Collins, Rich Vlietstra, Justine Gold, Polly Osborn, and Gill Richardson. North of the forty-ninth: Kevin Hanson, Nita Pronovost, Felicia Quon, Adria Iwasutiak, Jillian Levick, and Greg Tilney. And so very many others too numerous to name.

I am grateful to my legal representatives, Deneen Howell and Robert Barnett at Williams and Connolly, LLP. Thanks for having my back.

My family was infinitely patient. As were Skinny and Turk.

I send a great big crushing bear hug to all my readers. It's gratifying that you're so loyal to Tempe. I hope in the near future to be able to see you once again at signings and public appearances. Until then, visit my website (KathyReichs.com), like me on Facebook, and follow me on Twitter (@kathyreichs) and Instagram (@kathyreichs). You are the reason I write!

If I failed to thank someone I should have, I apologize. If the book contains errors, they are my fault.

Don't miss

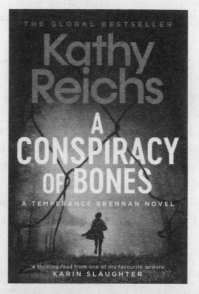

The *Sunday Times* bestseller and Richard & Judy Book Club pick

EVERY BODY HAS SECRETS
A corpse with no hands or face.
A decade-old missing child case, full of buried lies.
A connection between them that only one person can find.
And the more Temperance Brennan uncovers, the darker
and more twisted the picture becomes.

AVAILABLE NOW IN PAPERBACK, EBOOK AND AUDIO

SIMON &
SCHUSTER